FIRES
IN THE
DARK

LOUISE DOUGHTY

D0037119

POCKET
BOOKS

LONDON • SYDNEY • NEW YORK • TORONTO

First published in Great Britain by Simon & Schuster UK Ltd, 2003
This edition published by Pocket Books, 2004
An imprint of Simon & Schuster UK Ltd
A Viacom Company

1 3 5 7 9 10 8 6 4 2

Simon & Schuster UK Ltd
Africa House
64–78 Kingsway
London WC2B 6AH

www.simonsays.co.uk

Simon & Schuster Australia
Sydney

A CIP catalogue record for this book is
available from the British Library

ISBN 0-7434-4037-4

Typeset by M Rules
Printed and bound in Great Britain by
Cox & Wyman Ltd, Reading, Berkshire

ACKNOWLEDGEMENTS

In 1999, the British Council sent me to be Writer in Residence at the Masaryk University in Brno, in the Czech Republic, where I did the initial research for this book. During that visit, I received considerable help from Professor Ctibor Nečas, Renata Kamenička and the staff of the Museum of Romany Culture. Much of that work was written up while I was undertaking an Artists' Residency at the Banff Centre in Canada, the perfect place to write a novel. Further research was undertaken with the financial help of the K. Blundell Trust and a Writers' Award from the Arts Council of Great Britain.

The following historical works were invaluable to my research: Oldrich Misa's memoirs, published collectively as *Under the Sign of Pisces*, particularly Part I, *Childhood*, and Part II, *Escapes from War*; the series *The Gypsies During the Second World War*, published by the University of Hertfordshire Press; the work of Ctibor Nečas, in particular *The Holocaust of the Czech Roma*; Mateo Maximoff's articles on Kalderash language and customs in the *Journal of the Gypsy Lore Society*; *Na Bisteren*, published by the Museum of Romany Culture in Brno; *Lidice: Sacrificial Village* by John Bradley; and the definitive *Prague in the Shadow of the Swastika* by Jan Kaplan and Callum MacDonald.

Particular thanks to: Thomas Acton, Suzanne Baboneau, Moris Farhi, Ian Hancock, Antony Harwood, Jane Hodges, Jan Kaplan, Donald Kenrick, Jacqui Lofthouse and, of course, Jerome Weatherald.

For Jerome

Solidarity is not discovered by reflection but created. It is created by increasing our sensitivity to the particular details of pain and humiliation of other, unfamiliar sorts of people.

RICHARD RORTY
Contingency, irony, and solidarity

Today, at this very moment as I sit writing at a table, I myself am not convinced that these things really happened.

PRIMO LEVI
If This Is a Man

NOTE ON LANGUAGE

This novel is about a group of Roma or Romany people, more commonly known as Gypsies. The word *gypsy* is pejorative in many European languages and is often a racial slur. In English it is inaccurate but not generally considered offensive as long as it is spelt with a capital G.

'Roma' means The People. Roma people use the word *gadje*, or *gadže*, for anyone who is not-Roma or Sinti (another Romany group). *Gadje* may be imagined as *whitefolks* said with a great deal of scorn. Roma and Sinti societies are highly complex, with many different groups speaking different forms of the Romani language. The characters in this book are Kalderash (Coppersmith) Roma, who are travelling in the Czech lands but are originally from Wallachia, in present-day Romania, so I have used the Vlach Romani forms of most words.

There are some deliberate inconsistencies in this book. When using the plural, I have added an English 's', and I have occasionally used the Anglo-Romani term O Del, meaning God. When referring to street names in Prague, I have used the English equivalent of the most famous landmarks, such as Wenceslas Square and Charles Bridge, but in the interests of flavour, retained the Czech versions for others.

I am greatly indebted to Thomas Acton, Donald Kenrick and Ian Hancock for attempting to explain to me the complexities of Romani along with a great deal else besides. Any remaining errors or simplifications are entirely my own responsibility.

Rromale, phrálale, pheyale, me sim rromani feri ekh tserra, numa o mai lačo kotor si. Te yertin varesave doša me kerdem ande kadi paramiči, thai pačan ke čačo si o ilo murro.

CONTENTS

PART 1

1927

CHAPTER 1

Summer in Bohemia: high summer. The sun is furious, the sky a vast dome of bright and solid blue broken only by a few wisps of high, motionless cloud. It is 1927, July – the middle of the day.

The heat has deadened everything. No trace of breeze stirs in the grass, the trees are still. The cows can hardly lift their heads, so accustomed are they to indolence. Flies hang lazily over patches of dung already baked unyielding black. Daisies droop. Only the skylarks are in motion, ascending and plummeting with pointless enthusiasm.

At first glance, this small corner of the world seems uninhabited. The buildings at the edge of the field are disused. There is a tiny stone cottage which looks sound enough but the barn next to it is in ruins, sagging beneath the weight of its own dereliction. It is the sort of old barn which you would pass by and not even register.

Perfect for Gypsies.

Six women are inside – five of them crouching around the sixth who lies supine on the hard earth floor. A birthing sheet has been laid beneath her and two women sit either side of it waving inefficient fans made from twigs and straw. The woman wears only a loose chemise – the others have undressed her, folded her three-layered skirts and hastily unplaited her braids to allow the gold coins trapped in her stiff, oiled hair to drop loose. The coins have been gathered and, along with her elaborate jewellery and money belt, placed outside the barn. They must not become *marimé* – Unclean. Divested of her finery, how vulnerable the woman seems. Two of the women are supporting her at her shoulders, raising her when she flaps a hand upwards to indicate her position is uncomfortable. For the moment, she is pausing between contractions to close her eyes and pant gently. She has not yet reached the wild time, when she will move into a crouching position and lose all awareness of the processes of breathing.

The remaining woman squats between the labouring woman's legs, observing the blossoming of her vagina. She thinks it will be some time yet.

The boy will be called Emil. His mother is Anna Maximoff, a tall woman famed for her good looks, breeding and pride. She is also considered insightful but as she is currently giving birth to her first child she is temporarily deprived of the ability to see further than the next contraction.

Her cousin Tekla – the woman examining her – predicts that Anna is not nearly open enough for the pushing to begin and that a lengthy battle lies ahead.

Little Emil has other ideas.

The men of the *kumpánia* have been sent to find the nearest village or, if they cannot locate it, otherwise occupy themselves. The group was on its way to Kladno when Anna's time came early. They were hoping to reach the sour-cherry orchards on the westerly outskirts, Ctibor Michálek's orchards.

No man will be allowed near Anna for two weeks after the birth, while she is still *marimé*. She will not be permitted to wash or cook or perform any duties which might contaminate them. Instead, she will be tended by Tekla while she lies in the barn, feeds the child, sleeps and dreams of his future. When they are alone together, she will whisper his real name into his ear.

*

Tekla allows herself a small smile at her memory of the look on Josef's face as she ushered him away with the other men. Josef is her cousin and Anna's husband, famous for bursting into tears when his wife was stung by a bee at their wedding feast, while the assembled guests flung their arms up and burst out laughing, declaring that a bee-sting was good luck, the next best thing to bird shit.

For a moment, Tekla remains lost in this memory and has time to note that it – still – causes her pain. Then Anna lets out a strange, meandering howl, arching her back, as if the curve of noise is raising her body from the floor.

Tekla looks up in surprise. She sits up and commands the other women to lift Anna and turn her, the sharpness in her voice obscuring her alarm.

Tekla has dealt with sixteen births and never yet had to cut a baby loose of its mother. The thought makes the back of her neck prickle. She has a knife ready, as she does each time, cleansed in the fire that morning before they left the forest camp and wrapped tightly in clean cloth to keep it uncontaminated. It is hidden in the pocket of her apron. When she bends over, she can feel it resting across the top of her thighs. The cloth might be difficult to unwind in a hurry.

The women supporting Anna look to Tekla for instruction. Božena and Dunicha have borne five children between them. They know enough to sense that something is amiss. Božena is fond of contradicting Tekla but even she looks at her appealingly now.

Tekla does not trust herself to speak again, fearing the tone of her voice might convey alarm to Anna. She gestures with both hands, palms upwards. Božena and Dunicha lift Anna from her crouching position with one arm each over the nearest shoulder. They brace themselves to take her weight – she will push down towards the ground so that the powers of the Earth will help to pull the baby out. The women with the fans, Ludmila and Eva, instinctively increase the intensity of their flapping, as if the air they generate might wash away Anna's pain. All four have their gazes concentrated, breathing in time. Anna's face, normally clear and calm, is bathed in sweat. Her eyes stare wildly around, from one woman to the next, as if she is accusing each of them in turn of being her torturer. The veins on the back of her neck stand out in great twisted ropes as she strains. Tekla remembers that Eva and Ludmila have never attended a birth. It must be frightening for them to see Anna, their beautiful Anna, made ugly by this extremity.

Only Tekla herself is managing to maintain a distance, a coolness in her thoughts – if quick decisions must be made, they will be her responsibility. She feels as though her mind has gone numb, as if the insignificant has become hugely important and vice versa. She finds herself noticing that a supporting beam in the centre of the barn is full of woodworm. In a far corner, there is a rusted iron mangle which was once painted green. The bowl and rollers are missing. She hears a husky snuffling and glances round to see that the old dog Biri has worked his way loose from where he was tied outside and is scrabbling beneath the barn door, desperate for admittance.

They should have left the door ajar, Tekla thinks. It is completely airless in the barn. She can feel the sweat running down her back and chest, small rivulets between her paps and a stickiness which will be darkening the back of her blouse.

Anna throws her head back and lets out another howl, bearing down between Božena and Dunicha, her full-throated yell dying into a pitiful cry that sounds as if it is trapped at the back of her throat and whimpering for release. Tekla lies down on her side, turns her head and peers between her cousin's legs – and what she sees makes her realise there is no time to be lost.

*

The story about Anna's husband Josef and the bee was absolutely true. He did cry easily; but he only cried for others.

As a child, Josef had been trampled by one of his father's mares. His left leg was mashed, the bone splintered twice below the knee. There was no doctor in the village, so his father and uncle held him down while his mother strapped two wooden splints either side of the bone.

They were in Upper Hungary then, in a settled *tabor* by the River Dunaj, close to a village called Sap. His father bought and sold horses, across the river mostly, dealing with a group of Lowari Gypsies and a few *gadje* – he spoke fluent Magyar, Slovak and German along with Romani. His mother sewed and spoke only Romani and Czech. She hated being settled and begged his father nightly to take to the road, if only in summertime.

The *tabor* was squeezed between marshland at the southerly edge of the village and the river. The wagons were enormous square things with flat roofs and wheels sunk deep into the mud – they had been there for two generations. They would never move again.

In the summer the camp was plagued with huge swarms of bluebottles, plump and iridescent, buzzing and dancing in their anxiety to mate. It was particularly bad around the pea harvest, when the rotting matter left by the thresher gangs sent the flies wild. Each family would string washing lines around their wagon and hang up sheets of flypaper in rows – to get from wagon to wagon you had to duck beneath the sheets. When the flypaper became so dense with insects you couldn't see what it was any more, it would be taken down and burnt on the fire. Charred flakes would shoot upwards in a hot column – the area around the fire would become engulfed in a cloud, the puffing ash of little legs and wings.

The flies reached their peak in August, when the mosquito season started. The summer swarms drove Josef's father crazy but he did not want to take to the road while the horse business was so good. He was forever threatening to buy a little house in the village amongst the *gadje* – a threat which would send Josef's mother running to the other women for comfort, sobbing and flapping her apron.

It was a *gadjo* doctor who persuaded Josef's parents to break the leg again. He was a town doctor, a Hungarian from Nitra who had been passing through Sap one day on his way to Győr. He had stopped to visit a relative and had seen young Josef hobbling back towards the camp with an egg in each hand – the eggs lending tremors to Josef's limp as his stick was tucked under one arm. Assuming him to be palsied, a speciality of his, the doctor had followed Josef on foot to the Gypsy *tabor*, where he strode through the wagons oblivious to the hostile stares of the residents. He introduced himself to Josef's father and asked to examine the boy.

He was a little disappointed to discover that the limp was due to a badly set bone, but he offered to do the family a favour: re-break the leg and set it properly with a set of iron callipers which he had in the back of his carriage, parked outside his aunt's house in Sap. He would do it without payment as long as he was permitted to visit them every six months for the next two years and check on Josef's progress. Josef's father must give his word of honour that he would relinquish the callipers when the two years were up, or leave them on the aunt's doorstep if the family took to the road before then.

At this point, most men would have escorted the doctor to the banks of the Dunaj, and booted him in: but Josef's father was used to dealing with *gadje*, and he was a pragmatist. He wanted his son to follow him into the horse business. You needed two good legs to ride.

Josef's mother had to be carried bodily from their wagon.

They held Josef's nose and poured *slivovice* into his mouth until he coughed and swallowed. Then they broke his leg with a wooden mallet. At the first blow, Josef fainted. When he came round he vomited. Then he fainted again. The fainting and vomiting continued intermittently for a week, accompanied by a fever. By then the *gadjo* doctor had left with a cheery wave and a promise to visit them in six months' time. Josef's mother burned blackberry leaves in a dish and prayed to the Saints and cursed the day she and his father had ever met. Without consulting her husband – an unheard-of rebellion – she arranged for her uncle to summon a *drabarni* all the way from the Eastern Mountains, to be paid on arrival by one of the gold coins from her braids. When Josef's father found out he smashed all their wedding crockery and they didn't speak to each other for ten months.

The *drabarni* came, took the coin, and told them there was

nothing she could do for a child whose leg was still clasped by a *gadjo*'s implement.

It was a month before Josef left his bed and another two before he regained his strength and could walk without pain. Throughout all this, he never cried. He screamed sometimes – fainted and vomited on occasion. But there were no tears.

Then one day, when he still had to drag his leg behind him like a dead dog on a stick, he was walking past his mother as she kneeled before the fire frying potato cakes. She was in the process of wrapping her apron around the handle of the blackened pan. As she lifted the pan, the edge of her apron caught on the trivet and it tipped from her grasp, emptying its contents on to the embers and burning her hand as she tried to prevent it.

A child was not to realise it, but his mother's cry was more at the loss of the food than at her burnt hand. At the sight of her twisted face, Josef began to wail – and once he had begun, he could not stop.

After that, he would cry at the slightest excuse – but only when the pain or distress occured to someone other than himself. Bad news in the *tabor* was kept from him. If another child scraped a knee or brushed a thistle, Josef's mother would turn his head away from the sight. His father would not even whip a horse in front of him.

When the *gadjo* doctor returned two years later to prise off the callipers, Josef gripped his father's arm so tightly he drew blood with his fingernails – but shed not a tear.

When his wife Anna was stung by a bee on their wedding day, Josef Maximoff wept for the remainder of the feast. He was so in love with Anna he wanted to die. He wanted to weep every time he looked at her; her beauty, her strength and stubbornness. It was that very strength that made her seem so vulnerable at times. She would never admit to anything, so he felt it all, continually, on her behalf.

They were in Moravia by then. Josef's mother had finally won out and they had taken to the road, using Sap as their winter quarters. Josef's father's spirit had been broken long before. When the *gadje* had their Great War, a colonel had come recruiting for the Imperial Army and left with half the men and all the horses. Josef's father had pleaded to be conscripted so that he could stay with the animals but the colonel said the horses were not being allocated to the *gypsy* regiment. They wouldn't even admit Josef's father into the infantry. They said he was bow-legged and too old.

None of the horses or men ever returned from the *gadje*'s Great War. The horses were shot to pieces from underneath their Magyar lieutenants. The Roma regiments were the first to be sent into action to be mown down by the French.

Josef's parents were to die not long after he was married. Neither of them lived to see how inexplicably long it would be, seven years, before Anna became pregnant with Josef's first child. When she told him she was carrying a baby, he fell down on his knees in front of the entire *kumpánia*, stretched his arms and burst out sobbing – Josef Maximoff, crying for himself at last. All the women around had smiled and shaken their heads. Anna had laughed a huge red laugh.

No man was allowed near his wife when she was in labour, but everyone in Josef's *kumpánia* agreed – the minute Anna's pains began, he was to be hurried from the scene as quickly as possible.

*

As he walked along the edge of the field with the other men, Josef chewed at an ear of wheat and tried not to think about the

look in Anna's eyes as she had stirred the fire that morning. It
was a concentrated look. Her mind was elsewhere. At the time,
he had wondered if her belly was so large it was no longer
comfortable to squat. Now he realised that her pains must have
started.

Normally Anna would walk alongside the wagon while they
travelled – she liked to walk, even as her girth expanded and her
stride turned into a slow waddle. That morning, she had been
uncharacteristically quiet while brewing his tea. They had
loaded up the wagon together in silence. Josef had glanced at her
surreptitiously from time to time, then harnessed the horse and
climbed up on to the wagon. When he was settled with the reins
in his hands, he turned to look at her.

For a moment, Anna stood beside the wagon, frowning to
herself. The other families had loaded up and harnessed and
were waiting for Josef and Anna to move off before following.
Only Tekla was not quite ready, messing around by the fire.

Anna pursed her lips, bit at the lower one, unpursed them
and said in a small voice. 'Husband, move over there.'

He had gazed down at her. Anna had never used a small
voice in her life. As she climbed up carefully on the seat beside
him, he had thought, ah well, the sour cherries will wait.

For the rest of their journey, he drove as if the wagon was
piled high with eggs. Anna sat bolt upright next to him, her
hands on her knees and her arms locked, as though she lacked
a spine. She said nothing. Only her breathing betrayed her:
periodically, it would deepen, then she would exhale with
stealthy force, as if she was trying to whistle without making any
noise.

Tekla, Ludmila and Eva were in the back of the wagon, and
every hour or so Tekla would climb up and rest her forearms on
the seat, peering between them. She tried to persuade Anna to

come inside with the other women – which would have been a great deal more seemly than her riding up with Josef for all the world to see – but Anna was not given to being seemly at the best of times. She was breathing in the morning air and gazing around the fields. Josef guessed that she was searching out the best place to stop. He respected her need to feel that the place was right. There was no telling how long they would have to be pulled up, after all. Perhaps she would ask him to change course and head for the woods at Kralupy, where they would be able to pull into a clearing and be out of sight.

The sun was high by the time she lifted her hand and Josef pulled sharply on the reins. He looked around to see what she had spotted. They were still in open countryside.

The field to the left had no gate and was fallow. Cows grazed the neighbouring land but there were no dwellings in sight. Then he saw what she had seen. At the far end of the fallow field, almost obscured by trees and bushes and snuggling insecurely next to an old cottage, lay a derelict barn.

Anna's expression was glazed as Tekla helped her down from the wagon and issued orders to everybody else. The men were ignored while the women gathered around Anna, taking her from Josef and swallowing her in their women's care. His last glimpse of her as they led her to the barn – panting openly now – was of the back of her tall head, clearly visible above the others, her headscarf neatly knotted at the nape of her neck.

The men pulled the wagons round the high hedge that bordered the field, unharnessed and tied the horses in the shade, ensuring their tethers were long enough for them to grass. Josef was brisk in his actions, feeling the need for physical activity. He unloaded a bale of hay and pulled a fistful loose, then used it to wipe the sweat from the geldings, rough in his desire to do something useful, to think of anything but his wife.

His proximity to the horses calmed him a little. They were the finest in the *kumpánia*, four-year-olds. He was the only man who had a pair – they had cost him sixteen thousand crowns each. Wiping them down was the first thing he did each time they pulled up, no matter how thirsty or dirty he might be himself.

When he had finished, he assembled the others. They would find the nearest village on foot – the local *gadje* might not be accustomed to People and it would frighten them if they turned up in a caravan. They needed salt, and Josef needed new bellows. He had patched his old ones with pig skin so many times that air puffed from everywhere but the nozzle.

The wagons were still visible from the road, so they left old Ludvík Franz and his wife to look after them and the horses. Eva Winterová and her sisters were instructed to remain with them and gather firewood. As the men set off, Josef heard a twisted howl from inside the barn.

When the men had traversed the edge of the wheatfield, they climbed a sty and tramped alongside younger, greener wheat, infected here and there with bracken. Josef guessed that a generation ago, the whole area had been wooded. The ground began to slope gently upwards, towards a tended copse. When they had passed the trees, they could look down across more fields to see the smoky smudge of a village in the middle distance. Josef paused and removed his hat to wipe his brow with his handkerchief. He always felt the heat, particularly on his face. Walking when it was warm made his leg ache which exacerbated his limp.

It took them less than half an hour to reach the village, which seemed to comprise little more than a small crossroads and a mud-track main street with rows of cottages on either side. There was no one around. At the end of the street, they found a tiny chapel and schoolhouse, and close by a small shop which had sweets in the window – jars of fruit-flavoured toffees wrapped in coloured papers and burnt-brown sugar sticks.

They entered cautiously. No one was behind the counter but there were rows of shelves upon which household goods were piled; blankets and tin buckets and oil lanterns with foggy glass.

A man emerged from the back room as they entered. He glanced them over, then nodded, reserved but courteous. There was nowhere where they would get bellows, he said, they would have to wait until Kladno, but he would sell them a block of salt and a beer apiece. He had his own barrels. He was about to close for the afternoon, but he would give them clay mugs and they could leave them by the door afterwards.

Josef enquired about who owned the land with the old barn and the shopkeeper gave them the farmer's name, Myclík.

We must pay him a visit on the way back, Josef thought. It would be a good idea to get to him before somebody else went and told him there were *gypsies* on his land.

They emerged from the gloom of the shop to blink at the hot sun. Václav had unbuttoned his shirt to the waist. He flapped it so that it billowed outwards. 'Josef,' he said, 'those trees over there?'

Opposite the shop there was a small rise topped by cluster of oak trees which provided a canopy over the village well. Josef glanced around. The village still seemed empty but he didn't like the idea of sitting down and drinking somewhere so visible. 'Behind the well,' he replied.

They sat in a semi-circle and rested their backs against the rough stone; Josef in the middle, Václav on one side and Yakali and his two sons on the other. Each man tipped a little of his drink on the ground. There was silence.

There was a coolness between Václav and Yakali. In the quiet moment, Josef acknowledged that it had deepened recently. Yakali had Justin and Miroslav, two strapping lads, fifteen and fourteen respectively, both desperate to marry at this year's harvest. Václav had three young daughters; Zdenka, Pavla and Eva. A man with three daughters would always feel at a disadvantage next to a man who had produced sons. Yakali never lorded it over Václav but it stood between them like a stagnant pond.

Zdenka would be twelve in the autumn. She and fourteen-year-old Miroslav had begun to eye each other, but Josef knew Yakali had plans for his sons to marry elsewhere. The Zelinka *vitsa* would gather at the harvest and Yakali had a long-held understanding with a South Bohemian family who had two daughters the same age as his sons. Yakali's wife Dunicha was keen on the match. With three men to look after she couldn't wait to have a couple of *bori* to take over the chores. If Miroslav married Zdenka then Dunicha would have Zdenka's mother Božena in the next wagon, keeping far too close an eye on her daughter's well-being.

In the meantime, Václav was naturally becoming anxious about where he was going to place his girls. He wouldn't get much of a price for them, in Josef's opinion: they were short like their father and dark like their mother. Zdenka had receding gums and bad skin.

It was a pity, all the same. Josef would have been happy to see a tie between the Winters and Zelinkas. It would strengthen the *kumpánia*. Zdenka was a good girl, hard-working and modest. She would be disappointed when she realised Miroslav's parents were negotiating with another family. He hoped it would not cause bitterness.

The first sip of beer was so refreshing it gave Josef the illusion that his thirst was quenched. By the third sip, he was uncomfortable again. The other men had leaned their heads back and closed their eyes, grateful to be out of the sun. Yakali had pulled his hat down over his face and was resting his wrists on his knees with his hands hanging limply, his mug already emptied and discarded by his side. Josef tried not to resent how easy it was for Yakali to relax.

For once, they had plenty of time. Josef closed his eyes and tried to quell his unease. To stop himself thinking about Anna in pain, he thought about Anna on their wedding night. She had stood over him in the tent and he had waited for her to fling her long skirt and petticoats upwards in one swift movement – it was what a woman like Anna would do. Instead, she had gazed down at him, then grasped two great, full handfuls, raising her garments centimetre by centimetre, with exquisite slowness, gazing at him all the while, her smile growing broader and broader as the skirt rose higher and higher . . . He would never forget that moment, her delight in confounding his expectations of her.

He opened his eyes to lift his clay mug to his mouth. Halfway through the action he paused, knowing all at once that he would not be able to swallow. He lowered the mug again, sighing gently. O, that a man could relive his wedding night a thousand times, instead of all that followed; the worry, the responsibility – the thought that as he drank beer in the shade Anna was lost in the agony and mystery of whatever it was that women went through. It made him feel inadequate, his worry, less of a man.

'Josef . . .' Václav said without turning, his voice softly reproachful, '. . . drink your beer. Enjoy these moments. Today of all days you should drink. Your son is being born.'

A first-born was always referred to as a son until it was proved to be otherwise. Josef sighed again, more heavily. He didn't care if the child was a boy or a girl or a piglet with a blue tail, just as long as Anna survived.

Ahead of him were the fields on the edge of the village, a wide expanse covered by a mass of dark green corn, leaves glistening and the air above shifting and shimmering in the heat. A light breeze was blowing. A pair of buzzards were riding the warm air, lazy and inseparable. He had met a man in Mělnik once, an Elder who had lost three wives in childbirth, one after the other. Even though he had been left with five children to raise, he had declared he could not bear to marry again.

Josef closed his eyes once more, as if preventing vision might prevent speculation. It didn't work, but he allowed the breeze to play on his face.

Beside him, Yakali began to snore.

His eyes had been closed for only a moment when he was woken from his thoughts by a deep, bubbling voice which declared, 'So, *gypsies*, nothing to do but drink beer and doze, eh? You lucky people. God's favourites I'd say.'

Josef sat up. The man in front of them was a municipal policeman, his moustache bristling and unkempt, his eyes alight with a cold twinkle. He was on duty, his uniform jacket tightly buttoned. The only concession he had made to the heat was to push his cap up from his forehead so it sat at an unsteady angle on the back of his head, atop a mass of thick, mid-brown hair. On one shoulder he wore a small drum. Two short wooden drumsticks were clasped in the other hand. He had one foot up on the grass slope, right in front of them, and was leaning forward, resting on his knee.

'Good afternoon, Officer,' said Josef stiffly, embarrassed that the man should have been able approach with none of them hearing.

The Officer looked at him but did not return his greeting. 'Where might you be going, *gypsies*?' he asked casually.

Václav jumped to his feet. 'Officer, you must congratulate this man. As we speak, his son is being born.'

Never tell a gadjo where you are going or where you have been. If they know where you come from, they will close the road behind you. If they find out where you're heading, they will have a gallows waiting.

Václav was beaming with joy. 'We are smiths, heading up to Teplice. We have three months' work awaiting us. This man's wife was taken ill this morning. It is his first child, you can imagine how he is feeling. Do you have sons yet, Officer? Of course you do, a man such as yourself . . .'

The Officer stood upright and grinned to show he wasn't fooled. 'The whole village will be out shortly, *gypsies*. I suggest you make yourselves scarce.'

Josef rose. 'My name is Josef Růžička,' he said solemnly. 'And my family will be stopping in this area for a while. We were on our way to find a farmer named Myclík. Will he also be out shortly? We have business with him.'

'Myclík will be working his farm,' said the Officer. 'It's what farmers do, I'm told, but if you're determined to hang around then his son will be here. He's married to a villager but he works for his father in the evenings. He'll have just finished sleeping off his lunch.' His tone of voice suggested that he put Myclík's son in more or less the same bracket as *gypsies*.

He turned away from them and re-adjusted his cap. Then he lifted the drum from his shoulder and pulled the leather strap over his head, which involved re-adjusting the cap again. He descended the shallow slope, paused to cough, then lifted his drumsticks smartly. He began to beat as he walked.

'Stay here, brothers,' said Josef, then followed the Officer down the slope.

Three small children ran out of a cottage to greet the Officer as he strode smartly down the main street, beating his drum. Two were little girls who fell in beside him, clinging to each other and staring. The third child was a boy who stepped smartly behind the Officer, lifting his feet high to march in time with the drum. As the small parade progressed, villagers emerged from their houses, the women wiping their hands on their aprons, the men fixing caps on their heads.

Only a woman from the nearest cottage glanced behind and saw Josef, following at a respectful distance. Her eyes widened and she ran up to the two women in front of her to whisper at them. They turned and stared as they walked.

At the end of the main street was a crossroads with a wooden Calvary erected on a stone plinth. The Officer turned and stood facing the villagers, legs firmly planted. He continued to drum until he was sure they were assembled. They had all seen Josef now, who stood apart and watched the Officer with calm interest. The Officer gave a final roll of his drum and then lifted the sticks sharply, freezing in position for a second. The boy who had followed him stood to attention beside him, frowning self-importantly.

After a ceremonious pause, the Officer tucked the drumsticks into his top pocket, sat on the edge of the plinth and pulled a folded piece of paper from inside his jacket.

'In Prague today,' he began in a tired voice, 'it was announced that further to last year's coalition agreements between the government, the German Agrarian Party and the Christian Social Party, additional measures are to be introduced towards a general inclusivity of all national minorities. Immediate opposition to this proposal was announced by the Slovak Clerical Party . . .' One of the villagers began sneezing ostentatiously. 'Whose secretary today emphasised that their continued co-operation in Cabinet was dependent upon governmental support for the discouragement of Magyar Irredentism upon Slovak territory. President Masaryk has provided full assurances . . .'

Josef allowed himself a conspicuous yawn. White people. *Gadje. National* this; *national* that – the Empire had been dead for eight years and still they were scrapping over its corpse. How may one own the earth? Plant on it, travel it, dig it – but own it? *Gadje.* They would plant a flag on the moon if they could. *Gadje, gadje dile.* Truly, there was nothing wrong with the world that was not the fault of the *gadje.*

He glanced around the villagers – a small group, not wealthy by the looks of them. The women were stout and tired-looking, sallow-skinned. Odd how these Czech *gadje* could seem both dark and unhealthily pale at the same time. Josef preferred Eastern and Balkan *gadje.* They were swarthy and vicious, the lot of them, but you knew where you stood. These Bohemians thought of themselves as progressive and that often made them worse.

The Officer was talking about a new law to enable the commencement of the building of integrated town complexes in the spirit of constructivism and functionalism.

Josef wondered if Myclík's son was the slender youth to his left who was standing with his head hanging down, drawing circles in the dirt with the toe of one shoe. He had both hands tucked underneath his armpits and was bareheaded, as though he had just been dragged out of bed and could scarcely be bothered to dress. He felt a rush of sympathy for the unknown Myclík, followed by an inner glow as he realised he had been thinking, *children, what can you do with them?* A drop of sweat ran down his forehead. He blinked. *Anna, Anna, Anna . . .*

The Officer had paused to gain everybody's attention. He glanced at Josef.

'The implementation of Law 117 is today announced, being a Law to curb the nuisance caused by so-called Gypsies and other Travelling Persons and Vagabonds.'

Josef stared fiercely at the Officer, immediately aware that the stare of every other inhabitant of the village was now rested upon himself.

The Officer continued amiably. 'All persons who have no fixed abode or who are of a nomadic inclination must present themselves immediately to the nearest authority of the state for the issuing of detailed identification. Each member of the family over the age of fifteen must attend, although all family members may be registered upon the identification papers of the head of the family. Prints of all five fingers on each hand will be required along with a physical description of each individual. This paper will then supersede the previous identification papers upon which only the thumb-print of the right hand was required. In addition, each individual must provide evidence of means of income, along with a full account of the route their nomadising habits require them to take. Failure to comply with these regulations will result in an immediate fine of one hundred crowns, to be increased with each subsequent breach of regulations by a further one hundred. Prison sentences will be levied upon defaulters. This law is applicable immediately and all nomads must herewith present themselves to the relevant authorities without further hesitation or delay.'

At the end of this announcement, the Officer allowed a dramatic pause before rising, adjusting his cap and retrieving his drum and drumsticks. He gave a final, staccato roll on the drum to indicate to the assembled company that Law 117 was the final piece of news he had to impart that day.

The crowd broke into loud, spontaneous applause. One of the women gave a forced laugh. Two of the men whistled. The small boy rushed up to Josef and jumped up and down in front of him making derisive noises with his tongue between his teeth, eyes bulging, until his mother rushed over, grabbed him by his arm and dragged him away. The villagers broke into loud chatter as they turned to their homes. Several glanced back at Josef, to observe his reaction.

The Officer removed his cap, lifted the drum strap over his head and put the drum down beside him. He wrinkled his nose at the sun and wiped his forehead with his sleeve, then twisted his arm to frown at the row of silver buttons at the cuff. He shrugged without looking at Josef. 'Don't say I didn't warn you,' he said.

He rummaged in a trouser pocket and retrieved a voluminous cotton handkerchief with which he proceeded to wipe his buttons. 'I come here on Monday afternoons to do the news,' he said, 'but I don't stop. They expect me to cover eight villages in one day and my superintendent doesn't believe in bicycles. Imagine. My counterpart in the next district has a brand new Orion motorcycle and I'm not allowed so much as a pair of pedals. I'm here on Thursday mornings for other business. Old Jirout sets up a desk in his shop.' Satisfied with the state of his buttons, he rose and replaced his cap. It was only then he met Josef's gaze.

'You'll all have to turn up, men, women, everyone over the age of fifteen. Bring your papers with you, or any other proof of identity. Receipts for any purchases you've made in the last year would be useful, if you keep such things, although you probably don't, anything that will prove your route. I needn't explain that you'll all be liable for arrest if you don't show up. You look like a sensible man.' He nodded. 'My name is Slavíček. Good day to you.' He turned, smartly.

As Josef walked back along the main street, the villagers came to their doorways and windows to observe him silently. As he approached the well, he remembered that he had neglected to enquire after the farmer Myclík's son.

The others were standing, gathered round the well, watching his approach.

Josef stopped in front of them. He felt old. 'We must go back at once,' he said, and the others nodded, acknowledging the seriousness of his tone. Young Miroslav gathered up the clay mugs to deposit them in front of the shop. Václav shouldered the block of salt. They turned to walk back down the road.

The sun was more yellow now. As he descended the slope, Josef felt a rush of longing for the honest noon-day heat, the white noon when he had known nothing of the *gadje*'s latest Law. It is a bad omen, he thought, and he found himself hastening his step. It is a bad omen for my child. It became imperative that he return to the barn as quickly as possible.

In his anxiety, he forgot the stares of the villagers and almost ran back down the street. The others hurried behind him. The small boy leaned out of his window as they passed and called after them in a victorious treble, 'Run, *gypsies*, run!'

CHAPTER 2

The old dog Biri was a clever dog who acted stupidly, which was either stupid or clever, depending on your point of view. When the wagons were pulled up, he had been tied to the spoke of a wheel but with characteristic ingenuity had worked his way loose. Having failed to gain entry to the barn, he had then occupied himself by jumping around the field looking for mice or rabbits, a task he performed by bounding about almost vertically, as if on a spring.

At the sound of Josef and the other men returning, Biri abandoned his hunt and began to run excitedly towards them, across the field. The grasses were higher than he – all that betrayed his swift presence was an invisible finger drawing a waving line through the wheat, a line which snaked from left to right in a haphazard but inexorable route towards the men.

As they neared the barn, Josef watched Biri's hidden

approach. What news would the old dog bring? He felt he would know what had happened as soon as he bent to scratch his ear.

Biri gave a single bark of pleasure as he ran up to them. He described a figure of eight around Josef and Václav, then returned to Josef for a scratch, panting happily. *Stupid dog*, thought Josef as he bent down. *What would he know?*

He stood upright and looked across the field. He saw Tekla emerge from round the side of the barn. She stopped and leant against the wall, then bent double, as if she was weeping, or being sick. He started to run, crashing through the wheat, Biri jumping excitedly alongside. He was twenty metres from Tekla when she straightened and saw him. He stopped and stared at her.

She gazed back at him for a moment, an admonitory gaze, then her look softened a little. He blinked and realised that his eyes were full of tears. He had run a few metres but his heart was thumping as if he had sprinted from Bratislava.

'It was bad,' Tekla called out to him. 'But they will live.'

Biri was jumping in the air, again and again, letting out mock snarls to entice his master to play.

Josef looked back. The other men were striding across the field towards him, following the path he had cut through the wheat.

'Josef,' called Tekla, and he turned to her. It was only then that he saw she was clutching a bloodied knife. 'Return to the others. Go to the wagons and build a fire, open the flasks. Give praise to O Del. You have a son. Tell the others their women will not lie with them tonight. We all had to help. It was bad. It was a bloodbath. You have a son.'

*

It seemed extraordinary to Anna that Tekla insisted she lie still. She felt as if she could lift her son into her arms and whirl about the barn, but she felt it in her mind, her body somehow aware that such activity was impossible. This is what it means, she thought, to be a mother at last – to have a body that knows it cannot do things but a mind which tells you to fly to the skies if you wish, sit in the trees like a sparrow and sing to the world. There has never been a better baby. There has never been a baby at all, before now. I have the first, the only one. I have invented the baby. All the babies that come after this one will be as shadows, ghosts. Hang banners, dance and sing, line the highways with cheering hordes of peasants – here is my child.

He was suckling now, her boy, his tiny mouth fixed around her huge brown nipple, his head smaller than her tight, marbled breast. Cradled in her arm, his body was warm and still covered with fine white fluid, his face wrinkled tight with the effort of existing. You will learn how to do it, she thought amusedly. It will come naturally soon.

The other women had left, weeping and exhausted, but Tekla was still with her. She had propped Anna's legs in the air and had jammed clean cloth between her thighs. Every now and then, she lifted the outer layer of cloth to examine the blood-soaked bundles underneath.

Anna knew that Tekla was worried about the bleeding but she could not bring herself to be concerned. She had not even felt the cut, for by then her whole body had become one muscle, every cell of her being channelled into the vast effort of pushing down. In the midst of it, she had heard a distant voice, Tekla's voice, shouting, 'Don't push, don't push . . .' but by then the barn was full of the wild yelling that came from deep inside her and Eva and Ludmila sobbing in unison and the laboured breathing of Božena, a breath which became bellow as Anna bore down, a guttural cry on her behalf.

Then, suddenly, everybody was crying. A small red wet thing was flopped on to her chest and Tekla was calling out in hoarse desperation. Anna was only vaguely aware of the crying and busyness of the others, for every part of her was flooded with joy.

It was good the others had been there, Anna thought. The boy would belong to the whole *kumpánia* now. It would bind them. It was unusual for all the women to stay for the delivery but at no stage had Tekla given the others permission to leave. Anna had seen their faces as Tekla had shoved them towards the door afterwards; their shared joy in their achievement, the radiance.

Ludmila had returned briefly with lime blossom tea and unleavened bread, peering joyously at the baby before being shooed away by Tekla. Now, Anna and Tekla and the baby were alone, and this was the best of times. Now all was quiet and warm and the white sunlight burst jealously through the cracks in the barn's ceiling.

'Are the men back yet?' Anna asked Tekla, speaking without raising her head, unable to tear her gaze from where it was examining the deep crease of skin at the top of her baby's nose. 'Has Josef been told?'

Tekla looked round. 'I told him,' she said. 'They were just coming back when I took the cloths outside. I told him to build the fires. We will hear them singing tonight, no doubt.'

'He knows to choose a boy's name?' The father chose the daily name for each child, but the mother had the privilege of whispering the baby's real name into its ear. The mother did not even have to tell the father what it was. The fewer people who knew a child's real name the better. A real name was power.

Tekla nodded, and gave a small, twisted smile.

*

As Tekla turned away, busying herself by clearing more of the soiled garments into a bundle for burning, she realised she was feeling a raw pang of envy, like stomach-ache. She would never name a child. How strange, she thought, that I should be the one in pain, while she over there lies beaming and glowing. She was feeling the old, gnawing sensation, the dull unhappiness that she thought she had put behind her eight years ago on a night when she had foresworn any emotion at all. In all those years, she had not allowed herself the luxury of misery, not once.

It was bad to feel this way, a bad omen for the boy. Did she want to put the Evil Eye on him? What was she thinking of? She tried to direct the feeling away from Anna and her baby, to channel it into a generalised resentment against all the women who had taken her services for granted over the years. Mothers have it easy, she thought. They never see what goes on between their legs. It's me who has to do the work. It was me who dealt with this baby emerging shoulder first, the cord wrapped twice around its neck and the placenta bouncing out behind like a raft on a river of blood. All *she* did was push.

'How will the men eat?' Anna asked without lifting her gaze from her child. 'Zdenka will have to make soup, I suppose. There's barley. Božena can direct her. Will that be acceptable?'

'It is up to you,' Tekla replied, still busying herself.

Anna looked at her at last. They had always shared the management of the food for the *kumpánia* but Tekla was ten years Anna's senior and in the absence of Josef's parents had always assumed a certain seniority.

'You have a child,' Tekla said quietly. 'You are a proper Romni now. The decision is yours.'

'Tekla . . .' Anna said softly, her voice gentle and amused. 'You will always be half of any decision I make. Child or no child. I have no title that I do not owe to you.'

Anna's kindness irritated Tekla, with its implied graciousness, but she tried to quell her bitterness. She did not trust her own emotions on this matter. She should be grateful, after all. Few unmarried women were ever accorded the status she had within Josef's family.

'We are not through this yet,' she said roughly, to hide her feelings.

Anna gave a small laugh. 'Don't fear for me, Tekla. I have a boy to care for now. No ill will befall him or me. I will see to it.'

Tekla shook her head. She had seen this many times. For the first couple of days, the new mothers always thought themselves immortal. Then the weeping and the tiredness would come. Anna would find out soon enough.

*

When Tekla had left, Anna realised that there was one thing better than being alone with Tekla and her baby – it was being alone with the baby, just the two of them, her arm around him creating the perfect circumference.

He was sleeping now. Tekla had warned her to rest, she would need every minute, she said, but Anna could not bear to close her eyes: not when her son was there to gaze upon.

She gazed as it grew dark outside and she heard the crackle and leap of the fires. They would need two, dug into holes on separate sides of the field; one for Tekla to burn the bloodied things and another for Zdenka to warm soup for the men. They would be gathering in a circle at the far end of the field. In the stillness, their voices would carry, floating and mingling with the demented swooping of the bats and the exhausted chuckles from the women's circle. The women would be re-living the birth, swapping stories. Tekla would get to talk about how she had felt at each stage and at last receive her reward; the unqualified praise and admiration of the other women. The young Winterová girls would fall asleep gradually, grumpily, having been refused permission to come and see the baby. A boy for them all to spoil – what a perfect thing. What a little prince he would turn out to be.

A son, Anna thought, with all her new and sudden wisdom: a son is a blessing and a curse, a treasure and an agony. A girl would be a part of me, like a limb. But a boy, how long will he be mine? Before I know it, he will join the men. He will run from me without so much as a backward glance.

Little Stranger, she thought, exhaling softly over his head, to encourage him. *Tiny thing, of me, but far from me.*

He will have to have a name to give the *gadje*, Anna sighed: probably František. She and Josef had discussed it. Perhaps the *kumpánia* could call him Emil. She liked Emil. It was a name to linger over. Em*eel* . . .

His breathing was so slight she could scarcely detect it, even when she lowered her face to his. The smell of him, like new bread, or was it her smell? She could not tell. He and I smell identical, she thought, smiling in the darkness. The barn was softly warm, and the warmth and softness wrapped around mother and child as they curled together in the gloom, breathed together, smelled the same.

'Yenko,' Anna whispered in her son's ear. 'Your real name is Yenko.'

*

In the morning, Josef awoke with his mouth stuck solid. He had been snoring all night and the heat and closeness inside the wagon had baked his exposed tongue. He had drunk too much last night – it would have been impolite not to raise his glass with the others, even though they all knew he never normally took more than a single beer. Then he had reached a point when he had no longer noticed how much he was drinking. He had stood and sang a song about his love for his son. They had all become maudlin. He had gone to the wagon to sleep instead of

lying in the grass with the others, sobbing all the way because
the beauty of the stars was more than he could bear.

He rolled over and was suddenly aware of an urgent need to
urinate – so urgent that he lay still with his eyes closed, knowing
that further movement would be uncomfortable. After a while,
he turned slowly, lifting an arm in expectation of Anna, before
remembering that none of the women were in the wagon with
him. He opened his eyes. The dawn had drawn grey squares in
the wagon's interior. A glimmer of light through the shutters was
striking the tin frame of a picture of the Virgin and her Holy
Child on the opposite wall, lighting a single spark. He had never
woken alone in a wagon before.

His blanket felt clammy. He flung it back and let the soft air
play on his skin, pull him from sleep.

In this state of nearly dreaming, with all motionless outside
but for the gentle chatter of the dawn birds, he heard a sound –
tiny but definite, weak but demanding.

In the barn, a few yards away, Josef's baby son had also
woken. He was beginning to cry.

Josef lay still and listened, a smile of such warmth spreading
through him that it seemed absurd that a smile should occupy no
more than the limits of his mouth. His son's cry: what a minute,
unimpressive sound against the roars of the world, how small
and animal-like it came – there, again – more of a cough than a
cry, how helpless and reedy – how perfect. *I am the happiest man
alive.*

Josef's smile lasted until Thursday. In that time, he and Václav
had been to visit the farmer Myclík, a small mean man who had
required two hundred crowns and the promise of complete
anonymity to allow them to stay in his fallow field. If they spoke
to anyone in the village, they were not to say they had received

permission from him. They were to dig pits for the ashes of the fires. They were to spade over the furrows left by the wagons.

'I am surprised,' Václav remarked as they left, 'that he did not insist we replace the grass the horses eat, blade by blade.'

Even the mean Myclík did not dispel Josef's good humour – but on Thursday morning he woke and groaned before he had even opened his eyes.

Anna and the baby must be left alone in the barn today, with nobody but the old dog Biri for protection. The rest of them had to pay a visit to the village. Officer Slavíček would be waiting.

As they approached the top of the main street, they saw that it was a different village. The deathly hamlet of three days ago had been transformed into a place of life and purpose. There were people.

The first they saw was a small group of men gathered around the Calvary at the crossroads, talking to each other and nodding. They looked up as the Gypsies approached and stared. Josef inclined his head slowly as they passed.

At the top of the street, there were more. Two old men were sitting on the step of the first cottage wearing identical felt hats and plaited string braces, chewing on pipes and muttering to each other out of the corners of their mouths. As Josef and the others passed, they spat on the ground. Justin Zelinka, nearest to them, turned and bowed, smiling, while murmuring under his breath in Romani, *may you wake up one morning to find your chickens stiff in the yard with their legs in the air*.

Further on, four women stood in a row, arms folded, eyes screwed up against the glare of the sun. Others were walking from cottage to cottage, laughing and chatting. The men were mostly stationary, trying to look more serious. The entire village had come out to watch the Gypsies being fingerprinted.

'Don't they have work to do?' Václav muttered to Josef as they walked down the street.

'They've declared a holiday,' Josef replied.

Children ran alongside them as they walked, getting as close as their bravado would allow. Little Eva Winterová had dropped behind and was chatting to the two shy girls in Czech – she was a noisy child and always made friends easily. Too dumbfounded to respond, the shy girls were holding hands and grinning from ear to ear. Eva's mother Božena turned when they were halfway down the street and shouted loudly, 'Eva! Eva! Come away from those little girls, they're filthy!' She spoke Romani but her meaning was unmistakable. The village women glared at Božena and Božena glared back.

As they approached the shop in procession, the villagers fell in behind. Realising that an audience would be in attendance, Officer Slavíček had thoughtfully brought his table out on to the porch, neatly piling his official papers and inkwell in front of him, with the large, rectangular inkpad for fingerprinting on the side. He was perspiring heavily in his uniform. His thick brown hair was matted on to his forehead and his cheeks were shiny. He glanced at Josef as he approached – Josef had dressed properly for the occasion in his high boots, green trousers and leather waistcoat with huge silver buttons. He had even waxed his moustache.

The women were wearing all their skirts and their best red blouses. The gold coins in their braids had been polished so hard they outshone the sun. The tails of their patterned headscarves hung down their backs. Even the children had been forced into shoes for the event.

Josef mounted the wooden step and stood before the desk. Officer Slavíček greeted him with a broad grin, as if they were old friends.

'Good day to you, Josef,' he said, inclining his head. 'It is good of you all to turn out on such a warm day. I am sure relaxing in the shade would be a great deal more congenial.' He glanced around the villagers to see if his little joke had been appreciated. 'Now, to business. You are the Chief, I presume. The *Sheró Rom.*'

'The Gypsies you have dealt with before have been Polish,' Josef stated flatly. 'We are Kalderash.' *Sheró Rom* was a term used by the Polska Roma. Josef was the *Rom Baró*, the Big Man. He had met *gadje* like Slavíček before. One word of Romani and they considered themselves experts.

Officer Slavíček raised his eyebrows coolly. 'Kalderash. From the East?'

'Originally, yes. I was born in Wallachia but we settled in Slovakia for some time. My father was a wealthy horse dealer. Until our horses were stolen, that is, by *Kaiserlich und Königlich*. He had hoped I would follow him into the business but I trained as a smith like my uncles so that we could . . .'

'Yes, well, I get the point . . .' Officer Slavíček said. 'You are Coppersmith Gypsies, good, good. We don't get many Coppersmith Gypsies in these parts.' He was fidgeting with his papers.

He withdrew a form from the pile, clattered the pen from side-to-side in the inkwell, shook it once, and then held it poised above the paper.

'Name?'

'Josef Růžička.'

'A Czech name?'

'Yes,' Josef only just restrained a sigh. They had all used their Czech names for years. Only Anna's unmarried sisters still used their Vlach surname sometimes. Why was it necessary to explain these things all the time? Why did the *gadje* always have to write everything down?

Fortunately, Slavíček seemed happy not to press the point.

'Date of birth?'

'I haven't a clue.'

'Let's try your age, shall we?'

Josef shrugged.

Slavíček flicked him a derisive glance. The villagers tittered.

'Occupation.'

'I have already told you.'

Officer Slavíček frowned and shook his head.

'Distinguishing features . . .'

Josef remained silent.

Slavíček pulled a sympathetic face, downturning the corners of his mouth. 'I noticed as you came down the street, you have a limp. Is that permanent?'

Josef nodded.

Slavíček spoke out loud as he wrote. 'Medium height and build, limp to left leg. I think that will do.'

He opened the inkpad and pushed it forward. 'Place your fingers and then the thumb here, please, right hand first, then left. Firmly.'

At this, the villagers who had gathered on the step and on the grass below craned their necks forward.

Josef winced with distaste as Slavíček took his fingers from the pad and pressed them down on to the form he had just completed. He lifted his hands and glanced at them. The ink had left blackish-purple stains on his fingertips, ripe like bruises. As Slavíček folded the form into quarters, Josef asked, 'Is there a pump nearby where I may wash my hands?'

'Oh come, man, a bit of ink doesn't hurt.' Slavíček paused as he folded the paper. 'Your wife. Is she here?'

'My son is but three days old.'

Slavíček sighed heavily. 'I'm supposed to see all the adults in person, but I suppose we can put her on your form anyway.' He unfolded the form laboriously.

'Name . . .'

The process was repeated for Anna. When it came to distinguishing features, Josef drew himself up and said, 'My wife is of such indescribable beauty that she is impossible to imagine unless you have had the pleasure of setting eyes on her. A pleasure which I sincerely hope you will never enjoy.'

Slavíček looked up at him, narrowing his eyes to indicate that his patience was exhausted. 'You have other women there. Send them up. Don't go anywhere yourself. I'm going to need you to go through your route. I hope you've brought some papers with you.'

Josef nodded smartly and turned. Before he reached the step, Slavíček called him back.

'Josef, Josef! Your son. How can a man forget his own son?'

Josef had not forgotten his son. He was hoping that Slavíček had. He turned wearily. 'His name is František. He has no trade as yet and his distinguishing features are two arms, two legs and a body with a head on top.'

He turned back and descended the step.

Tekla and Anna's sisters came slowly forward. Josef watched as they answered Slavíček, each in turn, in quiet monosyllables.

When it came to the fingerprinting, Tekla snatched her hand away when Slavíček reached for it and indicated with a sharp, jutting motion of her chin that he should not touch her fingers. Slavíček lifted both his palms upwards and gave a grimace, a half-sarcastic apology. Tekla did not smile.

As the women descended, Václav mounted the step.

The villagers began to wander off, losing interest in the spectacle. A couple of the men made noises about having work to do. Many of the women were sitting now, perched on the edge

of the porch, fanning themselves with their hands. Josef's people
were still standing under the sun, all but naughty little Eva who
was sitting cross-legged underneath the porch and had coaxed
a small dog with a dirty white coat to join her. She was asking
the dog questions. Where did it come from? What did it do for
a living? Why did it talk so strangely? Was it stupid?

When each of the families had given their details in turn and
received their folded identification papers, Officer Slavíček rose
and tossed his pen on to the table. He seemed weary. He packed
up his papers and tucked them under one arm, beckoning Josef
to return.

As Josef mounted the step, Slavíček turned to Jirout the
shopkeeper and asked him to lift the table inside.

The villagers dispersed slowly, sighing.

'Tell your people to go and sit down by the well,' Slavíček
said to Josef. 'This will take a bit of time.'

Inside the shop, Slavíček led Josef past the counter and the
shelves of goods and through to a small back room where Jirout
had placed the table and added two large mugs of beer with
huge, light-brown heads of foam. Slavíček gestured Josef to sit
opposite him. Jirout re-entered from the back door with a tin
plate on which were balanced several large chunks of bread and
a small glass bowl of salt. He put the plate down and left without
looking at either of them.

'Help yourself,' Slavíček gestured towards the plate and mug.
'Jirout has a licence to brew his own, much to the irritation of the
brewery at Smečno who seem to think that nobody west of
Prague should drink anything but theirs. Drink. It's good.'

They raised their mugs and met each other's gazes as they
wished each other *na zdraví*. Josef apologised silently to the
Ancestors for not offering them a libation, pointing out that it

was filthy *gadje* beer and probably tasted like the water left over after Anna had washed turnips.

The beer was delicious. It was only then that Josef remembered he had drunk it when they had first arrived in the village three days ago. He felt he could hardly remember anything of that time. He had become a father since then.

Slavíček had removed his cap and was unbuttoning his collar with some difficulty. When he had extricated himself, he slung the jacket over the back of his chair, took another swig of beer, then wiped the foam from his overgrown moustache with the back of his hand. His shirt was dark with sweat and sticking to his chest. His braces dug into his shoulders. What an uncomfortable way to earn a living, thought Josef.

Slavíček saw Josef observing him and gave a small ironic nod. 'Lucky is the man who never wears a uniform.'

Josef was tiring of Slavíček's insistence on his good fortune. 'Jirout is a man of many abilities,' he said, gesturing behind Slavíček, where a dozen iron lasts were heaped against the wall.

Slavíček turned, saw the lasts and chuckled. 'Old Jirout hasn't cobbled for years. I suppose he can't bear to throw them away. Maybe they make him feel nostalgic. We could use a decent cobbler round here. None of your group I suppose?'

Josef shook his head. They all knew how to make clogs for their families but he didn't know of any Rom that cobbled. It had never struck him as a particularly dignified profession, caressing strangers' feet.

Slavíček had reminded himself of the business in hand. 'So are you the only smith then?'

'The others assist me sometimes,' said Josef, 'Sometimes I work alone.' *So far*, he thought. *One day my son will help*. At the thought of Emil, he gave an involuntary smile. *Emil*. He was still getting used to using the word. It gave him such pleasure to fantasise about the boy. What would he look like now? He felt he would burst if he didn't see his son soon. Tonight would be Emil's third night on earth. Anna would lay him on the ground and place three pieces of bread and three cups of wine in a circle around him, for the Three Spirits. In four more days, Anna and the boy would be able to join him in the wagon, although she wouldn't be allowed to handle food or dishes for another week. 'There isn't much copper any more,' he said mechanically to Slavíček. 'We work the orchards in the summer. I shoe horses sometimes – in the winter I make barrel hoops for the pickle factory. All the others help then. There is more work than we can handle. Our winter quarters are in Moravia.'

Slavíček picked up a piece of bread, dipped it in the salt and took a bite, leaning back in his chair. 'So what was all this about work in Teplice? Jirout tells me you're on your way to Kladno.'

Josef paused. He had forgotten what Václav had said on Monday.

Slavíček spared him the strain of further invention. 'Look, Josef, I'm sorry but you're going to have to be more detailed. I need the full route, including dates, and details of what you do at each stopping place. It all has to be listed here, then a copy of the list has to be attached to each individual's form . . .'

Josef remained silent.

Slavíček opened his hands to appeal to him. 'It has to be right, Josef. Once it's on this form, it's set in stone. You'll have to apply if you want to deviate from the route, register with the local police if you turn up anywhere that isn't on the list. If you are found deviating from it without permission you'll be liable for a pretty hefty fine, and this time they're really serious up there in Prague. Look, I'm not one of those who think that you're out to steal the hens from my backyard but you have to understand that there are plenty of people out there with very nimble fingers. They're not all real nomads like you. Alcoholics, people who've lost their farms gambling. They're all on the road these days. Something has to be done. If you don't co-operate then you'll just be put in the same bracket as all the others. Not every municipal officer is going to be as tolerant as I am, I can tell you that.'

Josef sighed heavily. The pile of lasts against the wall was bothering him. It was like a heap of human feet. The Ancestors had survived a thousand laws like this new one. Once upon a time they cut the left ear off Roma in Moravia and the right in Bohemia – or was it the other way round? At least Slavíček was not requiring body parts. Not yet.

'We spend August and September in Kladno . . .' Josef began.

As he emerged from the shop, the Winterová girls ran excitedly across the street towards him.

'Look, look!' Pavla was calling, waving something in the air.

They all ran up the step and jumped around Josef. 'A *gadji* went into the shop while you were in there,' shrieked Pavla excitedly, 'and we were all staring in the window at the sweets and our mouths were watering and she brought toffees for Eva and me and an apple-flavoured whistle for Zdenka because she is the oldest. It made a *real whistling* sound.'

Zdenka nodded in confirmation. 'I let the other two have a go,' she added hastily.

'Really?' said Josef. 'It really whistled? Can I try it?'

The girls looked at each other. 'We ate it,' Eva admitted sadly.

'But look, look . . .' said Pavla, perking up as she remembered what was in her hand. 'The *gadji* asked if there were any other children back at the camp and we said no but there was a new baby and she said was it a boy or a girl and we said a boy, and she gave us a crown.'

Pavla held the crown up on the palm of her hand, where it lay flat, displayed it like a precious jewel.

Josef was furious. Did these *gadje* think he needed their loose change to provide for his son? Add together his horses and his wife's jewellery and he was worth five of these peasants.

'Take it!' he snapped at the girls. 'Go on, go in the shop.' He pushed roughly at Pavla's shoulder. She gave him a brief, round-mouthed stare before turning.

'But it's for *Emil*,' squeaked Eva, although her sisters were already running into the shop, not about to query their unexpected fortune.

'He's too little to have sweets,' Josef said, more kindly. 'He'd like you to spend it. Go.'

Nobody spoke as they all processed back down the street, ignored by the villagers. Nobody said anything as they traversed the fields back up towards the copse, the girls still dancing excitedly at the rear. It was only as they strode down through the wheatfields that Josef spoke. Václav was immediately behind him.

'Tell me, Václav,' Josef said. 'I'm a man of medium height and build, notable only for the limp in his left leg. How about you?'

'Me?' said Václav. 'I am short and portly. I have a large nose, full beard and whiskers.'

'And you, Yakali?' Josef called over his shoulder.

'Average height, muscular build, red scar across the back of my right hand.'

'You've done better than us, Father,' Justin called from the back of the line. 'Neither of your sons have any distinguishing features at all.'

'God be praised . . .' muttered Yakali as they walked. 'Praise be to God.'

*

The farmer Myclík sent his son to move them on. It was twelve days after Emil had been born. Josef had only known his son for five days but had already forgotten the time when he did not exist. When the boy slept, he fitted snugly into the curve where Josef's neck joined his shoulder – he would undo his neckerchief and open his shirt to place him there. Even when Emil awoke and cried, Josef was unwilling to relinquish him. Anna had to demand the return of her baby for feeds.

The others laughed at him. Their enforced stay near the barn was losing them income by delaying their arrival at the harvest, but it allowed the wagons to be cleaned, horse tackle to be mended – and a little joviality at the expense of the *Rom Baró*, who seemed under the delusion that none of them had ever met a baby before and needed to be introduced to his repeatedly.

They were given no notice to quit the field. The farmer's son arrived one morning and stayed to watch them load up their belongings. Anna was still *marimé*. She had been keeping away from the men, taking Emil to the shade of the trees on the far side of the field to nurse him. The other women would gather around them and flap them with fans – smiling, talking, neglecting their other duties. She waited under the trees until Josef signalled to her that it was time to pull off. As she carried Emil towards their wagon, the other men paid her the courtesy of turning their backs, to save her the effort of having to skirt behind them.

They would stop twice on the way, even though it was a short journey. That way, by the time they arrived at the orchards, Anna would be able to step down from the wagon and greet the other families. Then the real celebrations could begin.

Myclík's son, the lazy, hatless youth, stood cross-armed while they loaded up, watching them with narrowed eyes as if he was cultivating his own insouciance. As the last wagon bumped and swayed onto the road, he spat on the ground and crossed himself. Josef was waiting nearby with a spade, to turn over the wagon tracks once they were all on the road. As he bent to the crumbled brown earth, he wished the soil bitter and the Myclík family a poor harvest. He had never minded the insults of the *gadje* all that much before, not the way that Václav or some of the other men minded. Now he felt as if young Myclík's phlegm was aimed directly at his newborn son. He would like to take the spade to the young man's shoulder, to teach him a lesson he wouldn't forget in a hurry.

He ran past the youth without looking at him, handed the spade up to Václav as he passed his wagon, then trotted to the front, where Justin was standing holding his harnessed horses. He jumped up on to the seat and took the reins.

It was sunny again, but cooler than the previous days. A small breeze fluttered the leaves on the trees. Fat, pure clouds raced in battle formation across a hard blue sky. Josef gave a joyous cry, '*Hey*-ooh!' as he flicked the reins and the horses gave a brief start and stumble before falling into step. There was no better feeling than that first lurch of the wagon. It was summertime; they were heading for the orchards; they were Kings of the World.

CHAPTER 3

The women waited inside the wagon. Tekla told Ludmila and Eva to check the cupboards and lockers to make sure everything was securely stowed. Anna nursed her baby, sitting on her bed with her knees raised to support him, her skirt a wide canopy, her unbuttoned blouse loose on her shoulders. The interior of the wagon was dark, the shutters closed against the bright sunshine outside, the cracks between them allowing a few thin strips of light. Anna hummed softly to her child.

Ludmila paused in the act of lifting down a tin-framed picture of the Holy Mother to bend over them, close her eyes and inhale deeply. 'I love that smell . . .' she murmured, as she slid the picture flat beneath the bed. 'Will he always smell like that? It's so new, and old.'

'Like fresh bread . . .' Anna said without lifting her head.

'No, more like meadows . . .' said Ludmila, sitting next to Anna and peering at Emil's forehead. 'Look at his scar.'

'I can't believe how well it's healing,' Anna said. 'Tekla, the paste you put on . . .'

'All babies heal quickly,' replied Tekla, as she squatted on the floor pulling string tightly around the stacked copper pans, to prevent them rattling. 'It's because they're doing so much growing all the time, everything heals. Once he has hair no one will even know it is there.'

'We will always know, though,' smiled Ludmila, 'won't we? My tiny *šav*?'

Anna lifted him up. 'Pat him for me, Ludmila. The feeding makes me sleepy.' She handed Emil to Ludmila, and lay down.

The wagon jolted forward. Eva, still standing, fell against the wagon's wall.

'You might as well go and sit up with Josef,' said Tekla to Eva. 'Ludmila and I can walk. There's no reason for all of us to be in here.'

Ludmila and Eva exchanged glances. Normally Anna would sit up with her husband, as was her right, but with a newborn she would stay hidden from the envious eyes of the *gadje* for the length of the journey. Tekla was next in status and the privilege of sitting up should fall to her.

'No, I don't want to,' said Eva quickly. 'Ludmila and I will stay here and mind Emil while Anna's asleep. You go.'

Tekla leaned forward and bit the string, tied the final knot in one swift, fierce gesture, then rewound the loose ball with a windmilling motion of her hands. 'I don't know what's wrong with the pair of you,' she said without looking at them. '*She* might have an excuse for being soft in the head but not you two.' She rose and climbed the two wooden steps, opening the small door to the seat of the wagon, knowing that Ludmila and Eva would be pulling faces behind her back.

As she turned to close the door behind her, Tekla saw in the suddenly light-filled wagon that Eva had sat down on the floor next to Ludmila and was stroking Emil's swaddled back, both of them staring at him joyously. Their exhausted elder sister slept behind them, her eyes closed but her mouth still stretched in a smile: a perfect tableau – the three beautiful Demeter sisters and their beautiful baby boy. Tekla pulled the wagon door shut with a bang.

*

In his whole life, Josef was only to be on first-name terms with one *gadjo*. That *gadjo*'s name was Ctibor.

Ctibor Michálek was a fruit farmer. His living was sour cherries and he had a lifelong relationship with them, one of great attachment punctuated by spells of disloyalty, for there were other fruit in Ctibor's life. Apricots were an important romance for him, although they were never as vital as the cherries – and then there was his passionate affair with the peach. Farming peaches on his land was folly but Ctibor Michálek could not renounce his lust and, contrary to all expectations, succeeded in producing three small crops on a gentle, southerly slope before the bitter winter of 1929 froze the trunks and cracked them to the heart.

That summer of 1927, he was still courting the peach, although he was anxious, as he explained to Josef while they walked round the orchards the day after the *kumpánia*'s arrival. 'They blossomed early this year, Josef,' Ctibor said, shaking his head at the memory. 'And then we had a chill wind from the Urals. I don't mind telling you, I was worried. The bees stayed at home. I came out myself and hand-pollinated each tree with a rabbit's tail.'

He sighed as if remembering a woman from his past. 'I can't pretend this year's peach crop was the best. The apricots though . . .' His face became radiant. 'Oh, Josef, you should have been here for the apricots. The taste of them. It broke my heart to send them off for canning. I could have eaten the whole harvest fresh.'

The two of them paused by a tree of Montmorencies, already ripe. They always made it before the English Morellos but they and the Russian Vladimirs were still planted in mixed groups, to allow them to pollinate. 'Self-sterile,' Ctibor had informed Josef once, explaining his farming methods. 'There's a lesson for Mankind in that, you know.'

Ctibor lifted a hand to cup a cherry in the tips of his fingers and twist it gently from the stem. It amused Josef to see the man hold up a cherry, for Ctibor Michálek liked his wine and his nose had acquired a deep reddish hue, not unlike that of his fruit. Had a jay alighted on Ctibor's shoulder at that moment, the bird would have been unsure where to peck.

'They are wonderful things, these beauties,' Ctibor was also fond of saying. 'Other men, they can keep their cows and pigs and – with respect – their horses. Animals. You shovel it in one end and out it comes the other. Me, I am a happy man, filling the world with fruit.'

It was early morning. Josef had paid his customary visit to Ctibor at sunrise and had already drunk real coffee and eaten a fresh meat and onion roll, warm and fragile from the huge new oven in Ctibor's tiled kitchen. Now Ctibor passed him a cherry from the Montmorency tree, and Josef took it from his hand, sliding it between his lips and tasting the dew from its skin before he applied gentle pressure with his teeth. The fruit became tense, then burst, splitting to the stone and flooding his mouth with sharp and purple flavour. It tasted of dawn.

They were standing at the top of the long, northerly slope, from where Josef could look down across the still-misty, grey-green orchard, where the pickers were already moving in the early light, their baskets hanging at the hip from wide straps across their chests. All his *kumpánia* were there and over a hundred others; Czech and Moravian Roma mostly, a few Lowari.

No other farmer in the whole of Bohemia employed as many Roma as Ctibor Michálek. His harvests had become famous as a place for the *vitsas* to meet and exchange news, for marriage agreements and the settling of debts. A series of *divanos* would be held throughout the harvest to settle disputes, lasting all the long, long evenings when the smell of ripe cherries would wash over the fields in slow waves, all the way to the ice-house near the railway substation where the canneries kept their trucks.

Ctibor's devotion to the Roma went back a long way. Ctibor had married young, and for love, a Jewish girl called Sarah whom he had met when he went to be measured for his first tailored suit. When he married her, his family had cut him out of their lives, his father declaring he would never see a penny from the shoe-polish factory in Kladno in which he was a partner.

Ctibor had left the factory after only six months of work and as a consequence the bank would lend him no more than the price of twenty acres, scarcely enough for a peasant to feed his family. Ten years later, he was worth his father, brother and cousins put together. Disdainful relatives whispered that a Jewish wife had brought him luck with money but Sarah was a mousy woman who took no interest in business. She had been cast out by her own family in her turn, for marrying a Gentile. Her father had held a funeral service for her.

It was not the Jews who had brought Ctibor luck, so he declared to Josef at least once each season. It was the Gypsies.

Less than a year after he had purchased that first small plot of land a Romni had come begging at the door of their wooden shack, with four small children in tow. Sarah was frightened of them, but Ctibor insisted that the woman and her children be invited in and given stew and bread, all the stew and bread, in fact, which he and Sarah had been saving for their supper.

The woman and her children had eaten swiftly and silently. As she was leaving, the woman paused on the step and turned back to Ctibor, beckoning. She walked him down the path, the children trotting anxiously behind her, to where Ctibor had begun to plant his first one-year-old saplings in neat rows. She told him he must replant them at once, nine trees in a circle for good luck, and always use Gypsy labourers to pick his fruit. Then he would become a fortunate man.

Josef had not the heart to tell Ctibor that the woman was probably more concerned with finding employment for her people than with Ctibor's future fortune. Ctibor swore that from that moment, his trees were blessed. 'I am a Rationalist,' he told Josef once, 'and a Humanist and a Socialist – but a man must be allowed a little superstition in his life, otherwise his life is grey. I allow myself this, and see, the combination of superstition and a regular spray of self-boiled lime sulphur has given me the best crops in the district.'

*

After Josef left Ctibor on the slope above the orchards, he descended to the far fields, swinging his stick lightly in the morning air. The real business of the day could now commence. He had told Ctibor about Emil, of course, and Ctibor had clapped his back and congratulated him, but the conversation had moved swiftly on. Ctibor's wife was barren. The two men had subtly lamented their childlessness to each other in the past. Josef would not have expected Ctibor to make a grand fuss of his news. There were limits to any friendship.

But now there were other Roma to tell, and a *mulatšago* to be organised, to christen the boy. The first who must be informed were his own distant kin, the Tent-Dwelling Kalderash led by Tódor Maximoff. He must get to their tents quickly. Nobody must tell them but himself.

Tódor Maximoff and his *kumpánia* had pitched their encampment, as usual, in a far field behind a row of fir trees, symbolically distant from the wagons and tents of other Roma. They did not mix easily. Josef they tolerated, because he was distant kin and Kalderash, although not quite Kalderash enough. Josef knew they looked down on him and his *kumpánia* because they did wage-work and gave their children Czech names sometimes – because Josef shaved his chin and waxed his moustache instead of keeping a black fluffy beard. He did not like the fact that Tódor Maximoff looked down upon him, and liked even less that he found himself looking up. Tódor was a giant – and his physical size seemed like no more than the literal manifestation of his status amongst other Rom. Most men's heads only reached Tódor's huge beard. The silver buttons on his coat were the size of hen's eggs and his wealth was rumoured to be fabulous. He was pure Kalderash. He made Josef feel assimilated, almost Czech by comparison. Sometimes Josef felt a little ashamed at how Czech they were – at others, he thought, *I live in the modern world, that's all*.

The Tent-Dwellers were especially nervous of Anna and the other women. Tódor's *kumpánia* were strict adherents to the purity laws – his wife Zága wrapped a cloth around the handle of a mug of tea before she handed it to him, so the contact with her flesh should not contaminate her husband's beverage. On the rare occasions that Anna accompanied Josef on his visits to the tents, she kept her distance, even from the other women, and the air around would become stiff with mutual disdain.

As Josef neared the circle of tents with their striped awnings, a small voice cried out from the trees that lined the left of the path, *'Devlesa arakhav tu!'*

Josef stopped and looked around.

By the side of the path, leaning up against the trunk of a sloping fir, was a boy aged eight or so dressed in an embroidered blouse and waistcoat but naked from the waist down. His hat was tipped at an unlikely angle and an unlit cigarette butt was hanging from his lower lip.

Josef bowed deeply.

The boy stood up, spat the cigarette butt on the ground, bowed in response and repeated solemnly, *'Devlesa arakhav tu.'* I find thee with God.

Josef restrained an amused smile and replied seriously, *'O Del anel tu.'* May God lead thee.

The boy grinned, turned tail and scurried back into the camp to announce Josef's approach, his bare feet kicking up leaves and twigs behind him.

Tódor Maximoff was seated on a small wooden stool in the centre of the tents, smoking a pipe, but at Josef's approach he rose and opened his arms.

'Jóno Maximoff!' he bellowed, abandoning the formal forms of address, as a compliment. 'It has been too long! You should have come to England. My wife's braids are full of five-pound pieces. She makes music when she walks!'

Tódor's expeditions to England were legendary. He went every three or four years and had, Josef inferred, just returned from one such trip. He was famous there. He had shown Josef a copy of his picture in a newspaper, disembarking at Dover.

Earnest young men with spectacles and worn leather briefcases came to his camps, he said, clutching notebooks and begging to study the way he and his *kumpánia* spoke. (They came in handy, the earnest young men, as Tódor had mastered French, Italian and Spanish along with his native Hungarian and Russian but English defeated him. The young men could usually get by in one or other European language and so acted as translators in return for permission to follow them around like puppies.)

'My wife will only wear Hungarian gold!' Josef declared in response, grasping the man in a hug then pushing him forcefully away. 'It takes two horses to carry her!'

'My daughters' knees are crippled by our wealth!'

'Aa . . . ah . . . *Phrála*, children are indeed a blessing . . .' Josef laughed, stepping back so as to fully appreciate Tódor's expression when he imparted his news.

Tódor looked at him quizzically.

'You have not heard . . . ?' Josef feigned astonishment.

Tódor showed him his palms. 'I am an ignorant man!'

Josef beamed, silently, his lips pressed tightly together, to force Tódor to guess. Tódor narrowed his eyes and shook his head slowly from side to side, trying to work it out.

Suddenly, Tódor's eyes popped open in surprise. 'Jóno . . . Jóno . . .' His voice became a growl as he spread his arms wide. 'This cannot be . . . *truly*?'

Josef threw his arms wide and yelled. 'I have a son!'

Tódor flung himself at Josef, grabbing him round the shoulders with his full weight still in motion, hurling them both to the floor. They rolled over in the dirt together until Josef begged the giant to stop by shouting. 'My coat! My coat!'

Tódor jumped to his feet and turned back to his tent. 'Zága!' He shouted merrily to his wife. 'Tip the soup into the horse trough! We have a celebration tonight! Kill the goat!' Zága stuck her head out of the tent, acknowledged the command without expression, then disappeared.

Josef was brushing himself down.

'My favourite goat! Tonight he will turn on a spit – we won't eat him he's as tough as old boots. We will fill ourselves with all manner of meat!' Tódor raised a finger. 'But on your son's wedding day, we will kill one hundred kid-goats. Every Kalderash in Europe will come. My cousins will return from Montevideo. I make you that promise, Jóno my brother.'

Josef regarded the sleeves of his best green coat, now peppered with leaves and dead grass. Anna would be furious. It was interesting how Tódor always became his brother when there was good news in the air. He couldn't recall Tódor being quite so brotherly four years ago when he had wanted to borrow his shovel and tongs to take on a job over at Krakovec.

Josef saw that the boy who had greeted him was standing nearby. He had donned knee-length trousers and was holding a stool. Tódor saw him too, and beckoned him forward, allowing him to place the stool before waving him away and gesturing for Josef to sit. Other men had begun to gather at a distance, to pay their respects, but they would not approach until Tódor indicated that he and Josef had finished the private part of their conversation.

One of the women came forward with a silver samovar and English china on an elaborated Japanned tray with small gilt legs. Tódor acknowledged her by nodding at Josef. 'Our new *bori*. Take a good look. What nationality to do you think?'

Josef observed the girl while she set the tray down upon its legs and poured the tea, a gold cloth wrapped carefully around the samovar's handle. She was wearing Kalderash dress; the loose red blouse and skirt with petticoats, and had a money belt and apron. Her hair was dark and braided but her face was round and freckled, her nose small and snubbed.

'English Kalderash!' said Tódor to Josef's silence. 'Did you realise there was such a thing? We met this one's family in Cambridgeshire. I bought her for my youngest, Andréas, that imp who welcomed you. They made me pay through the nose and my wife had to show her how to butter her hair, but she's a good girl so we have already honoured her with the tea-making duties for our guests.' The girl was backing away. Tódor waved at her with circular motions of his large hand. She came and stood close to him and he delved the hand into the small golden purse on side of her money belt.

'Have you seen one of these?' He held the coin out to Josef. It was large and thin, and had a small hoop at the edge for threading a ribbon. 'It's a British Gold Medal. We bought it in a pawn shop. This one is for something they call Long Jumping. The shopkeeper explained it to me. Grown men run up to a pit of sand and jump in it. Then they give each other medals. Next, they stand very still on boxes, wearing the medals round their necks.' He shook his head. 'We've started a collection but I can't permit the women to wear them until we have twelve for all of them, you know what women are like.' He spat on the coin and shouted at it. 'Your mother! Your father! Come here!' Then he slipped it back into the girl's purse.

As the girl backed away, not turning until she was a respectful distance from them, Josef noticed the approving look that Tódor gave her and guessed that there might be more than one reason why he had been prepared to pay through the nose. A less attractive new *bori* would not be on public display, however 'good' she might be.

'Where were you camped this time?' Josef asked, sipping his tea noisily to show his appreciation. The delicate china cup was awkward for him to hold and the liquid scalding hot.

Tódor's cup looked ridiculous in his large hand. He reached

forward with the other and scooped up a handful of sugar cubes from a china bowl, tossing them into his mouth before raising his cup and throwing its steaming contents over the cubes. He crunched once, then swallowed deeply.

'Liverpool,' he said, and belched.

Josef raised his eyebrows. 'Not London?'

Tódor shook his head. 'We went down there later but we had to go up to Liverpool to escort my cousins on to the boat. Do you know they are going all the way across the Atlantic? Crazy. Do not leave the high road for the lane, I told them. Montevideo. God go with them but it's madness. They won't find a living there, I can tell you. In South America, the *gadje* are black like us, and so poor, you can't make a penny out of them. I like my *gadje* fat and white. The English are slugs. All you have to do is squeeze.'

Josef now felt able to ask the question that any Kalderash wanted to ask when they met another.

'Was there any copper?'

It was the one topic about which Tódor would not boast. He rolled down his lower lip, pulled at his beard and shook his head gloomily. 'Even less than last time. We did the chocolate factories, and the hotels, of course, but even most of them have enamelled iron these days . . .'

Tódor fell darkly silent, by which Josef judged that the slug-like English were no longer as fat and juicy as Tódor had found them in the past. There was a pause. Behind Tódor and the tents, through the trees, Josef could see a furious-faced Zága dragging a stubborn, complaining goat. It reminded him of the business in hand.

He put down his cup, but Tódor was clearly not inclined to let him go just yet. He leaned forward.

'Tell me Jóno, this Law 117 that everyone is talking about. Is it true? Is it as serious as it sounds?'

Josef nodded. 'I think so, yes. We were forced to register on the way here. They can find us whenever they want to now. In Slovakia they called us cannibals and threw mud at the wagons as we passed. If a policeman wants me now, all he has to do is check with the central office in Prague and everything will be there written down, where I am, what I'm doing, the colour of the lining of my waistcoat.'

Tódor stroked his beard and sighed, murmuring to himself. 'Perhaps we should have gone to Montevideo after all . . .' He lifted his chin and fiddled with his red neckerchief. 'And will you bring business to the *kris*?'

Josef shook his head. Law 117 would be the main topic of conversation at the *kris*. Personal matters would have to take their turn.

Tódor rose to indicate that the conversation was closing. 'I hope we will not have time wasted with trivial matters, this year. Those Lowari from Ruthenia have come all this way, again. Last year they spent three days discussing whether a man could have sausage in his soup before St George's Day.'

And you would have rather spent three days discussing whether a man apprenticed less than seven years should call himself a metalsmith or a metalworker . . . thought Josef, without rancour. He loved Tódor, but he could understand why the others became so irritated with him at times.

As the rest of Tódor's *kumpánia* approached, Tódor grasped Josef in another hug and whispered to him joyously, 'A son, *phrála*, a son . . .' then turned to his fellow Kalderash with his arms spread wide.

*

This is what other Roma say about the Kalderash.

The Kalderash. If you're going to hold a kris with the Kalderash, then make sure you do it in their tent. They're the only ones who have tents big enough and they have eiderdowns to fall asleep on. You will certainly want to fall asleep, because nobody can talk longer than a Kalderash. When a Kalderash stands up to demand retribution because his brother-in-law told him there was copperwork in one town knowing full well it was in the next, then he begins by saying that his sister married when there was frost on the grass. He will then describe the frost.

Do not expect jokes from a Kalderash. The Kalderash take themselves extremely seriously, especially their appearance. They are famously vain. This is because it takes them so much time to polish their buttons and stitch ribbons on to their coats. A Kalderash likes to pretend he can drink and sing like any other brother but underneath his brash exterior is a Wallach as gloomy as a cow. A Kalderash always believes the worst.

Do not ask a Kalderash to lend you money. If he does, you will be bound to him forever and spend your whole life making rivets. When the Kalderash have a vessel to work, they do not stop, even to eat. They carry on working even when it gets dark. They make their women stand over them holding paraffin lanterns. Fortunately, their women are tall. Unfortunately, this allows their men to hammer and beat and hammer, right through the night, when the rest of us have to be up before dawn to pick cherries with nothing but a cup of chicory coffee inside us. They do their work outside their tents so that everyone can see how hard they work. They are immensely strong.

Do not marry your daughter to a Kalderash. By the following summer, she will despise you. Do not bother trying to open negotiations for one of their women on behalf of your son. A Kalderash would sooner see his daughter married to a bear.

*

This is what the Kalderash say about other Roma.

They are all right, probably. But they are not Kalderash!

*

Josef opened the door to his wagon slowly, to admit the light gently upon his wife and son. As he stepped in, he glimpsed them curled together on the lit at the far end of the wagon, both asleep. He pulled the door to behind him, re-establishing the gloom, put down his stick and made his way slowly towards them, moving with care so as not to bump into anything. What a privilege, to catch them both asleep for a few minutes. He kneeled by the side of the bed, and gave infinite thanks to God.

He was about to rise, when Anna's eyes opened. She glanced first at her child, curled against her chest, and then her eyes focused and she saw Josef. She smiled.

'He has not woken yet this morning?' Josef asked softly.

Anna shook her head once. 'No. The longest yet. He will be hungry when he wakes.'

Josef moved to sit beside them, to savour these few moments.

How wonderful it had been to wake in the night and hear the snuffling of the child feeding, to creep out before dawn and leave Anna and Emil warm together.

He and Anna stared at their baby for several long, tender moments, then glanced at each other and exchanged a disbelieving look, then returned their gazes to their child.

'His skin is too big for him . . .' said Josef. 'His hands . . .'

'He will fill it soon enough,' Anna replied. 'I have enough milk to feed every child at the harvest.'

'Good, a good sign. *Baxt.*' Good fortune – more than luck, blessing.

They were silent again, awhile.

'I paid a visit to Tódor Maximoff,' Josef said eventually, his gaze still fixed on Emil.

Anna yawned hugely. 'How are our Tent-Dwelling cousins . . . ?'

'As ever. They have a new *bori*, from England. They are collecting gold coins as big as dinner plates. He wants to provide the meat for the *mulatšago.*'

'Tonight?' Anna's tone was suddenly sharp.

'Well, yes,' Josef replied sheepishly. He had been anticipating her displeasure. Tódor was showing off, delighted at an opportunity to show how quickly and fulsomely he could provide. But Anna would rise to the occasion. She always did. He could not have objected to Tódor's generosity, after all.

*

Anna closed her eyes and groaned. She would have to get up, find Tekla, then go over to the Tent-Dwellers' encampment and talk to sour-faced Zága about what was needed – right now, if everything was to be ready by this evening. A competition, just what she needed! She had stopped bleeding but it still hurt to walk. Were there enough spices for maize cakes? She would have to beg cumin from Božena. Božena was never without cumin. She began to calculate. Eva and Ludmila would have to help as well. Taking them from the harvest work would mean lost income for the *kumpánia* but it would be shameful to be outdone by the Tent-Dwellers. Zdenka could fry the cumin and coriander seeds while Ludmila and Eva pounded the maize. Golden God take the Tent-Dwellers! She had hoped for at least one quiet day with her son. It was too hot for a woman with a baby strapped to her back to be frying and beating. Men! Let's have a *mulatšago*, they say to each other. Where did they imagine the food was going to come from? Out of thin air? They didn't have a clue.

'Ctibor Michálek wanted me to dine with him and his wife tonight,' Josef continued. 'He will want to talk politics as usual.'

Anna saw a glimmer of hope. 'Tell Tódor Maximoff you have to dine with the Big Gadjo. He will understand. They all like you to stay close to the fire.' *If you want to stay warm, stay close to the fire* – the Magyar proverb had been a favourite of Josef's father. He had mumbled it on his deathbed, continuously, as if he had invented the phrase.

Josef shook his head. 'They have already drained the blood from the goat. Zága will have teams of her daughters plucking chickens. I will go and see Ctibor. I can invite him. It will please him to be the guest of honour and the others will think I am doing my job.'

Anna sighed, resigned. There were disadvantages in being married to a mild man. She raised herself on one elbow and kissed Josef lightly on the mouth. At her movement, Emil rose swiftly through his layers of slumber and began to screw up his face. She smiled down at him and parted her blouse to extract a heavy breast, already leaking sweet, cloudy milk.

Josef sat watching them as Emil began to turn his head restlessly, gaping his mouth.

'Shall we get a priest for him?' he asked.

Anna winced as Emil latched on and began to suckle. *Black Birds* her family had called priests. They thought it an ill-omen to have a *gadjo* in a dress come and lay hands on your child. Her father used to touch his privates if a priest passed by, to restore his manhood.

'As you wish,' she said, knowing that Josef would like one. His mother had had so many icons and crucifixes in their wagon you could hardly get in the door.

'I will find one of the girls and tell them to go and find Tekla for you,' Josef said.

Anna frowned. Tekla had been behaving so oddly the last few days. 'Zdenka and Pavla are weaving baskets at the shed,' she said, 'but Eva is around somewhere. She was standing in the door earlier and begging to see Emil. You can tell her if she gets Tekla quickly then I will let her hold him when they get back.'

*

When Ctibor heard that his invitation had been reversed, he demanded that Josef come and eat lunch with him immediately.

Josef agreed on the condition that Ctibor be not offended if he left the table sooner than usual. There were arrangements to be made. What arrangements? Ctibor demanded to know – and sent one of the farm boys to fetch a priest and another to count the wine bottles in his cellar. Ctibor was the only *gadjo* in the whole world as generous as a Rom, Josef thought, and like a Rom had little sense for when his generosity would be more welcome if less immediate.

'Sit! Sit!' Ctibor cried expansively, ushering Josef into his kitchen, where his wife Sarah had dumplings boiling and a goulash simmering on the stove, filling the kitchen with steam and the heavy aroma of meat. Josef preferred to eat lightly on a hot day, but Ctibor could not be refused without offence.

'Sarah, you too, come, my friend and wife at the same table. Make me happy.'

Sarah turned from the stove, wiping her hands on her apron, and acknowledged them with a nod. Josef glanced at her and they exchanged a look of mutual forbearance as she sat down. It was clear she no more enjoyed sitting at table with a Gypsy than he did with an Unclean white woman, but they both cared for Ctibor and for him, they would do it.

'I hear the Sinti are worried these days,' Ctibor said as Josef sat.

Josef shrugged. 'There will be a meeting on Sunday. I will get the news then.'

Ctibor shook his head. 'They're having a hard time of it. I had five families last week, never seen them before, queuing at my door. You've heard about the riots in Vienna? Those bastards got away with it! But I don't see it's going to affect us. The Germans living in this district are realists.'

Sarah rose from the table, muttering about the goulash.

Ctibor winced and leaned forward. 'I shouldn't really discuss politics in front of Sarah. It makes her angry, and sad,' he said quietly to Josef. 'You know, Prague is filling up with Viennese Jews who can't stand it any more, and of course the Czechs aren't exactly pleased either. Bloody German refugees, they say. I keep telling her, she mustn't worry. As you know I had my doubts about the wisdom of leaving the Empire, economically I mean, but look at us now. Do you know, you can buy a thing in Prague that sends blue electricity through your fingers and cures melancholia?' He leaned forward, confidentially. 'Actually, Josef, you'll forgive my demanding your time, but I wanted to talk to you of Prague. It's a matter of some urgency. I have a scheme going. I've bought a place there, in the Old Town, an office with apartments above. I'm thinking of supplying the stores directly. Things are so good at the moment, business is booming and I've got to use my capital. I'm desperate for good men, Josef.'

Sarah returned to the table with beer. She stared at her husband and Ctibor sat back in his chair. 'Politics and business!' he declared, lifting his hands. 'Both are banned at my table. But I can't help myself, you understand me, Josef. We'll go through the details after we've eaten.'

Poor Ctibor, Josef thought, as they raised their glasses to each other. He should have had sons, a whole houseful of them, great strapping boys who would eat all the time and argue with him and run his orchards and his businesses – and maybe a small, quiet daughter for Sarah, so she wouldn't feel lonely. Truly, childlessness was a curse. Why else would Ctibor be so keen to adopt the Roma? He would never see it that way, of course. He was too big-hearted, with his large belly and red face and fluffy hair.

'Now is the time,' Ctibor declared as he set down his glass mug with a flourish. 'Look around you, Josef. Have you ever seen my fields so well tended? This winter I had to hire factory workers to dig my irrigation ditches. A man has flown across the Atlantic all on his own, like a stork. The *Spirit of St Louis* has come to Europe! Now is the best of times, for your people too, you'll see.'

Josef did not mention Law 117. *When things are good for the gadje, they are bad for the Roma. When they are bad for the gadje, they are even worse for us.*

Sarah had brought several bowls of pickles and salads to the table, with white squares of cheese crumbled on the top.

'Look,' said Ctibor, gesturing at the abundance of food that had appeared merely as accompaniments. 'I don't believe any real harm can come to the world. Just look.' He raised his hands to indicate the whole of his large kitchen with its copper pans in ascending sizes and huge blue ceiling and decorative plates on the walls. 'We sit here in this lovely house which hard work and God has granted me, and around this table we three diverse souls. Doesn't it fill your heart with hope?'

Ctibor beamed at his wife and at Josef, and his wife and Josef beamed back at him, but not at each other.

PART 2

1933

CHAPTER 4

Justin Zelinka was the only man in the *kumpánia* who could read and write, so he read Ctibor Michálek's letter to Josef out loud as the men huddled in the wagon, one freezing dark January night.

'*Greetings Brother*,' he read, and Václav gave a contemptuous snort. He did not approve of the fact that Josef and Ctibor called each other brother.

Justin paused. Josef gave Václav an annoyed glance. Václav became interested in the contents of his unlit pipe. Josef nodded at Justin to continue.

'*I hope this letter finds you well,*' Justin read, '*my wife sends her greetings to Mrs Růžičková. We think often of your young boy in this bitter winter. Has the Jihlava frozen to its bed? Here, everyone is saying it is as bad as '29. I have wrapped the trees on the north side of my fields with blankets, round the trunks, but I doubt it will help . . .'* At this, the assembled men grinned at each other. How absurd, swaddling trees like babies.

Josef was smiling too. 'They are like horses to him . . .' he said, shaking his head.

'I hope your winter quarters are proving . . .' Justin frowned at the page and shook his head. *'. . . ress . . . ressy . . .'*

'Resilient?' suggested Josef. Justin shrugged.

Václav snorted again and this time there was a murmur of agreement in the wagon. Their winter quarters were far from resilient. They were supposed to reside at the Black Huts until March, according to their papers, but the barrel factory in Třebíč had closed and there was no more hoop-making to be had. They had to take to the road every few days, illegally, just to feed themselves and the horses. They were working the small towns and villages around in a wide, anti-clockwise arc. The women sold charms. The men cleared snow and dug ditches. They only went out one wagon at a time because it was now against the law for Gypsies to go anywhere in a group larger than one family. Law 117 was growing new clauses every season. They sprung like snowdrops.

'Tell him our winter quarters are proving as overcrowded, freezing cold and miserable as ever!' declared Václav, stabbing the air with his pipe. Václav was a bitter man this season. He now had five daughters. His oldest, Zdenka, was still unmarried, although she was nearly sixteen. Eva and Pavla were marriageable but could not be betrothed before their sister, so Václav had five little spinsters on his hands, slipping around the Black Huts like dark ghosts and taunting him with their small, stubborn good health. Then, last autumn, Václav's wife Božena had finally given birth to a boy, Martin, a sickly thing who now had whooping cough and gasped and wheezed all night. They were all terrified for him. Václav had become religious and self-blaming, asking Josef what sins he had committed against God to be punished so.

'We will get to the reply in a minute . . .' Josef said gently. 'Justin, go on . . .'

Justin read the rest of the letter without interruption. '*My offer of work still stands, Josef. I go to Prague every month now and am pleased to report that the office is running as efficiently as can be expected under the current circumstances. It was the right decision to sell those acres last summer, although as you know I was most disappointed by the poor price I received. I am still of the belief that my expansion into timber would have succeeded were it not for the entry of the Russians on to the market. Far more experienced merchants than myself were taken aback by the sudden price drop. I cannot regret my attempt to diversify. Do not forget that I do not forget you, Brother. Warmest regards, Ctibor Michálek.*'

Justin folded the letter and replaced it in the rough, crackling envelope, then handed it to Josef. There was a general murmur and shifting amongst the men as Justin picked up his quill. Then he raised his inkpot up to the lantern light and said, 'Brothers, you have a few minutes to debate our reply. I still have ice in my ink.' He cradled the inkpot in his hands and began singing to it.

There was a sudden burst of laughter from the adjacent wagon. The women were becoming raucous.

'Someone go and tell those women to keep quiet! We are doing business here!' growled Václav. The other men glanced at each other. No one was minded to go out in the cold and dark. 'She'll feel the back of my hand tonight . . .' muttered Václav. He could not forgive Božena for giving him five healthy girls and one sick son.

'Laughter keeps us warm . . .' said Yakali reasonably, quoting the proverb. 'Laughter and song . . .' As if on cue, the women's voices could be heard raised in a chant.

'Miroslav, please . . .' said Josef. He no more wanted to quiet the women than Yakali, but Václav must be placated if they were to get anything done.

Miroslav rose from where he was squatting and, pulling his blanket tight around his shoulders, opened the door.

The men braced themselves for the flood of freezing air that rushed through the wagon. Justin took advantage of Miroslav's exit to move closer to the stove. His father Yakali moved back to allow his son to warm himself.

Yakali was an example, Josef thought. He had just been released from two years in prison, because a *gadjo* picked a fight with him in a market square, but he remained as philosophical as ever. Justin and Miroslav had married the South Bohemian girls and had two children each. Miroslav's first child had died of the measles but his wife was now carrying his third. The Zelinka family seemed to have the knack of managing misfortune, of refusing to let it overwhelm and defeat them.

What would they do with Václav when his son died? It would destroy him. It would be hard for Josef to comfort Václav without sounding smug. Emil was five years old and the toughest, healthiest boy a man could wish for – his hair still fair, his looks marred only by the thin red scar on his forehead. He was the prince of the *kumpánia*.

It was hard not to love the boy too much. Josef felt full of fortune every time he looked at him. It was as if all the other children he should have had by now, all the unborn babies, had given the gifts of their tiny souls to be poured into Emil, to fill to full his store of perfection.

Another wave of cold air rushed into the wagon as Miroslav

returned. He was rewarded by a place next to the stove where he squatted down and began to shudder melodramatically.

'I think we should discuss whether or not the *Rom Baró* goes to Prague,' said Václav.

Josef looked at him in surprise.

'I know,' said Václav. 'But how else do we survive this winter? Our horses are so bony you can hardly keep a harness on them. Josef, how much longer will the fodder last?' Václav's question was rhetorical. They had been rationing the hay for weeks now. The horses had begun to eat their filthy straw bedding.

'I'm more greatly concerned about the harnesses . . .' Josef said. The straps were nearly worn through, where they fed through the brass rings. A new harness would cost thousands of crowns and the women's jewellery was long since sold. When the current tackle went, he would have to sell one horse to harness the other. He had two mares now, once clean and brisk, now bony and plodding, with bleeding gums and textured patches on their flanks.

'Well then,' said Václav, looking round at the others. 'What choice do we have?'

'Prague . . .' said Yakali uncertainly. It would be like sending Josef to the moon.

Josef had been to Prague once, when he was a boy. His uncle had taken him. He could remember the trams, the screeching noise they made, the people crammed together, men and women pressed up against each other. The women didn't even seem insulted. The men wore brown suits, cravats, funny round hats that looked ripe for knocking off with sticks – all those people all herded together like hens in a coop, but a coop that hurtled along the streets and screamed as it shot around a corner. It made Josef's hair stand on end just to think of it.

But then he imagined being in a warm office with windows to
protect him from the wind and rain. He would be the boss,
Ctibor had told him. He would tell all the *gadje* in the office what
to do. The first order he would give them would be to keep the
stove so well stoked that the windows fogged up.

'What does the farmer Michálek actually want you to do,
Kakó?' asked Miroslav, and at that everyone glanced at Josef, who
pulled a face and shrugged.

'I say he goes,' said Václav. 'Let's write the letter.'

'I say we wait until the end of the month,' said Yakali. 'See if
something turns up.'

Václav snorted in derision. They all looked at Josef.

'Václav,' said Josef, 'what would you write?'

'I would write this,' said Václav firmly. *'Dear Gadjo, I will work
for you in Prague but I will not demean myself. I will abide by our laws
at all times. My food must be prepared separately and I will not work
in the same room as filthy gadji whores. I expect fifty per cent of
everything, half of it advanced to me to send to my kumpánia. O Del
is the one true God and the Roma his only people. Josef.'*

Václav gave a single firm nod, then glared at them, defying
them to compose a better letter.

'Yakali?' Josef asked.

Yakali frowned. *'Dear Farmer Michálek,'* he began. *'I am most
sorry to hear that frost is cracking your fruit trees. Our horses' hooves
are also cracked. We wish you all advancement and hope that God may
guide you through this bitter time. I am sorry that my people cannot
spare me from my duties caring for them, but very much hope to see you
in the spring, when we may travel to your lands earlier than before.
Your honest friend, Josef.'*

Josef glanced at Miroslav, who said, 'His timber business
failed. Who's to say his canning is going to do any better? I say
go for a wage rather than a cut. When you have collected a

bucketful of beetles you feed them to the chickens straight away, you don't give them a chance to run off.'

Justin said. 'My ink is now unfrozen, *Kakó.*' He held his quill poised above the brown sheet of paper that quavered on his lap.

Josef exhaled heavily.

'*Dear Ctibor,*' he began, and paused. The wagon was silent but for the scratching of Justin's quill. '*Greetings to you, Brother. Our winter quarters have proved sound again this year. I feared that both my horses were lame last week but my fears proved groundless. The road is long. May God bless you and your house and keep you from harm. Your Brother, Josef.*'

There was a silence, during which a certain puzzlement amongst the men was apparent. Had the *Rom Baró* made a decision or not? Václav exhaled shortly through his nostrils.

Josef looked from one to the other, then raised his hands as if to say, *well, it's a compromise.* He gave an uneasy, conciliatory smile, before declaring with a flourish, 'Brothers, I declare this *divano* concluded!'

The next morning, the sun shone so brilliantly that when Josef opened the door to the wagon, the sparkle from the snow hurt his eyes. He sat down on the step, tugging a blanket round his shoulders, and lit his pipe.

The wagons had been pulled up in a circle, rear entrances facing in, so that his group had their own small enclave on the edge of the Huts. From his vantage point he could watch the men leading the horses out so that they could sweep out the Huts, and the women running from wagon to wagon, busying themselves with all those women's tasks that suddenly became so important once the weather turned fine.

After the grey gloom of the last few days, the bright white light was irresistibly beautiful. Justin and Miroslav were laughing and joking as they brushed down the horses. Eva and Ludmila were chattering as they sliced up the huge grey block of soap which rested on a stone, and wrapped the individual pieces in cloth. Even Václav raised his hand in greeting to them all as he emerged from behind his wagon and hung his copper washbasin on a nail by the door.

It was a source of great amusement to the other Roma in the settlement that Josef's *kumpánia* stabled their horses in the Huts and slept in their wagons. Josef thought the Huts disgusting, barely fit for the animals, let alone decent Roma. He had never slept in a house in his life. Not even a winter as bitter as this was going to make him start.

There was only one other nomadic *kumpánia* at the Black Huts, over-wintering there like them. The rest of the inhabitants were settled Moravian Roma who were there all year round – and there was one family of poor, filthy *gadje* who had fallen on hard times and stank to high heaven. All the other families lived in the Huts themselves. Their children would come around, when they were bored, and gallop up and down the wide river of frozen mud between the Huts, shaking their heads and making whinnying noises. The joke amongst the other Roma was that the Kalderash loved their horses so much they gave them their beds to sleep in.

A group of children was running his way now, delighted that the bright sun made it temporarily warm enough to play. Josef saw Emil at the head of them. He was popular with the other children because of his light skin and hair – he could almost pass for a white boy. They were all playing horses, about twelve of them, mostly boys with a couple of small girls trailing in the rear.

They came to a halt where the other men had tied the horses and stood around watching them work. Miroslav raised a broom and shook it playfully at them, and they squealed in mock apprehension, retreating a few steps, then creeping forward again.

Josef observed the group. He did not like his son mixing with Moravian Roma. He had talked to him about it, but Emil was a spoilt boy, and disobedient. It depressed him sometimes. He would have sooner thrown himself into a furnace and slammed the door shut behind him than disobeyed his own father, Andreas – a man always ready with the whip. Children had no respect these days. *Maybe the problem is me. Maybe I am too weak with him. I don't like him associating with that riff-raff. He should be learning Vlach ways from other Kalderash boys – but there are no other Vlach families round here, and if there were they probably wouldn't associate with us because we've become so used to Moravian ways. There is no one like our strange, mongrel group. What are we doing here? Why don't we go back to Wallachia, or Russia, where we belong, and stay put? Hardly anyone travels these days. Ach, relax, Josef, and let the boy play. It's not his fault.* He sighed heavily. At Emil's age, he was holding bellows for his uncle while he worked. He could remember the heat from the open furnace, how he had appreciated it in layers: the bidding warmth as you approached on a cold winter's morning, then the growing fury of it – and finally, a pain behind the eyes as you stared at the motlen metal. Staring at it hurt but it was impossible to look away. His uncle's forearms were speckled with rough spots where the sparks had burnt him over the years – his hands were rough as tree bark. Josef would push with all his might on the bellows, wanting so much to do it hard enough, to be like his uncle: silent and hugely powerful. He was tooling and polishing by the age of eight and receiving a cut of the take for his efforts. He could not remember a time when he had not earned money. Emil was nearly six. He didn't work because there was no work to be had. He fetched water. He helped his father insulate the Huts with piles of brushwood and swept straw, and he played with the Moravian Roma boys. When would the boy learn a trade?

'Emil!' Josef called out to him. The boy did not hear him immediately, too busy giggling with the others. 'Emil!'

Emil turned and saw his father beckoning. He spoke briefly to his friends and then trotted happily over. Josef slung an arm around his shoulders and pulled him to his chest in a bear hug. Emil squirmed and wriggled free.

'I've told you about those boys,' Josef said. 'That big one especially, the black one. They laugh at us. They're a bad influence on you. You should play with your own group, learn something from the men. You should keep busy with us.'

Emil let his chin protrude and looked at the ground, itching to return to his playmates. *I would never have dared show such a face to my father*, Josef thought angrily. He grabbed Emil's arm. 'That big boy, the one who follows you around,' he said harshly. 'He is not your friend. They make jokes about us, about our horses. It is time you learned how a Rom responds to people who insult him.'

Emil looked at his father, intrigued. Josef knew he had appealed to the boy's pride. Emil was impulsive, and strong, and used to being adored by a *kumpánia* full of girls and women. Adoration was his due.

Josef leant forward and said, 'Show me you are a big boy, Emil, a boy a man can be proud of. I heard that boy over there making jokes yesterday, jokes that insulted your mother and father.'

Emil stared at him, wide-eyed.

'Go, show him,' said Josef.

Emil turned smartly on his heel and strode back to the group of children. Without preamble, he stepped up to the large, dark-skinned boy. He withdrew his fist and, aiming upwards, smashed it soundlessly into the side of the boy's head.

The boy staggered, howled, and turned away, fleeing over the frozen mud, the other children at his heels.

Emil returned to Josef with a triumphant smile. 'Good,' said Josef. 'Now go and help your Uncle Yakali sweep out that hut, go into the dark corners where he can't see, his eyesight is bad.'

The door to the wagon opened and Anna descended, stepping around him with a bundle of clothing in her arms. The women had strung up a line and were trying to air as much as possible while they had the chance.

'What was that about?' she asked Josef.

'Your son is learning to be my son also!' Josef declared. Anna looked at him, then shook her head.

A few minutes later, Josef saw that a group was storming up the mud track, led by a dark-faced woman who was clutching the boy's hand. *Here we go*, he thought.

A stream of children and four or five other women were in the group. The woman stopped in front of their wagons.

'Where is the mother of the Kalderash boy!' shouted the woman. 'I call her out! Where is she?'

Anna turned calmly from the line, a pile of clothing still in her arms, a wooden peg between her teeth.

'It is I,' she replied calmly, then spat out the peg. 'Who calls me out?'

The woman seemed inclined to skip the formalities. Perhaps it was the cold – or maybe she had left something boiling over a fire. She squared up to Anna without another word, lifting her fists.

Anna sighed, then handed the bundle of clothing to

Ludmila, who stood open-mouthed on the other side of the line.

The men had stopped sweeping to watch, grinning at the show. Emil had come to the door of the shed and stood next to Miroslav, staring from his mother to the woman.

Time we had a bit of fun round here, thought Josef. This should warm things up.

Anna was rolling up her sleeves.

The two women had just begun to circle one another, when the door behind Josef swung open and Tekla jumped down from the wagon. She ran up to the Moravian Romni and said, 'I told our boy to punch yours! We are sick of him causing trouble round here. You Moravians don't know how to behave!'

Anna was still staring at Tekla in disbelief, when the Moravian Romni thumped Tekla neatly on the nose, turned quickly away and strode back down the mud track.

Anna and the others felt obliged to scream a few insults at the departing crowd – and the departing crowd felt obliged to scream a few back – but the matter was clearly concluded.

'Tekla!' Anna exclaimed, rounding on her cousin, whose nose was dripping fresh red blood on to the snow.

'Shut your face!' Tekla responded. 'I'm still good for something. Your arms are like twigs! You couldn't punch a petal!'

The men turned back to their work, shaking their heads. *Women!*

Anna tried to take Tekla's face in her hands, to examine the damage, but Tekla knocked her hands aside and turned back to the wagon. As she pushed past Josef, she muttered fiercely from beneath the rag she held over her nose, 'If you men have no work to do then O Beng himself makes work for you!'

'Tekla . . .' said Josef sheepishly, raising his hands. 'It was only a little fun.' *A man has to teach his son something*, Josef thought to himself, uneasily. *Well, all right, it was a stupid thing to do. But I meant no real harm.* 'Come, Tekla, don't be angry with me. There was no malice in my mischief – a boy's game. Forgive me!'

Tekla stared down at him. He was silenced by the look on her face. 'I have long since learned to do that, Josef,' she said quietly. She closed the wagon door behind her.

When Josef turned back, Anna was standing in front of him holding a small wicker basket of pegs. 'You are a fool, husband,' she said, her look indecipherable.

Women! Their strange looks! What were they on about now?

She turned away, shaking her head. 'All men are fools . . .'

*

Inside the wagon, Tekla held her head over a bowl and squeezed the bridge of her nose. A clot would soon form. She shouldn't be doing it inside the wagon but if she went outside the other women would gather round and she could not bear sympathy. While she waited for the bleeding to stop, she wept salty tears of self-pity that had nothing to do with her nose.

Afterwards, she wiped her nose and peered at her reflection in the hammered-smooth piece of tin which hung from a piece of string on the back of the door. She would have to go outside soon, or one of the others would come in. How many opportunities did she have to cry alone?

Her nose was still the same shape, flat and flared, red with the cold. Her eyes were still too close together, the brows heavy and dark. Her skin was still sallow and pitted. A punch. What else was she good for?

She ran her tongue over her lips. They were cracked and sore with the cold. Sometimes, at night, lying next to Ludmila and Eva, she would press her lips against the soft skin on the inside of her wrist, just to imagine what it must be like to have another person's mouth against your own.

She turned away from the piece of tin and closed her eyes. She lifted a hand, still in her fingerless woollen gloves, and stroked her cheek, knowing her expression was a frown of pain and glad she could not see herself any more. It was always a mistake to look. When Anna and Josef had married, she had re-braided her hair and pulled her best skirt over her workaday one without ever once running down to the river with the other women, who stood above the water like a bunch of silly geese, swaying and admiring their wavery reflections. At the dance after the feast, she had celebrated with greater gusto than anyone present. How she had danced – and how the two families had laughed at short, squat, ugly little Tekla losing her inhibitions for once and kicking up her skirts. She knew they were laughing at her – she had drunk so much that she was horribly sober – but it suited her fine. If they enjoyed the sight of funny, dumpy little Tekla Maximoff making a fool of herself, then maybe they would be too busy laughing to guess the truth.

The truth was, she had loved Josef for years, ever since they were children together in Sap. Once or twice, she had even dared to hope her feelings might be reciprocated. Josef had married late for such an eligible Rom – he had been hard to please, and many a family had paraded their daughters before his parents over the years. Then came the news of his engagement to Anna Demeter.

Tekla could remember the first time she had set eyes on Anna. The betrothal had been tentatively agreed but the Demeters were lowly stuff in comparison with the Maximoff clan. The girl was instructed to prove herself in a variety of domestic tasks before Josef's parents would give their full consent.

One grey-green dawn, Anna and her sisters were to join the women of the Maximoff *kumpánia* at mushroom-picking. It was a chilly, foggy morning: first light. Tekla had waited with the others at the edge of the forest, all standing in a row and staring down the lane. She could recall her grim satisfaction at the solid line of women, waiting for these chits from the Demeter clan who thought themselves equals. How intimidating we will seem as they approach, she thought. *She had better get used to it.*

Then, the Demeter girls walked down the road together in a line, three tall, slender women emerging from the mist, the gold coins on their belts and braids clinking softly in the silence. Tekla had inhaled, struck breathless by the knowledge that that was what Josef had been waiting for, that vision. *I was there when he had chicken-pox at the age of twelve*, she thought tremulously. *I was outside the wagon and heard the snapping sound when they broke his leg. My mother stayed with his family when his mother disappeared for six months after his father cracked her jaw. I cooked for my beloved cousin every night.* And still the three tall women drew nearer, Anna in the lead, her face a smooth-skinned picture of graciousness, her eyes alight, her fine lips turned in a seraphic smile. Even the older women had been temporarily struck dumb. It had been an effort not to turn and run.

On the wedding night, Tekla shared the wagon with her mother and Josef's parents who lay drunk and hating each other at the far end. The newly-wed couple were in a specially erected tent outside, with a double canopy to protect them from the light summer rain. The families had stood around and clapped as they retired.

Tekla huddled on her small cot and drew her knees up underneath the blanket. The worst thing she could do was think about what Josef and Anna were doing now, she said to herself, and proceeded to think of it in great detail. She imagined Josef's forearm around Anna's back – she loved his forearms, the strong muscles, the dense, dark-brown hairs, the immaculate hands. She imagined their mouths upon one another, Anna's braids falling down and around Josef's face . . .

At the beginning of the betrothal, she had comforted herself with the thought that many first marriages ended in bitterness or divorce and it was not uncommon for a man or woman to return to a true love many years later. But when she had seen the look on Josef's face when Anna had been stung by a bee, just before he crumpled into tears, she knew that this marriage was a great deal more than an arrangement. She had lost Josef as irrevocably as if he had gone over the edge of a waterfall in a pickle barrel.

Tekla squeezed her eyes tight shut to hold back her bitter tears and dug her fingernails into the palms of her hands. Josef had got what he had been waiting for. All the small, shy beauties that had been paraded before him were wasting their time. She, Tekla, each loving meal she had cooked, the sewing she had done for him – it had all been a waste of time. He had been waiting for a woman who held her head so high it was amazing no one slapped her for insolence. Why was it that people thought it charming when a beautiful woman was headstrong? She, Tekla, was headstrong too but nobody had ever remarked of it approvingly. Anna had long arms that seemed to lift in the breeze when she danced. Tekla had plump shoulders, short arms and large, muscular hands. Anna could lose her temper and the men around her – even the women – would sigh at the dark flash of her eyes. If Tekla got cross, it only made her more ugly.

Now, right now, as she lay curled under the blanket, with Josef's parents out-snoring each other after the feast, the man she loved would be lifting Anna's skirts, their eyes fixed intently upon one another. While she, Tekla, had nothing but a hard cot for comfort, they would be melting flesh with flesh. Anna was beautiful. Tekla was ugly. The sun would drop from the sky in flames before those two basic facts were altered.

Finally, bitter tears rolled down her cheeks. At first, she tried to stifle her sobs, but soon she lost all sense of restraint and wept openly, her mouth a harsh rectangle of grief and her cries strangled at the back of her throat so as not to be detected outside the wagon – she wasn't concerned about waking Josef's parents or her own mother. A horse falling from the sky and crashing through the ceiling wouldn't bother them.

It seemed at that point that her pain was infinite, located somewhere in the very core of her, and that she loved Josef more at that moment, yearned for him more, than she had in all the moments of her youth and childhood put together. It was only later she realised. The moment she most grieved was also the moment she ceased to love him quite so badly. As she wept in desperation, a small desire for self-preservation began to grow in her.

Gradually, over the next few years, Tekla fell out of love with Josef and in love with Josef and Anna, with the idea of them as two beautiful children, well-meaning but irresponsible, who had no idea of the pain they caused by their innocent devotion to each other. When Josef's parents died, Tekla found herself with a new role, new status. She took over the bulk of the cooking duties and began to organise more and more of the chores, distributing the work between herself and Anna's sisters but bestowing on Anna only the lighter duties. She, Tekla, was now mother to this strange grown-up family, the new *Rom Baró*, his beautiful, carefree wife and her charming siblings. It was she, Tekla, who kept the wheels turning. It was a role which remained secure so long as Josef and Anna were childless.

Emil's birth had changed everything: Anna was a mother, not only more beautiful than Tekla but also more respected. It was galling to see how good at it she was. If only she had been a poor cook, or unable to sew. At least when she was barren then she had a flaw – and an all-consuming one at that. What had she left Tekla with, after Emil? Nothing. Now Emil was five years old, and perfect, and loved by everyone, and she, Tekla, still did the chores and picked up the pieces, except that nobody noticed any more because they were always too busy noticing how perfect Emil was. Not even Anna's failure to give him any little brothers or sisters detracted from his virtues, so strong and impudent was he. Perfect.

Well, Tekla thought grimly, poking the rag into a nostril to remove the last trace of encrusted blood. I know how to take a punch, that much I can do.

The door to the wagon opened. It was Anna. Tekla turned away quickly, picking up two folded blankets from the top of the oak chest.

'Here,' she said, holding them out without turning to Anna. 'You forgot to take these out.'

'I thought they were too heavy,' Anna said gently. 'I unfolded them but then I thought the sun didn't look as though it was going to last and we can't risk them getting damp. We'd never get them dry again.'

Tekla turned to Anna and raised her eyebrows, downturning the corners of her mouth in an expression which indicated that in *her* opinion there was not the remotest chance of the blankets becoming damp on such a fine day. 'As you wish,' she said, tight-lipped.

She pushed past Anna, leaving her holding the folded blankets and gazing at the floor. At the door she paused. She wanted to say, *it has been an effort not to hate you, and at this very moment I am losing the battle.* Strange how a small incident like today's could bring it all back – how she could go for years hardly thinking of all the pain Josef and Anna had caused her. She closed the door gently behind her. *Let me keep my bitterness at least,* she thought. *It is the only thing I have that is truly mine.*

CHAPTER 5

Václav Winter's son died at the beginning of February. They all heard him gasping for breath one black night, as the whooping cough closed his throat at last.

The ground was too frozen to bury him, so they took him in procession to Třebíč, to the brick crematorium on the far side of town, opened specially each winter. Václav carried the tiny coffin in his arms all the way, his face a mask of grief. The women supported Božena, who could scarcely walk, her five small daughters trailing weepingly behind. Every single inhabitant of the Black Huts followed them into town, the musicians playing, and the *gadje* they passed in the street removed their hats and stood with their heads bowed as a mark of respect.

Martin Winter's death was the first – others followed swiftly, as influenza ravaged the occupants of the Huts. Each day it seemed to leap from shack to shack, advancing with unbelievable speed. Two old Moravian Romnis went first, followed by another baby and a boy. The disease progressed along the Huts until it reached their encampment. Old Ludvík Frank, bedridden and enfeebled already, went first. His wife came down with it but pulled through. All five of the Winterová girls fell sick and Zdenka – poor, toothy, unmarried Zdenka – did not survive.

The night Zdenka died, Václav ran out into the freezing darkness in the middle of a tuneful snowstorm, and shook his fists at the sky. Josef and Yakali tried to pull him back inside but Václav took no heed of them, his feet planted firmly in the fresh snow, his face tipped upwards as he howled, 'I said *instead*, O Del! Are you *blind*? Are you *deaf*? I said *in-STEAD* . . . !'

A week later, Emil fell ill.

He had been lethargic and complaining all day, but Anna assumed his whiny mood was due to hunger – there was nothing but a little farina to eat, and there would be nothing else until the current snowstorm lifted. She did not detect his high temperature until that evening, as they all retired. He started complaining that he wanted to go to sleep – unusual for Emil – and when she asked him why, he said his head hurt. She placed a hand on his forehead and felt at once that he was burning. She told Josef to sleep on the floor and Eva and Ludmila gave up two of their blankets for him. Anna wrapped herself around Emil and held him close as he fell asleep. He was just over-excited, she told herself. She would hold him so tightly the fever would not dare penetrate her embrace.

In the morning, there was no doubt. He was awake before any of them, crying out that he was thirsty. While Tekla pulled a shawl around her shoulders and went to break the ice on the water bucket by the step, Anna pulled Emil's clothing away from his chest and pressed her cheek to it. He pushed her away, moaning that he was cold, although he felt as hot as a little roast chicken. He continued to shiver and complain even when she wrapped him in blankets and lay down next to him, clutching him. 'It hurts,' he cried, his voice tiny and baby-like, but when she asked where, he closed his eyes and wouldn't answer her.

'So,' Tekla said simply, as she sat down on the edge of the bed, nursing a tin mug of water and gazing down at them. 'We are not immune, after all.'

As soon as dawn broke, Josef and Ludmila and Eva were banished from the wagon, the girls to sleep with Pavliná Franzová who was still weak and needed company anyway, and Josef to lodge with the Zelinkas – Anna dared not send him to the Winters' wagon. Two of their girls were still sick.

Tekla went to make tea for the men. Then they would see if they could persuade Emil to take an infusion.

While Tekla was gone, Anna lay curled around her son, stroking the damp hair back from his forehead, tracing the length of his scar with her finger, until he pushed her hand away, saying she was hurting him. Tekla had said there was a freezing mist outside. That was a bad omen. The mist would pull poisons from the earth. When Tekla came back, she would tell her to stay in or out and stuff rags beneath the door, to prevent any more evil air entering the wagon. The crisis would come today or tomorrow – the Sweating Sickness was always a quick killer. She would soon know.

She felt strangely calm, lying next to her sick son. *It is very simple for me*, she thought. *For those with normal size families, it is more complex. Božena had six children and has lost two of them – a third of her life is now grief. My mother had eleven of us in all: us three in quick succession; then the twins, Chachu and little yellow Arniko, who died at*

six weeks; then Pavla; then Andreas; then poor Malilini who fell from a
cart and broke her back and took four pain-filled years to die; two more
boys – how she had doted on blond Emanuel; then a stillborn girl. What
a mad tangle of joy and misery was there – what strange pattern of loving
and loss must have grown around my mother's heart. I have but one child
to worry about, so as long as I can protect just this one, then I am
completely happy. But if I lose Emil, I lose everything. My life will be a
void.

All day, Emil's temperature soared up and down. He would eat
nothing and sip only cold water. Towards evening, he seemed to
sleep a little, then was suddenly awake, tossing and turning, unable
to get comfortable.

'Go and eat with the others,' Tekla said to Anna, 'you've been
in here all day,' but Anna refused, only consenting to lie down on
Eva and Ludmila's bunk and close her eyes.

She dozed for a while, then awoke when Tekla was lighting
the kerosene lamp.

'How is he?' she asked, sitting up, realising that she was
hungry and thirsty, despite herself. Perhaps if Emil was quiet,
she would go and see if there was a little bread.

Tekla shook her head.

Anna slipped from beneath the blankets and went over to
Emil, still wrapped tightly in his. He was deadly pale and hardly
conscious, his lips fluttering gently, as if he were reciting a story
to himself.

Tekla said, 'If you won't leave him, I'll cook you some farina.
The last thing we need is you falling ill as well.'

'Is the fire still going?'

'Yes. I'll go now.'

Anna sat next to Emil, a blanket around her shoulders,
watching his face in the shadows. Darkness must have only just

fallen but it felt like the middle of the night. She closed her eyes and prayed that her son might see daylight again.

She had been praying for a while when she heard a gasping sound. She opened her eyes. Emil was fighting for breath. He began to cough. She raised him a little and grabbed the edge of her apron, holding it to his face so that he could cough into it. The spasm lasted several minutes. When he had finished, she laid him down again, stood and held her apron up to the lamp. In the yellow light, she saw that Emil had coughed up sputum streaked pinkish here and there. She had heard of this. People drowned in their own bloody fluids. 'Oh God in heaven . . .' she whispered to herself, her legs suddenly weak with fear. She raised her face to the lamplight. *Who will save my child?*

She turned and dropped to her knees, opening the door to the locker beneath their bed, and pulling out the largest of the copper vats. Then she flew to the wagon door and wrenched it open, jumping down outside and falling on her knees beside the snowdrift that was backed up against the side of the wagon.

A few metres away, the dark shapes of the other women were huddled around the orange glow from the fire. The rest of the camp was hidden in the darkness. The mist had gone and it was a clear night, the sky above her bright with stars. 'Anna?' she heard Tekla call.

'Help me, Tekla!' she responded weakly, the freezing air cramping her lungs as she exhaled in great clouds. She was using both her arms to pull the fine, powdery snow into the copper vat.

Tekla ran to her. 'What are you doing?'

'He's dying,' she sobbed. 'We must pack him in snow, it's the only thing left.'

'No,' said Tekla.

Anna scrambled to her feet and tried to lift the vat – God give her the strength. Tekla tried to prevent her. Anna shouted. 'Tekla! I am not going to lie next to my son and just wait for him to go blue! He can't breathe!'

Tekla lowered her voice and hissed fiercely, 'It doesn't work. It doesn't bring the fever down. Božena carried Zdenka out into a snow drift and half buried her, what good did it do?'

'We must do something . . .'

'Listen to me! Put that down. On your son's life, *listen* to me.'

Anna dropped the vat down and sank down next to it. Tekla took a rag from inside her blouse and turned it in the snow, then handed it to Anna. 'Put this inside your clothes until the snow melts and it is damp but not too cold. Lay it on his forehead. I will take the vat to the fire and melt the snow. We have to get the water not hot but not cold either, like a body should be. Then we will bathe him. If you freeze him he will only shiver more and his temperature will go *up*, not down. Do this!'

Without waiting for her to reply, Tekla bent and lugged the vat on to her hip, then turned back to the fire, where the other women were peering anxiously towards them.

As Anna rose, she felt herself sway and her vision blur. She loosened her shawl and put the snowy rag inside her blouse, as Tekla had instructed her, and the freezing shock of it suddenly clarified everything. Tekla was right. She must not panic. If she did, her son would die.

Emil did not die. They bathed him, and sat up watching him all night. By the time dawn broke, they knew he was out of danger, although Anna insisted he stay in bed for an entire fortnight, so frightened had she been by his illness.

In the meantime, Tekla fell sick, but she did not die either. The others waited to become ill and just when it seemed the danger had passed, Anna, Josef and Ludmila fell sick for a day or two in turn, as if they were passing the disease around themselves like an apple, for each to take a bite. None of them became seriously ill like Emil and Tekla. Eva escaped altogether.

As soon as they were all well again, Anna examined her behaviour during the crisis. She was ashamed. She had behaved like an ill-bred, superstitious Romni. If it had not been for Tekla's presence of mind, Emil might have died. Some women keened as their children faded, rocking themselves, beating their heads against trees, crying out against what Fate had dealt them. She should have been above such panic. The illness had come amongst them because they were at the end of their resources. It had nearly taken her child because she had been weak and inadequate. She must work harder, be stronger, more like Tekla. Fate must never again have the chance to play a part in whether her child lived or died. It would be she, Anna Sariyia Maximoff, Kalderaška, who decided that from now on. God forgive her presumption.

There were ways for a mother to feed her child, now that the weather was improving – ways in which the father took no part. These ways would be how Emil survived until spring.

Freezing February became a bitter March. Each morning, she would lift her shawl from the hook on the back of the wagon's door and slip outside, instantly awake as the air embraced her. With any luck, Tekla would have already started the fire. The other women would join them silently in the icy darkness, taking it in turns to make tea for their men in order of precedence but as one in their misery.

It is the only time we all hate our men, Anna sometimes thought, when we stand before the fire, waiting for the water, while our husbands and sons have a few more moments in the sweet land of sleep. We hate them then, with all our hearts.

As she was wife to the *Rom Baró*, she stood nearest to the fire, bent over it so close that sparks stung her cheeks and the smoke made her cough. None of the warmth ever spread to the rest of her body. The others would huddle either side of her, Tekla muttering to herself, praying or chanting sometimes. Božena would puff on a pipe. Although it was still dark and the Black Huts no more than shapes in the gloom, there would be the occasional tweet of a dawn bird, a sign that light was there, around the corner, light if not warmth.

By the time she returned to the wagon, Josef would be rising. She would hand him tea in his tin cup without speaking, then go to rouse Emil. He would sit up sleepily, his light brown hair in fluffy disarray and eyes glittering as she pulled the blanket up round his shoulders and handed him his tea. He had recovered his strength only slowly, but in the mornings he still had a little of the old mischievousness in his eye.

'Are we going from door to door today, *Dalé*?' he would whisper, putting the hot tin cup to his lips then away again, pulling a face, nodding hopefully.

She would nod, sigh, smile. 'Yes, Little One,' she would whisper in return, reaching out a hand to smooth the hair back from his face. 'We are going from door to door.'

Ostensibly, the women and children went out each day to sell the charms that Josef made from small pieces of beaten metal and coloured pebbles. They brought in no more than a few hallers which the village women only gave them to get rid of them – those hallers hardly justified the amount of times Anna and Emil were chased down the path with a broom. But sometimes, while they paused on the doorstep while the village woman fumbled in her apron, Emil would have time to squeak, as Anna had taught him, 'Look, *Maminka*, the lady is chopping vegetables. Do you think she might give me a piece of carrot?' Or sometimes it was. '*Maminka*! *Maminka*! What is that wonderful smell?'

Anna always snapped, 'Hush, Little František, don't be so rude. The lady will think we are beggars.'

Sometimes, it drew no more than a shrewd look. Mostly, the woman of the house would give Emil an indulgent grimace and go back into her kitchen, returning with a piece of carrot or a vanilla roll.

Once, only once, that winter, were they ushered inside.

It was three weeks after Emil had recovered from his illness. He was still thin and pale. The woman who stood at the door to the large stone cottage stared down at him for a long time, glanced once at Anna, then tilted her head to indicate they could step up.

Anna observed the woman as she led them through into the kitchen. She was small and soft, wrapped in several woollen shawls, like a bundle of blankets. She was a pious woman, Anna could tell. It was her bent look. She moved slowly, and made a clicking sound as she breathed through the phlegm at the back of her throat.

The small soft woman seated Emil on a wooden bench at the kitchen table, and then turned to the stove where a huge iron pan sat steaming. They had killed a pig the day before, she explained over her shoulder to Anna. The boy could have a bowl of strong soup.

Anna remembered pig-kills from her childhood, when her family had been sedentary for a few years in South Bohemia. She could recall how the children would be given the job of stirring the blood with their hands. The blood was in huge buckets, black and smoking. They would sit round the buckets up to their elbows, stirring and stirring to prevent the blood from clotting. Her mother and the other women would be boiling barley and frying spices. A *gadjo* butcher would be hired to twist sausage skins from the intestines. Later, they would be given titbits as a reward. Anna's favourite piece was the cheek.

It never lasted long, a pig, not among the Roma, for it would have been shameful not to invite all your neighbours around to eat it. It was why the pigs were kept for fattening and selling and rarely killed. When the *gadje* killed a pig, they kept it hidden from their neighbours. They froze the meat in ice-houses, smoked it, stored the sausages. They tried to make a pig last forever.

The woman turned from the stove and placed a bowl in front of Emil, whose eyes became full moons. He glanced up at Anna for permission to lift the bowl to his lips, but she nodded towards the woman who was going to the wooden dresser to fetch a spoon.

Anna remained standing against the kitchen wall while Emil ate. The woman had not invited her to sit and she knew better than to push their luck, though the smell of the soup made juices run in her mouth, bathing her gums in acid. Her stomach was full of air. She felt herself sway, lightly. She had missed her bleeding time that month – she should have had one while Emil had been ill – but it was hard to believe she could have conceived during such a lean winter. She had long since given up hope of having another child. She would not say anything to Josef until she was sure.

She exhaled slowly while she watched Emil, forcing herself to concentrate, to stop her knees from buckling and her mouth filling with bile.

It was a joy to watch him eat, her small son with his eyes sparkling and his little legs swinging. The small soft woman was sitting next to him, revelling in his satisfaction, handing him more bread – he had finished the first lot with extraordinary rapidity – encouraging him to dip it into the soup and suck the gravy from it.

'It's good, eh? My soup? Good? Good?'

Emil nodded happily. The woman clapped her hands together and rocked back and forth, smiling at him, then reached out a hand and ruffled his hair.

Anna watched and felt all at once as though the bitter juices in her mouth were also the fluids running through her veins. She realised she was feeling pure, unadulterated hatred. The woman was a thief. She had stolen Anna's joy – her rightful joy, the joy of sitting next to her child and feeling happy in the knowledge that she had provided for him. Look at how he was feasting. And look at how the woman was congratulating herself. Thief.

She felt herself sway again. Small white spots appeared before her eyes. After the bitter cold outside, the kitchen was stuffy, the air thick with the smell of meat. Anna closed her eyes briefly, then opened them. If she fainted, Emil would not get to finish.

On the opposite wall, above the dresser, was a set of delicately carved wooden shelves on which were rows of engraved eggs; purple, red and black, with gold tracery and tiny figures carved out of coloured wax. They were beautiful. They must have taken hours.

There were some man's boots by the door, old boots, a tin bucket and two little spades carved out of wood – children's toys, spades for children who played at digging, who thought digging was a game. This was a house where the woman had time in the evenings to decorate eggs, not to sell at Easter but to put on a shelf for her family to enjoy. The children played at digging. Their father carved them spades. There was enough wood to make toys out of. Where were the children now? At a school, probably, one of those large buildings where *gadjis* sent their children to learn numbers and letters and forget how to gut chickens or raise a shelter – to be turned into foolish *gadje* like their parents. What kind of mother hated her children so much that she sent them away from her each day when they were scarcely big enough to walk? No wonder the *gadje* sometimes came and stole children from good Roma families. They could not bear to see how much they were loved. It shamed them.

Anna looked at the woman, who now had her head bent over Emil, close enough to inhale the vapours from the soup. Perhaps that explained her indulgence. She felt bad about sending her own children to school, so she was spoiling Emil, reassuring herself that she was a good mother after all. At church on Sunday, she would feel calm and satisfied because she had done a kind thing. She had fed a starving little *gypsy* boy a bowl of good strong soup. (Being good to a *gypsy* child got you into Heaven – whereas being good to a *gypsy* adult made you a sap.)

The woman glanced up and saw Anna observing her. Anna had not the time to compose the venom from her look. She forced her lips into an unconvincing smile.

The woman rose to her feet and said hastily, 'Finish now, boy, and be off.'

Emil looked from his mother to the woman, confused by the sudden change of tone. He hurriedly scraped the last of his soup and snatched up the piece of bread that remained on the table, cramming it into his mouth. He swung his legs over the bench, jumped down and ran to his mother.

With Emil back at her side, Anna felt strong enough to thank the woman convincingly.

The woman flapped her hands to acknowledge the thanks and indicate they should leave. She was unable to meet Anna's gaze. She knew she was the one who should be giving thanks. Anna had shared her son for a few brief moments and given the woman a chance to save her self-satisfied *gadji* soul. The woman

would remember how she had been kind to the poor little *gypsy*
boy for years to come. She would remind herself of it every time
she did an unkind thing. Every time she beat one of her own
children she would say to herself, *they have no idea how lucky they
are.*

They backed out of the house and the woman slammed the
door shut before they had even descended the step.

As they strode down the lane, Emil – his mouth crammed
with the last piece of bread – looked up at Anna and said, *'Dalé,
why didn't the gadji give you any soup?'*

Anna marched along, her fury and hunger adding needless
haste to her steps. Emil was trotting to keep up, spitting
breadcrumbs as he went.

'She gave you soup because she wanted to feel good about
herself,' Anna replied. 'And she didn't give me soup because she
wanted us to think that she was good but not weak. She thought
that if she gave us both soup we would think she was stupid.
Then we would go back again, and take more and more from
her.'

'But we won't be coming back to this village . . .' Emil said,
frowning.

Anna slowed down her walk. The cold was biting at her
shoulders. She managed a small smile. 'I didn't mean she
thought *we* would go back. I meant us, any of us. The People.
White people always think that if they are generous to one of
us they will have a hundred on their doorstep. That's why they
are afraid of us. Men and women who have lots of things are
always afraid. They are afraid of losing them.'

She stopped, bent down, and took Emil by his shoulders,
turning him towards her to pick the crumbs from his coat and
push them into his mouth with a finger. 'Remember that, son of
mine. It is a great weapon. We have nothing at the moment.

Things are very bad. But having nothing is also a strength. We are hungry now but it was worse when we had just a little. I know it's hard to believe when a *gadjo* sends his dog out of the house to chase us away. But he does it because he is frightened and because we are powerful.' She had finished. She brushed down the coat, out of habit, even though all the crumbs were gone.

Emil looked at his mother and gave a small, sly smile. Then, from inside his coat, he withdrew the piece of bread that he had concealed there while eating the soup. ·

He lifted it to his mother's mouth and her teeth snatched at it, nipping his fingers. He pulled the hand back and yelped in mock pain, then threw his hands up in the air and whirled around, shrieking with delight.

Anna squatted on her haunches, chewed at the bread and watched as her small and perfect son spun round in the middle of the road, suffused with joy at his own cunning.

They had arranged to meet Josef by the small cluster of trees outside the village. Tekla was there already. Ludmila and Eva had been left behind at the Black Huts.

Tekla was watching their approach. She nodded at Emil, tripping happily along beside his mother. 'You have had luck . . .'

Anna nodded. 'You?' she asked, and instantly regretted the question. She should have been able to tell from Tekla's demeanour that she had had no luck at all.

Tekla made a small *tsk* sound between her teeth and spat on the ground. 'What luck am I likely to have? We need more children to take along. No one is interested. It is stupid that Božena takes all her girls. You should have backed me up.'

Božena's performance to the *gadji*s involved displaying her daughters in descending rank and pointing out how many mouths she had to feed. With Zdenka and the baby gone, the ranks had been diminished. When Tekla had asked if she could take one of the girls door-to-door, Božena had raged at her for being so cruel as to deprive her of another child – and Tekla had pointed out that it was cruel to deprive her and the Little One of the food she might be able to acquire. It had been a bitter scene.

Anna sighed, remembering the bread she had swallowed almost whole. If she had produced a decent-sized family then the dispute would not have arisen. 'Take Emil with you tomorrow,' she said, grudgingly. Tekla did not reply. Emil was swinging from a low branch of a nearby tree, his shirt riding up from his breeches to expose a white, flat patch of skin. It made Anna shiver just to look at him.

As they waited, a family of peasants passed by; a broad-shouldered farmer and his equally broad wife, three children who stared across the road in honest curiosity while their parents averted their gazes.

Emil dropped from the branch and stood staring back, offering mute solidarity. The children continued to gaze behind them as they entered the village.

'Dalé . . .' Emil said, still staring after the family.

Anna did not reply. She was leaning in the shelter of the tree.

'Dalé . . .' Emil turned and wandered over to her. 'Dalé, why are the gadje all so ugly? Their faces, they are white and pudgy, and they have big noses and ears, and they're so clumsy when they walk. They are like cows.'

'They can't help being ugly,' Anna responded listlessly. 'They are born that way. You mustn't be unkind about their faces. It's not their fault.'

'They can help being dirty,' said Tekla. 'That is their fault.'

'Do they ever wash?' Emil asked. Like all children, the thought of dirt fascinated him – the forbidden and disgusting, the opportunity to give a melodramatic squirm. He started wriggling in front of his mother and aunt, wanting them to join in the joke.

'They call it washing,' Tekla replied, squatting on the ground and beckoning Emil to her. 'But what they do is put water into a huge copper tub, then lower themselves into it, completely . . . unclothed. The dirt floats off their skin and dissolves into the water. Then they lie there in the water for hours and hours, soaking themselves in their own filth.'

Emil and Tekla pulled faces at each other and made disgusted noises. Emil was jumping up and down.

'And do they really sleep with their animals, Tekla?' He flung himself forward, his arms around Tekla's neck, knocking her backwards.

'Emil!' declared Anna in shock, 'Who has been talking to you of such things?'

Tekla and Emil were picking themselves up from the ground, grinning. 'Pavla,' said Emil happily. 'She said that the *gadje* have cats and dogs and rabbits in their beds at night and that they love their cats and dogs and rabbits more than their own children. They make their children go to school so that they can spend more time with the animals.'

'Well, it's true they let animals into their houses,' Tekla said, pulling Emil towards her by the arm and brushing at his coat. 'They let them just walk across the door like guests and wander around and sit in chairs, animals that do nothing to earn their keep. Especially cats.'

'Pavla said she was in a house once and the *gadji* had a cat on her lap and she was stroking it and *eating* at the same time and the cat was licking itself and swallowing its own dirt and . . .'

Anna stepped forward, grabbed Emil's other arm and pulled

him away from Tekla, then dealt him a swift, vicious cuff across the head, hard enough to make him stumble. 'František!' She always used his *gadje* name to reprimand him. 'You will not talk of such things in my presence. You are old enough to know better. It is disgusting. The filthy things the *gadje* do. It is better not to even think of these things.'

'Sorry, *Dalé* . . .' Emil mumbled, rubbing his head where she had struck him.

'And you, Tekla,' Anna turned on her. 'You should know better than to encourage him in such talk. How am I supposed to raise my boy?' She had not meant to place an emphasis on the word *my*. She had made an effort not to do so. But it had been there, nonetheless, as slight as a breeze but just as unmistakable. Tekla turned away, her arms crossed, and leant against the tree, her back to them.

Anna sighed, closing her eyes briefly, then turned away herself, leaving Emil to stand confused between them, rubbing his head and looking from his mother to his aunt.

This bitter winter, Anna thought. When will it end?

*

As Josef approached the two women, he saw at once that there was discord between them. They stood leaning against the tree-trunk, half-turned from each other. Emil was squatting between them, a small spirit between two stone statues, chin in hands and lips moving as he sung soundlessly to himself.

The boy jumped to his feet and ran gratefully to the wagon. 'Can I ride up with you, Dad? Please? Please?' he begged as he scrambled up beside Josef.

Josef pulled him on to his lap, ruffled his hair and said, 'No, Emil, it is too cold. In the back, it is late. It will be dark soon. The others will be waiting for us. Go.' He pushed the boy behind him.

Anna and Tekla were wandering slowly to the back of the wagon. Neither of them greeted him. He rolled his eyes and sighed, waited until he heard the thud of their feet inside, then flicked the reins.

The journey back to Třebič was tortuously slow, the single horse clumping painfully between the shafts, as if her hooves were made of lead. Josef lifted the reins half-heartedly every now and then, his head drooping, thinking grimly about how he was cold and tired and hungry and fed up with being cold and tired and hungry as well. Never had a journey seemed so long.

They were about an hour from the Black Huts when the mare plodded to a halt. Josef raised his head, wondering if he had dozed off. He flicked the reins, but the horse did not move. He sat up and looked around. The road was long and empty, with open fields either side. They were later than they had meant to be – the gloom was gathering. It is hardly light these days, Josef thought, as if the darkness waits behind each turn in the road, each tree, waiting for its chance to gather and swallow us. They were level with a small cluster of trees on the left of the track, a dark blur in the gathering dusk. Horses could see ghosts. A horse would not advance if there was a spirit in the road before it.

Josef glanced over at the group of trees, set back slightly from the road. He saw that there were dark shapes on the barren ground between the trees; tents, three small ones, huddled close together. They could hardly be called tents, more loose constructs of branches and twigs with blankets and rugs thrown over them in layers. They sagged, the middle one hanging dangerously to the left.

The horse gave a whinny, shook her head and trotted forward. Josef pulled on the reins and she halted.

On either side of the track, the wide expanses of field were brown and lumpen with a light covering of snow. The area around the trees had some scrubby, dead undergrowth and a small ditch through which, Josef guessed, must run a tiny, frozen stream. Why else camp in this forgotten space, with the town less than an hour away? Unless, of course, you could go no further.

A wind moaned across the deserted flatlands, rising and falling with unnatural monotony. The black branches of the trees bent slowly, unevenly. The barren fields were darkening. The tents were probably derelict, Josef told himself. There was no reason to stop. He held the reins loosely, fingering them.

It was the crows. There were half a dozen of them, huge crows waiting in the trees, in a row on an upper branch, motionless but for the one on the end which flapped its wings and worked its feet sideways along the branch impatiently. On the ground nearby, a couple of magpies were pecking fruitlessly at the frozen earth, waiting at a respectful distance.

Tekla stuck her head out of the wagon. Josef handed the reins back to her and said, 'Wait here.' Then he threw the blanket from his shoulders and jumped down.

His feet were numb. When he reached the ground he stumbled. He fell on the palm of one hand and cursed, shaking the hand as he hobbled towards the tents. In front of them, he paused and called out a greeting. The magpies rose from the ground in alarm, wheeled once in the air, then settled again. The crows did not move.

He heard his name and turned to see that Anna had followed him, her hands wrapped in her shawl, lips pursed against the chill wind. 'What is it?' she asked as she drew level with him, panting.

He indicated the tents.

They hesitated for a moment, a pause to gather their strength, then walked carefully over the frozen mud. As they approached, the wind changed and there was a sudden smell, strong and sweet. They halted. Josef called out again.

The entrance to the left-hand tent flapped open and a crow emerged backwards, with something in its beak.

'God preserve us . . .' said Josef, crossing himself, and Anna drew breath.

From the middle tent, there came a low groan. They exchanged a look and approached.

The tent was no higher than Josef's waist. He bent to the entrance, and lifted a flap of dark grey blanket, dampened recently and now frozen stiff. At first, he could see nothing, then, a glistening gaze.

He lifted up the flap and flung it back over the side of the tent.

An old man lay inside, a grey bundle in the gloom. He was tiny but nearly filled the tent, which stank of urine. He was wrapped in tattered blankets. All that was visible was his pale face and shiny head, completely bald. As Josef's eyes adjusted he saw that a white moustache drooped over the old man's slack mouth and there was a little rough white stubble on his chin.

For a while, he seemed to be staring through them. Josef wondered if he was blind. Then he saw the old man's eyes focus on the buttons on his coat. Josef's silver had been sold long ago, but he had made some pewter buttons as replacements and polished them to a dull sheen.

'Wallach . . .' the old man said huskily. His Romani was heavily accented, difficult to understand. 'Go back where you belong. It's bad enough without you nomads. They don't care about us. It's you that have caused all the trouble. Thieves. You've spoiled everything . . .' His voice became an incomprehensible mutter.

'What is your name?' Josef asked, edging forward as much as the restricted space in the tent would allow. The old man's breathing was effortful, his chest rising and falling in huge, swift curves. He was very close to death.

The old man shook his head. 'I was the fastest man in the village. I pulled more water than the lot of you. That Helka was a cold bitch.' He paused and coughed, shuddering his chest cavity so furiously he looked as if he might fall to pieces if the blankets weren't holding him together. 'I fought . . .' he said. 'I still have my Iron Cross . . .'

Josef reached inside his coat and brought out his water bottle. He leaned forward awkwardly, and with his arm full stretch, managed to get a hand underneath the old man's head. The old man wet his lips on the water but did not swallow. Josef lowered the head and put the water bottle back inside his coat. He stared at the old man. A man who could not swallow was close to the end. The old man stared back.

'Where are your people?' Josef began to say, but the old man interrupted.

'Take me outside,' he spat, his voice husky, barely audible. 'I want to die in the open like a proper Rom.'

Josef nodded. He backed out of the tent on his hands and knees.

Anna was standing a few feet away. She had her shawl pressed against her mouth.

'It's an old man,' Josef said. 'He's dying.'

It was easier to dismantle the tent than to drag the old man out, so together they lifted the stiff, frozen layers of muddy blanket and pushed away the branches, until he lay exposed to the open sky beneath the overhead lattice of trees.

'You'll freeze,' Josef said, kneeling beside the man and trying to tighten the blanket around him.

'Can't feel the cold any more,' the old man whispered. His face was completely white, the eyes sunken and unnaturally dark. His mouth hung slack when he was not speaking, a downturned gash dividing the lower half of his face from the upper.

'I thought I was going to die in the tent,' he said hoarsely. 'I couldn't get out. The stars.'

'You will die in the open,' Josef promised him.

'Put stones over my face, so they won't get my eyes.' His empty gaze lifted to the trees, where the crows waited.

'We will bury you,' Josef said firmly.

The old man exhaled, a hoarse, huffing sound. 'Not in this ground. Put stones on my eyes and my mouth, and don't . . . and don't . . . 'He was unable to finish the sentence, although his mouth moved as if he was still trying to speak, gaping open and shut, as if he was a fish.

Josef knelt by the man and began praying. He had scarcely begun the second prayer when the old man died.

The light was almost gone.

Anna had not moved, standing a few feet away with her shawl still wrapped tightly around the lower half of her face. She stayed there while Josef looked around for some heavy stones and heaped them, one by one, over the man's face.

'Yakali and I can come back with the pickaxes and try to bury him tomorrow,' he said as he stood, clapping his hands together to brush the dirt off his gloves, 'what's left of him.'

Anna had not spoken a word while they waited.

He stared at her. 'The other tents?' he asked eventually.

Anna nodded, and he saw that her eyes were full, her gaze dark. 'That one is empty,' she said, breathing in deeply, her breath a shudder.

Josef looked at the other.

'Two children. Girls. They are still warm,' she said.

He bent to pick up more stones but she stepped forward and placed a hand on his forearm. 'It is too late.'

They walked back to the wagon, where Tekla was peering anxiously for them in the near-dusk. Behind them, the crows descended from the trees.

*

That night, as Josef and Anna lay on their bed, Emil dozing between them, Anna thought of the bodies of the old man and the little girls, lying out there in the dark. She thought of the crows. Crows knew how to fly around until they found dogs to lead back to an injured animal. The dogs would then make the kill and begin the dismemberment with their teeth. The crows would take over when the dogs were sated.

How close we all are, she thought, how nearly we walk the edge of that precipice. Our lives have been precarious ever since the winter set in, when they closed the barrel factory. It could happen in a moment. Josef could fall from a horse and be injured. A new disease could come. The townspeople could turn us from the Black Huts. Another law. All it takes is a moment, and suddenly we are tumbling, the end a cluster of trees by the side of the road and a tent so derelict that nobody even bothers to stop and take a look at what is inside. The crows are waiting.

How close they were. Another month without work and everything of value would be sold – the horses, maybe even the wagons themselves. What would happen to them then? They would be trapped in the Black Huts, with no way of moving or earning a living. In the spring, they would have to try and get back to Bohemia on foot. The crows.

Josef was motionless beside her but she could tell by his silence he was still awake. She knew he was thinking of the old man, of what was happening in the dark as they lay together with their child between them and the other members of their family breathing warmly in concert at the far end of the wagon.

She felt him reach out a hand to touch her shoulder. Then he asked softly, 'Was it a good day, today?'

Anna knew what he was asking. *Has my son eaten?*

They never told Josef about the food Emil was given by the village women. Emil was taught not to mention it. It would not be fair on Josef, to let him know that his son came home Unclean each day because his father could not provide.

All the same, he knew. How could he not know? Emil was still weak after his illness but he had yet to acquire the listlessness of the truly starving child. He was always hungry of course, but each day they found a little something for him. Josef knew.

'Yes,' Anna whispered. 'A good day.'

Josef drew breath as if he was about to ask a question. Anna knew what it would be. He had asked it of her many times. *Promise me I will die in the open, so that my soul can leave my body. Promise me you will put coins on my eyes and mouth so that my ghost cannot return to my dead body. Promise me this.* It was his one great fear, that his soul would be trapped in his corpse after death and he would spend Eternity screaming for release. Her reply was always the same. *You will die in the open if I have to tear away the roof of our wagon with my bare hands.*

Josef released his breath and Anna knew he did not want to refer to what they had seen. It was bad luck.

He withdrew his hand from her shoulder, settled himself to sleep.

It *had* been a good day, Anna thought, despite that terrible discovery. Emil had eaten strong soup. Whatever else happened, she could repeat that like a chant. *My son has eaten today. Yenko has eaten.* No other failure, no amount of burning wind could take that victory from her. The main object of the day had been achieved – and if tomorrow it took all day to achieve it, then so be it.

She would see her son through this winter, and the child inside her would grow somehow, even if it had to feed on the marrow in her bones. It was simply a matter of being fierce enough, and her store of ferocity was a bottomless well, deeply dark and infinite.

My child, my children, will not end up in a tent by the side of the road, Anna swore to herself in the moment before sleep. Fate will not decide what happens to them. It is I, their mother, Anna Maximoff, who will decide that, Anna the Blasphemer. God forgive me. Between them, Emil turned in his sleep, lifted a hand briefly to grasp at nothing, then let it drop. He pressed his face into the pillow he shared with his mother and gave a short, contented sigh.

CHAPTER 6

The men came at the end of the month. Josef was with the horses, bending and feeling down a foreleg thigh on the black mare, trying to find a swelling that might betray a sprain. He saw the two *gadjos* pass the open doors of the Hut but had no reason to believe they were looking for him. Miroslav came to fetch him a few moments later. Josef emerged from the stable slowly, stopping just outside the door and regarding the men where they stood looking round, a few metres away. It never did to hurry when summoned by a *gadjo*.

The elder of the two was short and portly. He was wearing a pigskin coat which was too large for him and had enormous fur lapels, turned upwards like a salamander's collar. He wore whiskers and a peppery beard tucked into the coat for warmth, which made it seem as though his facial hair grew upwards from his chest, fulminating over his chin and cheeks before burrowing under his fur-lined cap.

The younger man was thin and wore spectacles and glanced around nervously, as though thinking to himself, *coming here wasn't my idea*.

Miroslav spoke to the men as he passed on the way back to his wagon. They turned and regarded Josef, who returned their stares, standing his ground. The two men glanced at each other. Eventually, they were forced to approach.

The bearded one spoke first. They were looking for a smith. Someone in the town had told them there were Coppersmith Gypsies at the Black Huts. They had tried the local Guilds but no one there could help them. They wanted something very specific, particular skills which were – how could they put this? – not necessarily current nowadays. They were employed by a local landowner, nobility, to renovate his nearby estate and restore it to its natural glory. The Count was most specific that everything had to been done in a way which was historically accurate.

Josef listened, wiping his hands on a cloth in an effort not to appear interested.

It was not a large job, two or three weeks' work perhaps, a little casting but mostly repair work. He would be paid by weight. They could provide some of the materials but not the tools. The hours were strict. He would be fed at lunchtimes.

Josef remained impassive while they talked, to draw them out. Eventually, there was a long pause.

'Do you . . .' said the bearded one, 'do you, perhaps, have any examples of your work which you could show us now?'

Josef turned without speaking and strode over to his wagon, lifting his leg high to mount the steps in one stride and push back the door upon a surprised Anna who was sitting cross-legged on the floor and knitting, singing softly to herself, with Emil asleep in her lap.

Leaving the door swinging open – something he never usually did – he crossed the wagon in two steps, ignoring Anna's frown, and opened the cupboard. He withdrew their copper spice box, made by himself at the age of seventeen; six square compartments and one long one at the side, for cinnamon sticks. It was one of the few pieces of his handiwork not yet sold.

He carried it from the wagon, kicking the door shut behind him.

The men were standing and gazing up at the sky, as if they did not care to look around the Black Huts or return the stares of the children who had come outside in the freezing cold to gaze at them.

Josef strode over, stumbling on the frozen, rutted mud.

'Gentlemen . . .' he said, holding out the box. He lifted the lid. 'The compartments are lined with tin. I hand-lined them myself, using molten tin spread with an oakum wick.'

The man with the beard growing out of his coat took the box from Josef and felt the weight of it. 'Most interesting,' he said, handing it to his fellow. 'Did you pickle it first?'

'Of course,' Josef replied.

'Vinegar and salt?'

'I used salt and cream of tartar. It removes the annealing more thoroughly, in my opinion.'

'What sort of alloy would you use if we wanted, say, a decorative horse brass, to hang in a library?'

What a stupid idea, thought Josef, while replying quickly, 'Bath copper. Six per cent zinc.'

It was the younger man's turn. 'And say we had a number of vessels that needed cleaning, no wild patinas, they've just been in storage.'

'Which recipe do you prefer, the German or the French?'

The men stiffened and the one with the beard barked. 'French, naturally.'

Josef thought the German recipe much the simpler but was not about to lose the job by saying so.

'I would require large vats in order to boil the vessels in water with lemon rind. I would then hand polish with fine sand. The grading of the sand is essential if we are to avoid scratching.'

He was pleased with himself for that 'we', the implied inclusion of all three of them in a joint endeavour. He felt it redeemed his previous error. (The Czech *gadje* went purple if you even *said* the word *German* these days.)

The men looked at each other. The bearded one nodded.

'You have work,' the other said, with a polite nod.

Josef bowed deeply and offered them tea, but the men were keen to leave. They gave Josef instructions for finding the house and asked him to report at dawn the next morning.

As they walked away, Josef heard one of them saying, 'He's absolutely perfect.'

*

They rose when it was still dark. Josef and Václav took a horse each and Emil rode up in front of his father, sidesaddle, wrapped in a blanket and still half asleep. Třebíč slept while they skirted the town. Smoke rose from one or two chimneys. Now and then, geese awoke and clucked as they passed. The horses' breath condensed in ghostly clouds.

Josef had miscalculated how long it would take for them to plod there with the animals so weak and Emil across his lap, so it was already light by the time they clopped down the long track that led to the mansion, a grey edifice in the mist. They skirted the building along a path, turning the vast corners of a side wing, alongside a row of firs and past a disused well.

At the back of the house was a deserted gravel courtyard. The high windows of the house hung in serried rows. A few brown leaves danced against the stone walls. Deep within, a dog barked.

Václav dismounted first and Josef handed the stirring Emil down to him. His blanket slipped to the ground as he woke and stood upright. Václav picked it up and tried to wrap it back around the boy but he wriggled away from it, saying simply, 'No.'

Václav shrugged and placed the blanket over his own head and shoulders, shuddering and performing a small, skipping dance to show how cold it was. Josef led the horses to an iron ring set in a wall and tethered them, then returned to Emil and Václav. Emil looked up expectantly. Josef lifted his hands and let them fall. He had been given no instructions other than to go round to the courtyard at the back.

They stood for a moment, then they all looked at the floor. Eventually, Václav wandered over to his horse and threw the blanket over her rear, then went and leant against the animal and talked to her.

'Father,' Emil said, scuffing one shoe in the gravel, 'Why are there so many windows?'

Josef sniffed. 'To look out of, *muro šav*, to see what's outside.'

Emil narrowed his eyes and looked up. 'But *we* are outside . . .' he said thoughtfully, gazing from one window to the next, as if he expected to see a different *gadjo* at each, staring down at them.

At last, a nearby door opened, with ancient slowness. The younger of the two men who had hired Josef stepped out. He gestured at them.

Inside was some sort of stone ante-room, narrowing to a low-ceilinged passage at the back. Empty iron hooks were inserted into the walls at various heights. A leather apron was tossed carelessly over a wicker basket in one corner. The light was dim.

The young man looked at Václav and Emil, then at Josef.

'We are paying you by weight, not the man-hour,' he said.

'I am well aware of that.' Josef's tone was firm. This man was a junior member of the household staff and unsure of himself. Josef could smell it.

Physically, he and Václav made a good team; Josef of average height and build but with, he liked to think, a thoughtful, intelligent air; Václav, short and muscular, bullish-looking and expressionless. Josef was actually the stronger of the two, but Václav's physique always impressed the customers. They had worked together, on and off, for years. In times such as these, Josef could not have taken a job without including Václav. It would have been dishonourable.

'Very well.' The young man turned sharply and led them down the stone passage. Josef and Václav followed. Emil trotted behind obediently, having been promised that he would feel the weight of Josef's hand if he got up to any of his mischief. The boy would have to concentrate today. Today was one of his few chances to learn.

The passage was so narrow that Josef brushed his shoulders against the walls. The floor sloped sharply down and they turned a corner. The light from behind them vanished and left them in almost total darkness. There was a rattle of keys and the clunking mechanics of a lock.

When the young man swung the door, Josef was half-blinded by the flood of yellow electric light that lay beyond. They stepped into a huge, vaulted kitchen, blinking.

The young man turned and said with a supercilious air, 'We have electric lighting in every room in this house, including the employees' quarters. The Count is eager to restore this building to its former glory but at the same time believes one should also take advantage of the best of modern conveniences. The Count is a most comprehensive man.'

'If you will show me the vessels,' said Josef with a small bow, in a tone which he hoped implied he did not care whether the Count was comprehensive, narrow-minded, or a three-legged imbecile.

They spent most of the first day building a kiln in the small, enclosed courtyard outside the kitchen. Once Václav had helped him pile up enough bricks, Josef sent him back to Třebič, to visit the local smith and hire some larger pieces of equipment – he wanted to weigh the vessels himself, if that was how he was being paid. He had bought a bag of smaller tools, and set Emil to mixing mortar while he inspected the vessels. The supercilious young man proved friendly, eventually, and sat with them for much of the morning, taking an interest in Josef's plan of work. The lunch he provided was more than enough to feed all four of them. Emil's eyes nearly popped out of his head when he saw the pastries. Other staff from the mansion came in and out of the kitchen now and then, and paused to observe what was going on.

By the time the light was fading, the kiln was built and covered with brushwood and sackcloth to protect it from the cold overnight. By the next day, it would be hard enough to use. The vessels for cleaning were lined up by the kitchen door – there were some beautiful shallow copper pans with unusual wrought-iron handles. Josef felt happy for the first time in months.

Emil was exhausted. Josef was all for starting the cleaning there and then – they had electric light to do it by – but the

young man came and begged them to stop work because he
could not go home until they had.

'A beer, Václav!' declared Josef as they mounted the horses. 'A
small *pivo* for us working men!'

Emil fell asleep on the way back to town. Josef knew the
hostelries in the centre of Třebič were not friendly, so they went
back around the outskirts until they found a stone building with
a wooden sign outside and a little golden light gleaming from its
shutters.

The tavern was in the middle of a row of cottages and
consisted of one room with a stone floor covered in sawdust and
two long tables with benches either side.

They had to bend their heads to enter the tiny doorway. The
only other customers were two old men playing backgammon in
a corner, empty glasses beside them.

The innkeeper was cleaning glasses with a cloth. He looked
them up and down when they entered, then continued to
clean.

Josef and Václav sat on one of the benches. Emil was still
asleep, lying across their laps. 'We may have a long wait,'
muttered Václav.

Josef shrugged. He was in too good a mood to mind.

After a while, however, it became clear that the man had no
intention of serving them at all. He continued to clean his
glasses, and when he came to the last one on the counter top,
paid special attention to it, holding it up to peer in the poor light
from the lanterns strung above the bar.

Josef could feel Václav's antagonism growing, as if he was a
kettle coming to the boil.

Such behaviour did not bother Josef as a rule. Life was too
short. But if Václav became angry then there would be a scene,

maybe a fight, and the last thing they needed was for one of them to become injured when there was work to be had.

The only sounds were the wind blowing outside, whisking dead twigs against the shutters, and the small *squeak-squeak* as the innkeeper turned the glass round and round against the cleaning cloth.

'It is a cold night,' one of the old men playing dominoes said suddenly, loudly, without looking up from his hand. His companion did not lift his head. 'Serve these men, Lukeš,' the old man said.

The innkeeper put down the glass and gave the two old men a long, expressionless stare. Then he walked around his counter and approached Josef and Václav.

Václav's face was bright red with fury. Josef said quickly, 'Two beers.'

The innkeeper stood in front of them, without moving. Václav muttered under his breath, *'Te tasarel les O Beng . . .'* May the devil choke him.

Josef reached into his pocket and placed some coins on the table. The innkeeper picked up the coins, examined them, then dropped them into his apron pocket. Only then did he turn to fetch their beer.

Josef's spirits would not be dampened. He even thanked the innkeeper when their beer finally arrived. He was thinking about the fire they would build in the kiln the next morning, the smell of scorched brick and tang of molten metal. The glow from liquid metal was brighter than the mortal eye could take, the sheen of it unearthly. God made us Roma metal-workers for good reason, Josef thought. There is something Holy in it.

'Oh *phrálá,'* he sighed to Václav, 'Do you remember when every day was like this, day after day, hard work that we were trained to do, not digging ditches for cold *gadje* who think they are doing us a favour by giving us a few crowns. That woman last week. I nearly broke her skull.' Josef had been cheated the previous week, by a woman who had promised him twenty crowns for the job and then only given ten because she said he had cleared the wrong side of the path.

'I remember . . .' said Václav, and the shortness of his reply suggested he was not quite as nostalgic as Josef about their smithy days. It suddenly occurred to Josef that Václav resented him, and always had.

He fell silent, staring moodily into his beer, annoyed that Václav had punctured his happy mood and trying to work out how much of Václav's shortness was the innkeeper's fault and how much his. Václav had not been the same since his son had died – he had to allow the man his grief. But there seemed something more personal in his bad mood now. Perhaps it was because he always had to work as Josef's subordinate – he didn't have the training to take on a job in his own right. But that was hardly Josef's fault. Josef had his uncles to thank for his training, after all. Blood mattered in these things, and foresight. Weak blood, maybe that was Václav's problem. Perhaps that was why he had produced so many girls. Josef sat silently, thinking bitter thoughts.

Václav's voice was conciliatory when he spoke. 'Come, Josef, don't brood on what is past. It is not our way. Live lightly.' He seemed recovered. 'Come, you know I'm right. We have food for today and work for tomorrow, God save the *gadje*. Where would we be without their cake tins and their ornamental horse brasses and all their little foolish things? They were sent to this earth for a good reason – to put food in our bellies, and even beer sometimes. They may be stupid as a flock of starlings, but they keep us alive.'

That much was true. Josef raised his glass, and he and Václav toasted the *gadje*.

PART 3

1942

CHAPTER 7

Emil stayed crouched beneath the bush, head down. All he could see was the clear water of the river, running over the glossy brown stones. His back ached but the slightest movement would make the twigs above him rattle and the green leaves shudder. His trousers were hitched uncomfortably around his crotch but to loosen them he would have to stand. He was sweating. Somebody was crashing downstream towards him. Until he knew who it was, he wasn't going anywhere. Beyond the row of bushes were the open fields. He would not stand a chance.

The gunfire had come in brief bursts, punctuated by shouts. It sounded as if it was coming from the village but the summer breeze blew erratically; it was impossible to tell.

Crouched painfully, Emil thought briefly and disbelievingly about death, about the fact that he had disobeyed his father to cross the fields and climb the rise to see what was going on down in the village. He thought, I am only fifteen. The others would be waiting for him – his father pacing round the cart, his mother sitting very still, her lips fixed, with Parni leaning against her sucking two fingers and Bobo asleep on her lap. He could just picture them. He thought, I'm all right, *Mum* and *Dad*, don't worry so. Trust me. I am fifteen.

The person who was crashing through the water came nearer, then stopped, very close by. Emil could hear the person taking raw gulps of breath, a pause between each gulp. He recognised panic in the sound, and the panic gave him the daring to turn his head slowly and peer through the leaves of the bush. A twig caressed his cheek. There was the smell of earth, and something sharper, a tang.

The man stood in the middle of the stream, legs planted wide on the brown stones with the clear water rushing over his white bony feet. He was dressed in rough trousers and a vest, a brown cap askew on his head and face reddened from sunburn. He was glancing from side to side, fearfully. He saw Emil peering through the bushes, and froze, like an insect paralysed by its own reflection.

Emil stared back, heart thumping. He knew he should turn and run, but he was mesmerised by their mutually captivated stare.

The man broke first. 'Have you got anything to eat?' he asked. He pinched his fingers together and lifted them to his mouth. 'I need to eat.'

Emil shook his head while pushing his hands into his jacket pocket, meaning, no, only this.

He held out the small piece of flatbread that his mother had given him that morning with a fried mixture of potato and cabbage. He had eaten half of the bread and kept the rest for later.

The man glanced around, then mounted the bank in two swift strides. Rounding the bush, parting the twigs, he reached out and grabbed the bread from Emil's hand. He nodded while he chewed and swallowed.

Emil said. 'It's all right. I know what it is to be hungry.'

'Who are you?' the man mumbled.

They were squatting next to each other beneath the bush, like two old *drabarnis*. Emil said, 'My name is František.' He glanced around. 'Are you being followed?'

The man shrugged. 'I don't think so. They shot the others. Four of us made a run for it. I heard them go down.'

'Do they have dogs?'

He shook his head. 'No. We wouldn't have run if they did. It was my fault. I said, they're going to shoot us anyway after what we've seen. They'll never let us go back and tell everyone.'

Emil looked around uneasily. He wanted to hear the man's story but they couldn't just sit there while Germans scoured the area. His family was only two fields away. He stood and beckoned to the man. 'Come,' he said.

He led the man upstream, through the water, then turned and, gesturing for him to crouch, ran along a low hedge, up to the copse. At least from there they would have a vantage point. He made the man wait in the bushes, then went to the edge of the copse so that he could look down to where smoke still drifted above the village in the afternoon haze. He had a clear view of the fields. There was no one making their way towards them.

He returned to the man and squatted down beside him. 'So,' he said. 'You are a prisoner. You have escaped.' He had never seen a prisoner before. He's filthy, Emil thought, and he stinks. Maybe he's a robber, or a murderer.

The man nodded. He had recovered his breath. 'I think I'm the only one who got away. I heard the shots but I didn't look back. There were several bursts. When I reached the stream I paused but nobody was behind me. It was my fault. It was my idea.'

'Where are you from?' Emil gestured towards the man's prison uniform.

'Terezín. You've heard of it.' He hesitated. 'I am a Jew.'

Emil shook his head. 'We try and stay as far away from the news as we can. But I know the Jews are having a bad time.'

The man gave him a long, steady look; a look at once empty yet full of hostility. 'A bad time,' he said eventually. 'Is that how you would describe it . . . ?'

There was a long silence. Emil was anxious to get back to the others. If he was much longer, his father would set out to find him – maybe he would even go as far as the village and who knew what would happen then. This area was not safe, that much was clear. But what if the man followed him? He rose tentatively. 'Well, God be with you . . .'

The man grasped his arm and looked up at him, bony fingers digging into his arm and eyes huge in the thin face. 'No. You must help me. I have to get away from here.'

Emil sat down. 'We must be fifty kilometres from Terezín.'

'They brought us in trucks, thirty of us. They brought us to dig the graves. I've done a lot of jobs since I became a Jew. Bricklayer, carpenter, tailor. I was a Geography student before they closed the university. My parents had converted before I was born. I didn't even know I was Jewish until they came for us.'

'Dig graves for who?'

The man fell silent, then lifted his chin in the direction of the village. 'The men who killed Heydrich, that's what they were saying. Or their friends. I don't know. None of them looked like trained men to me. They were just villagers, a schoolteacher, a policeman, peasants. They sent the women and children to the camps. Some of the children were being taken to Germany, the blond ones, the ones they thought would make good Germans. I heard them talking . . .'

Emil thought, if they are clearing this area, then we must leave. It won't be safe any more. He glanced around the copse. The few large trees gave them enough shelter but he could see down across the fields. He would see his father if he crossed the field and made for the stream.

'What happened?' he asked.

The man looked at him with wide, searching eyes, as if weighing up the possible benefits of telling Emil what he had seen. 'You're just a boy . . .' he murmured. At the same time, Emil could see him calculating. *This boy holds power over me. He must be humoured.*

This is what desperation does, Emil thought, pitying the man briefly. It makes your thoughts wide open, so that any stranger can see exactly what you want.

'You're a local?' the prisoner said, looking him over.

'No, *Biboldo*, Unbaptised One,' said Emil indignantly, glancing down at the shiny buttons on his waistcoat. 'I'm not a *gadjo*, I'm a Rom, a Gypsy man. Do I look like a white man?'

The man ignored his indignation. 'So you don't have relatives down in that village, whatever it's called?'

Emil shook his head. 'I was born near here. We were living in Moravia when the Order came through. They gave us two months to settle, so we tried to head back here. There's a *gadjo* my father knows we thought would help us. The police made us settle. They burnt our wagon. They come to the hovels where we are staying and count us all the time. I have to go to school.'

'What I meant was, did you know them? They are all dead, that's why I ask. All of them.'

Emil glanced down over the fields, keeping an eye open for his father, then brushed the loose dirt from an angular stone at the foot of the tree and sat down. '*Everybody*? They just came and shot everybody?'

'The women and children were already gone by the time we got there. The Schupo' had sealed off the village the previous day, then the Gestapo moved in. They brought along some farming experts to tell them if any of the machines were worth keeping. It was all piled up by the side, along with the bicycles and perambulators and sewing machines. The rest of the village was burning, the church, the school, every house. They said it took them two trucks full of barrels of petrol. In the truck I arrived in, from Terezín, there was a barrel of lime and a whole pile of shovels and pickaxes. They took us to an allotment . . .' His voice drifted. Then his gaze hardened again. 'I was staring so hard at the green plants that I bumped into the man in front of me. That was when I saw the corpses, row after row, a hundred and fifty, two hundred. Some of them had many bullet wounds. They had all been shot in the head. I saw brains spilled out. The rats had started already. The Commander had come along and he showed us where they wanted the grave dug. It had to be done by nightfall, he said, and if it wasn't we would be joining the traitors in there, he said, and they gave out the pickaxes and spades. There were mattresses and hundreds of bullet cartridges on the ground and empty bottles of beer and vodka. Some of the Gestapo were drunk. There were explosions and shouting in other parts of the village, and the smell of burning and petrol. We could hear the banging and leaping of the flames. I didn't know flames could make so much noise.

'To start off with the soil was light. It was just on the edge of the orchard, well cultivated. Then it got harder and they began to beat us. Some of us were sent to get firewood so that they could build a fire and we could go on digging after dark. After dark, the corpses next to us were just black shapes on the ground . . .'

He sighed deeply, and removed his cap. 'I got this cap from one of the corpses, towards the end of the afternoon. To protect my head. It was the only one I could see that didn't have blood or brains on it.'

He turned the cap over, then replaced it on his head.

Emil looked up at the sky and felt momentarily surprised to see that it was still a pleasant, mid-June blue. He shook his head, as if he had something in his ear he wanted to dislodge.

'They cooked geese for the Gestapo the next day,' the man was saying. 'But nobody gave us anything . . . I saw him, Frank himself, come from Prague to take a look. He's tall . . .'

'Why did they do this?' Emil asked, but the man gave him a scathing glance and ignored his question.

'Finally the grave was deep enough for them, they kept measuring it all the time and shouting and beating us. As we were lowering the bodies in, the Commander said if anyone stole anything from one of the corpses they would be shot, and I was terrified about this cap. I nearly threw it into the grave but I had already been wearing it for a day, and I thought if I removed it then that might draw attention to it. So I left it on my head, and the whole time I was waiting for one of them to notice that I had arrived without a cap and now I had one. The bodies felt heavy. There was a Czech policeman with a big moustache. And some boys who were just children. A priest, old men. Strong men, small men. It didn't make any difference. They had killed them all. Some corpses had no fingers or eyes. Then we scattered lime over them. As we piled the soil on top, the breeze started to blow. We were coughing . . .'

Emil blew air out from his mouth, puffing out his cheeks. His *kumpánia* should go back to Moravia, like his father wanted. Emil saw himself at the *divano* that night, sitting amongst the other men, revealing what he knew.

He rose. 'I must go,' he said to the man.

The man looked up at him beseechingly. 'I have to get back to Prague. I have friends there who will help me. My parents, they've been sent to the East.' From his crouched position he seemed much younger than he claimed to be.

'I'll try to return,' Emil said. 'If I can, I'll bring food. I don't know, though, they might not let me. I can't promise.'

The man nodded.

Emil did not meet his gaze as he turned and walked swiftly to the edge of the copse, scanning the fields below to see if it was safe to cross.

He heard something behind him and turned. The man was still crouching where he had left him, hissing something in a harsh, urgent whisper.

'*What*?' Emil hissed back, pulling a face as he strained to hear.

'I *said* . . .' the man hissed. 'I said, my name is also František . . .' He nodded his head and grinned, nodding and nodding.

Emil turned without reply, and ran down the hill.

When Emil returned to the cart, his parents were doing precisely what he had imagined them to be doing. His father was pacing beside the cart, up and down the dirt track, gesticulating. His mother sat pale and determined-looking, Parni leaning against her and Bobo on her lap, his face buried between her breasts. Bobo always behaved as though he regretted being born and would much rather be back inside his mother.

Emil ran up to the cart, breathing in swift, excited gulps. 'They have killed the villagers,' he called out to his family, as he approached. 'Over the rise, they shot them all, we have to get back . . .'

His father took a step towards him, drew back his hand and smashed him across the face. Emil spun a full circle in the air before he hit the ground.

His father dragged him up by the lapels of his coat and slammed him against the side of his cart. Emil felt his chest cavity thump inwards as the breath left his body. His teeth made a mechanical *vuh-vuh* sound as they clattered together.

His father's face was very close to his. 'If you ever disobey me again Emil, if you ever leave the cart without my permission, I will beat you so hard that you will be crippled for the rest of your life. You will limp worse than your father ever did, I make you that promise.' He pulled him by the shoulder to the back of the cart, lifted him bodily and threw him in.

As the cart pulled off, he huddled into a corner, licking the salty blood from his burst lower lip. His mother sat rigid-backed next to his father. Only Parni turned round to gaze at him. He turned away from her, staring back down the road to where wisps of smoke were just visible upon the horizon.

His father's anger had not abated by the time they reached the hamlet. Tekla was there to greet them and she looked from one to another as they descended from the cart.

She stepped forward and gathered him in her arms, even though he was a head taller than her now. Only then did Emil begin to sob. He tried to stifle the sounds, ashamed of them, but the more he tried to stifle them the louder the sobs became, until the great, hollow noise of them shook his body.

Sensing his wounded pride, Tekla turned him away from the

others and led him away from the cottages, down to the stream. She sat him by the stream and said, 'Stay here, I will fetch a cloth to wipe your mouth.'

While she was gone, Parni came down to the stream to stare at him, two fingers stuck in her mouth, her eyes round and wondering. Emil said wearily, 'Go away, Parni.' His little sister didn't move. He waved a hand at her, uselessly, without anger, but she did not stir until Tekla returned and dismissed her with a toss of her head.

While Tekla wiped his mouth she said, 'Your mother told me. Fear can make a man very angry, you should know that.'

'He didn't even give me a chance,' Emil mumbled resentfully. He had swallowed blood and saliva. He felt sick.

Tekla made a sceptical clucking sound. 'Boys, men, you and your explanations.'

'You listen, Aunt . . .' Emil said, and told her about the Jewish student in the woods and the bodies he and the other prisoners had buried.

Tekla sat very still while he told her. Then shook her head. 'Ever since they killed that Big Hitlerite, it was bound to come to this. I don't know what they're playing at. Are they trying to get everyone in the whole damn country killed? The Hitlerites have gone crazy now. How stupid can you get?'

'I will tell him. Then he will see,' Emil said, unable to keep the resentment out of his voice.

'Stay away from your father,' Tekla said. 'I will tell him.'

'It's my story. I found the Jew.'

Tekla shook her head. 'Emil, no . . .' She fell silent for a moment, chewed at her lip, then sighed. 'We cannot help that man. I'm sorry but it's true. We have enough to do trying to save our own black hides. Think of your little sister and brother. Think of your mother.' She crossed herself. 'God forgive us. But the Germans are sending the Jews away and you can bet whatever they do to the Jews they will do next to us.' She rose. 'I'll tell your father what he needs to know. They can discuss it tonight.'

Emil jumped to his feet. 'I will be at the *divano*. I'll tell them myself.'

Tekla shook her head. 'You will stay indoors with us tonight, *šavo dilo*, until you learn to be more prudent. Don't even let your father set eyes on you . . .'

She turned and mounted the rise.

Emil sat back down and cried, gently, at the shame of having to remain with the women and the children while the men decided what was to be done.

CHAPTER 8

'Anna . . .' Josef said, stroking her long hair, right from its roots on her fine skull down the length of the oiled braids to the fluffy tips, light as rabbits' tails. 'Anna . . .'

They were lying in the shade of the tall bushes that lined the fields. Anna had her back to Josef and her eyes closed. He was spooned against her, his head propped up on one hand, the other hand stroking her braid, his voice a whisper.

'Anna . . .'

She smiled but did not reply, her eyes still closed. She loved this habit of his, after they had lain together, the way he spoke her name; softly, firmly, sighingly, as if after all these years he could still not quite believe that he had a wife, and that her name was Anna.

His hand became still and she opened her eyes, turning her head to look at him. His face was drowned.

'Do not think of it,' she said calmly. 'He's alive. We're all alive.'

'This afternoon . . .'

'Think of me, of us . . .'

Josef rolled over on to his back. Anna turned to him and rested her head on his chest, her face turned up to him. He put both arms behind his head to pillow it, and she played with the buttons on his shirt, inhaling the soft smell of heat from his skin.

'When we heard the shots,' he said. 'And I looked at you, and our eyes were locked, and we were the only two people in the world right at that moment. We were both thinking, *our son has been shot*. I wanted to run, to follow him. Your eyes were locking mine.'

'I know,' she sighed, dropping her head.

'And I thought, this is just the beginning. Emil is dead. I will go to find him and they will kill me too. Then they will come and find you, and the Little Ones. I swear, when he returned, I had to hold myself back from beating him into the ground. I could have killed him with my bare hands. I thought he was the murderer of all of us.'

'He didn't die. None of us died.'

'Not today . . .'

'Not tomorrow!' she raised herself up, her face close to his, glaring at him.

'We might all die tomorrow.'

'Hush!'

'No, Anna, don't hush me, listen. We must talk about it. If it happens it will happen so quickly there will be no time for talk. Even the Little Ones. We must make them understand what they must do if they are separated from us. I've been putting it off, just like you, like all of us. None of us wants to believe it but we'll be sorry if we don't talk now.'

Anna sat up and adjusted her skirts, wincing. Josef had hurt her a little in his fury, but it had never been the same after she had given birth to Bobo. She had torn along the length of the scar tissue still left from Emil. It had taken months to heal. Three children, it was enough, whatever anyone said. Her body felt turned inside out, wrung out. She was a bag of bones. This was the best bit, the afterwards; a pleasant, sticky warmth between her legs and the smell of Josef, the quiet talk. She lay back down beside him.

'What do you want to say . . .' she said coaxingly.

Josef hesitated. 'Remember our wedding night . . . ?' he said eventually.

She smiled, lying next to him. She loved the redundancy of the question. It was his way of saying many things by saying nothing.

She turned to him and propped herself up on one elbow. 'I remember the arguments between our parents. Lord! Five thousand crowns and three copper basins. You were lucky my mother didn't persuade my father to hold out for the kettle.' She enjoyed deflating Josef when he became sentimental.

'He knew well enough,' Josef growled. 'He knew if he didn't palm you off on the Maximoffs no one else would take you, headstrong girl!'

She thumped him. 'Liar!'

'Five thousand was a fortune to your father. He would have done the deal for half the amount.'

'You begged your father to pay. He could easily afford it. You showed him my needlework and told him I would make it back for you in six months.'

Josef pushed her off him, groaning. 'I should never have told you that, girl, you've been big-headed ever since!'

They lay next to each other for a moment, smiling up at the sky. Then Anna sighed. 'Your poor father . . . your mother . . .'

Josef's parents had died within three months of each other, the winter after their son was married. His mother had contracted peritonitis and perished in agony in the small hours of a freezing January morning. Josef's father, who disliked his own wife so much he had hardly spoken to her in years, contracted pneumonia in sympathy and withered the following month, three weeks before the first thaw. It had taken ice-picks and two days' labour to bury him.

She could not bear for them to become serious yet. 'Do you remember, the bee . . . ?'

'You smashed it with your fist. Everybody laughed . . .'

'Our wedding night . . .'

She rolled over on top of him, her face very close to his, looking down on him with her smile growing wider and wider . . .

He pushed at her, grinning. She rolled off him and sat up, tipping her face to the sky. *No skylarks, today*. She glanced down and saw that there was some dry grass on her skirt. She picked it off. Tekla was with Emil – or maybe she would have gone down to the stream by now and started the washing. Eva would have found some excuse not to help. Ludmila would be looking after Bobo who would be clinging and whining because his mother had dared to leave him for an hour. There would be stony looks when they returned to the cottage.

'What are we going to do about Emil?' Josef asked sadly. 'He's so naïve and immature. What if something happens to me? How could he be the man of this family?'

'He was an only child for so long. Only children stay children much longer. He still thinks he will be looked after all the time.'

'Oh, Anna . . .' Josef was still lying on his back, his face upturned to the sky. She looked down at him and saw that he was crying, although his features remained still. The tears carved shining lines from the corners of his eyes, across his temples and into his hairline. He blinked, and put his hands over his face. 'This stupid war. Didn't they orphan enough children last time round? Wasn't it enough misery for them?'

Anna looked down at him. 'Husband . . .'

Josef removed his hands from his face and opened his eyes, wiping them with the back of his hand, his voice suddenly brisk again. 'I must persuade the others tonight. We should have flown East while we had the chance. Every week, things get worse.'

Anna stood and brushed down her skirt. She held out her hand, to raise him.

He grasped her hand and sat upright but did not stand. He looked out across the fields, then up at her, frowning slightly. 'The seam of my waistcoat is going, here, on the left-hand side . . .'

'Oh . . .' Anna said, keeping the impatience out of her voice. She adjusted her apron with her free hand. She hoped Tekla had had the good sense to start baking the potatoes. Eva would be wandering around the cottage waving a duster as if she was cleaning up. She never did anything unless Anna was there to berate her.

'Tekla noticed this morning. She said you only have the grey thread left,' he added as he stood, dropped her hand and ran both of his palms over the creases in his trousers. He buttoned his flies and buckled his belt. 'I am hoping she's wrong.'

Anna gave a small smile. 'I'll look.' Tekla was absolutely right, as usual. They turned to walk back along the hedge.

When they returned to the shack, they found Eva in floods of tears and Ludmila singing at the top of her voice at a screaming

Bobo who appeared to be trying to tear out his own hair. Parni was sitting in the corner on the dirt floor, blithely scraping the rust from a bucket with a wire brush.

'I see the war is still on,' Josef remarked drily.

Eva rounded on them. 'She cannot expect me to help her with the sheets as well! Haven't I enough to do! I do everything!' she shouted. Tekla was nowhere to be seen.

Josef picked his best hat from the peg just inside the door. 'I must organise the *divano*,' he said, with an air of great purpose. Anna ignored him. Looking a little deflated, he turned away.

'Where is Tekla?' Anna asked Ludmila.

Ludmila stopped singing, thus achieving the purpose of Anna's question. 'Washing sheets. She knows I can't take Bobo down to the stream. You know what happened last time.'

'Bobo could have stayed with me!' spat Eva.

The boy was still crying, accompanied by the regular tsk-tsk of his sister's wire brush against the bucket.

'Why is she doing that indoors?' Anna demanded of Ludmila, pointing at Parni.

'Tekla told us all to stay inside,' replied Eva. She dropped on her knees, grabbed a cloth from a nearby chair, wrapped it over her head and pulled an ugly grimace. 'Don't you know the Germans shoot people just for walking down the road?' she said, mimicking Tekla's deep, thick grumble of a voice. 'Do you want to get us massacred . . .'

'Stay inside and help me with the sheets!' declared Ludmila, dropping to her knees and joining Eva in her mimicry. 'Go to the stream and be sensible! Help me and don't help me!'

Bobo had stopped pulling his hair and thrown himself at his mother's legs, clinging to them so desperately that she had to bend and prise him loose in order to be able to hoist him into her arms.

'Wooden God give me strength!' she shouted as she lifted him up, simultaneously spying the basket full of unwashed potatoes behind the door.

*

No one came to eat with them, which was unusual – and discourteous. After his solitary meal, Josef sat outside the shack on a stool while Tekla took the pan to one side so that the women and children could take their share. Normally, he had Emil for company, but Tekla had banished him down to the stream to eat from his tin plate alone. Josef's anger against his son had melted now. He missed him.

He took his pipe and pouch from his pocket. He had only a few shreds of tobacco left, mixed with dried grass and leaves, but the action of filling and lighting the pipe was comforting. A single puff and it went out again, which gave him the luxury of relighting the taper from the embers of the fire, each time managing to fool himself he was about to have a smoke.

Anna came, lugging a zinc tub of damp earth, to clod down the fire before blackout. She put the tub down and squatted next to it, looking up at him. The evening had become cool; she had a shawl wrapped around her shoulders.

'Have you eaten?' he asked. She nodded.

There was a silence. Their shack stood apart from the others, at the end of the lane. There were no other houses in the vicinity. Only their *kumpánia* inhabited the deserted hamlet. There was an old barn for the horses and room for the carts. The nearest *gadje* village was five kilometres away. Josef and Václav had managed to find farm work after they had returned from Kladno, unable to find Ctibor Michálek. The local council had given them permission to use the hamlet. It had been empty even before the invasion. It wasn't a bad place to wait out the war.

Anna said quietly, 'You know that Václav will speak against you tonight, don't you?'

Josef paused in the action of raising the taper to his pipe. He put the taper down, removed the pipe from his mouth and frowned, still staring straight ahead. His voice was expressionless. Anna was speaking out of turn. 'Václav is my oldest friend. We are brothers. He is Emil's *kirvo*.'

Anna did not respond. After a moment, she rose and went back inside the cottage.

The sky was beginning to darken. The fields were grey by the time Josef buttoned his coat and walked down the lane. As he passed the other shacks, he glanced in. Božena Winterová was pulling the blackout curtains across her window, tweaking the old cloth gently across the wire. She glanced out as he passed and gave the cloth a swift, violent tug. Next to the Winters', the Zelinkas' home was yellow-lit and the door open but nobody in sight. It was unusual for no one to be sitting on the step. The evening was mild. He wondered if everyone was staying indoors now they all knew of the killings at the village. Even the children were out of sight.

He climbed the stile. Across the rapidly darkening field, the other men were already gathered, awaiting him. No fire could be lit, but they were seated in a circle around a symbolic pile of twigs. A couple of faces turned towards him at the sound of his approach, and continued to stare as he strode across the scrubby grass towards them.

When had Anna ever been wrong? Pray to God she was wrong now. If Václav spoke against him, it meant the end of the *kumpánia*.

He knew as soon as he took his place that Anna was right. Václav gave him a coldly courteous nod as he arrived. The others would not look at him. Everybody seemed morose.

After the greetings, he rose immediately. There was no point in delaying what had to be said.

'I have been saying for some time now that we should keep moving,' he said, 'and the events of today have proved me right. The Devil Germans have gone completely mad. We must flee to Slovakia immediately. We must try and forge papers or find a *gadjo* who will do it for us. I have said all along that we should leave Bohemia, as soon as we failed to find the *gadjo* Michálek. He was our only reason for coming here in the first place. We should have gone straight back to Třebič there and then. We are sitting ducks in this hamlet. They can come and get us whenever they want. This morning proved that. They know exactly where we are. Those villagers they killed, they thought they could just sit tight as well. It will be our turn next.'

After he had finished, he sat, and in the silence that ensued, he realised that every other man around the fire was waiting for Václav to speak. Was he the last man in the *kumpánia* to realise he would be opposed?

Václav glanced at him as he rose. Then he bowed slightly, turning in a semi-circle to include all of the seated men. He lowered his head and directed his remarks to the pile of twigs. Above him, the bats swooped soundlessly in the gloom.

'You know with what regard I hold our *Rom Baró*,' he began, acknowledging Josef with a brief dip of his head. '*Kakó*, you know it too.' Josef wondered if there was not a slightly sarcastic edge to that *Kakó*. Chief. He was unused to hearing it from Václav's lips. They were normally just brothers.

Václav had turned back to the others. 'He and I have travelled together many long years. I am *kirvo* to his first-born, his son. But I must oppose him now. Slovakia is not the place for us to go. In Slovakia, the Roma live in holes in the ground. I would rather die than go back there. It is a land of darkness and ignorance.

There may not be so many Germans but the Slovaks will be doing their job just as well, you can be sure of that. Josef is sincere but misguided. I believe he is weak in his thoughts. It was seven years before his wife bore him a child – I do not mean to offend you, *Kakó*, but I must speak as I find. Seven years is a long time. He is a good man but not strong. He has hesitated all his life. We all know he is led by influences . . .'

The silence of the men had acquired a stunned quality, broken only by a distant shout from the cottages, a mother calling in a child. Josef stared at Václav. They all knew he hated Slovakia and was determined not to go there but he was speaking against Josef in such personal terms. Such words could only mean that a dam was breaking, that years of withheld bitterness and resentment were coming to the fore.

Josef became aware that he was drawing breath very deeply, his eyes staring wide and unblinkingly at Václav.

'We knew where Law 117 would lead,' Václav continued. 'Czechs, Germans, Germans, Czechs. They're just as bad as each other.' He began to slap the back of one hand into the palm of the other. 'A *gadjo* is a *gadjo* is a *gadjo*! Getting away from Germans will do us no good whatsoever. The truth is, all *gadje* are evil. The Slovaks too . . .'

Josef rose to his feet. To rise while another man was still speaking was a clear breach of etiquette. The other men looked from Josef to Václav and back again. Yakali murmured in alarm.

'They are not the same,' Josef said, unable to do more than quietly assert what he knew in his bones to be true. His voice was low. 'They are not.'

Václav faced him, speaking quietly too. 'To us, they are.' Then he shouted. 'I say they are!'

In the face of his vehemence, Josef wavered. 'What are you suggesting we do?' he said.

Václav shrugged. 'We have no choice. We hide out here. We wait. We work the farms while we can and live off roots if we have to, we've done that often enough before.'

'We have a few hours' work each week. This winter we will freeze to death in those hovels, or starve. That's if the Germans leave us alone that long.'

'Now you are certain. Now, all of a sudden, because a few *gadje* have been shot, that makes your mind up, after we have been debating all these months? How do we know you won't change your mind halfway down the road? How, *Kakó?*'

Josef felt anger rising up within him again and was suddenly overwhelmed with it. *First my son disobeys me when I forbid him to leave the cart, now this. Does no one heed me, value me? Am I of no consequence? I am Rom Baró!* 'It doesn't matter what I have said or thought in the past. I am saying what I think now. That is what matters! Does it matter to you, Václav?'

Václav looked at the men around him, lifted his hands and let them drop, as if to say, *see, I was right.* He shrugged, and sat.

Josef felt breathless. He had been about to step forward to Václav and raise his hands to him, to shake him for his insulting behaviour, but Václav seating himself had made that impossible.

What am I? Josef thought. Am I losing my dignity? I nearly hit him then – nearly began brawling like a common drunk, a *gadjo*. It is vanity. I am arguing because I cannot bear to think that I may be wrong and Václav right. I am intent on avenging a personal slight without stopping to wonder whether, however clumsy his speech, Václav's opinion could be correct. A true *Rom Baró* thinks only of his *kumpánia*, not himself. But another voice in his head said, *let them go. The fewer the better. If it is just our family trying to get into Slovakia we can dress as peasants and go on foot. If we try and take this whole lot with us, we don't stand a chance. Václav has just insulted me. The rest of them sit there like sheep. I owe these people nothing, myself and my family everything. Walk away. Let them go.*

Josef drew himself up to his full height. 'This *divano* is broken!' he declared. 'I will not wait for a vote from Elders who have seemingly lost their tongues. You have conspired before this meeting. If you wish Václav Winter to be your new *Rom Baró* then you are free to elect him. I and my family will be leaving for the East just before dawn. Anyone who wishes to do so of his own free will is welcome to join us.' He turned to Václav. 'If you ever speak of my wife again, I will cut out your tongue.'

Václav leapt to his feet. He slammed his fist into the palm of his other hand. 'How dare you threaten me!' He advanced upon Josef. The other men scrambled up from the grass. *'Me mangar kris!'* Václav bellowed. I demand justice!

Josef stepped towards him. Václav squared up. The others were between them, all talking at once.

Yakali cried out, 'Beat him with words! Beat him with *words*!'

Justin said, 'How can we have a *kris*? Who will adjudicate?' He was right. Where would they find *krisnitoria* in the middle of a war?

'How can we *not* have a *kris*?' Václav shouted in retort. He was right too. If there was no *kris*, then there was no justice, no law, nothing. It meant anarchy. Josef felt dizzy. They were all shouting like children. The *kumpánia* was unravelling before him, like a shawl being pulled by a thread. Everything he had worked for, it was all dissolving. How could he have threatened Václav like that? He must restore order immediately or his reputation would be gone.

He hesitated for a moment, then turned sharply and limped off into the darkness. Behind him, there was a moment of shocked silence before the men's voices broke out again. Someone called after him – Yakali, perhaps – but he continued striding away as fast as his bad leg would carry him. They could say what they liked. He was sick of being a Rom. He would dress like a cowherd and lead oxen when they got to Slovakia – Anna could take in washing for all he cared. They would pretend to be *gadje* for as long as it took to stay alive.

No one came near them for the rest of the night, not even to bid them farewell. The others slept but Josef stayed awake, watching the night sky, chewing dried oak leaves and thinking bitter thoughts. While it was still dark – while it was darkest – a single, bent figure made its way up the lane, dragging a sack of belongings which clattered and chinked as if the pots and pans inside might be protestingly alive. It was Pavliná Franzová, the Ancient One, an extra mouth to feed but a mouth that spoke fluent German. *She's not stupid*, Josef thought, observing her approach, *and she knows the Germans better than any of us*. She and her long-dead husband had joined up with Josef's *kumpánia* after the last war, when they had been hounded out of their homes during the riots between the Czechs and Germans in Sudetenland. Josef was reassured by her decision to join them. It was not just him, then, leading his family into doom.

The women rose an hour before dawn. Anna infuriated Josef by insisting on digging up the tubers and seedlings from the vegetable patch behind the cottage and storing them in wooden trays. He ordered Emil to help her. As his wife and son dug, side by side, he heard Anna hissing to Emil in the dark, 'All your father worries about is whether we will be shot. He doesn't seem to think we will need to eat if we *don't* get shot. He thinks food appears out of thin air.'

As he helped Emil carry the boxes to the cart, Josef hissed to his son. 'All your mother thinks about is the next day's dinner! When we could be shot!'

The edges of the sky were tinged with silver by the time they left. Josef was furious – he had wanted to make as much headway as possible before full light.

Anna was sitting next to him. Tekla, Eva and Ludmila had tied their braids up underneath their headscarves and sat with their heads bowed amongst the things in the back of the cart, Parni and Bobo asleep across their laps, Old Pavliná hunched in a corner. Emil was leading the horse so it should not stumble in the rough lane – when they reached the road, he would take over the reins for the daylight travel. He was the most fair-skinned of them all.

As the cart lurched away from the hamlet, Anna, seated up front next to him, placed a hand on Josef's thigh. He did not respond, twisting the idle reins about his fingers and staring straight ahead.

Above them, the moon was misted by fine cloud, as if it was dissolving into the night sky, its form unable to hold. It was a cool, soft night, so still a whisper would carry across a field.

When they were a safe distance from the hamlet, Anna said carefully, 'It sits heavy with you, Josef.'

Josef nodded. Anna meant, *leaving the kumpánia*. He could not tell her that what bothered him was wider, greater. I have realised, he was thinking, what kind of man I am. I am a coward.

When Václav had demanded *kris*, justice, he had told himself that he would not argue more with him because it was obscene that one Rom should fight another when the *gadje* were trying so hard to kill them all. He had told himself that the only course of action for a wise man was to walk away, and walk away he had.

But now, in the still grey night, the wheels of the old cart creaking with each slow turn, he knew in his bones that the process of thought he had believed himself to be undertaking was a lie, a construct he had hastily devised as he walked away from Václav and the other men, the ridicule burning behind him. He was a coward. He had not argued with Václav because he had known he would lose. In the past, he had always chosen the course of modesty and in the good times, the peaceful times, this had made him seem wise, a man of restraint. But now that forces of destruction stalked them and O Beng was to be found behind each bush, his wisdom and restraint were worth no more than a girl's sigh. Václav's little daughters had more courage than he. Never in his life had he been more afraid than now. He was a coward.

What kind of man am I? His hands gripped at the reins. Tears smarted his eyes. *Am I a true Rom? A Rom's first duty is to his family. I must save my family.* Yes, a voice whispered, and save your own hide into the bargain. How convenient to have a family. How comfortable to hide behind your wife's petticoats. A true *Rom Baró* saves his whole people. You are no true Rom.

Anna, next to him with her hand still resting on his thigh – she was little comfort, though she meant to be. Were she a man, she would have argued with Václav, and won.

He thought of Parni, his tiny girl, the wideness of her eyes in her small face. He had given her a piece of apple yesterday, cut from his own. It was all there was. She had looked at it, tasted it, then handed it back saying, 'Father, it is bitter.' She had gazed at him, trusting him to find a piece for her that was not. Václav's children would have snatched the apple and wolfed it down, knowing that if they did not eat it there would be nothing else. His Parni, small and calm and huge-eyed, had believed absolutely that if she returned the piece of apple her Father, her *Taté*, the *Rom Baró*, would find a better one for her.

And he had taken the piece of apple, and chopped it and mashed it with his knife until it was brown and foamy. Then he had gone to where Anna kept a small supply of precious milk powder in a wooden keg beside the spice box and added half a spoonful, along with a few grains of cinnamon which he lifted from the empty box with a dampened finger, and he had stirred it and taken it to her.

She had received the bowl from him solemnly, as no more than her due.

My daughter believes in my power to save her, and she does not care what I think of myself. The thoughts swam in Josef's head: above him, the dissolving moon. *I am a coward. I am no true Rom. What is prudence but cowardice? How would I like my son to behave? My son. I beat my son today. I behaved like my own father, whom I grew to hate. Is that what all this is about?* He felt tired, so tired. Anna laid her head on his shoulder. She was tired too but would never say so. She could have sat in the cart and dozed with the others, but she would stay up with him until they reached the road. Her head was heavy on his shoulder, the weight of it uneven, rolling on his bones in concert with the rocking of the wagon. The horse snorted and shook its head, as if it was only now awaking from a long sleep. *What kind of man am I? What kind of man?* If they came through this, if they lived, he would have his answer: a wise *Rom*, a living one.

CHAPTER 9

They took their usual route East, skirting south-west of Prague. Prague: who knew what was happening there? Ctibor Michálek had been swallowed by Prague and his farm occupied by the SS, his beloved fruit orchards hacked to pieces. The restaurants and cafés in Prague were full of Hitlerites now, they said, all in black with those stiff caps with skulls on them. Bored of Paris, the Devils holidayed in Prague. Prague had always been a hell-hole, in Josef's opinion. Now it was truly a seething city of Evil, the heart of all that was rotten amongst the most rotten of the rotten, stinking *gadje*. Not until they crossed the Vltava did he feel well clear of Prague.

They stuck to the small roads, the winding tracks between the villages where they could pretend to be a family taking goods to market. On the fourth day, they pulled up behind a deserted farm for the night, and in the morning a man in a suit came and told them that the old building belonged to his brother. If they cleared it for him and restored the vegetable patches at the back, he would let them help themselves to some of the produce. Josef regarded the man and surmised that there was probably a good reason why he did not want to ask the local people to help clear his 'brother's' farm. That was good. If he had something to hide, then he would be telling nobody about them. They stayed at the farm for three weeks, until the man in the suit came by one lunchtime, in a great hurry, and told them to pack up and be off immediately.

They continued the journey slowly, stopping often. While they were still in Bohemia, their papers were legal, at least. Josef realised he was trying to delay the moment when they would reach the highlands and cross into Moravia. After that, they would have to get their story straight. But the longer they delayed, the harder it would be to explain. Travelling was strictly forbidden. *We are forbidden*, Josef thought. *We are becoming more forbidden with each passing day.*

It was late one afternoon when they approached the Moravian hills. They were on the forest road, a rise that led up to the highlands. As they rounded a bend there was a roar, and passing them was a convoy of twenty trucks full of German soldiers. Josef was driving and kept his head down as the convoy passed, afraid that if he glanced at it he might meet the gaze of one of the Devils. Unable to look, he was aware of the Evil Ones and their vehicles only as a thunder of noise, a vibration from the road that shook the decrepit, overloaded cart and shuddered his bones. He had heard stories about Roma being stopped on the roads and arrested, their carts overturned into ditches. He felt the tremors long after the convoy had passed.

They pulled off the road well before the light began to fade.

It was time to find a clearing in the forest and wait until dark before they crossed into Moravia.

*

The cart had been rocking her for so long that Anna felt she had achieved an hallucination, a strange nothingness where she would doze for a second, to be jolted awake, doze for a second . . . Looking at the faces of the other women, she could see they were doing the same, heads lolling, eyelids descending, then shooting upright at a shudder from the cart. Only the children managed any real rest.

When they were in the middle of the forest, with no sign of life ahead or behind, Josef pulled up and asked them all to get down and carry as much as they could.

Anna handed Bobo to Eva. For once, the plump, clingy boy did not protest. The Little Ones were both exhausted. Parni was half asleep, so Anna put her on Emil's shoulder. Ludmila and Pavliná would have to carry the bundles. She and Tekla would help Josef manoeuvre the cart. She handed a bundle of clothing to Pavliná, who shook her head and reached for her own sack, the noisy one full of pots and pans. Anna sighed in wonder. Pavliná had always been a terrible hoarder, so obsessed with her possessions she would insist upon her own heavy bundle rather than carry someone else's lighter one.

Josef chose a narrow gap in the trees to lead the horse off the track. They would find a clearing as soon as they were out of sight, then wait until the middle of the night before continuing. While Josef led the horse, Anna and Tekla pushed at the cart on either side, trying to prevent the wheels from getting stuck on fallen branches or in ruts. Anna grazed her hands grasping at the rough wood. Tekla made grunting noises as she pushed, until Josef turned and hushed her. 'Who's to hear . . . ?' Tekla grumbled, but was silent.

They had not gone far before the trees became too dense for the cart to progress. 'We will be all right here,' murmured Josef, then turned to slip back to the road and kick over any traces they had left behind.

Emil tied the horse while Anna unpacked the few things they needed to eat and rest.

She lifted down the wooden box of their remaining supplies. Inside was a small sack with a little flour, some hard biscuits, the two last wizened apples and her clay pot. She removed the lid of the clay pot and unwound the heavy string of flatbread dough. The raw dough was unpleasant but filling – after tonight, even that would be gone. They would have to barter for food in Moravia, which meant contact with the *gadje*. It might take another week, or more, to reach the Slovak border. Slovakia – a hated, backward country in her mind till now. Now it meant relative freedom, safety. Unless, of course, Václav Winter was right, and the Slovaks would prove as bad as the Hitlerites. She pushed the thought to the back of her mind.

Parni had awoken now they had stopped. She came and stood next to Anna and rested her head against her thigh. 'Mummy, I'm thirsty,' she said.

'The water is finished,' Anna said. 'We will find some in the morning. We are going to eat.'

'But I'm *thirsty* . . .' She gave a small, exhausted sob and leant against her mother's thighs.

'I know, Little Daughter,' Anna said softly, wearily, stroking her head. 'I know . . .'

*

Emil was unrolling his mat when his father came and said gently, 'Emil, let the women settle. Sit up with me for a while.'

Josef turned and walked through the trees, stepping lightly on the spongy forest floor, the dense, textured carpet of dead pine needles, twigs and leaves. Emil followed him.

They chose a fallen tree trunk. The moss upon its side felt soft and damp. Emil tried sitting in three different places before he found one without an uncomfortable knot or ridge. Josef was filling his pipe with debris picked from the ground beneath the log. He couldn't light it but it comforted him to suck on it.

'See?' said Josef, pointing with the stem of his pipe.

Emil looked back at their tiny encampment, just visible in the half-light. Through the black crowd of trees, he could see the cart to one side, the horse standing tethered to a pine, still as a statue, and Tekla and his mother gently shaking out their mats. The Little Ones, Pavlína and his two aunts were already asleep on the forest floor. What a small, depleted group they were, a few women, an old one, the babies . . .

'That is what we have to make live . . .' Josef said softly, tapping his pipe on the trunk. 'If I die, the responsibility will pass to you. Never leave them, Emil, I don't need to ask you, do I?'

Emil shook his head, even though his father was not looking at him. 'No,' he said. 'You don't.'

'I know,' Josef added quickly, 'I know I don't. I just needed to say it to you, for myself.' There was a long silence between them.

'It has not been easy, these weeks on the road,' Josef said eventually. 'You have been kind to the Little Ones. They can't help complaining. That is one of the hardest things, not being able to make them understand. You have been very patient with them.'

Praise at last, thought Emil.

'If something happens.' Josef paused and drew a deep breath, then repeated, 'If something happens, happens to me, I mean, and if you have to make a choice, ever, then save your mother,' Josef said. 'The others would die without her anyway.'

'You think it will come to that?' Emil asked, flushed with pride that his father was talking to him like an equal, discussing frankly who they might or might not save.

Josef shrugged. 'I hope not, but if we can't get into Slovakia then there is another possibility, somewhere we could go, but it's dangerous, I'll explain to you, everything, while we're on the road. You never know when something might happen to me, so you must know everything I know.' He fell silent.

The gloom gathered around them. They watched first Anna and then Tekla lie down. Soon the small dark mounds of their bodies became invisible, and all they could see of the camp was the solid black shape of the cart.

'It still feels strange to be without the others . . .' Josef murmured. 'I keep thinking we are on the way to meet them. We are so few now, alone . . .'

I am all he has, thought Emil, his happiness a little spoiled by the thought that his new-found status in his father's eyes had as much to do with necessity as respect.

'That day before we left, near the village,' his father said. 'I was angry, but I shouldn't have hit you like that. I was frightened.'

It was almost completely dark. Darkness fell quickly in the forest, as if the trees were grateful to be claimed. Above them, the first stars were appearing in a fathomless sky.

'Are you still frightened?' Emil asked. He would not have dared ask such a question by daylight, when he could see his father's face.

'Hardly, any more,' his father sighed. 'Not now we're on the move. At least we're doing something. It's sitting waiting for them to come and get us that's worst. I'm so used to being worried I think I've forgotten what it's really like. I was more anxious in the beginning. Now I'm just tired. It isn't the thought of dying . . .' He paused, exhaling heavily. 'It's the madness of it. You start to think, maybe it's me that's crazy. That is frightening. Do you know when I first realised the world was truly going mad? When we had to get a gas mask for the horse. That day we spent, going from shop to shop in Třebíč, trying to find one with a strap big enough. A hundred and fifty crowns. They were still glued to their radios and weeping over Austria. We hadn't a clue what was coming. It seemed so ridiculous at the time but what would seem ridiculous to us now?'

Emil leaned towards his father and rested his head on his shoulder. 'I can't remember anything before the war,' he said.

'Really . . . ?' Josef murmured, comfortingly.

Emil sat up and rubbed his eyes. He sighed. 'I can remember when they made me go to school, the teacher sitting us at the back of the class. I remember the first day, when we were making pictures with glue and sunflower seeds and dried peas and I ate the sunflower seeds and put the peas in my pocket to give to Mother.'

Josef exhaled shortly, an amused sound. 'It was a good job I met you on the lane. If you had told your mother you'd been beaten on the first day she would have gone there the next morning with her sleeves rolled up.'

Emil smiled to himself in the dark. He had quite liked school. He had liked the Easter parades, the girls in their white dresses. He had even made friends with some *gadje* boys in his class. And he knew how to read and write, and speak German. He knew things his father didn't know, about the world. He knew how big it was, and how different types of *gadje* thought they were different from each other and would be insulted if they realised that to the Roma they were all just *gadje*. 'Afterwards, after the invasion, the teacher took me out of the class one day and put me in a room with all the books. Cutting England and France out of the maps – I remember this pile of Englands on the floor. It looks like an old lady feeding a bird.' It had been frightening when the Germans came but thrilling too. Those boys who had bullied him, from the class above, and the others who just never spoke to him, all those white boys who thought themselves so superior, they had watched the Germans march right in and had to realise they weren't top dogs any more. It was something, that.

'See, you can remember . . .' said Josef.

Emil shrugged in the dark. He remembered the excitement of the invasion, the people on the streets. They had all crowded in front of the announcement, the poster pinned up in the window of Frieder's Tapestry, Millinery and Parlour Goods. A man at the front had been reading aloud. The assembled *gadje* had all gasped in dismay at each phrase. Josef had pushed at Emil's shoulder to indicate he should wriggle to the front, hissing, 'See if we can still use our crowns . . .'

A man beside them had overheard. 'They've pegged it to the mark. Won't be worth nothing now . . .'

They had hurried away, to try and buy as much as possible before the shopkeepers realised, but the shops had all closed. 'Rabbits,' his father had muttered as they went from shop to shop, 'digging their holes already, much good may it do them . . .'

I do remember, Emil thought, small flashes, scenes like that. But I can't remember how I felt. I can't remember what it was like not to wake up quickly knowing I must have my wits about me, because today might be the day, and there is no time to waste. I can't remember what it was like not to feel like that, keen and quick, and so exhausted at nights I'm asleep as soon as I'm lying down, not like Father. He stays awake all night and is old and sluggish in the morning. He worries so. His moustache is going grey.

'Your moustache is going grey,' Emil said.

'Nothing to do with the war,' sighed Josef. 'It's been going grey since the day I married your mother.' He sat up straight and eased his shoulders back, wincing. 'That raw dough. It sits in my stomach like a little dog. What kind of world is it, when you can't have a fire in the dark?'

Emil awoke with a start. He was lying on the ground and something was poking in his shoulder, a sharp twig. It was pitch black but for a few tiny, pin-prick stars high in the sky. He was sweating and short of breath.

'Emil . . .' his father was whispering, his face just above him. 'It is time to move . . .'

Emil sat up in the darkness, recovering his breath. A few feet away, his father was waking the others. He shook his head, disorientated, wondering why the twinkling stars were on the ground to his left rather than above him. After a moment or two, he realised that they were not distant stars but fireflies, very close by. The night was stiflingly hot. His shirt was sticking to his back.

*

By dawn, they were in Moravia. They pulled off the forest road again, and slept. Mid-morning, they woke, and Josef decided that they should risk daylight travel. They had avoided the dawn and curfew patrols. If they hid by day and travelled by night it would be obvious to anyone who stopped them that they were engaged in subterfuge.

A few kilometres out of the forest, as they were descending from the highlands. Josef saw, in the distance, the approach of a single vehicle, shimmering with sinister indistinctness on the long, straight road ahead. They could not take the risk of pulling off

the road – they might have been spotted already. The only option
was to continue and keep their heads down.

As the shimmering vehicle came nearer, it resolved itself
into a German army jeep, travelling at some speed. *Welcome to
Moravia*, thought Josef. They had their story prepared. The jeep
began to slow down, its approach progressively delayed the
nearer it came. Then suddenly, with an engine roar, it was
upon them. It braked sharply, swerving across the road a few
metres ahead. Two soldiers seated in the back stood and raised
their rifles. An officer in the front passenger seat jumped down
and strode purposefully to where they had halted.

The officer was short and fat, with a ruddy, cheery face. He
did not bother to address them but merely extended his hand
palm upwards. Josef had jumped down and stepped forward,
moving to one side so that if the soldiers in the jeep shot at him
they would not hit the cart.

He opened his jacket wide, then slowly pushed his other
hand into the inside pocket and withdrew their identity cards –
his, which included everyone in his family, and Pavliná's.

The officer unfolded the cards, flicked through them,
frowned. '*Zigeuner . . .*' he muttered, glancing up at Josef's
face.

Josef pulled his cap off his head. He clutched it in his hands.
'We don't normally leave our settlement,' he said in Czech. 'But
my mother is sick.' He indicated the cart, then leaned forward
towards the officer and spoke quietly. 'She's dying. Nothing
infectious. Just old age. She begged me to bury her alongside my
father. We used to live in Třebíč. You can see there. It's on the
papers. We only returned to Bohemia a few months ago. We
have all the relevant documentation. Our ration cards were re-
issued. We had work. We're going back there as soon as
possible.'

The officer stepped up to the cart and peered in. Pavlína
Franzová was huddled between Ludmila and Eva. Ludmila was
stroking her brow. 'Pity a dying Gypsy woman, sir . . .' said
Pavliná, in fluent German. 'I just want to rest in the earth next to
my dear dead husband. He died in Třebič but he was born in
Schwarzenberg, do you know it?'

'No,' replied the officer shortly. 'Where are you going?'

'Back to Třebič, our old quarters. It is where I want to die,
sir . . .'

'Yes, so you said.'

Josef realised that the officer had not understood his
explanation in Czech. He cursed his poor German. He hoped
Pavliná would remember the details.

The officer turned from the cart and handed the identity cards
back to Josef. 'You have not heard, about Registration?' he said
to Pavliná.

Pavliná gave Josef an anxious glance. 'We are registered in
Bohemia at present,' she said. 'Our papers are in order. You can
see . . .'

'No, I mean next week. Registration Day.'

'We have been travelling, sir,' said Emil. He had dismounted
the cart to stand next to Josef.

The officer turned to regard him. Josef felt the cold prickle of
sweat on the back of his neck. He had told Emil to remain quiet,
whatever happened. If Emil told him they had been on the road
for seven weeks they would be arrested on the spot.

'You speak German?' said the officer.

'Yes, sir, of course,' said Emil smartly, drawing himself up to
his full height.

The officer seemed pleased not to have to address Pavliná any
more. 'Tell your father and the others that the second of August
has been designated Registration Day for all Gypsies throughout

the Protectorate. You must report to the nearest authority on that day, the complete family. A new census is to be taken. You'll be in Třebič by then. It will be an opportunity for you to get your papers in order. If you wish to re-register in Moravia then I daresay you will be allowed to, under the circumstances. But you must all present yourselves. Anyone not legally registered after that date will be arrested and imprisoned. Do you understand?'

'Yes, sir,' said Emil, all but clicking his heels together.

'Very well,' said the officer, nodding at Emil politely, before turning back to his jeep.

They waited by the side of the road until the jeep had pulled off.

Josef turned to Emil. 'Well done,' he said quietly.

They camped outside Třebič, on the outskirts of a village called Kamenice, making a lean-to with branches and blankets. The weather stayed fine. Josef managed to barter with a local farmer for some old beets. He had to give him the last of the carved serving forks he had fashioned while they were still in Bohemia. There was nothing left to barter now, for the whole of their way across the rest of Moravia – his last object was his gold ring, and that must be saved to help get them across the Slovak border.

Registration Day was announced by a sign on the village shop, and now they were known to the local *gadje*, Josef decided they had no option but to go along and re-register. If they could get their Moravian rations cards reinstated, then they would be legal in the district. Maybe he and Emil would be able to get a few days' work, to give them some resources for the last leg of the journey.

The Registration was taking place on the outskirts of Třebič, the opposite side of town from their old winter quarters. On their

way there, they passed the mansion where Josef had done the
copperwork, all those years ago. The main gate was chained
shut, but Josef caught a glimpse of the front of the house as they
passed. The windows were boarded. There was black painted
graffiti on the old stone walls. He thought of the beautiful copper
vessels he had restored, once more languishing unused in the
Count's electric-yellow kitchen. And where would the Count
himself be now, he wondered, the comprehensive Count that he
had never met? In prison maybe, impoverished certainly, dead
perhaps. Truly, nothing lasted.

Two kilometres past the big house, they took a turning down
a track to a small cluster of sheds surrounded by a high wooden
fence. As they approached, Josef saw that there were over a
hundred local Roma already in the yard. Most had come on foot,
by the look of it. They had few possessions with them. They
stared at Josef and his family as the cart wobbled into the yard.

To the left of the sheds, there was a row of half a dozen large
trucks. This must be some kind of depot, Josef thought. A group
of gendarmes had placed a large table outside one of the sheds
and were trying to form the assembled Roma into a line.

When they had all dismounted from the cart, Josef told them
to take as many of their belongings as they could carry, then
threw the canvas over the remaining items and tied it down
tightly. He led the horse to a tree next to the trucks and tethered
it, still harnessed to the cart. With any luck this wouldn't take too
long. He had only just turned to join the queue, when three
Czech gendarmes descended upon the cart and began tugging at
the rope that tied the canvas. Josef turned. 'They are just our
things,' he said. 'Food and clothing, and some tools of mine. I am
a smith.'

The gendarmes threw back the canvas, ignoring him. One
extracted a wooden tray of Anna's seedlings, removed the lid,

and pulled a face. 'Here, Miroslav,' he said to another of them who was standing on the other side of the cart. The other one looked up, and the first tossed the tray casually over the cart. A few of the seedlings and a scattering of soil spun out in a wide arc as the tray flew over the cart. The second gendarme caught it clumsily. The third gendarme was holding Josef's tool bag in one hand and shaking it up and down, feeling its weight and listening to the sound it made.

Josef stood, unsure about the wisdom of protest. He couldn't prevent them stealing from the cart. He would have to do an inventory when the cart was returned to them, and then go and complain to the registration authorities if necessary. As he turned away, one of the gendarmes was kicking one of the cart's wheels, to see how sound it was. He could hear the wood cracking under the force of the man's boot.

They stood beneath the hot sun for two hours, while each family presented their papers and had their fingerprints checked to confirm identity. Every now and then a case arose when a member of a family was missing or someone was registered in a different district. Then the offending family would be taken into a hut by one of the gendarmes for interrogation. Ocassionally, raised voices could be heard from inside.

By the time it came to their turn, the gendarmes were weary. A group of German soldiers were lounging nearby but they seemed in no hurry to help the Czechs with the administrative task. They were drinking from their flasks, laughing.

Josef began to talk even before the gendarme behind the desk had opened their cards. 'We used to live round here,' he said, 'but we moved to Bohemia. Now we need to come back . . . This old woman is trying to trace her daughters . . .' Sighing, the gendarme rose, and indicated one of the sheds with a sideways toss of the head.

Inside, the matter proved surprisingly easy to settle. Once the gendarme had established that everyone on the two identity cards was present, he told them that they were entitled to residency in Moravia. He did not meet Josef's gaze as he said this, stamping their card, then staring at the floor as he handed it back.

'We are free to go?' asked Josef.

The gendarme removed his cap, smoothed his damp hair across his head and said, 'You will all be going as soon as everyone is registered. Wait in the yard with the others, please.'

As they emerged from the hut, Josef saw that two German soldiers were unharnessing the horse from their cart. 'Emil!' he called out in alarm, running over.

Emil followed in his wake. 'Tell them,' Josef called over his shoulder. 'Tell them we have registered the horse too. It's on our papers. They can't take the horse.' All at once, he had a sick feeling in his stomach, a hollow dread, like black air.

They ran up as the soldiers were leading the plodding mare out of the yard and round the back of the fence.

'Sirs!' called Emil in German. 'Sirs! That is our horse! Everything is in order. We have already been dealt with!'

'We will deal with the horse, *Zigeuner!*' called one of the soldiers. They continued around behind the fence, to where there was a wide, shallow ditch – beyond it, open fields. One of them led the horse down into the ditch. She stumbled and whinnied, then stood there, stepping her hooves, shaking her head restlessly. As the soldier climbed back out of the ditch, he said to the other one, 'Are you sure we're not supposed to keep the harness?'

'Did you look at it?' laughed the other one.

Josef, standing next to him, was staring down at the horse. It was only out of the corner of his eye, and with utter disbelief, that he saw the soldier extract his pistol from his holster. He had time to shout, 'No!'

The mare's head jerked and her foreleg knees buckled. A neat, perfect stream of bright red blood shot from her forehead and spurted forward in a huge arc. By the time she fell, the blood had already made a huge puddle in the scrubby grass at the bottom of the ditch.

The soldier was replacing his pistol in his holster. 'You have to make sure it is right between the eyes with horses,' he was saying to the other one. 'Anywhere else, you split the skull open and get brains scattered everywhere. Always make sure they are in a ditch or something, lower down than you are. That way you avoid getting soaked. That one yesterday was borderline, we probably should have kept that, but this . . .' he shook his head.

From the compound, there was screaming, commotion. The soldiers turned and ran back. Josef and Emil followed.

Inside the yard, the trucks' engines had all been started. The noise was deafening. Above it, Josef could hear Ludmila and Eva crying and Anna shouting. He looked around for them but the yard was suddenly full of gendarmes and soldiers. Women were running, arms outstretched, crying. Just inside the gate, two soldiers were beating a man to the ground.

Out of the crowd, Parni hurled herself at Josef's legs, screaming with fear. Then Anna was upon him shouting, 'Where is Emil?'

Emil was right beside him. She clutched at both of them, crying out, her voice high and hollow. 'We thought it was you! We thought they had shot one of you!'

The gendarme in charge of the registration was striding around the yard shouting, 'Calm down! Calm down everybody!' He spotted the soldiers who had shot the mare and marched up to them, waving his arms in remonstration. 'We are *trying* to do this in an *organised* manner!' he bellowed. The soldiers lifted their hands.

'They shot the horse . . .' Josef said weakly. 'We won't get the cart back. They've shot the horse.' How will we reach Slovakia now? he thought despairingly.

The gendarme in charge was shouting at the soldiers. 'Do it now. Quickly! Get them all in now!'

'In now! Time to go!' Another gendarme was bellowing in Czech, above the sound of the trucks' engines. 'Come on! Stay together everybody! Families stay together! Up you go!'

Tekla and the others appeared by Anna's side. Eva was weeping. Ludmila was saying over and over, 'Oh, dear God, oh Lord save us, oh God . . .' Josef turned and saw that everyone was being loaded into the back of the waiting trucks.

*

Emil stood by his father, feeling nothing more distinct than a need to be physically close to him. It was hard to take in the screaming and weeping of the people around him, for he still had an image fixed in his head, the perfect curve of the arc of blood as it had sprayed from the horse's forehead, the clean beauty of it, the sudden stagger of the animal as she had fallen.

Then the noise of the engines and the weeping people rushed over him, like a waterfall, and he felt himself awaken. His mother thrust a bundle of clothing into his arms, then picked up Bobo. His father was holding Parni. His aunts were standing by clutching bundles. Old Pavliná was twisting her apron between her hands and wailing that she had left her things on the cart.

They were the last to be loaded up. By then, the yard was thick with the exhaust fumes which puffed and popped from the trucks' engines in huge, intermittent black clouds. Even the soldiers were coughing and waving their hands. As they approached the back of the truck, Emil smelt diesel oil, the hot, dark chokingness of the haze which surrounded them. He blinked. It hurt the back of his throat. He would always think of that smell as the smell of the *gadje*. He heard his mother whisper to herself, her voice cracked and broken, '*Devla, arakh amen. Mule sam.*' God preserve us. We are dead.

PART 4

1942

CHAPTER 10

There is a town in South Moravia, let us call it Orlavá. It's a small town, no more than a large village really, but its situation is a relatively happy one. *Well* . . . the Jews have gone, German soldiers patrol the streets every night and anyone owning more than six ducks or geese is liable to sudden arrest – but otherwise, Orlavá is surviving the war relatively unmolested. Most of its inhabitants are well used to privation. When the fat ration is decreased they over-feed a goose and slaughter it for lard – and they find a way to hide the odd illegal chicken. They share each other's pig-kills. They give their relatives firewood. It is the kind of town where if you mention to a neighbour that your eiderdown is getting thin, they will go and unstitch their own to bring you a fistful of feathers!

At the edge of Orlavá is a hamlet. It is close enough to be part of the town – certainly the residents of the hamlet would say that

they live in Orlavá, although the residents of Orlavá would say
that the residents of the hamlet live in Romanov – the *gypsy*
village.

Romanov consists of eight stone cottages in a curved row like
teeth, not far from the brown canal owned by the Baťa shoe
factory. Behind the cottages is a small wood, through which runs
the River Morava. The hamlet is bracketed by these waterways
which are bracketed in their turn by two railway lines; the local
one that runs through Orlavá and down into Slovakia, and the
fast Northern Railway which runs up through North Moravia to
Poland, the country which hosts small, insignificant towns such
as Trzebnica and Oświęcim.

In the first of the whitewashed cottages, the one furthest from
the canal and set apart slightly from the others, lives a family by
the name of Malík.

Jan Malík is patriarch and ruler of all he surveys. When he
smiles, the sun shines. When he frowns, his wife, daughter and
both dogs hide beneath the kitchen table.

His wife is called Líba. She is small (her husband is tall) and
her face closed and pinched. It is a secretive, dark-little face, with
neat, expressionless features. She wears clogs like all the other
women, but unlike them has learnt to walk across the dirt floor
of her cottage with tiny, sliding steps that are virtually soundless.
She even manages to keep her skirt from rustling. She wears her
headscarf tightly wrapped around her skull, as if the dark cloth
might keep captive any thoughts that are in danger of escaping.
She has learnt, over time, that to let a thought escape is a very
dangerous thing indeed.

The daughter is called Marie. More of her later.

*

The reason Jan Malík got into so many fights was – his brother
Karel once said to him – that he looked like Charlie Chaplin.

This was absurd. Jan Malík was a clear foot taller than the Little Tramp. His skin was four shades darker, his hands twice as big and his moustache three times as bushy. But there *was* something comic about Jan. His arms were too long – his jackets never fitted properly and he always displayed a length of wrist. He had a narrow waist for such a big man and his trousers always hung haphazardly around his hips. His feet were huge, his shoes bulging from beneath the loose flare of his trouser legs.

This comic look was unfortunate, for there was nothing comic, or even happy, in Jan Malík's nature, as many men had realised only too late. Another man could look at Jan and fail entirely to take him seriously. Surely there could be no harm in such an odd and slender figure – surely if Jan got into a fight he would be all arms whirling windmill-like and clumsy, half-meant punches? It was a misapprehension with sometime tragic consequences, the opponent would realise at the first blow, as the solid mettle of Jan Malík's fist made contact with his soft flesh or smashed into and splintered brittle bone.

Jan Malík liked a fight, and he liked to practise fighting. He fought with other men – any man – and he practised on his wife.

There was a way to hit your wife, the men of Romanov agreed, and Jan Malík went way beyond the way. You had to keep a woman in line, of course – and there were some women who were never happy until they had provoked a good slap. But Jan Malík did a great deal more than that, and he was inventive. To lash out in anger was one thing, to use your imagination quite another.

His wife was ill one day – jaundice it later turned out to be – and Jan Malík believed that she was shirking because he had told her to stop being dreary round the house and go and collect nettles from the river bank, to feed the geese. He knew she hated nettle-collecting. He knew that as she turned obediently for the door, she was giving a gentle sigh. The predictability of this reaction enraged him. He took his wife out to the front of the cottage, where the whole of Romanov could watch her humiliation, and beat her with a leather strap until her blouse was shredded and stained with blood. The others came to their doors to watch with narrowed eyes, but no one intervened. Later, when her eyes went yellow and a doctor had to be summoned, he accused her of becoming ill to draw attention to herself, to advertise her rawness to the world.

On another occasion, he caught her sobbing in the back yard as she plucked a chicken. It was winter. Her hands were swollen and chapped from carrying water to and from the pump and the skin had cracked across the knuckles, leaving tiny red crevices of open flesh. The chicken's plumage was sticking to the knuckles where they bled. Extracting the tiny white feathers from the wounds was making her weep and rock with pain.

Jan was furious. She was weeping to shame him, he said, to tell the whole of Romanov that she was miserable at having such a bad husband. He would show her how bad he was. Let him give her something to cry about. He grabbed her hand and rubbed it up and down against the frozen, splintered bark of a nearby tree trunk.

Everyone disapproved of Jan's behaviour but nobody took responsibility for doing anything about it. If she had been a girl from a respectable Roma family then her father or another male relative would have reclaimed her long ago – but Líba belonged to nobody. She was an orphan, sold to Jan by an uncle when a group of itinerant farm-workers passed through Orlavá during the cucumber season. She knew nothing of her family history – the aunt and uncle who raised her had told her nothing. As she had no background and no trade, Jan had got her cheap.

He was an orphan too, so he handled his own negotiations.

His brother Karel tried to act for him but Jan dismissed his help – as he dismissed everything that Karel tried to do. Karel was the good brother, the well-thought-of one. He was the only person who might have brought pressure to bear on Jan to desist but apart from a few quiet words, Karel did nothing.

(On his deathbed, in 1962, Karel Malík, a survivor of Auschwitz and Buchenwald, was to confess to his daughter. All his life, he said, he had told himself that he never stopped his brother Jan from beating his wife because it wasn't his place to interfere. Only when his body was rotting inside-outwards from stomach cancer had he the courage to admit the truth. Jan's bad reputation had suited Karel fine. Having such an ill-thought-of brother was obliquely gratifying. People said, *Karel Malík is so kind and wise and modest, what a shame about that terrible brother.*)

There were sixty-seven people living in the eight cottages of Romanov, counting the half-derelict one that housed only Shabba, the beggarwoman-drunk. Collectively, they all had a vested interest in doing nothing.

Líba Malíková had committed other sins apart from being poor, unskilled and having no lineage to speak of. She had produced but one child, for a start, a girl.

Líba had been afraid of how Jan would react to the birth of a daughter – every man was disappointed not to get a son – but for a while, Marie seemed to soften him. She was born in the summer. As soon as autumn threatened, he was the first man in Romanov down at the woods collecting pine cones. With a baby in the house, he said, they would need a good stock for the winter. Líba watched him labour up the lane bent double underneath the weight of the huge wicker basketful. Sometimes, he even sang while he chopped wood. Things were not so bad when Marie was a baby.

Then came that night. Líba and Jan were lying together on the wooden bed, Marie between them. Jan suddenly lifted himself over the baby and flopped down on top of his wife. She had jumped, her breath pushed out of her, then lain obediently still, feeling the rough pressure of his knees pushing up her skirt and forcing her legs apart. His left hand grasped a fistful of her hair – the other was fumbling with his trousers.

After a few minutes of fumbling, he seemed to give up, lying motionless on top of her, his stubbled cheek resting against hers and his other hand still grasping her hair. She was holding her breath, his unsupported weight heavy upon her. Her lungs began to ache with the effort. Eventually, he lifted himself from her and slid carefully over the baby, to his side of the bed, where he lay turned away from her, facing the wall. Líba kept her breathing shallow, undetectable, until she was sure he was asleep.

The beatings resumed the following day. They seemed worse now. Perhaps they had always been that bad and she had just forgotten in the brief interlude when she had not been beaten. But there seemed to her an extra element of disgust and repulsion in the way he handled her. If he came upon her breastfeeding, he winced and turned away. I am revolting to him, Líba thought. Maybe it was simply that she had always revolted him. On their wedding night, he had gestured for her to lift her own skirt – he would not contaminate himself by handling her lower garments. She was always careful to stand still and fold her skirt out of his way as he passed, wrapping it tightly around her legs until he was safely out of reach. The only useful thing her aunt had ever taught her as a girl was that if one of the male harvest workers insulted her in the field, she was to shake her skirt at him. The threat of such defilement would send the bravest youth running back to the safety of the other men.

As their daughter became older, as she showed the first signs of puberty, Jan's behaviour worsened further. Líba knew it must be difficult for him – it was hard for any man to be outnumbered by women in his own home. She worked at her duties with extra diligence, and she taught Marie to stay out of his way.

Jan never beat his daughter. He never needed to. She was used to standing in the corner and watching as her mother was hammered to the floor, so one of her father's dark looks was always enough to make her drop to her knees and bow her head in submission.

One day, while Jan was sitting at the table, finishing his lunch, he said to Líba, who stood in the corner. 'Where is the girl?'

'I sent her to the pump, Husband,' Líba replied, looking at the ground – it would have been insolent to raise her head when Jan addressed her. 'She must learn to draw water cleanly. Yesterday, the bucket came back muddy. I had to send her back three times.'

It was essential for any Roma girl to know how to draw water cleanly. Her future husband's family would judge her on that. Some of the women in Romanov talked of nothing but how their daughters could fill a bucket to the brim and bring it home without ever once resting it on the ground or allowing it to brush against their skirts.

Líba liked to pretend to Jan that she was hard on Marie. It was the best way to protect her. 'She didn't want to go,' she added, 'but I told her, she has to learn.' It was already the longest conversation Líba and Jan had had for some months.

Jan was silent for a moment, wiping his plate with his bread. He gave a small snort. 'I suppose so. I will want clean water.'

Líba raised her head swiftly. Jan was not looking at her. She lowered her head again, drawing breath slowly, then approached the table to take away his empty plate. Head still down, she turned away.

Jan stood. He gave a small sigh of satisfaction and ran his hand along the length of the table. It was new. He had made it himself. Lately, all the men in Romanov had taken to making chairs and tables and eating from them instead of squatting on the floor like the Old Ones.

He went over to their bed and dropped down upon it. Líba followed him and removed his boots, placing them carefully side by side on the floor. By the time she had finished, he was already snoring.

Líba returned to the fireplace, placed the dirty dishes in the tin bucket next to it, and only then did she allow herself to properly exhale.

She had foreseen her daughter's future.

I will need clean water . . . he had said, casually. *When you are gone*, he might have added.

It had not occurred to Jan that Marie must learn the ways of a Romni in preparation for marriage. He had clearly never considered the possibility that she might one day belong to another man. She was his daughter. His wife Líba would die before him: she was small and weak and her health was poor. When she was gone, his daughter Marie would take her place, to save him the bother of remarrying. Líba would die and Marie's sole inheritance would be her father. There would be nobody else for her. She would never have anybody else.

Automatically, Líba took the carpet beater from the alcove and went out to the yard. Her one pride in their poor cottage was the small piece of rug which Jan had brought home one day and which she lifted from the dirt floor every morning and hung over a piece of rope she had tied between two trees in the yard.

She began to beat it.

It was a close afternoon, warm and still. Most of the hamlet was dozing after lunch. The dull *thwumping* noise of the wicker beater against the rug returned a soft echo in the quiet of the day. Beyond the canal and the railway track, in the fields, the tall grasses swayed gracefully. Líba set up a rhythm of beating until the rug swayed on the line like the grasses. Her heart was pounding in time: her head felt as if it might explode. Her daughter, her girl whose bleeding had only just begun, was going to *become* her, identical to her in every way. There would be nothing in her life that her mother had not also had.

Thwump. Thwump. Líba increased the power behind her beating. I will kill him, she thought, suddenly flooded with strength and purpose. I will kill him for what he is going to do to my daughter. *Thwump. Thwump.* The rug bounced on the line. I will take a boiling pan of water and pour it over his face while he sleeps. I will find the axe and break his skull open and watch as the blood leaps from it. *Thwump.* It seemed as though the fury in her head was running through her limbs and her arms were tense as steel. She felt hugely powerful, as though she was going to hit the rug hard enough to make it fly through the air, high up above the hamlet of Romanov, above the town of Orlavá, over all Moravia and beyond.

'Woman.' The word was spoken softly, simply.

She froze, the carpet-beater limp in her grasp, her breath coming in huge gulps from her exertions.

Jan was standing in the doorway of the cottage. He had a sleepy look on his face. He had pulled his boots on but they were still unlaced.

'You woke me up,' he said. 'Are you trying to rouse the village?'

She bowed her head, as she always did before a beating. Words only increased his fury.

He stepped towards her and took the carpet-beater from her grasp.

'Call this clean?' he said. She looked up.

He nodded towards the rug. 'Every day you beat this thing and every day it comes back into the house looking worse than when you took it out.'

He motioned with his head for her to stand back, then he lifted the beater backwards, way back, and brought it down on the carpet with a huge swing of his long arms. The *thwumping* sound had a depth and resonance Líba could never have achieved, a sound which seemed to fill the air around them and the field below. The brown dirt puffed out in clouds.

Líba watched as the rug flapped and danced under Jan's beating.

When he had finished, Jan turned and rested the carpet-beater up against the cottage wall, then nodded at her to come to him and tie his boots.

She knelt before him. When she had finished, he bent and raised her by pulling on one of her arms. He held the arm tight in his fist and squeezed it, then shook his head. He chuckled.

'What stupid, stringy arms. I've seen more strength in a squirrel.' He laughed, a full, open-mouthed laugh. 'You are really are pitiable aren't you?' He grabbed her chin in one hand and shook it playfully from side to side. 'Pi-ti-ab-*bull*!' He turned away from her, laughing still. His laughter echoed as he strode off down the lane.

CHAPTER 11

The way it works is this. The man in charge of public order in this forgotten backwater is Officer Sergeant Holt. Holt considers himself to be a decent man. He was sorry when they took the Jews because he didn't have anything against them personally. They never troubled anyone as far as he could see. He has no such scruples about *gypsies*. He wouldn't care if he never saw one of them again. But he does like Karel Malík, whom he doesn't really think of as a Gypsy, as such.

He and Karel Malík go back a long way. They were at school together, before Karel left to help his father at the factory. They didn't see each other then for some years, but when Officer Sergeant Holt was promoted to his public order post he found that Karel was by then an Elder in Romanov and their lives began to intersect again. Now, they meet once a fortnight to play cards – Karel always lets him win, which is a standing joke

between them. And Officer Sergeant Holt is confident that
Karel respects him and keeps order in Romanov, as much as he
can.

There is a world weariness about Karel Malík that Holt
recognises and imagines he shares. They are both men just
trying to do the right thing for their separate communities, after
all. He thinks of Karel as a white man trapped in a brown
heathen skin. And he sees himself as a happy, abandoned fellow,
by nature, enclosed by his own sense of duty as an officer of the
law. *Gypsies* – the Devil take the lot of them! But Karel Malík is
all right.

That brother of his, however, is another matter. Jan Malík
nearly got Romanov burnt down just before the war. A local
pedlar went to Romanov selling cleaning materials, a harmless
boy, half-simple, with blond hair and a withered arm. Jan Malík
accused him of looking at his daughter – which the boy might
well have done, as it was easy enough to look at someone when
you were selling them a dishcloth. Jan had kicked the boy
down the lane. Unfortunately, the boy was the nephew of one
of the town merchants, a popular man with a lot of friends.
Holt had been forced to dissuade them from going down to
Romanov one night with their faces covered, holding flaming
torches.

Sergeant Holt made Karel Malík pay for that. Two gold
bracelets found their way on to the wrist of the popular
merchant's sister. Where they came from, he didn't like to think.
As long as it was out of his district, he didn't care.

The war has put an end to vigilante threats from the residents
of Orlavá but Sergeant Holt knows that a far worse threat to
Romanov is looming. He meets with the local *Landrat* each week.
He receives regular circulars from the Ministry of Interior. Back
in May, there was the Government Decree on the Preventative

Fight Against Criminality. Gypsies and *persons wandering in a gypsy fashion* are now officially asocials, which means they can be arrested at any moment. Ever since last year, the Ministry has been asking him to fulfil certain quotas. Each district has to arrest a certain number of miscreants, vagabonds and general layabouts to be sent to the punitive work camps. If he can't find them, then Sergeant Holt is obliged to arrest the nearest thing he can get. So far, he has managed to keep it down to well-known ne'er-do-wells; men from the workhouse, a couple of old down-and-outs who camped on the other side of town and were not related to the Romanov lot. He has not had to touch Romanov, or anyone liked or respected in Orlavá itself. But it is only a matter of time.

Then, in July, it comes. It isn't even marked confidential. The General Commander of the Civil Police in the German Protectorates of Bohemia and Moravia has issued the order for *The Elimination of the Gypsy Menace.*

It is to be called Registration Day, and every Gypsy must register. The date is set for the first week in August. Deportations will take place the same day. Holt sends one of his men to fetch Karel Malík.

When he arrives at his office, Karel seats himself unhurriedly on the other side of Sergeant Holt's desk. Holt stands with his back to Karel, staring out of the window. Beyond the courtyard outside his office, the lane swoops down, revealing an uninterrupted view of fields where treetops sway gently in an old summer breeze. He thinks how innocent those breezes seem, and how simple compromises are, morally simple. If a man points a gun at a child's head and says, *I will shoot this child, or I will shoot those two children over there,* what are you supposed to say? You say, all right, shoot him and spare those two. Shooting one child is half as bad as shooting two. *Men who can't admit that are more than cowardly*, thinks Sergeant Holt, *they are morally corrupt.*

He hears himself saying to Karel Malík. 'I don't know what the transports are for. For one of the camps, I suppose, but I hear some of those places are not so bad. You have to work but you get fed. You're all on file. I can't see what anyone can do. You can hardly take off down the road in a big gang. You won't get ten kilometres.'

Karel is sitting on the other side of Holt's desk, leaning back in his chair with his arms folded, as relaxed as if they were discussing a rabbit hunt. 'There must be something . . .' he insists simply, calmly. Success with Holt depends on him behaving as little as a man like Holt would expect a *gypsy* to behave. As a consequence, Karel is so relaxed he appears almost somnambulant.

Holt is still staring out of the window, watching one of his men sweep the yard. That is all the authorities are asking of us, he thinks, to keep the place clean. Eventually, he turns and looks at Karel, although he still does not sit. 'There is a possible loophole . . .' he says thoughtfully. 'But I can't get all of you through it.'

Karel nods, to indicate that he appreciates what Holt is doing, and that he will agree to the price.

'We can try and say that you've been settled so long that you don't count as Gypsies. You can apply for Christian status, but we'll have to do it straight away, before Registration Day. Several of you have jobs. That makes a difference. Normally, it wouldn't work, but I know the local Commander . . .' There is another pause, another nod, another tacit agreement to the local Commander's price, whatever it may be. 'But . . .'

Holt allows that *but* to hang in the air while he wanders over to his desk and seats himself. 'It is known that we have a

Gypsy settlement here and there will be talk if I do not send you off to be registered. I have to be seen to be obeying the law or they will simply replace me with someone who will. You must give me some of your people. Half. A truckload. Once they have been sent off, we can begin an appeal procedure immediately. Maybe we'll get them out. But the rest must stay invisible in the meantime. You know what I mean. Anyone who is known in the town must go, otherwise people will notice you're all still here and someone will tell. You yourself are in great danger. I don't know whether I will be able to protect you.'

'I cannot give you half,' Karel says reasonably. 'How would I persuade them? It would mean splitting up families. Half is out of the question.'

'Give me twenty, a dozen even. I can fob them off with that, for a while at least. I can't do it for less. You know what I am risking even agreeing to that.'

Karel regards Sergeant Holt with a steady, clear-eyed gaze. Karel is a man who understands a bargain, particularly a bargain with a *gadjo*. It is how he has lived his whole life, and he knows that his whole life and the whole lives of every man, woman and child in Romanov is what is at stake.

'Four,' he says evenly, after a pause. 'I can give you four.'

*

Considering she was a poverty-stricken beggar, and a drunk, and stank to high heaven and was a universal embarrassment to everyone, Shabba had a surprisingly haughty demeanour. Líba would watch the old woman sometimes as she shuffled up and down in front of the cottages, pausing occasionally to importune the fresh air. Líba enjoyed watching Shabba, the only inhabitant of Romanov ineluctably lower in status than herself. The old woman was not as old as she made out, Líba decided.

Shabba was tall and large-faced, with deep grooves that led down from either side of her nose to the edges of her mouth. Her skin was so filthy it was impossible to tell how black she really was, but her hair always looked surprisingly clean and white, falling loosely around her heavy features like the branches of a weeping willow.

Sometimes, Shabba would pause in front of Líba's cottage and turn and stare knowingly at her, her haughty expression defying Líba to pity her. The hooded eyes would look her up and down, as if she was saying, *I know you. I know what goes on in your house*. At other times, her expression would be glazed and drunken, and Líba would go swiftly into the cottage and place a piece of bread or some potatoes on a plate, cover them with a chequered cloth and take them out to her. All the women fed Shabba. She was one of their own, after all, and the fewer times she went into Orlavá the better – she shamed them all.

They had an even greater interest in keeping Shabba off the streets now. The rumours had begun some weeks ago. The Roma were to be rounded up and sent north, like the Jews. Karel had tried to reassure them. He was good friends with Officer Holt, wasn't he? Holt would warn them before any round-up. But in the meantime, they had to keep their noses clean. They had to try to be forgotten. If anyone saw Shabba heading for the town, she must be brought back immediately. The women were to see to it.

Líba believed what Karel said. Karel was Jan's brother, and if Jan was all-powerful and believed his brother then she must too. But sometimes, at night, she would lie awake listening for the sound of trucks – the sound of a motor vehicle approaching Romanov would only mean one thing. She realised that it was impossible to distinguish the exact point at which a sound began. Sounds did not have starting points. They grew from nothing, from silence, which meant that all silence could be the nothing immediately prior to the start of the sound.

The next morning, tired and bleary-eyed, she would curse herself for her fears. Nobody cared about them, a small bunch of Roma stuck out on the edge of an insignificant town like Orlavá. What would be the point of taking them anywhere? Wasn't there a petrol shortage?

Jan was over at Karel's house, so Líba was taking the opportunity to sit on the step of her cottage and wait for her daughter. Marie was at the well, lingering because she knew her father wasn't around, talking to the other girls perhaps. Líba hoped so. She herself never mixed with the other women, she didn't dare, but her daughter was allowed a little more freedom, and it pleased her that she had been able to develop a few friendships in the hamlet. If Marie had friends, it would protect her. *When I am gone* . . . Líba thought sadly. She had nearly died of pneumonia last winter. Her hair had a few white strands, already. I suppose I am in my mid-twenties, she thought to herself. Already.

Marie was thirteen, and as tall as her mother, which was short. Her skin was a few shades lighter, but other than that, they were identical. This much I have done, Líba comforted herself, when she thought of her child. She has got this far at least, my small sleek girl. And I can tell, just by looking at her, that she is cleverer than the rest of Romanov put together.

Down the lane, she heard a small laugh, like water. Marie was walking slowly towards her with another girl, her pretty cousin Ilona, Karel's oldest daughter. They were both carrying two buckets, walking slowly in the late afternoon heat.

Marie stopped when she saw her mother sitting on the step, bowing her head.

Líba nodded at Ilona. 'Off home now,' she said, with all the sternness she could muster.

The two girls exchanged sly looks as Ilona turned away. Líba felt a rush of envy for their conspiracy. *Let me join in*, she thought helplessly, *oh, let me be one of you. I'm not on his side, not really. I never have been*.

Marie put the buckets down on the ground and, seeing her mother's forlorn look, rushed over to her. She knelt in front of her, then glanced over her shoulder.

'Your father is out,' Líba said.

Marie smiled, then put her arms around her mother's waist and her head in her lap. 'I will never leave you,' she said simply.

I fear you may not, Líba thought, but said nothing, stroking her daughter's headscarf until she became worried that Jan might return and find them so affectionate. 'Come,' she scolded. 'It is nearly evening and I was waiting for that water so I can cook, as you well know.' Her daughter disentangled herself with a small sigh.

Jan returned from his brother's house with a puzzled air, an air he did not explain until he was seated at his table, food in front of him, his wife and daughter standing by the dresser awaiting his commands.

'My brother asked to see me,' he said, frowning at the air in front of him. 'But when I arrived he behaved as though he didn't want me there. Then when Dalia asked me to eat with them, he interrupted her and told her not to be insolent. Just as I left, he told me he wanted me to take care of a watch that he was worried about losing and pushed it into my pockets. Then he called me back, then he dismissed me . . .'

Marie and Líba remained silent. Comment from them was not

necessary. Jan shook his head. 'They were having chicken livers,' he added, glancing down at his own plate of thin stew. He tapped the side of the plate with one finger, which meant he wanted more bread.

Líba had just placed a slice of rough black bread on the edge of his plate, when they all heard, simultaneously, an unmistakable sound. It was the sound of an approaching motor vehicle. Líba froze. Even Jan was rendered motionless as they listened. The noise came nearer, grew, then divided into two different sounds – that of a large vehicle and something smaller, lighter, a motorbike perhaps. The sounds reached their cottage. There was the screech of brakes, applied roughly. The engines died.

It was a pleasant summer evening. The door stood open. Sergeant Holt stepped into the room.

Marie and Líba stared at him.

Jan glanced up from his supper. 'May I at least finish this?' he asked, gesturing at his plate.

'No, I'm afraid you may not,' said Holt politely. 'Two minutes to put your things together. Clothes only. Valuables are to be surrendered to me.'

Jan spoke as he rose, his mouth still full. 'Since when has anyone in this household had any valuables, Holt?' He looked at Líba. 'Get our things,' he said quietly.

Líba ran to their cupboard and drew out Jan's spare shirt and trousers. Thank God he was still wearing his boots. Marie had hurried to her alcove and brought over what she could grab. Together, they threw the things down on to the bed and rolled the blanket around them.

'Mama, your shawl,' said Marie as they turned to the door. Líba looked at her daughter. It was August. Her daughter was only thirteen but had realised straight away that that if her mother survived the next few months, she would need her winter shawl.

Outside, there was a truck and Holt's motorcycle. Four German soldiers were ranged in the yard, their guns displayed across their chests.

Jan looked at the soldiers. 'Expecting trouble from the Gypsies, eh?' he said to Holt, indicating the other cottages with his head. 'Sure you brought enough? We don't go quietly as a rule.'

Holt exhaled sharply through his nose. 'Expecting trouble from you, Jan. We're well aware of your reputation.' Jan looked at him. 'We're not taking any of the others,' Holt said, looking at the ground, then the sky. 'You're the only ones, you three, and the tramp.'

Jan stared at him.

Up the lane, from the derelict cottage at the far end of the hamlet, Shabba was being led by a young soldier who was pulling her by the elbow. She was muttering happily to herself in a tuneful sing-song. The young soldier was grimacing extravagantly. He called out in German to his compatriots and the others laughed.

'You won't see any of the others coming out to give you a send-off,' Holt said as he mounted his motorcycle. 'They'll have made themselves scarce, I think you'll find.' With a single bouncing motion, he kicked the motorcycle into life, then turned and pulled it into position in front of the waiting truck.

Jan and Líba and Marie stood waiting for Shabba as she hobbled and rocked towards them. The young soldier was clearly disinclined to pick her up and carry her. Her clothes hung from her body, wrapped around her head and feet in layers, despite the heat. Shabba had no bundle to carry to the truck – she was the bundle.

Líba glanced around. The others might be staying inside their houses but she knew their departure was being observed by every inhabitant of Romanov. She wanted to shout at them, to scream. Were it not for her fear of Jan's displeasure and the reaction of the soldiers, she would have run into the middle of the lane and howled her fury at everyone hiding safely inside their little stone walls. Then, she saw that somebody had emerged after all, silently, like a ghost. It was Karel. He was standing on the verge in front of his cottage, watching impassively, knowing his watching was being watched by the rest of Romanov. Nobody would ever say that Karel Malík had not the courage to face the brother he had betrayed.

At the back of the truck, there was some hiatus. The soldier was trying to lift old Shabba up, pushing at her while trying to keep her at arm's length – she stank of urine as usual. Had Shabba been sane and frightened, the soldier might have been more brutal, but faced with the unmistakable authenticity of her derangement, he was wincing and coaxing, glancing at Jan appealingly – how do I deal with this one? The other soldiers stood by watching, laughing at him.

Líba saw her chance. Still holding Marie tightly by the hand, she marched the few steps towards Karel, then stopped and faced him squarely. She spoke quickly and quietly. Even as she spoke, she heard the sureness of her tone and had time to wonder that her own voice, so little used, was so lucid and calm.

'Jan is your brother, Karel, and you will answer in Heaven for what you have done to him. God may not count my life and the life of my daughter as worthy of retribution, but I tell you this. Look at me. Look into our eyes.' Karel said nothing, but his gaze flicked from mother to daughter. 'Do you see?' Líba continued. 'Do you see us? We may be nothing to you, any of you. But this look, this will pursue you until the day you die. On your deathbed, you will remember it. Tell the others. You will see us.'

Karel did not move, but she saw his gaze shift to look past her. Jan had seen them. She turned back to the truck.

As she and Marie walked the few paces back to the truck, she watched her husband's face to see how he would react to Karel. This would be the moment that Romanov had been waiting for.

Jan looked at her as she approached, then held out his hand to assist her into the truck.

*

Karel Malík observed as his brother Jan helped his wife into the truck, as gently and as chivalrously as a Count assisting his Countess into a carriage.

When he had helped his daughter, Jan picked up the bundle that lay at his feet and handed it up to them. Then he climbed up himself, his long legs easily gaining the floor of the truck. The remaining soldier jumped up beside them and Jan assisted him in lifting the tailgate, each of them pulling on one of the chains at either side. The soldier fastened it, then shouted to the driver.

Jan was seated opposite the soldier, still fully visible to Karel as the truck began to bump down the lane. Karel waited for him to turn and stare at him, a lethal stare – but Jan remained impassive. He gazed mildly out of the truck, as if Karel did not exist.

As the truck swayed away, leaving intermingling vapours of grey diesel exhaust and brown dust, Karel Malík realised that that blank look was his brother's revenge.

Behind him, the residents of Romanov began to emerge from their cottages. They were whispering, and Karel Malík knew what those whispers meant. He was finished. He had saved their lives, for the time being, and he had done the unforgiveable – he had given up four of their people, one of them his own brother, to be taken by the *gadje*.

Karel took two paces after the truck, then stopped. He watched as it disappeared down the dusty summer lane, bathed in light.

PART 5

1942–3

CHAPTER 12

The policeman had a fine mare; a great long-legged thing, coal-black, a high-stepper. Emil stared at her as they trudged along the lane. He and his family were at the head of the column, the policeman on his horse directly ahead of them. Sometimes, when the lane widened, the policeman pulled the mare back so they were trotting alongside. 'Not far now!' he would call out, encouragingly, the horse dancing lightly on the verge, lifting her legs like a show animal and shaking her fine, narrow head. When Emil looked up, it seemed as if the policeman and his mount were almost floating beside them. White light flashed beyond their combined silhouette.

The sky was blinding. Sweat poured down Emil's forehead – he could feel his hair sticking beneath his hat. He and Josef were taking it in turns to carry Bobo who was semi-conscious and moaning with thirst. The only sound was the child's low groaning and the musical jangle of the horse's harness.

His mother and little sister were a few paces behind them.
Every now and then he glanced back to see if they were all right.
Parni was clinging to her mother's skirts, hanging her head on her
arms. Anna was murmuring to her as they walked. His three
aunts were helping old Pavliná. Behind them was everyone who
had been taken by truck from Třebič, and others who had joined
them in the railway yard at Brno. When they had all stumbled
from the train at Nědvedice, his father had jostled their family to
the front of the crowd as they lined up to be marched from the
station. He needs to control something about this journey, Emil
thought, to impose order upon some small element of it.

His shirt clung to his back, clammy with sweat. The back of
his throat was raw. He felt sick and dizzy and he wanted to stop
and urinate. 'Not far now,' the guard kept calling, until the
words drained of meaning and made no more sense than the
jangle of the harness or the soft slap-slap of the guard's thighs
against the horse's leather saddle.

The lane entered woodland and led them up a small rise
surrounded by forest, into some sort of camp. As they passed
through the tall wooden gate, Emil saw three large barracks to
the right, and a row of smaller ones. The camp was surrounded
by a high fence topped with loose rolls of barbed wire. Sentries
stood in watchtowers at the corners. A group of Czech
policemen, guards, was waiting to greet them, gesturing towards
a long row of trestle tables behind which half a dozen officials
sat.

They were at the head of the queue. As Emil gazed around,
his father spoke to the first man seated behind the table. The
ground of the camp sloped sharply upwards, so the barracks
rose above each other on the terraced earth. On the far side of the
camp, beyond a wide dirt square, there was an area annexed by

open fencing that had pens of some sort. Emil looked up. The
sky was baked blue; honest-seeming. I was born on a day like
this, he thought vaguely. His mother always told him that, on hot
summer days. She told him it so often that he would groan to
make her stop. I am fifteen, he thought. Time to think about
getting married.

He stepped forward, to where his father was waiting in front
of the table while a woman seated next to the official was making
notes. 'Taté . . .' he said, glancing around at the high fence and the
Czech guards and the long queue of Roma behind them.' Taté,
rrobija si kado than?' Dad, is this a prison?

Josef turned but before he could speak one of the guards – a
large man in a shabby black uniform – strode forward from the
row that was waiting by the desk.

Emil saw the man coming towards him, then felt the man's fist
on the side of his head. There was a moment of sightlessness, a
brief glimpse of the crazy, tilting sky, then the taste of dirt on his
lips and tongue. As he spat out the dirt, someone grabbed the
back of his shirt and hauled him to his feet. He felt the cloth rip
and staggered as he came upright. He said in Czech, 'My shirt . . .'

The guard hit him again, less hard this time. Emil bent double
but did not fall. The guard pulled him upright, then began to rip
the shirt forcibly from him, tearing at the fine cotton and
wrenching the seams. Emil staggered and swayed. The other
guards in the line were laughing.

When he had finished, the guard held the tattered remnants
of the shirt clenched in his two fists. He shoved it in Emil's face.
He caught a glimpse of pink skin stretched over knuckles, plump
fingers. The man smelled of sweat, layers of it; sweet sweat from
the hot afternoon and sour sweat from days ago.

'Ein hemd!' the guard declared. Why was the man speaking
German when he was a Czech policeman? 'Ein hemd!'

Emil moved back a step but the guard advanced upon him, shoving the shirt in his face. *'Ein hemd!'* he said again, and Emil understood that the guard wanted him to repeat it.

'Ein . . . hemd . . .' Emil said, uncertainly. If the guard wanted him to say it, then why didn't he just ask him to say it?

The guard tossed the shirt aside and Emil got a proper look at him – a fat man, fat-faced; large nose, bulging cheeks, no neck, a chin that joined directly to a chest that rose and strained from beneath the tight uniform jacket. He rejoined the other guards, who were smiling and shaking their heads.

Emil turned to where his father stood watching, his face a mask. His mother had moved to stand beside him and place a restraining hand on his arm. Emil knew his own glance was bewildered. He tried to compose himself. He wanted to signal to his father that it was okay, that he was glad he had not intervened, and that he was beginning to understand the way things were.

The woman seated behind the table said in a quick, low voice, in Czech. 'It is forbidden here to speak anything but German. It is the same for us. We have to speak German too.' She switched to German. 'You must hand over your possessions,' she said, loudly, clumsily. Josef nodded and began to empty his pockets. On to the table went their identity papers, Josef's leather wallet, a small stitched purse where he kept a few hallers and crowns, his tobacco pouch and pipe, an embroidered handkerchief and, last of all, his gold ring, the ring they had been saving as a bribe to get them into Slovakia – the last thing they had left of any value. Emil stared at the ring as it lay on the table. Finally, he comprehended. They were in prison. Their escape was as likely as his being able to crawl through that tiny, yellow circumference.

The man at the table picked the ring up and turned it over. He glanced back down at the queue of waiting people, then drew a huge book towards him, a ledger.

As they walked away, one of the guards was gesturing at Emil and Josef to hurry up a small rise towards one of the barracks. Emil kept his head down to avoid the fat guard's gaze as they passed. It was only when they were halfway up the rise that he glanced behind and realised that his mother and the others were not being allowed to follow.

'Do not look back,' Josef said quickly, speaking under his breath. 'Do not draw attention to yourself.'

The barrack was low and wide and long. Inside, there were concrete pillars and a central island on top of which sat huge zinc tubs of water. Lining the walls were wooden bunks in tiers. The guard who had escorted them to the door told them in German to take off all their clothes and wash. He spoke slowly and loudly, and Josef replied, '*Jawohl, dankeschön.*'

Emil was half-naked already but his father beat him to it, undressing swiftly and plunging his hands into the cold water then rubbing them over his body. Emil stood close by, his skin suddenly goose-pimpled. It was gloomy and dank in the barrack despite the heat outside. He had hardly ever seen his father naked. In winter, Josef slept in one of Anna's nightgowns, wrapping it around his legs before pulling his trousers on top in the morning. Emil noticed the hairs on his father's chest were a light sandy colour, much lighter than the rest of his father's hair. He felt a flicker of curiosity – the pale hairs, the loose stomach. Emil's own body was still so narrow and hard: his father's was a portent.

While they stood shivering, an orderly in shabby, dyed shirt and trousers stepped into the barrack holding a sack and a stick. Josef had folded his clothes neatly and placed them on a bunk. Emil had copied him. The man lifted up the clothes with the stick, item by item, and shoved them into the sack.

The guard saw them observing the procedure and said. 'They will be disinfected and stored. You will be given a uniform.'

Emil saw a muscle on his father's cheek twitch and felt the pain of such an insult to him. His father – his father who would not even hold a teacup until he had scrubbed beneath his nails when he paused from work – his father's clothes were going to be disinfected.

Outside the block, the guard walked ahead and they followed, still naked, to where a row of huge black vans was parked on the hill just inside the perimeter fence. Emil glanced back down the slope. The queue of people at the trestle table looked endless, but other men were being escorted up towards the barrack. One of them looked up and saw them, his eyes widening in shock at their nakedness. Emil turned back quickly, his hands over his genitals. The guard gestured at them to mount a small set of wooden steps and to enter the back of one of the black vans.

Inside, there were two long wooden benches, the length of the van. Four men waited.

'The first!' one of the men exclaimed happily in Czech. 'Our first customers of the day!' He gestured for them to sit down on one of the benches and moved forward towards Emil. Another of the men approached his father. They were holding razors. The first man bent and dipped his into a bucket at Emil's feet, then wiped it on his apron and began to shave Emil's head with swift, rough movements. The razor was blunt and there was no soap in the water. Emil winced.

The men were in civilian clothes and seemed to be happily ignoring the prohibition against any language but German. Josef asked them rapid questions as he was shaved. 'Why are you shaving us? Where will they put our clothes? Do we get a receipt? My boots were good boots.' The man shaving him ignored him, whistling to himself. Josef tried again. 'When do we get something to drink and eat? They gave us nothing in Brno.'

'You've missed lunch, *gypsy*, a fine goulash!' one of the other men said, grinning and showing a row of black teeth. 'There's a grand restaurant in this holiday camp, you'll love it!'

Realising he would get no useful information, Josef fell silent.

The man shaving Emil took hold of one of his wrists and lifted his arm. 'The body hair as well,' he said, as he began to shave Emil's armpit. When he had done the armpits and chest, he indicated for Emil to stand. He grimaced, then reached down and flicked the razor either side of Emil's genitals. A few of the longer pubic hairs fell to the floor. Shaving him properly would clearly be a complex business.

'How many are they checking in today?' the man asked his compatriots rhetorically. He waved a hand. 'Oh, that will have to do.' He pushed Emil lightly on the shoulder to indicate that he should be seated again, then stepped back to allow one of the others to come forward.

The man was holding an aluminium bottle with a stained label, and a cloth. He had the bottle's screw-top lid clenched between his teeth. He tipped the bottle on to the cloth and then rubbed it, first over Emil's shaved head, then Josef's. Emil felt a freezing, stinging sensation on his raw skin. Inhaling, he smelt kerosene.

Josef at last gave way to fear. 'Dear God!' he exclaimed. 'Are you going to set fire to our heads?'

The four men burst out laughing, one bending double over the bench, another slapping Josef merrily on the shoulder. They sat together with their scalps stinging while the laughter echoed around the black van, back and forth, until the guard outside opened the door and snapped at them to get a move-on. Didn't they know there was a line of prisoners coming up the path?

They emerged, shaved and naked, into the sunlight, blinking at one another. Emil stared at Josef, his look wide-eyed in disbelief at the rapidity and severity of the transformation. The man who had been his father only minutes ago was now a bald, shrunken derelict. His head was red-raw in patches, with strands of black hair clinging limply here and there. A trickle of blood ran down his forehead until it was partially diverted by a rough black patch where his eyebrows had been. He was wide-eyed with bewilderment.

Emil stared; his father stared back, their gazes mirrors of incredulity.

Emil turned away and looked up at the sky, gazing at the silver disc of the sun. He closed his eyes and saw he had burned a circle into his retina, black against the orange interior of his lids. *I was born on a day like this*, he thought, his eyes still closed, his face turned upwards. It was the last time he played games with the sun.

*

Anna prised Bobo's plump fingers away from her blouse, one by one. He was screaming – a high-pitched tone that rapidly soared beyond the limits of normal human sound to become a single singing note. A woman in uniform was pulling him around the waist and Anna knew that if she did not disengage her son's fingers from her blouse he would be hurt.

The woman turned swiftly when Bobo was in her arms. Anna was relieved when she could no longer see his face.

Parni stood by, staring, her eyes dark and expressionless. Anna stared back at her, trying to communicate reassurance in her gaze, trying to say, *it will be all right, be good, do whatever they tell you to do, I will come for you, look after your brother*. Parni gazed until another girl, three or four years older, came and took her by the hand.

'Come,' said the other girl. 'We have to go now.' She seemed almost cheerful.

Parni stared over her shoulder at her mother as she was led away.

It was only then Anna realised that Bobo was the youngest child who was being taken – the nursing mothers in their group were allowed to keep their infants with them. As he was carried away, she felt a slight swell and tingle in her breasts, even though there was hardly any milk left in her and she was only letting him suckle once a day. She remembered how Ludmila had accidentally dropped Bobo on his head when he was eight weeks old, and how her breasts had sprung with milk at the sound of her newborn baby's wail.

The two families immediately behind them in the queue had also been registered. Their children, along with hers, were ushered away to a block in the middle of the camp. Most of them were crying as they walked away but Parni still seemed composed, holding the cheerful girl's hand. She had made a friend already. That was good.

A mother next to Anna was biting her own hand, staring after her children, tears streaming down her face. With her other hand, she was punching herself in the head.

When Anna looked ahead, she saw that Josef and Emil were already being led away from her, up the rise.

She breathed in deeply, closed her eyes once, then turned to face Tekla and Eva and Ludmila and Pavliná Franzová, all of whom were staring at her, waiting to take their cue from her behaviour. She straightened her back and tilted her chin towards the two women orderlies who stood a metre or so away, windmilling their arms, gesturing impatiently towards one of the large barracks. Our block, Anna thought, *the place where we are to be kept*. As they turned away, there was some commotion at the desk. One of the men was protesting in fluent German that there had been a mistake. He owned his own business making belt buckles, essential war work. He employed sixteen people. He shouldn't be here. There had been a mistake.

In the barrack, Anna sank on to a lower bunk near the door as the women around her undressed and washed. One of the orderlies stood in the doorway and told them to wash, then put their clothes back on. There were some uniforms, she told them, old Czechoslovak army uniforms, dyed black, but only enough for the men. The orderly waited until the barrack had filled up, repeated the order, then left them to it.

Eva and Ludmila had a brief but vehement argument, then agreed that they could not bear to be parted and should share the bunk above Anna. Tekla had chosen a bunk next to them. Pavliná scuttled to the far end where there was more room and chose a bunk with empty bunks either side, a move that rapidly became redundant as the block filled up.

Eva and Ludmila began to cry as they undressed; soft, timid sobs of distress. The women around them were whispering to one another, glancing at the open door. Two guards were patrolling outside.

Tekla removed her clothes with swift, determined movements. When she turned and saw Eva and Ludmila weeping, she snapped loudly in Romani, 'Shake out those blankets!'

A couple of other women lifted their heads.

'How are we supposed to dry ourselves?' Tekla continued, holding her own blanket up to the light, tutting and frowning. 'Golden God! Is that all the water they have given us? For all of us? Start using that bucket, Eva. Ludmila, stand close behind her. We'll all use that one. I'm not sharing a bucket with anyone I don't know, I don't care what they say.' Some of the other women had stopped what they were doing to listen to Tekla's scolding.

'What are you crying for, you stupid soft girls?' she snarled at her cousins. 'It could be a lot worse. Golden God, Eva Demeter, STOP that snivelling! You could be stuck in Brno prison or lying dead in a ditch with a bullet through your head! What are you snivelling for? Think you'll grow wings if you cry hard enough? Ha! Stupid girl! You've always been witless. I'm surprised you found your way out of your own mother's belly!' Eva was cupping her hands and lifting the water slowly to let it run down over her naked chest. She was still weeping softly. 'So they've put us in a camp, men, women, babies,' Tekla continued. 'Did you ever expect any better from the *gadje*?'

Anna listened to Tekla's monologue, the only voice in the large block. Tekla. It would take more than the Moravian police force to keep her quiet. Around them, the other girls and women were sitting on their bunks awaiting their turn at the buckets, pretending not to listen.

'At least we are still alive! All we have to do is obey the rules and survive. The war will be over before winter sets in. We're a lot safer here than on the road. It was the best thing that could have happened to us. Whose mad fool idea was it to try and make it to Slovakia? May we all die! It was craziness! If we'd got to the border we would have been mown down by machine guns or torn to pieces by dogs ... Praise to God we were arrested! We're so lucky! He's keeping an eye on us, the Lord, thank Him for that!' She was speaking loudly enough for them all to hear, her voice a rough, determined sing-song, rising and falling as she shook out the blankets. 'La-di-la-di-la! Filthy! Who DO they THINK we are?'

Anna gripped the edge of her bunk tightly with her hands, grasping at the rough-hewn wood. She thought, *I must not go mad. If I am to protect my family and save my children's lives, then I must think clearly and calmly the whole time we are here.* She could still hear Bobo's singular scream in her head, as if the sound of it had lodged in her brain like a piece of food stuck between two teeth. *I must not go mad.*

CHAPTER 13

The whistling sound had a derisive quality. It was derision that awoke Emil at 5 a.m. precisely each day.

The orderlies were called kapos. They were mostly Czech prisoners from Brno, sometimes Roma or Sinti, and they were given all the duties that the guards declined to perform. It was a kapo who woke them each morning, flinging back the door with a crash. Like Anna and the others, Josef and Emil had chosen bunks near the door, to quell the claustrophobia of imprisonment, but being near the door had its drawbacks. The morning reveille had a personal, abusive quality. *Back* banged the door, *open* snapped his eyes – to painfully white light. The chill morning air rushed over him and the whistle pierced his ears with a shrillness so sharp and unpleasant it seemed to originate inside his skull.

Within a week of their arrival, their block had become so crowded that he and Josef were sharing a bunk. When Emil awoke he would feel both annoyed by and grateful for his father's proximity. It was good to have human warmth but Josef seemed constructed of angles. (He had refused to eat the soup the first week, saying he could not lower himself to such filth. Many of the men had done the same. None were doing it now.) It was less than a month, but Emil had to struggle to remember the time when his father had been a bulky man; solid-chested, with muscular arms and a paunch that betrayed a fondness for meat puddings. Josef had altered so quickly – the stubble growing on his head was grey. Emil had been so narrow already that the change in him was negligible. He glanced at Josef sometimes and thought, is this man my father?

After the initial shock of being woken, Emil would close his eyes, snatching another second of nothingness. As the shriek of the whistle perished, he could hear the minuscule clatter of the dried pea inside it, spiralling crazily in its prison of tin.

That morning, there was something else.

'Raus! Alles raus!' shouted the kapo, a short, white-haired convict who fancied himself to have a sense of humour. 'Time to get up and earn a living you gypsy scum!' he added in Czech. This one was lazy about his German. When he spoke it at all it was with a heavy, mocking accent.

'Come on! Come on! Schnell, raus and all that goddamed nonsense, you scumbags. Up!' He strode down the centre of the block pulling blankets from the men and throwing them on the floor.

The kapos were not normally enthusiastic about the reveille, preferring to lean against the doorway while their charges roused themselves. As the men staggered towards the door, he was shouting, 'Line up outside, directly outside. Appel just outside today!'

The men pushed their way out of the block. The kapo was shouting names from a list, in alphabetical order. Confusion reigned. What did he want? He said to go where?

The kapo finished his list. 'The rest of you can go and wash!'

Josef turned to Emil and pulled a face. 'We're on the list. We have to line up at the gate.'

As they trotted across the camp, Emil glanced over to the women's barracks but the shutters were still closed. His block had been woken early.

The sky above was white and the air light and cool. The hills above the camp, beyond the forest, were soft, grey, kindly almost. Emil yawned and ran his tongue over his teeth to clear the sticky, metallic sensation in his mouth. The cold air made him shudder as he ran.

At the gate, a guard duty of ten policemen was waiting, including Emil's old friend from the registration line, the one who had ripped his shirt from his back. They called him Čacko, Emil had discovered, and so far he had managed to avoid him. He had seen him beating other prisoners, twice, both young ones like himself. He had been drunk at the time but the other guards either didn't notice or care. He was popular with the others, loud-mouthed, jovial – drinking on duty was common anyway. Most of them had been sent to the camp as a punishment, for dereliction of duty elsewhere. 'We get the scum,' Josef had put it when he told Emil. He had befriended a Roma kapo from North Moravia who was a useful source of information.

The guards seemed in high spirits that morning. Čacko stood in the middle of them, buttoning his uniform with one hand, glancing around and grinning. In his free hand he clutched a length of black pudding, lifting it to tear off ostentatious chunks with his teeth and talking while he ate. *Black pudding. The guards get black pudding.* Emil ran his tongue over his teeth. They had not even been given the vile *ersatz* drink they called coffee, that morning. His breath tasted sour. Now he was properly awake, the dawn air was damp and unpleasant rather than refreshing. A thick mass of cloud was banked above them, waiting to be burned off by the sun. He gave a slow shudder which travelled the length of his body.

Čacko left the group of guards and strode amongst the prisoners, still eating, pausing here and there. He stopped by Emil and stood in front of him while Emil concentrated on his clogs. He belched. 'How's your German lessons coming along, my little schoolboy?' he asked eventually, in Czech. Emil caught a wave of the fat man's breath. It smelled of meat.

'Fine. Sir,' he replied sullenly.

Čacko's baton came swinging down on his shoulder. Emil bent under the blow but did not fall.

'In *German*!' shouted Čacko in Czech, and the assembled guards laughed.

Čacko moved back to join the others, gesturing and shaking his head.

Josef stood close to Emil and said softly. 'It has become a joke, the way that man treats you. They have talked about it amongst themselves. It's an act. You must stay away from him, especially when he is with the others.'

Emil rubbed at his shoulder with his hand. 'I know,' he replied shortly. *Drop the advice,* he thought bitterly, turning away. *If I'm old enough to take the blows I'm old enough to work out where they are coming from.* He did not expect his father to fight back – that would be lunacy – but he felt angry that Josef could not think of some way of distracting Čacko, of drawing his attention away from his son on to himself. Wasn't that the kind of thing that fathers were supposed to do? Anyway, it was his father's decision that had landed them all in the camp. The rest of the *kumpánia* were probably still lying low in Bohemia, making fruit puddings out of berries and moaning about the sugar ration.

'I don't need you to tell me . . .' Emil muttered to Josef, but his father had already moved away to speak to someone else.

'Form them up!' the shout rang out from the steps of the staff hut, several metres away. The prisoners and the guards all jumped. The Camp Commandant was striding towards them, shouting as he approached. The guards wiped the smiles from their faces. Emil caught a gratifying glimpse of Čacko looking panic-stricken and swallowing hard.

The men formed a squad – drill was the one thing they had learned so far in their three weeks in the camp.

At a motion from the Commandant, two of the guards ran down to the gate and pushed it open.

Emil knew that they were only going to work, to the quarry or the road-site, but he permitted himself a moment of joyous longing at the sight of the gate swinging back, at the thought that for the first time since their arrival they were about to get out of the camp. He felt suddenly strong – as if he could march all the way back to Bohemia, leave behind this thin, weak father and stride back to the strong, healthy Dad and the others who were waiting back there in the Bohemian cottages, in the past.

That night, as he sat on his bunk, Emil eased off his wooden clogs, one by one. A layer of skin came away from each heel, and when he looked inside each clog, the wood was stained with blood. There were huge blisters on both of his large toes, great white bulbs on the point of bursting. His eyes prickled with tears. How would he be able to walk the next day?

Josef was standing by the bunk, massaging his shoulder with one hand. They had been carrying and breaking rocks for ten hours. He picked up one of Emil's feet and examined the heel, wincing. 'Why didn't you take these off earlier, as soon as we were back? We could have swapped clogs for the rest of the day.'

'I told you my feet hurt.'

'Yes, but I didn't realise it was this bad.'

'You thought I was just complaining about nothing . . .' mumbled Emil resentfully, still holding the other foot, rubbing the toes gently.

'No,' insisted Josef. 'I just didn't think you meant . . .'

'Anyway,' said Emil, lifting his head. 'What happened to your deal with that kapo, about getting our boots back?'

Josef's look darkened. 'Hush. You will be heard.'

'So what . . . ?' mumbled Emil, glancing from side to side, where the other men were preparing for bed. 'You haven't done anything, have you?'

His father glared at him in response, but the debate was ended by the whistle from the doorway. Immediately, every man in the block turned to his bunk. Josef climbed up beside Emil.

Emil turned swiftly away from his father. They slept head-to-toe, Emil with his head to the wall, so that his father had the luxury of sleeping with his face pointing outwards, maybe getting a little air. Emil hated being jammed inwards. The ceiling was right above him, and the air so thick and fetid he had to close his eyes as soon as he was lying down to stop himself from panicking.

He lay still as the men around him fell swiftly asleep, resenting his father beyond measure. He did not think he would sleep at all – the pain of his feet was too great. An insect of some sort was crawling up his left leg but reaching down was impossible with his father packed so tight against him. The man on the next bunk always rolled towards them in the night. It was like being trapped in a coffin made of flesh.

Then, all at once, he snapped awake, aware that if he was now conscious that meant he must have slept. It was pitch dark and he was gasping for breath. The other men were silent. His father's foot was in his face. When he tried to roll over he found that his blanket was wrapped around and trapped beneath him. He couldn't move. His face was bathed in sweat. He managed to free an arm and push his father's foot away, then scratched at his scalp which was burning and itching. His fingers felt damp when he took his hand away. He lifted them to his nose and sniffed, trying to discover if his head was bleeding.

His father stirred in his sleep, groaning, and shoved his foot back in Emil's face. Emil gave a sigh of desperation and managed to turn. The man sleeping on his other side had his head towards the wall, like Emil, and his face was so close to his that his exhaled breath was like a furnace blast. Emil clamped his eyes shut and tried to slow his ragged breathing. Last night, a man at the other end of the block had had a screaming fit. His neighbours had pulled him from his bunk and thrown him on the floor, then beaten him into silence. Emil wanted to jump down from his bunk, kick at the door in a fury, but if he disturbed the others then he too would be thrown to the ground and punched into unconsciousness, and rightly so. The next night he would be back in the same bunk in the same position with a few extra bruises. He squeezed his eyes even tighter, willing himself to lie still and think of the only thing that gave him comfort, his favourite fantasy.

This is what I would like to do, he thought. *I will do it, one night. I will sneak down from the bunk, quietly, waking not a soul and find the door surprisingly unlocked. Then I will steal like a spirit across the camp and I will find my mother sitting on the step of her block. She will look up at me and smile her beautiful smile and say, 'Yenko, I wait here every night, just in case you manage to sneak out.' Then she will open her arms, and I will get down beside her and lie my head in her lap while she strokes my forehead. The air will be cool. She will talk to me about the stars.*

He lay still, replaying the fantasy over and over again, adding more detail each time, more soft words, more stars . . .

*

In the children's block, the night-shift kapo walked up and down, bouncing a crying infant on her arm and waiting impatiently for dawn.

As she passed the bunk where Bobo and Parni slept, the crying infant woke Bobo and he began to wail. The wail woke Parni, who joined his cry with hers, a groaning, adult sort of cry – and the cry was passed from bunk to bunk down the length of the barrack, each child waking the next in turn.

The kapo bared her teeth with frustration. This was the way it was in the children's block. For a brief time, they would all sleep. Then every half hour or so, sometimes less, one would wake, then wake the others, and a susurration would begin, a slow collective tide of cries which would rise in intensity until the kapo would lose her temper and shout and the wailing would subside to snivels as each child forgot the other children around them and, wrapping themselves in their own misery, gradually sobbed themselves to sleep.

Each night, every night, every half hour or so – sometimes less: the kapo could not stand it, this constant rise and fall of small, wretched voices. God bless the little ones, she was sorry for them, but it drove her crazy.

*

In the women's block, Anna lay awake, listening to the whispers of the dark. She often did this, close to dawn, her eyes open, straining to hear a recognisable wail from the small ocean of cries that came in waves from the children's block. Sometimes, she would strain not to hear.

There was a small window close to Anna's head. She often watched it, trying to distinguish the exact moment when the blackness in front of her showed the first glimmer of grey. There, she would think, and there – but it always seemed as though, when dawn began, she had missed it.

She reached out a hand and splayed her fingers against the smooth pane of glass. She watched as melting night defined her hand.

O Del, she thought. *Enough. Devla yertisar ma. . . Forgive me. It is enough. I deserve this perhaps, but my children? Must my children suffer too?* She knew her sin. *I thought I was so strong, so capable, whatever was thrown at us. I congratulated myself often enough. We were surviving the war so well I thought, thanks to my resourcefulness. I always fed the children a little something every day, even when we had to beg. Other mothers lost their tempers and shouted when their little ones were hungry but I always managed something. When our ration cards went missing I marched all the way into town with Bobo on my back and went straight into the meeting of the Landrat and told Emil what to say in German. They couldn't believe their eyes, this woman had just marched right in. I charmed an egg out of that old man in Brno. When Bobo was thirsty on the train I spat in his mouth to moisten it. Right up until we got here, I thought my strength was limitless. Other women would falter, their children would suffer and die, not mine. I would always save mine. Forgive me my pride, O Del. I admit that I have failed. I thought I was God and I am not. I am penitent now. Will you forgive me now?*

She waited for her prayer to be answered but the greyness around her hand continued to gleam, stronger and stronger. *God, Holy One*, she thought. *Enough!* But the greyness grew and grew until her hand was trapped in a clear square, whitening with each passing moment.

Silently, her tears came. *Devla yertisar ma . . . Forgive me. Forgive me my pride in believing I could protect my children.* She kept her hand pressed against the window but closed her eyes against the coming day. She thought of each of her children in turn, of how, when they were born, she had held each in her arms and whispered their real names in their ears; Yenko, Doikitsa, Branko. She thought of how she had sworn by the moon and the stars to defend them, always. *By the moon and the stars, I have failed.*

She opened her eyes. It was dawn.

*

In the men's block, Emil lay awake, trapped in his blanket, while the wooden wall a few centimetres from his nose gradually gained texture in the light.

*

In the children's block, the night-shift kapo paced up and down, bouncing the infant in her arms, oblivious to the fact that it had fallen asleep.

CHAPTER 14

September brought a sudden plunge into autumn.

Emil awoke to leaden skies. As he stood sipping his *ersatz* coffee beside the *ersatz* coffee-hut, he looked up and saw that the clouds were heavy with weather, dense, as though the weight of portent in them made them sag down from the sky. The air had altered. There was a briskness in the atmosphere, a bite.

They were marched out of the camp as usual, before the other blocks were stirring, so it was only when their lunch arrived – a piece of dry bread each – that the story went round the work detail. A whole family had escaped in the night. Their name was Murka. They were from Blansko. The father had been in the infirmary, with swollen feet. It was easy to get out of the infirmary. The mother had somehow evaded being locked in the women's block at night. Then she had succeeded in getting four children past the kapo in the children's block – some said the kapo was asleep, others that she must have been bribed. All six of them had climbed on to the roof of one of the wagons that was being used for storage and got over the perimeter fence.

The news was talked over and over, the few known facts repeated endlessly. Others had run, of course, in the first few weeks, but they had all been young men, and a couple of girls, who had made a dash for it when out on a work party and were brought back beaten within hours. This was different. This was planned. Who knew where the Murka family was now? Perhaps they had friends or relatives on the outside – perhaps even now they were sitting together around a pot of boiled chicken, drinking the broth while they waited for the bird to cook.

For the rest of the afternoon, the men worked with renewed vigour, even their Sinti guard shared a joke with them. Who could not be happy that someone had managed to get away?

When they returned to the camp that evening, they discovered that their joy was not shared by the women and the rest of the men, who had stood on the *Appell-platz* until lunchtime while the alarm was raised and the camp searched. Those in the infirmary had been turfed out to sit or lie on the ground. The children were kept locked in their block without food or water, screaming in fury and fear. The kapo who had looked after them since their arrival was seen being frog-marched out of the camp by two guards. The woman sent into the children's block to replace her could be heard shouting for quiet.

Emil and his father managed to spend a few minutes with Anna and the Little Ones after the supper of turnip soup had been served, in the wide dirt space between the women's and children's blocks, now unofficially designated as the area where the families could get together. It was the only time they were allowed free association, after supper but before the evening roll-call. His mother seemed fiercely gloomy, Emil thought. She pointed at the two Little Ones as they ran around in the evening light: after a day's incarceration, Parni and Bobo were maniacally grateful to be allowed outside.

'We will lose this,' Anna said, 'when the bad weather comes. We won't be able to sit around together. They might not even let the Little Ones out. It is cold already, today. I can't believe it. What is God thinking of? Haven't we got enough to fight against without an early winter?'

Neither Emil nor his father replied. All three of them were squatting in a row, watching Parni and Bobo. Around them, other families huddled or stood talking. Tekla and the others were grouped a few yards away. Eva and Ludmila had made friends with some of the Moravian Romnis and were talking with them. After the ordeal of the morning, there was a general sense of release. Anna alone seemed sunk in gloom.

Josef was chewing thoughtfully on a twig. It help eased his hunger pangs, he had told Emil, and reminded him of that time, back in another life, when it had been his habit to have his single smoke of the day, after supper.

'At least someone has got away . . .' said Emil awkwardly. He had never known what to say when his mother was unhappy, ever. Any comfort he tried to offer her seemed so paltry in comparison with what she could offer him.

Anna spat on the ground.

Emil glanced at his father and saw that he was indicating with raised eyes and a slight movement of his head that it would be a good idea for Emil to leave them alone. He rose resentfully and went over to Parni and Bobo. Typical of his father, to want his mother to himself. It was selfish, Emil thought, unbecoming of a true Rom. His father was forgetting how to behave, hoarding his wife. It would be roll-call soon, and who knew what would happen then? There would be more punishments for someone, after the escape.

Parni ran up to him. 'Emil! Emil!' she called. 'Bobo is putting stones in his mouth. I told him he's not allowed.'

Bobo was sitting in the dirt playing with a pile of pebbles which he and Parni had accumulated. His cheeks bulged. Emil went over and grabbed his brother's chin, forcing his mouth open, then hooked his finger in and prised out the pebbles. Bobo began to cry. Emil grabbed one of his upper arms and squeezed viciously. Bobo threw back his head and howled.

Anna appeared behind them.

'He was eating pebbles. He'll choke!' Emil exclaimed. Parni was nodding furiously, backing him up, pleased that their mother's favourite was in the wrong.

Anna shot Emil a venomous look and scooped Bobo up into her arms, then turned back to Josef.

Parni and Emil gazed at each other, disconsolately. Parni kicked loosely at the pile of pebbles.

*

For the next few days, the mood of the guards was ugly. All leave had been cancelled because of the escape. Emil balanced his fear of them against the pleasure he derived from their being trapped in the camp as surely as the prisoners.

One morning, when the work detail gathered, the guard in charge came and pulled him from the line, then sent him to the staff hut to ask for Officer Čacko, who had a job for him, apparently.

Čacko emerged from the staff hut, grey-faced and sunk in gloom. He glanced at Emil but said nothing, then set off across the camp. Emil trotted behind him. When they reached the men's block, Čacko strode round the side to the washroom, then pointed to a broom made of twigs tied in a sheaf to a branch. 'It's overflowed,' he said wearily, waving an arm across the washroom floor.

The latrine was in a small annexe off the washroom. Brown filth had washed across the cement floor. The filth lived and bubbled with the insects crawling through it. Emil turned his head, swallowing.

'I'll be outside,' said Čacko, and left him to it.

Emil stood for a moment, overwhelmed with misery. What was he supposed to do? The latrines were nothing more than pits. If they were full, they were full. New ones were being dug outside, surrounded by wicker fencing, but they were not yet finished.

There were six zinc tubs full of dirty water left over from that morning, ranged on a central concrete block. Emil put the broom down, picked up one of the tubs, and carried it carefully over to the latrine doorway, his arms shuddering with the weight of it. Little by little, he tipped the water out, swooshing it gently to wash the filth towards the outside door. When there was a large brown puddle at his feet, he put the tub down and took the broom, swishing the puddle outside.

The sluicing process took nearly an hour, by which time he had used up four of the tubs of water and washed out no more than the top layer of dirt. He was standing wondering what to do next, when Čacko re-entered and, with him, a strong smell of tobacco.

Čacko looked at the floor, then at Emil, shook his head and nodded at one of the remaining tubs of water. Emil realized he was being given permission to wash himself. He removed his shirt and tucked it between his legs, clasping it between his knees.

As he leaned forward over the tub, Čacko stepped up behind him, grabbed the shirt in his fist and yanked it out from between

Emil's legs. Then he went over to the wall of the washroom, leant against it and watched Emil splash water over his upper body. As Emil stood upright, Čacko tossed the shirt back to him. Emil rubbed the shirt over his chest to dry himself, avoiding Čacko's gaze.

As he pulled the shirt over his head, Čacko said with sullen malice, 'Got lice yet, schoolboy?'

Emil forgot himself. He looked Čacko straight in the face and replied quietly, 'No, I haven't.'

They held each other's gazes. Emil felt the elision from one moment to the next as an almost physical sensation. The point at which he could look down and avoid the confrontation passed without a flicker and he found himself locked in a battle of wills. He could not stop staring at the man, as if he had lost all reason and was only able to relish the brief illusion of courage that such a moment bestowed.

Without breaking his gaze, Čacko crossed the few steps that separated them and grabbed him. One of his fat hands clutched the scruff of his neck, the other the waistband of his prison-uniform trousers, and in the same swift movement, he began to whirl him round.

As his feet lost balance and his body twisted, Emil divided into two. The logical part of him recognised, slowly and quite calmly, that what was about to happen would be beyond the casual beatings he had endured from Čacko before. There was an air of fury and sadism about the man, at that moment: the exercise with the latrines had been no more than an excuse to assuage it. Emil thought, Čacko has me by the scruff of the neck, and trousers, and he is flinging me round so that I gather speed. He is about to smash me into the wall. There was even a fleeting but distinct moment in which, as his feet left the ground, he had the sensation of flight.

The thinking part of him and the feeling, animal part, were re-united as his face slammed into the wall. His head exploded with pain. There was a gushing sensation from the lower half of his face. Then he was on all floors on the filthy floor and Čacko was kicking him in the stomach, grunting with exertion. He fell on one side, his face towards Čacko, and as he opened his mouth to give an uncontrollable, nauseated howl, Čacko's boot rammed into his face and his head exploded again, with a pain beyond pain. He was nothing but pain.

Čacko fell back against the latrine wall, his breathing ragged. Emil rolled into a crouching position and opened his eyes to see a pool of bright red blood swimming in the liquid brown shit on the floor. Strings of blood dripped from his mouth and nose. His whole body was shaking, the lower half of his face completely numb. *What has he done to my face?* he thought in terror, lifting a hand and touching it gently with his fingertips. His hand felt a pliancy, but in the face itself he could feel nothing. Was anything still there? Then the pain became overwhelming again and he hung his head, gasping.

They remained like that for some moments, Čacko leaning against the wall, panting, and Emil crouched on the floor, now heedless of the stink around him, his only sensation the burning pain of his face. This is just the beginning, he thought, *oh God.* This is going to happen over and over again.

Čacko stood and hitched up his trousers, then worked both shoulders backwards and gave a single, loud sniff. His breathing had returned to normal: his voice was casual. 'Go and see your block Elder,' he said, 'he'll sort you out.' He remained standing over Emil for a moment or two. Then he stepped over him, quite carefully, and was gone.

After a short time, Emil tried to stand. He was shaking. It hurt to breathe. Using the washroom wall, he managed to limp to the entrance. Outside, the air was cold. Nobody was around. With excruciating slowness, he hobbled around the side of the block. He lifted his shaking hand to see that it was covered in blood from where he had touched his face. He paused, touched his nose gingerly, and realised it was twice its normal size. He was sobbing, gently but uncontrollably. He stood for a few minutes, trying to compose himself before he went in to the Elder.

The Elder was a white-haired Rom from Brno. He was sitting in his cubby-hole at the back of the block. When he saw Emil, he sighed. 'What is it with you, brother?' he asked, shaking his head. 'You and that guard. Were you born under an unlucky star or something?'

Emil did not reply. His tongue felt so thick, he was not sure he could speak.

'Here,' the man stood, beckoning him towards a tiny, square window, 'let me see in the light.' He winced. 'It sounded bad. Looks pretty bad too.'

'You heard?' Emil mumbled carefully.

The man huffed, 'You were screaming like a pig!' Seeing the look in Emil's eyes he added quickly. 'Don't worry, no one else is around. It's the shock. Here, let me pull at your teeth, see if they're loose.'

Emil moved the muscles that would normally open his mouth.

'Can you feel that?' the Elder asked. Emil shook his head. The Elder pulled a face. 'Well, your teeth are still stuck in there but if you can't feel anything then that's not good.'

'What has he done, to my mouth?'

'You don't have a mouth any more, *chavo*, you have a beak!'

'He said you would sort me out,' Emil mumbled resentfully.

The man shook his head and sighed again. 'Go to the infirmary and tell the kapo I said you're to jump the queue and see the doctor. Tell the doctor I said he should open his little drawer.'

The doctor's hut stood alone, a few feet from the infirmary block. A kapo was sitting on the step smoking, watching over the queue of sick, mostly women and children. Emil hobbled towards the kapo with a hand carefully in front of the lower half of his face, ashamed. The kapo looked up at him as he approached and said, with his cigarette still between his lips, 'Yes, *Brother*?'

Emil lowered his hand. The kapo stared at him. At that moment, a man emerged from the doctor's hut and descended the step.

The kapo tossed his head.

As Emil mounted the step, he heard the protests of the women waiting at the head of the queue.

Inside the hut, he kept his hand over his face as he turned and closed the door behind him. The doctor's coat was hanging from a large nail on the back of the door. It fell to the ground in a soft swoop, a gleam of black velvet, with a nap so deep it was almost like fur. A yellow star was stitched to the lapel. Emil lifted his hand.

'Nice coat, eh?'

Emil turned, his hand still covering the lower half of his face. The doctor was sitting behind a large, polished desk, a desk so huge it almost touched the two walls of the hut. On the edge of the desk was a porcelain bowl of water with several cloths folded neatly and hanging over the edge.

The doctor beamed, peering over a pair of half-moon spectacles that were perched perilously on the very end of his nose. 'It belonged to my father. It is the only thing of his I have left. It's stayed beautiful all this time and I can't bear to be parted from it even though I should bury it somewhere if I want it to survive the war.' He had shocks of hair sprouting from his head in extravagant display; white, grey, peppery-brown. He placed the tips of his fingers on the huge desk as he eased himself past it. 'Now this desk here was confiscated from a surgeon in Brno. It's got big drawers, small drawers, tiny spring-loaded drawers that pop out, so! Ach! What good did it do him?' His face darkened briefly. 'And now I see my patients in a shack – a cracked window and the most expensive walnut desk in the whole of Moravia. Excuse me, young man . . .' he lifted his hands and let them drop. 'But when someone comes in and stares at my nice coat and fine desk I always feel obliged to explain that they are not really mine. Now,' he looked at Emil over his glasses, 'What is it? Cat got your tongue?'

Emil lowered his hand. There was a pause while the doctor eased himself around the desk and approached him. He made a whistling noise between his teeth, then said soberly, 'Please forgive me for wasting your time talking about my coat and my desk. I'm sorry.'

The doctor's kindness made Emil choke. To have someone speak softly to him at that particular moment was hard to bear. He swallowed. 'My block Elder said you were to open . . . one of your little drawers.'

'Ah . . .' said the doctor, returning to his desk. 'He means this. It's a salve, but to be perfectly honest I'm not sure it's going to help in your case. Come sit on the edge of my desk. For some reason they refuse to put a chair in here. I think they think it will speed things up.' He turned back with a small tube and one of the cloths. 'Let's have a proper look at you. I suppose it would be foolish of me to ask how this happened?'

Emil didn't speak. The doctor gently prodded his nose, and wobbled his front teeth just as the Elder had. 'Anywhere else?'

Emil lifted his shirt to show his ribs. The doctor winced. 'Let's hope that's just swelling, shall we? Can you cough for me?' Emil coughed obediently while the doctor watched. 'Well, you can do that, that's something. I'm going to try and clean you up a little bit, then we'll apply my magic salve. It's all I have and I ration it very strictly.' He put his face close to Emil's and pulled a mock-strict expression. 'Only for my most privileged patients. My name is Dr Steiner, by the way. Who might you be?'

Emil shook his head, then sat still while the doctor dabbed gently at his swollen face. The doctor did not press the question.

After a few minutes' silence, Emil began to sob, dry sobs which shook his shoulders. Humiliated, he tried to control himself, but the sobs seemed to engulf his chest cavity. The doctor continued dabbing the salve, slowly and carefully. 'In God's name don't tell anyone I put this on you,' he said after a while. 'It's more than my life is worth, you know . . .' He replaced the lid on the tube, then took it back to his desk and locked it into a drawer. 'No offence, but I'll be emptying this drawer and putting the stuff somewhere else when you've gone. I just don't want you to waste your strength breaking in here sometime. I'm sorry, but things go and I can't replace them. It's usually the kapos, looking for things to barter.'

Emil remained seated on the edge of the desk, still sobbing in a hollow, gulping fashion.

The doctor came and sat next to him and put a hand on his arm. 'Listen, young man. Let's be practical. I think you've killed the nerves in those front teeth, but at least they're still in place. Your nose is broken, not much doubt about that. You might have a fractured jaw but we won't know until the swelling goes down.

At least the nose is still straight. Try and stay out of trouble and in a week you'll be surprised how much less painful it is. You've had beatings before. Now, they stopped hurting after a while, didn't they? You'll see. This one will too. You just have to stand it. You will stand it, because you don't have any choice.'

Emil shook his head. He tried to speak but only a gasp came.

The doctor inclined his head. 'What? Something else?'

Emil shook his head again. He managed to say. 'My fingernails . . .'

The doctor frowned a query.

'My fingernails . . . they've stopped growing . . .' Emil lifted a hand up, then let it fall back, uselessly.

The doctor gave a wry smile. 'Your hair too, eh? Well, you can't grow hair and fingernails on one piece of bread a day. Your body is saving energy, just so's you can walk around.'

'But I liked it!' Emil burst out furiously. 'I liked paring my fingernails. I liked sitting down and doing it carefully, and cleaning underneath. I *liked* it!'

The doctor sighed heavily, and nodded. 'I know . . .' he said quietly. 'I know . . .' He looked up at the ceiling, then down at the floor, as if he might spy in those two opposing planes some small picture of all that had been lost. He sighed again, and spread his hands.

'It's the little things, always the little things. Just when you think you're getting by. They took away my job, cut off the telephone, told us we couldn't have ration cards for apples, sugar, vegetables, tobacco, soap, nuts, cheese, fish. We're not allowed caps or suitcases. Buy a newspaper? Forget it. Travel on a trolley-car? *Nein!* We even had to give away my son's dog. Jewish children not allowed pets any more. One thing after another. Want to know when I cried? The only time I cried? When they revoked my fishing licence. And I hadn't fished for ten years.'

Emil stood awkwardly, wincing. He resented the doctor for
trying to cheer him up. 'At least you're not locked up,' he
mumbled.

The doctor gave a wry smile. 'You're right. Whatever
happens. It's always important to remember how lucky we are.'

From then on, Emil spent his days at Čacko's side. While his
father, thinner each day, marched out with the rest of the work
detail, Emil joined the others on the *Appell-platz* at the regular time,
and then obeyed the toss of Čacko's head in whichever direction
Čacko indicated.

Čacko's duties seemed less regimented than the other guards
– it transpired he was a distant cousin of the Camp
Commandant. He was assigned to Camp Maintenance, which
meant he could wander at will, finding fault with the prisoners
and kapos, and take breaks whenever he felt like it.

One afternoon, when a bitter wind ruffled the prisoners' thin
uniforms, a premonition of the winter's onset, Čacko decided
that they – Emil – should work on water detail. Two wooden
buckets had to be filled to the brim at the pump, then carried
carefully to each block, to refill the tubs for washing the next
morning. It was impossible to hold the buckets and walk
without some of the water slopping over the brims. When the
water spilt, Čacko would either laugh, or shout at him, or hit him
– sometimes just two of those things, sometimes all three. So
Emil's arms would ache with the effort of keeping the buckets
upright as he waddled across the uneven ground, Čacko behind
him all the time, out of sight, goading him. His trousers would
get wet – and now the weather had turned cold they would not
dry. They chafed against his legs. The effort of the carrying
would make him sweat but he was never allowed to drink from
the buckets and a thirst would clamour within him far greater

than the one he had suffered when he was breaking rocks
alongside his father. Just the sight of those buckets of water, the
silver light on the surface glinting at him as he walked, filled him
with a harsh, dry-throated rage.

It was a week after Čacko had smashed his face into the wall.
The swelling had gone down and hard scabs had formed across
Emil's upper lip. He still had no sensation in three of his teeth but
if he tried to bite his bread then tiny pains sparked around the
lower part of his face, like small electrical impulses. The bruises
around his ribs were going green and yellow at the edges.

Čacko had spent his lunchtime drinking, that was apparent as
soon as he returned from the staff hut. His face was florid. He was
muttering to himself. When they returned to the pump for the
third time, he sank down on to the concrete step and leant against
the well while Emil filled the buckets. He sighed heavily and
muttered something about dumplings. Then he closed his eyes.

Emil stood by the well, pumping slowly. The cold iron handle
resisted his efforts, forcing him to lean his weight against its
protesting creak. From the depth and tenor of Čacko's breathing,
it became apparent that he had fallen asleep. Emil slowed his
efforts and stood a little away from the pump, pushing lightly on
the handle with his arm at full stretch, which made it creak as
though he was pumping much more effortfully. He had a chance
to take a good look at the man he hated more than anybody in
the world.

At some stage in Čacko's life, Emil thought, something had
gone wrong with his face. It was as if the separate elements of it
had started to grow out of proportion to one another. The
bulbous nose had put on a spurt to get ahead of the rest of the
features, becoming globular and producing a few fine, downy
hairs. The cheeks had puffed in jealous fury, the blood vessels
bursting to sketch a myriad of tiny bright red tributaries. The

eyelids had formed fleshy twin dewlaps. And finally, the lips
had ripened. They were now a deep, damp purple-brown, like
figs on the point of bursting. He is a dead man, Emil thought to
himself, still pumping slowly lest the cessation of the handle's
creaking wake Čacko from his stupor. His face is that of a corpse
which grows plump with decay instead of desiccating, like a
man who has drowned.

Emil knew that Čacko's unhappy features should excite pity
in him, but it merely made his hatred more refined. One day I
will kill you, he whispered to himself. The plainness of the vow
tasted cool and clean in his mouth. *One day I will kill you*. He
allowed himself a brief panorama of fantasies – Čacko's
disgusting features becoming more and more livid as he felt the
grip of Emil's hands around his throat; the top of Čacko's head
exploding upwards as a bullet entered his eyeball; white flesh
blossoming outwards from the thin slicing of a knife down his
solid white chest.

Suddenly, Čacko's eyes popped open, as if the virulence of
Emil's thoughts had woken him. Emil dropped his gaze, leaned
over the handle and increased the ardour of his pumping. The
first bucket was now full to overflowing but hidden from
Čacko's sight on the other side of the pump. Emil did not dare
reach down to exchange it with the empty bucket. He would
pump for a while longer in the hope that Čacko might go back
to sleep. A change of movement was always unwise. It prompted
response. It was far safer to keep doing whatever you were
doing, to be tedious to observe.

'Finished yet?' Čacko asked indifferently. He coughed once,
then closed his eyes.

They did two more trips, then Čacko decided that he had had
enough and needed to go and sleep it off somewhere. They

returned the buckets to the store. Čacko stood outside for a
moment or two, yawning and stretching as if he had done a hard
afternoon's work. Emil stood next to him, head bowed. He was
aware that Čacko was staring at him, looking him up and down.

Suddenly, Čacko reached out a hand. Instinctively, Emil
ducked, but instead of striking him, Čacko grabbed him round
the head and pulled him into his chest. With his other hand, he
ruffled the downy stubble on Emil's head. 'Your hair is growing
back soft,' he murmured. Then he pushed him away. 'What shall
we do with you this afternoon, while I take a rest, eh? We'll find
you a seat somewhere, so's you won't go wandering about all
over the place and get yourself into trouble.'

They walked over to the kitchen block, passing a guard who
stood in front of it, round the back, to where there was a small
door in a lean-to adjacent to the main part of the block. 'Go,' said
Čacko cheerily, clapping him on the shoulder. 'Go and join the
mad Hoover salesman, little František. He'll know what to do
with you. Later on we have some building work to do.'

He gave Emil a friendly shove, friendly enough to send him
stumbling headlong towards the door. As Emil pulled it open, he
was assailed by a damp, putrid smell. The stink was so acidic in
his nostrils that his eyes began to water and he blinked as he
mounted the step.

The hut formed a small wooden ante-room, with a door that
led through to the kitchen on the other side. The kitchen door
was ajar and steam bellowed through it, carrying the putrid
smell. There was shouting from inside. Emil was so taken with
disgust that it was a moment before he noticed a small man in
the middle of the room, seated on a stool before a huge pile of
turnips. The small man looked up. He was in prisoner's uniform
but had a yellow armband like a kapo and a shock of thick
brown hair that stood upright on his head like a brush.

Emil gestured towards his head. Unable to think of anything else to say, he said, 'You've kept your hair . . .'

The small man pulled a face. 'We all did to start off with. Then we all didn't. The fuss . . .' While he spoke, he rose from his stool, opened the door to the kitchen and disappeared into the steam.

Emil stood for several minutes. The smell was not so bad once you got used to it. It was warm in the shed; and nobody was beating him. These were reasons to be pleased that he was standing there doing nothing, wondering what to do.

The small man with the shock of hair re-entered and pulled the kitchen door closed behind him. He was still talking. Emil had the impression that he had continued their conversation while he had been out of the room. '. . . myself in a position of authority but sometimes you don't always get to choose, do you?'

He was carrying another stool which he placed next to his own. As Emil sat down, the small man handed him a short blunt knife, picked up another knife from beside his stool, leaned forward and grasped a turnip. Emil copied him.

While they peeled the turnips, the man kept up a ceaseless flow. 'I was the very first prisoner, yes. In other camps you get a tattoo with a number. I should have liked one of those. I would be number 0001. I was the only mistake. The first one, and the only administrative error. I would have been okay if I hadn't been so good at my job. I had sold the last Hoover, you see. My papers were back in my lodgings but I couldn't possibly give them the address because my landlady had been arrested by the Gestapo and had her toes broken one by one so she would tell them where the ammunition was hidden. I'm no fool. It was only the police holding me, on the orders of Brno County Council, they said, but I still wasn't going to tell them I lived there. I thought they'd release me when they went to check with the

lady who bought my Hoover but she was so frightened about
having enough cash to buy it she denied all knowledge, the
prune. Find the Hoover, I told them. Then you'll know I'm
telling the truth. Go back, if she's thrown it down the well then
check the state of her floors. You're not telling *me* she got them
that clean with a broom. Listen, I'm an honest salesman, I don't
take any job unless I believe in it, and I'm telling you, those
machines are a bloody miracle.

'That was back in 1940. It wasn't much fun then. All in one
block, we were over two hundred in the summer. We built your
block, you know, with our bare hands. I'm a sort of intellectual
really. I asked them, couldn't they make me a politico – I didn't
like being an asocial. It was demeaning. Okay they said, if you
insist, but the politicos all get sent to the Reich to work in bomb
factories. I thought better of it. Then this spring they told us they
were closing everything down and it wasn't going to be for
asocials any more, only Gypsies. They asked for volunteers to
stay behind and help run things, sort of prisoners still but a bit
better off, like staff. Any more building barracks? I asked. When
they said no, I said, grand, count me in. Do you know, I was the
only one who volunteered to stay?' He shook his head. 'People
are strange . . .'

While he was speaking, the Hoover salesman had been
casually sticking the dirty turnip peelings up his sleeve. He
performed the action automatically, as if his brain had no idea
what his hands were doing.

Emil had been watching. After a while, he began to copy; peel
a turnip; toss it in the zinc tub between the stools; stuff the
peeling up your sleeve and reach for another turnip. The Hoover
salesman's sleeves were already bulging. When the left sleeve
was full, he transferred the small blunt knife to his other hand so
he could perform the action more easily the other way around.

'Imagination,' he was saying. 'That's what you need. You have to make yourself useful in some way if you want to survive. Of course . . .' he gave Emil a knowing look. 'Some people manage to make themselves useful to other certain people without even realising it. Some people make themselves so useful that they get introduced to other people who might be useful to *them*.'

'What do you mean?' asked Emil. It was the first chance he had had to speak.

The Hoover salesman rose from his stool. 'Excuse me,' he said. 'Must perform a certain duty. It's this soup we make. Drops right through and out the other end – excuse my coarseness, you'll have discovered that for yourself by now.'

When he had gone, Emil put down his blunt knife, allowed his shoulders to sink and closed his eyes. It was wonderful to be sitting down, but who knew what Čacko had in store for him later? He was so tired. Each night, he plunged into unconsciousness on the hard wooden pallet, only to wake an hour later, fretful, unable to rest for the pain in his jaw. The electrical impulses that fired around his mouth were fading, to be replaced with a dull, agonising ache. He got nosebleeds every day. ('Pinch the end of your nose, not the bridge,' Dr Steiner had told him. 'You want it to heal straight, don't you?')

Čacko himself never referred to the injuries he had inflicted, not even to gloat, and Emil's father had only stared at him when he saw him later that day, just stared, his mouth a disbelieving O as he clenched and unclenched his fists. Emil felt as if everyone in the camp knew who he was, now, and knew about how Čacko treated him. He had to walk around each day with the marks of it on his face, advertising his inability to defend himself to anyone who cared to glance at him. He was ashamed to look another man in the eye.

I could cope if only I wasn't so tired all the time, he thought. Even the hunger, I could cope with that. But then I am tired because of the hunger, I suppose. Who would have thought that I would ever look forward to that terrible soup?

He raised his head and lifted a finger to scratch at his arm. The turnip peelings were itchy.

When the Hoover salesman returned, Emil saw that his jacket sleeves were empty. The Hoover salesman resumed his position on his stool and picked up his knife. They began to peel again in silence.

'František,' the mad Hoover salesman said, and Emil looked at him, surprised that he knew his name. The Hoover salesman did not lift his head. 'Cultivate a little eccentricity, František. Lick the dirt off the peelings and spit it out before you eat them. You'll have to chew on the side of your face with a mouth like that. Chew them as slowly as you can, break them down with your saliva before you swallow. Don't share them with anybody, and don't tell a soul. These blunt knives will be taken away from us soon, when they realise there's no point wasting resources peeling the turnips, so make the most of this opportunity. Winter is coming, and however indigestible you think turnip peelings are, you are going to need all your strength when the snows come. It hasn't even started yet.' He sighed. 'Keep your eyes open. Stay quiet. Don't give in to lethargy. Pick fights if you have to. Cultivate a little eccentricity.'

The Hoover salesman had kept his head down throughout this speech, talking softly. 'Ta-da!' he cried suddenly, leaping to his feet. 'My hundredth turnip this afternoon. I've been counting, you know.' He performed a small jig around his stool, then sat down again. 'My best ever performance was seven Hoovers in one week. I bet you don't believe me, do you? Neither did my bosses. I kept sending them urgent telegrams to get more stock to me and do you know what my Regional Operator accused me of doing? He said I was burying them in the woods and stealing money to send the company. I ask you. Can you imagine? In years to come do you seriously think that somebody is going to dig over the copse near Troubky and find *seven Hoovers*? Some people have a problem with reality, that's their problem . . .' As he was talking, he was filling his sleeves with peelings once more.

CHAPTER 15

Anna and Tekla were stitching blankets in their block with a group of eight other Romnis. Eva and Ludmila were on a work detail at the workshop. Autumn was beginning to bite.

They were sitting just inside the open door, where the light was good but they were sheltered from the wind. The Moravian Romnis were on upturned boxes but Anna and Tekla were cross-legged on the floor. Of the many *gadje* habits she could not get used to in this place, Tekla said, the most uncomfortable was sitting down. In the workshop one day, a kapo had insisted they use the benches and the only way Tekla could do it was to squat on her haunches on top of the bench seat.

Anna didn't have a problem with sitting, but she squatted down next to Tekla to keep her company. The Moravian Romnis were laughing at them and shaking their heads.

'They're virtually *gadje*, some of them,' muttered Tekla. 'Do you know some of them don't even speak Romani? Black on the outside, soft and white in the middle.'

The woman sitting nearest them overheard. 'Wanderers!' she said with casual scorn. 'You think you're the only ones!'

'I've run out of thread,' said Anna, holding up her needle, and one of the Moravian Romnis passed the spool down to her.

Anna had just re-threaded her needle when a shadow fell across her work. She looked up.

Two girls were standing in the doorway, new arrivals; sisters, maybe twins. They were the exactly the same height, and they were holding hands. They were standing close together, their shoulders touching, two small women fitting snugly into the doorway like dolls.

Anna peered up at them. The light was behind them and she couldn't see their faces properly. 'Come in then,' she grumbled in Romani, gathering her blanket on to her lap. 'I'm trying to see what I'm doing. Come in and take a proper look around. I can tell you now it won't get any better if you stand in the door staring at it.'

The two girls entered and it was only then that their faces became visible. Anna saw that they were in fact mother and daughter, identical but for the mother's face being several shades darker than the daughter's. They were dressed in skirts and blouses with shawls and headscarves, wooden clogs on their feet. They were still holding hands.

Anna tossed her head. 'You can put your stuff on that bunk there for now,' she said in Czech, 'it's mine. The block Elder will assign you a bunk when she gets back but you'll probably be dumped next to us. Don't help yourself if you know what's good for you. I chose this end when we arrived because I wanted to be close to the door. Stupid. I get no heat from the stove and no light from the lantern. The others had more sense. If you want more warmth you can separate and ask some others down there to share. You might get lucky.'

'We want to stay together,' the daughter said firmly.

A woman sitting on a chair opposite the door whistled to signal the approach of a kapo. Anna lowered her head over her stitching.

The kapo, a Czech woman with a shaved head, stepped into the block and folded her arms. 'You two, take your things off and get clean. Use that there.' She pointed at the zinc tub on the concrete island in the centre of the barrack. The water in it was dirty, left over from that morning's ablutions. The kapo's German was halting and heavily accented. She had been shipped over recently, from Brno prison. Probably a prostitute, Anna thought, a *gadji* whore.

The two women were looking at each other.

Dear God, thought Anna. Where have these two been? Helpless little rabbits: they won't last long.

She mimed removing her blouse to the daughter. The daughter comprehended and, nudging the mother to copy her, began to undress.

The kapo stood in the doorway, rubbing her upper arms with both hands against the chill. 'Headscarves too,' she said in a bored voice, leaning against the doorframe to wait.

Anna bent her head over her sewing, raising it to her face to try and see in the poor light. When she lifted her head again, the mother had undressed and turned to the tub of dirty water. In the dim light, Anna saw that the woman's back was a criss-cross of scars, ridged and lumpy, with the skin so thin in places it showed the speckled red of the flesh beneath. Anna glanced at the kapo and saw that she had seen too. They exchanged a look that transcended the boundary between prisoner and guard.

The daughter saw them looking and said in Czech, defensively, 'When do we get our clothes back?'

'Soon,' the kapo replied hastily, lapsing into Czech herself. 'Wrap yourselves in these blankets for now.'

She handed over two blankets, snatched the clothes from the girl's outstretched arms and left the block.

The mother was still turned away from Anna. Anna motioned towards her with her chin. 'What are your names?' she asked the girl.

'I am Marie Malíková,' the girl replied. 'This is my mother.'

Anna could not take her eyes from the mother's back. The woman was still washing, slowly, unselfconsciously. 'Your father?' she asked.

Marie was drying herself. She stopped and cast her eyes down. 'Where do they put the men?'

'If he arrived with you they'll be shaving and delousing him. The men work ten hours a day breaking rocks. So do we sometimes. The men's block is at the top of the hill. Where have you come from?'

'The workhouse in Brno. We've been there for eight weeks. They took us straight from Orlavá and said we would get sent on to Poland. The old woman they took with us died in the cell and it took them three days to remove the corpse. I think they brought us here because we're appealing against our arrest. My uncle will get us out. He's an important man.' One of the listening Romnis gave a snort of derision. Marie put down the blanket she had been using and unfolded the other.

'Just use one for now. Keep the other dry,' Anna said. 'It will turn cold tonight.'

Marie handed the damp blanket to her mother, waited until she had finished drying herself with it, then took it back and wrapped the dry one around her mother's shoulders. She wrapped herself in the damp one, then gestured for her mother to sit on the concrete island.

Anna wondered if the mother was mute, but as she thought this, the small dark woman lifted her head and said. 'It is only women here, in this block? No husbands?'

Anna looked at her. 'The men are not allowed within metres of this block,' she said evenly. 'If any man tried to come over here, the guards would take him to the *Appell-platz* and beat him to a pulp.'

The small dark woman looked up at her daughter. The daughter nodded.

*

There were over three hundred of them in the women's block now. About twenty had gone mad. The mad ones were herded together in a far corner; but they seemed to feed off one another there and make each other worse. The women nearby complained to the block Elder – a large, unsmiling woman – and she suggested that the mad ones were separated and spread throughout the block. Everyone agreed that this was a good idea but nobody wanted to share a bunk with one of them. They were awake all night. They scratched themselves and kicked and screamed. (Everybody scratched themselves but most still had the self-possession to do it surreptitiously.) So the mad ones stayed together in the darkest corner, young and old. The unfortunates who had bunks beside them cursed and shouted at them in the night and slapped them sometimes, and nobody minded that.

One of the mad ones was a Kalderaška, the only other in the block, apart from Anna's group. Anna tried to talk to her one evening in the Vlach dialect, thinking that maybe she didn't understand Czech Romani. The woman mumbled at her, her eyes glistening in the gloom of her lower bunk, flapping her hand in front of her face as if attempting to bat away some invisible threat.

A woman sitting on an opposite bunk shook her head. 'That one is lost, sister,' she said to Anna. 'She was on my transport. I watched her go mad. Her children are all dead.'

'What happened?' asked Anna. She went and leaned against the bunk. They both watched the mad Kalderaška lying on her bunk, flapping her hands and muttering.

'She was half-mad already. Most of the children were gone. They starved in Transdnistria. The Romanians aren't even building camps, just dumping them in the open and letting them live on grass. Five of her children and her parents and everyone else were dead already, she told me. Her husband is in the Romanian army but she couldn't get word to him – he's on the Eastern front. Somehow, she got all the way up here. She only had one child left, a boy. He was almost dead, anyone could see that.' The woman shook her head again, and sighed. 'We were in the train for three days,' she continued, 'just standing in the station, waiting to leave.' Anna crossed herself. 'They passed some water in but a couple of women at the front got it all. This one's boy was crying for water, getting weaker and weaker and more hoarse . . .'

Anna stared at the woman on the bunk. She seemed insensible of their voices, her gaze rolling crazily.

'She hit him,' the other woman said simply. 'Nobody blamed her. We all just wanted him to shut up. Our children were thirsty too. But this boy was crying and crying and everyone knew he was dying and it was driving us all mad. And eventually she started hitting him. And then his crying changed and he was pleading with her but she carried on hitting him and he died.'

Anna stared at the woman. 'We should kill her,' she said quietly. 'It would be a kindness. Put a blanket over her face.'

The woman shrugged. 'She'll go soon enough. She doesn't eat. I grabbed her by the arm yesterday. Her flesh was like clay. They'll all die, the mad ones. First the mad ones, then the old ones, the children of course, then us. The men will last longest . . .'

Anna returned to her bunk as the kerosene lamp was doused. The kapo slammed the door behind her. There came the deadly thunk and clunking of the lock.

She had just closed her eyes when the Kalderaška at the far end of the block began to scream, a hollow, siren sound. *She was listening to us, after all,* Anna thought. She waited for the noise to fade but it rose in intensity, paused briefly, rose again. The women in the neighbouring bunks began to shout and exclaim: the women next to them shouted back. Eventually, there came thumping and grunting noises. The mad Kalderaška shouted for help, gasping out. The tone of her cries altered. Then there was silence.

Anna heard a small sob, not far away. A soft, 'Oh God . . .'

'Who is it?' she hissed.

'It's me, Marie,' said a tiny voice. 'What's happening?'

'Don't be frightened,' whispered Anna. 'It's the mad woman at the end.'

Tekla was lying between them. 'Shut up you two,' she said in a low voice.

In the morning, there were two corpses in the block: the mad Kalderaška who lay over the edge of her bunk, eyes staring, and another woman at the opposite end of the block. The block Elder merely nodded as they carried out the corpse of the Kalderaška; when she saw the other one, lying on the dirt floor floor between the bunks, she cursed. She bent and examined the woman's neck, then crossed herself.

'Who was *she*?' asked Marie, as they gathered round in a tight crowd. She was pressed against Anna, peering around her arm.

Anna pulled a face and shrugged.

As they queued for their *ersatz* coffee outside the hut, Eva came up to them and said, 'I just heard. That woman they strangled was Murková, the one who got over the fence with her husband and children. They did it while there was all that fuss going on at the other end. That's why no one heard it.'

'The Murkas got caught?' said Anna.

'She got back yesterday. The husband got away but the children were sent back with her. She was attacked by those two from the North, the big ones who always stick together? When the Murka children escaped, their children were beaten because their bunks were next to theirs.'

They all huddled together against the wind. Marie and Líba were standing very close to Anna. Eva elbowed them out of the way, glaring at them.

'Don't be unkind,' Anna said to Eva, distractedly. 'So the children will have no one now. The father won't even know. How come he got away?'

She was filled with an overwhelming desire to see Bobo and Parni. It came and went in waves throughout the day. Most of the time, she tried to quell her longing, knowing that if she didn't she would go as crazy as the Romanian Kalderaška, but it caught her at unexpected moments, like now. She swayed with it. There was pneumonia in the children's block. Two had died of it last week, three the week before.

'Do you have children?' Marie asked Anna, as they all shuffled forward in the queue.

'Three,' Anna said, exhaling carefully. 'My eldest is in the men's block, my two Little Ones . . .' She drew breath before she was able to continue. 'You are lucky, to be with your mother.'

'Yes,' Marie said simply.

Anna looked at Marie, observing her in the morning light. 'Your hair still has some shine to it, Small One, I hope they let you keep it. Your cheeks are still plump.' She gave a half-smile, then brushed Marie's cheek with the back of her hand. 'It is nice for us all to have something pretty to look at in here. We have forgotten so quickly what normal people look like.'

'It won't last,' muttered Tekla, behind them.

Anna turned to her. 'What's wrong with you?' she hissed.

'Stop making such a fuss of that house-dwelling *chava*,' Tekla hissed back. 'It's upsetting Eva and Ludmila. They rely on you.'

'Golden God,' swore Anna under her breath. 'When this war is over the first thing I'm going to do is find you all husbands, get you off my back.'

Tekla collapsed.

Eva and Ludmila shrieked. Other women gathered round in a huddle. Anna knelt beside Tekla and put a hand on her brow. Ludmila had her hands beneath Tekla's head and tried to raise her but Anna pushed her away. 'Leave her,' she said sharply. Tekla's eyes were flickering open and shut. 'She's burning,' Anna said.

'I'm all right,' Tekla mumbled, trying to raise her head. 'Leave me, I'm just hungry, that's all.'

'She had a headache yesterday,' said Eva. 'It was nearly killing her. She was holding her head in her hands.'

'Why didn't anybody tell me?' demanded Anna, and Eva and Ludmila exchanged looks.

Tekla was rising, pushing them all away. 'Leave me alone. Give me some air. I'm strong as an ox.'

Anna lifted her head. The women crowding round them had turned to take their place in the queue. 'Get back in there and make sure we get something to drink,' Anna said to Eva and Ludmila, who did not move.

'We'll do it,' said Marie, turning to her mother and pulling her by the arm.

Tekla scrambled to her own feet, shoving them all away as they tried to assist her. 'I'm perfectly capable of getting my own muck to drink.' She glared at Anna. 'Worry about the children, not us.' Supported by Eva and Ludmila, Tekla turned away. Anna was left standing at the back of the queue, the cold wind in her face making her blink.

They were sent to the workshop for an hour. Then they were sent in a group to dig the vegetable patch. After a piece of bread at lunchtime, which they were allowed to eat squatting by the freshly dug patch, they joined with another group to paint some wooden planks with pitch. A building programme was under way. The camp was going to get bigger.

After a supper of cold soup, there was the brief period before roll-call when it was possible to go and visit the children. Hurrying lightly over to the children's block, Anna suddenly felt it was almost worth this terrible separation for the sheer, pure joy she felt in those few hasty steps towards them. Her heart was thumping with the anxiety of the wait, but her whole body was suffused with a brief, wild euphoria at the thought that in a moment or two she would be holding her children in her arms.

As she opened the door, she saw that the older children must have been kept late at the workshop – there was a little space in the teeming block. Ten or so mothers had got there before her and were holding their little ones or talking to them. A couple of women sat disconsolately by the door – if the older children were not released from the work parties soon then there would be no time to see them before roll-call.

Some of the Little Ones close to the door raised their heads as Anna stepped in, their faces bright with anticipation. A wail announced their collective disappointment. A small boy, not much bigger than Bobo, flung himself against her legs, crying. Anna placed her hand on his head and patted his hair while she scanned the block for her two. Most of the children were sitting on the dirt floor between their bunks. Some were clambering about. A few simply stood and stared at her, their expressions blank. One large girl had her arms about the iron stove, still unlit despite the recent drop in temperature. She was clinging to it with a contented expression. Anna opened her mouth to breathe in. The stink in this block worsened daily. So many of the children wet themselves at night that their wood-chip mattresses were rotting.

Since the escape, an *Aufseherin* had been brought in to take charge of the block, with a team of kapos beneath her. She picked her way over to Anna now and lifted the small boy clinging to her legs. As she turned away, she pointed towards the washroom.

Inside the washroom, there was a small row of children against one wall, standing above tin buckets. Parni was in the corner, wiping Bobo with a rag. He looked round and saw Anna. He pushed Parni away, his face set, and ran the few paces towards his mother, fists clenched purposefully, legs moving quickly and clumsily. He slipped on the wet concrete floor and she had to dive forward to catch him, allowing herself a brief rush of joy as he fell into her arms.

She seated herself swiftly, her back against the wall, raised her knees and lifted her blouse. Bobo's fists clawed at her. She wrapped her arms around him and pulled him in close. Parni came and stood next to her. Normally, she placed an arm around Anna's shoulders while Anna was feeding Bobo, communing silently with them, but this evening, she came near her mother but did not touch her, standing with her head slightly bowed.

It was gloomy inside the washroom – the one small window was dirty and let in no more than a cold promise of light. The children shivered as they stood huddled over their buckets.

It was a moment or two before Anna lifted her head and noticed her daughter's demeanour. Parni was staring into the middle distance, vacantly, her arms wrapped around herself. She was wearing a man's jacket over her sackcloth shift. Her footwraps were filthy.

'Where is your hat?' Anna asked. She had told Parni to wear her woollen hat at all times.

Parni stared into a corner of the room, her face dark.

Anna struggled for a moment to remember the last time she had seen Parni stare like that. It was in Bohemia, last summer, when Parni had kicked over a bowl of milk in her haste to run outside and play with Eva. Anna had slapped her for that. A precious bowl of milk.

'What is it, *shei*?' Anna asked gently. Bobo whimpered on her lap and Anna pulled him closer. His mouth pulled at her greedily. There was nothing but a trickle inside her now but it was enough to keep the boy quiet for a short while.

Anna repeated her question.

Parni did not answer.

With her free hand, Anna took one of Parni's thin arms and pulled her closer. She reached up and pushed her fingers into Parni's tight black curls.

'The hat was itchy,' Parni said. Her voice was always so calm and pure.

'See this hair?' Anna replied. 'Where did you get these curls and knots? No one in our family has ever had such hair. And now, they trap the dirt. I know the hat was itchy, I told you, you have to pick the insects out of it each night before you sleep. You think you don't have insects in your hair?' She peered closely into Parni's face. 'When the war is over, *shei*, I will have to cut this hair of yours, only once I promise. I will cut out all the dirt and the knots, and then we will oil it and comb it and it will grow sleek and shiny, like mine used to be. It will grow back straight. You will be old enough for braids then. I will oil it until it is soft . . .'

'*Dalé* . . .' Parni interrupted. Anna shifted Bobo again and made a soft, noncommittal sound of encouragement.

'*Dalé* . . . when the war is over, will I not be a *filthy gypsy* any more?'

Anna kept her voice soft. 'You will always be a Roma girl, *shei*. Who has been calling you a *gypsy*?'

'We are all *dirty gypsies*. That's why we're here. We're here to be punished for telling lies and stealing all the time and for being a race that God hates, like the Jews. The Jews are even worse, though, because they killed God, in real life, only we just kill him in our hearts. The Germans look like God. They are big and have white eyebrows. We are being tested, and only those of us who have any God in us will ever be allowed out. And to have God in us we have to get rid of the *gypsy* inside ourselves and be decent and sit on chairs and use spoons and our parents are going to burn in Hell because they're too old to use spoons but maybe if some of us Little Ones work very hard and pray very hard God will let us be not-*gypsy* and then it will all have been worth it, our suffering, and we will thank God with all our hearts and we won't mind that our parents have burned in Hell because we will be glad . . .'

She paused to draw breath, then stopped and glanced around fearfully. She leaned towards her mother and whispered.

'Mummy, don't tell them I told you. You're not supposed to know . . .'

Bobo had fallen asleep in Anna's lap. She hoisted him carefully on to her shoulder. He mumbled. She patted his back and stared at her daughter.

'Who has said these things?' she said, but Parni shook her head defiantly, her lips pressed together.

The doorway through to the main barrack darkened and the *Aufseherin* stepped towards Anna with her arms outstretched. 'Come. They have blown the whistle,' she said in German.

Anna rose unsteadily with Bobo on her shoulder.

As the woman lifted him from her, he stirred. Anna suddenly felt tears spring to her eyes. *So short, so short a time. Why can I not hold my son for a few moments more? Wooden God, what reason is there in all this?*

Suddenly, her knees weakened. She collapsed against the wall, her arms angling inwards as she descended like a wounded crane.

'*Mummy!*' hissed Parni, petrified, and Anna realised that Parni thought she was responsible for her mother's collapse, that the small sudden drama might betray what she had told her mother.

Parni's tiny fingers grasped her mother's arm, pinching and pulling. 'Get up,' she hissed urgently. 'You promised. Get up.'

The *Aufseherin* had turned with Bobo, unconcerned by Anna's sudden display of emotion.

'In a moment . . .' Anna found herself able to say to her daughter. 'Just leave me, stay there. In a moment . . .'

Through her misted gaze, she watched the *Aufseherin* leave with her son. She closed her eyes to squeeze the tears on to her cheeks. They stung like acid. Parni still plucked anxiously at her arm. Anna's head swam. *Parni is right*, she thought, *if God is merciful, he will make his people gadje and release us from this Hell.*

With an effort that cost her the last of her strength, she pushed against the wall and stood. She brushed at her cheeks with her hands. On the *Appell-platz*, the whistle shrilled.

Parni was staring up at her. Anna patted her shoulder. She inclined her head. 'It's all right,' she managed to whisper hoarsely. 'I promise I won't tell.'

They left the washroom together. Somewhere at the far end of the barrack, she could hear Bobo. He had woken and realised his mother had left him and was howling in misery. 'Go to your brother quickly,' she said to Parni. Parni nodded obediently and began pushing past the children seated on the floor.

To leave, Anna had to step over a girl lying on the ground and wearing nothing but a blanket. She was white-eyed and staring, making strange gurgling noises and banging her head against the floor. It was only after she had stepped over her that, glancing back, Anna recognised her as the cheerful girl who had taken Parni's hand on the day of their arrival.

It was dark by the end of roll-call. Anna stumbled around the crowds of people on their way back to their blocks, looking for a glimpse of Josef and Emil. Her feet were numb with standing still for so long and she nearly tripped over an elderly man who was bending over one of his clogs. The elderly man pushed at her with a sharp elbow. 'Watch out, sister . . .' he muttered, then said, 'Anna.'

Anna stared at Josef as he stood upright. 'Your hair is *white* . . .' she said, unable to check her incredulity.

Josef ran a hand through his stubble. 'Maybe that's why we're all here . . .' he said. 'They thought they would whiten us.'

Anna grimaced, then felt a rough shove at her shoulder.

'Back to your block!' a guard shouted in her face, before moving on.

'Are you well?' Josef asked as Anna turned. There was no time for her to respond. 'I'm worried about Emil, since that beating . . .' he called after her.

Anna trotted back to her block with the other women. *Thank you, husband*, she thought, *a wonderful thought for me to sleep on. For a moment there, there was one member of my family I was not thinking of. But now that is the lot. Tekla is sick. My Little Ones miserable beyond measure. Now Emil.*

As they settled into their bunks, Anna told Tekla what Josef had said.

Tekla shook her head, coughed impressively, then shook her head again. 'He's a strong boy. The way that guard treats him is making him stronger. He's doing better than any of us. He gets extra food from that brute. You can tell just by looking at him.'

Anna hauled herself up on to her bunk and lay down. 'I don't think Josef meant like that. Not physically.' She tapped her temple. 'It's here, in his head.'

Tekla clambered up next to her, manoeuvring herself awkwardly in the small space. 'He's a strong boy,' she repeated.

'Are you sick?' Anna asked.

'I can't be sick.'

'Are you sick?'

'Shut up your face,' Tekla replied, pulling her blanket over her and wrapping it around. Her tone was matter-of-fact. She added softly, 'We're not in Bohemia now.'

*

Outside, the air held a quietness. The sky was misty-black. In the forest, the trees were still.

A few white flakes began to fall, sparse yet textured, like fragments of feather: the first snows of winter, tumbling in the dark.

CHAPTER 16

Čacko and another guard were sitting on a log outside the staff hut drinking coffee from tin mugs. Čacko was in expansive mood.

Emil was standing a few feet away, awaiting orders. Čacko circled a fat hand at him saying, 'Come, my little friend, it's no good today, I'm finished.' He held out his tin cup to Emil. In the bottom was a small amount of grainy liquid, cold. Emil lifted it to his lips hopefully but it tasted just like the *ersatz*. He drank it anyway. It was a long time since his dawn drink and he had eaten his bread ration the night before.

'I wouldn't mind,' Čacko was saying to the other guard, 'but every single man in my unit was at it. That bastard only picked on me because he hated me. I tell you, if I ever see that Captain . . .' he raised his fist and shook it in a slow, threatening manner.

'We all say that . . .' the other guard replied sceptically. 'It's easy to say . . .'

Čacko stood. 'Have you seen my boy?' he said, gesturing towards Emil. 'He does tricks. Here, boy!' Čacko patted the top of his thigh.

Emil approached reluctantly. Čacko pushed his hand into his trouser pocket and withdrew a small, hard biscuit, which he handed to Emil. 'Here, take it. They gave us each a box, last week.'

Emil took the biscuit and lifted it to his mouth, nibbling cautiously at first. It was as dry as sawdust. He swallowed with difficulty.

'What do you say?' Čacko asked in a sing-song voice.

'Thank you,' said Emil.

Čacko's hand flew from nowhere. His open palm cracked against Emil's cheek. 'What do you say to *that*?' he said.

'Thank you,' said Emil, keeping his face blank.

The other guard made a small noise of amusement, and shook his head.

Čacko nodded. 'I like to look after my boy.' He hitched his trousers. 'Keep an eye on him for me.' He walked over to the bushes behind the staff hut to relieve himself.

While he was gone, Emil became aware that the other guard was staring at him.

'Boy,' he said.

Emil glanced at him, then mumbled, 'Yes, sir . . .'

'Tell me, is it true what they say about *gypsy* girls . . . ? Eh?' The guard was grinning coldly. He wiggled his bottom from side to side. 'Eh?'

Emil dropped his gaze and stared at the patch of ground immediately in front of him. The top layer of mud was frozen. Soon, the ground would be hard as rock.

'I wouldn't know, sir' he replied.

The guard threw back his head and laughed alarmingly loudly. 'No, I suppose you wouldn't.' He rose from the log. 'Čacko's *Piepel*.'

Čacko was returning to them, buttoning his uniform trousers with apparent difficulty. He stopped and fiddled, grimaced, succeeded, then adjusted his balls. 'God, it's too cold to stand around here,' he was muttering. 'Come on, boy, I have a job for you. Later, you can feed the pigs, as your reward.'

'Send him with one of the girls,' said the other guard, clapping Čacko on the shoulder. 'It would do him good. Pick him a nice plump one, eh, if you can find one.'

'He'll need warming up all right,' said Čacko humourlessly. 'A little warm pussy is what he'll need . . .'

They crossed the camp, towards the infirmary. Beyond the *Appell-platz*, four teams of prisoners were at work constructing two new blocks, a small one and a large one. The large block was ready-made, bought from Brno Land Office. It was up already and six men were on its roof laying tar paper. Emil scanned the men for sight of his father. Some work details were still being sent to the quarries but he had hoped his father would be allowed to stay in the camp. His cough was worsening. His legs were sticks.

'You *gypsies* need more room, apparently,' Čacko said over his shoulder, as Emil followed. 'You're all giving each other diseases. That doctor is jumping up and down. You know what Jews are like.'

There was no sign of Josef amongst the men that Emil could see – but perhaps he was out of sight, helping with the smaller block.

When they reached the infirmary, they went behind it, to where the mortuary wagons stood. There were plans to erect another hut as a proper mortuary but for the time being they were using three wagons confiscated from incoming families.

'Wait here,' said Čacko, and disappeared.

An icy wind had been blowing all morning. Emil went and stood between two of the wagons for shelter, crossed his arms and tucked his hands into his armpits. He began jumping gently on the spot to try and keep warm.

The wagons were cheap, canvas-roofed ones: shameful old wagons, thought Emil, glancing at them, remembering their beautiful carved home from the days before the war. It was unbelievable the way some Roma lived. Had they lost their pride? Some of those people were better off in a camp, he thought. The roof on the wagon to his left had not been tied down properly and in the cold wind the corner of it rose and danced. Each time it lifted, Emil glimpsed the white protruding hand of one of the corpses.

Tired of jumping, he began to perform a small jig, hopping from foot to foot and singing a ditty. 'Yugga-dugga, yugga-dugga, soft-white-hand! Yugga-dugga, yugga-dugga, cold white hand! Hand! Hand! Cold white hand! I love coffee! I love stew!' He turned round in a circle as he danced and sang softly to the corpses. 'Yugga-dugga, yugga-dugga. I love stew!'

As he completed his turn, he gave a small cry and stumbled backwards.

A girl was standing between the wagons, staring at him. She was very small, with a steady, penetrating gaze. Her clothes were clean and her hair unbraided but tied neatly beneath a headscarf. She was gazing at him in disbelief.

He stood still, panting. He raised his face to the sky, squeezed his eyes tight shut and bit his lip.

'I like stew as well,' said the girl. 'But I prefer bread to dumplings. Dumplings take too long to cook. Are you Emil Růžička?'

'Depends who's cooking them. Yes. Who are you?'

She glanced around. 'I was told you would be with a guard.'

Emil shrugged. 'He'll be back.'

The girl's hands were beneath her shawl. 'Your mother sent me.' She stepped forward quickly and pressed a small, rotten potato into his hand. Emil could feel its pitted surface as his fingers closed around it.

'Thank you,' he said.

'So!' Čacko was returning with the infirmary kapo. 'You've been managing without me, I see.'

The girl bowed her head and turned away. Čacko grabbed her by the shoulder. 'Don't be in such a hurry, little one. We need more hands here.'

'I am sorting clogs in the workshop, sir,' the girl replied quietly.

'Koreff,' Čacko said to the kapo. 'Go over to the workshop and tell them I'm keeping the girl, then get two men and tell them to come here. These two can start the first wagon.' As Koreff turned, Čacko ordered, 'Get the sheeting first.'

The girl made no attempt to hide her dismay. Instead of spending the morning sitting in the workshop with the other women, she would now be out in the cold. The expression on her tiny face was sour.

Čacko had noticed. He reached out, grabbed her chin and brought her face near to his, an action which pulled her on to tip-toe and forced her to clutch one of his arms for balance. 'Cheer up, my dove,' he said lightly, 'just think how nice it will be for František here to have company.' Her face was so small that his hand could reach from ear to ear, her expression distorted by his grip. With his free hand, he clutched at one of her buttocks and squeezed. She hung suspended between the large hand grasping her face and the large hand clutching her bottom.

Emil looked at the ground, ashamed. The girl was meeting Čacko's gaze. He would not like that. Emil waited for the inevitable thump and cry. Čacko liked beating girls.

When Emil looked up, Čacko had dropped her, and turned to help the kapo who was dragging a huge roll of stiff cloth towards them. Emil stared at the girl, who was carefully brushing down her skirt. She looked up at him and gave him a cool, defiant gaze.

'Pull this out!' Čacko called to them.

They bent to tug at the fat roll. Sheets of cloth flopped open on to the ground. Čacko removed his hat to scratch his head. 'I think we need to do one at a time, package them up, put them in a pile. They'll bring a cart. If they'd left the wheels on the wagons we wouldn't have this problem. You.' He nodded at Emil, indicating with a jerk of his head that he should climb up into one of the wagons.

The corpses had been piled close to the entrance, so once Emil had hauled himself up, he had to push his feet beneath a child's leg before he could stand, holding the wagon beams above him for support. His eyes adjusted to the gloom.

The corpses in the first wagon were those of children, their flesh creamy-white, with bluish-purple patches here and there. They had been stripped naked and placed in rows. The first row had been placed neatly before rigor mortis had set in, their legs straight, arms by their sides. Since then, others had been thrown in anyhow and lay in distorted attitudes as if they were attempting to rise from the pile.

Emil reached out and pushed at one upraised arm. The skin still had a slight pliancy, like clay, but the arm was frozen stiff. Emil stepped carefully over the dead children so that he could

make his way to the back of the wagon to see what was there. It
was dark and empty.

Although he was sheltered from the wind, the interior of the
wagon felt colder than the outside – the corpses seemed to
radiate a chill in the same way that a living body gave out
warmth. The canvas roof trapped the cold. He picked his way
forward again and called out to Čacko. 'It would be easier if we
took the roof off, then I could see what I'm doing.'

'Leave it on,' Čacko called back nonchalantly.

The first corpse that Emil passed out was that of a newborn
baby, light as a twig. He passed it down to the girl.

The girl laid the baby's corpse, carefully, on top of the pile of
cloth. She closed her eyes briefly, then began to fold the top cloth
over the child. The sheets of cloth were intended for adult
corpses and far too large. Once she had folded, she had to roll the
wrapped corpse over and over to use up the excess. Čacko was
holding a roll of twine which he was unravelling into long
strings and cutting with his penknife, letting the lengths drop for
the girl to tie the bundle.

He glanced up at Emil. 'Stay there. She can manage.'

The kapo returned with two male prisoners as Emil was
handing down the next corpse, the one with its arms frozen
uplifted – a girl of three or four. They stopped and stared when
they saw what Emil and the others were doing.

Čacko glanced over at them. 'Start unloading that one,' he
ordered, indicating the second wagon. 'Pile them up next to the
sheets then we'll wrap them one by one.'

When they had finished, there was a pyramid of bundles
wrapped in cloth tied with string. They stood around silently.
Even Čacko had become morose. 'This is the last lot for Černovice,
you know,' he said, to no one in particular. 'The villagers won't

have any more. The whole damn cemetery is full of *gypsies*. We'll have to dig our own holes in the woods from now on.'

*

The pigs were housed in pens in a separate enclosure a short distance from the main part of the camp, within the perimeter fence but with an additional, securely guarded fence and a patch of no man's land overlooked by two sentry towers. Feeding the pigs was considered a privilege because of the possibility of picking titbits from the swill. On the three occasions Emil had done the job, the slop had been rotten, completely liquid, and he had been observed by a sentry every step of the way.

The girl was still with him. Čacko had sent them off together with two buckets each. The guard let them through the gate and they began to walk slowly across the no man's land. The buckets were heavy and the girl could scarcely manage hers. Emil went slowly so she could keep up. As they walked, he let out a long sigh at the pleasure of their momentary release. He glanced at the girl and she gave a small half smile, without opening her mouth. They walked in silence for a few paces.

Eventually, Emil said, 'When Čacko had hold of you, I thought he would beat you.'

'Me too,' she said simply.

'You were stupid to stare at him like that,' said Emil.

The girl did not respond.

'Weren't you frightened of him?' Emil asked.

The girl shrugged.

A flight of birds passed overhead. They both stopped and gazed at them, resting their buckets on the ground.

'You don't say much, do you?' Emil said.

The girl shrugged again.

They walked. The cold wind pulled strands of hair from the girl's headscarf. They fluttered across her face. She kept having to stop, put down the buckets, pull the strands out of her eyes and tuck them back into the scarf.

Emil glanced sideways at her, not wanting to stare too obviously. She was thin but her skin was still unblemished. Most of the women and children had sores on their faces now. She's a bit high and mighty, he thought.

'There's no point in being afraid,' she said suddenly, as they were walking. 'If you are afraid it makes a man like that enjoy it. It makes it worse. It's best just to seem bored if you can. Then they get bored too.'

Emil gave a sardonic snort. 'You don't need to tell me, girl. That animal beats me every day. I know just how much he enjoys it.'

She fell silent again.

'What is your name?' Emil asked.

'Marie Malíková,' she replied shortly.

'And your father?' There was a Jan Malík in their block, a new arrival, that must be him. He was a dark-skinned, unsmiling man who didn't talk to anyone.

For the first time, the girl smiled, showing a perfect row of tiny white teeth. 'You travelling men . . .' she said. 'My father? My grandfather? Their trade? My great-grandmother's maiden name? Just because you're all related to one another.'

'How else do you get the shape of somebody?'

She shook her head, still smiling.

'No, tell me, what am I supposed know, then?'

She stopped and put down the buckets again, looking upwards, sighing. 'How big and white the sky is today. Perhaps it always is. I don't normally get a chance to look.'

Emil stopped and stared upwards too.

'It stretches so far,' she continued. 'I've always thought that, even when I was little. And I had never even left our settlement. I've only ever lived in two places, there and here.'

They stood in silence for a minute.

'In Bohemia,' Emil said eventually, 'they have cherry orchards that stretch as far as you can see. There are so many cherries, at harvest time they fill whole trains with them. One winter we helped carve blocks of ice out of the frozen river, taking a chunk of river and storing it in the ice-house. We rolled it over logs. The horses' flanks ran sweat. My job was to wipe them as they pulled forward so the sweat would not freeze. Springtime is the best. We were in Moravia or Slovakia normally, but once we were staying at the orchards the whole winter, right through to the harvest. The spring was wonderful. I was about ten. You know how the sky looks at sunset sometimes? Pink and soft. The blossom on the trees was like a thousand thousand pieces of that sky. I saw a white horse once, running through the blossom.'

Marie looked at him. 'A ghost?'

It was his turn to shrug.

Emil looked back at the camp. One of the grey coils of barbed wire over the gate was loose and sagging. In the watchtower, a sentry would be observing them. If they stood talking for too long, he might report back to Čacko.

'Let's feed the pigs,' he said.

As they approached the pens, the pigs galloped towards them and stuck their snouts sideways through the gaps between the wooden slats, snorting with excitement, saliva dropping from their mouths in cloudy rivulets.

'They haven't built troughs,' said Marie.

'There's one here in the corner,' said Emil, emptying the first bucket. 'We do the buckets one by one.' The pigs crowded into the corner, scrambling and mounting each other, shoving and biting.

Marie handed her buckets to Emil, in deference to his superior experience at this task. While he poured the swill, she pointed at the nearest pig, a huge sow with black patches. 'Wouldn't you like to carve a schnitzel out of that one?' she said, smiling again. 'I had a schnitzel once, at a wedding. My father made my mother stay at home but he took me. He let me dance. I didn't know how to dance but I watched the women and made it up. I flapped my hands. The men all gathered round and laughed. The food was just for the men but at the end of the day when they were all drunk one of the women took me aside, round the back to where the women were cooking at a great long row of fires. I watched her carve this slice from a carcass. It was so thin you could see through it. She fried it for me in butter and lemon juice. I squatted on my heels to watch. I was so close to the fire it singed my eyebrows.' She was smiling at the memory. 'It was the best thing I have ever, *ever* tasted in my whole life . . .'

She stopped, a dream-like smile on her features. Emil wanted her to continue. If I could hear about a good thing every day, he thought, a good thing like that schnitzel, I would survive okay.

'Why couldn't your mother go to the wedding?'

Marie's smile froze.

Emil bit his lip. He turned back to the pigs.

Marie watched him while he emptied the buckets over the side of the pen, one by one. The pigs were in a frenzy. Their snorting would be audible back at the camp.

Suddenly she laughed. 'I ate a bit of the pig, and then a little dog ate a bit of me! I hope I was as tasty as the pig!'

Emil looked at her.

She shook her head. 'I'm not used to talking so much. At home. . .' Her expression darkened again.

'Tell me,' he pleaded. Her sudden silences were terrible. 'I told you about the white horse and the cherry blossom.'

'I told you about the schnitzel.'

'You haven't finished. Tell me about the dog. It bit you? On the way home?'

Somebody had left a rake next to the pen. He picked it up, leaned over the fence and began pulling over the pigs' filthy wet straw. A stench arose – but if the sentry was still watching them, it would at least look like they were doing something.

'It was the next week. There was diptheria in the district. We all had to go to a *gadjo* doctor who lived in a big stone house, all the children in the settlement. Nobody wanted to go but the Town Council summoned my Uncle Karel and the Elders and said if we didn't go we would be taken away and put in orphanages. The doctor had a little dog, a dachshund, it was famous in the town for being the fattest little dog that anyone had ever seen. The doctor's maid used to take him for walks. It took her forever to go up the street and back because the dog was so fat it could hardly walk. He was a snappy little thing. The boys used to make jokes about what they would like to do to that dachshund.'

The pigs had finished the swill and were snuffling disconsolately around the straw. Emil tapped at them absent-mindedly with the rake.

'We all had to line up outside the door and go in one by one. As the others came out they had cloths over their mouths and some of them were crying. They couldn't tell us what the doctor had done to them. I was at the very end of the line and by the time it got to my turn my knees were knocking together. When I went in, the doctor smiled at me. They put me in a big leather chair that leaned back and the nurse put a cloth over my chest. The doctor said. "I'm telling you heathen *gypsy* children because I know you didn't want to come. This is very important. Every year we lose some of you and you are all very precious. You all belong to Christ. Do you understand?" I nodded, but I was shaking.

'The nurse opened my mouth and the doctor reached in with a scalpel. He cut my tonsils off, then the nurse levered me upright and told me to spit them into a metal dish. My mouth was full of blood. As I spat into the dish, I saw that it was full of blood already and all the other children's tonsils were swimming around in the blood. "You're the last?" the doctor asked as the nurse wiped my chin. I nodded but I couldn't speak because my mouth was full of blood and I was in agony.'

Emil had stopped raking the straw and was staring at her.

'The doctor nodded to the nurse and the nurse put the metal dish down in the corner of the room. Then I saw that the dachshund was sitting at the doctor's feet. The doctor said, "Okay, Mr Tutti," and the dachshund ran over to the dish and began lapping up the tonsils.' She stopped and looked over at Emil.

Emil could see small spots before his eyes. 'You're making this up,' he said weakly.

She shook her head, laughing. 'I'm not, I promise,' she said. 'It was only later that I thought how funny it was. At the time, I was just relieved.'

Unable to speak, Emil gave a questioning frown.

'It meant they couldn't count the tonsils,' Marie said, looking down and brushing casually at her skirt. 'I was so relieved. I thought I might be in trouble. When my mouth filled up with blood I gagged. I'm sure I swallowed one.'

As they walked back to the camp, the empty swill buckets bumping against their legs, Emil said, 'Marie Malíková, next time you tell me how to deal with a beating, you can be sure I will listen.'

CHAPTER 17

At the beginning of December, it was announced that a number of prisoners would be released from the camp and transferred to a sanatorium in Northern Moravia. Priority would be given to the sick and the elderly, they were told, although other prisoners were free to apply to the camp authorities. The procedure for application was not explained.

It was the first large-scale release since they had arrived in August. For four mornings, Anna queued with a crowd of other women outside the camp administration offices to try and get Bobo and Parni on to the transport. Bobo's eyes were weeping and sticky – half the children in the block seemed to have infected eyes now – and Parni was dull and listless; a sanatorium? What did it mean? Whatever it was, it had to be better than the camp. For four mornings, the women were told to come back the next day, then they were informed that no children would be going this time – sick and elderly adults only. Maybe there would be a transport for the children in January. Anna was disappointed but not downcast. If they were starting to take the sick and elderly somewhere better then it meant that someone out there had realised how badly they were being treated. Things would gradually improve from now on, surely.

She joined Marie and her mother at the workshop. Tekla had been admitted to the infirmary and Eva and Ludmila were on a work detail.

'Any luck?' Marie asked as Anna sat down on the bench, nodding to the kapo, who registered her late arrival with a slow blink.

Anna shook her head. 'They're not sending children this time. God willing, they will on the next.'

The kapo raised her head briefly and glanced at Anna, then returned to nursing her tin mug.

Anna lowered her voice. 'How is my son?'

'I saw him this morning, crossing the yard. He was with that man, so I couldn't speak to him, but he glanced back at me and nodded when that man wasn't looking.'

Anna nodded. Marie was her conduit to Emil now, his guardian angel. She, Anna, had sent her, to look over him. She could not bake him bread or stitch a waistcoat for him, but she had found a girl to lighten his thoughts. This much she had been able to do. She glanced past Marie at Líba. The mother never spoke, but she seemed grateful to Anna, grateful that they both could shelter under her wing. Tekla had taken a dislike to Marie, and Eva and Ludmila had followed suit. Such things should hardly matter when they were cold and hungry all day, every day, and most of the time they didn't, but when they did, they mattered very much.

Marie seemed so small and self-possessed, so accepting of what was happening to them. It is hard not to enjoy someone who doesn't need me, Anna thought, when all around I am surrounded by need. She doesn't know it, this little thing, but she gives me strength, just by looking and sounding normal. The world is not quite mad, not yet.

After the workshop, they were sent back to the block. The block Elder brought some dark, stale loaves over and divided them under everybody's watchful gaze. There was something called salad, in addition, some stems of white cabbage floating in a tub of acidic vinegar. It stung the roof of the mouth, but it made a change from bread alone. Things are looking up, Anna thought. From the far end of the block, there were discontented murmurings while they ate. A group of old women, including Pavliná Franzová, had been in the block all morning, sewing, but they had not been allowed cabbage with their bread because they were not officially part of the work detail. Anna shook her head and pulled a face at Pavliná, trying to convince her that she wouldn't have wanted the cabbage anyway. 'Only those with teeth get this stuff, for your own good!' the block Elder called to the Old Ones.

They had just finished eating, when the door to the block opened and a few minuscule snowflakes danced in on a flurry of cold air. A woman kapo followed. They all looked at her. The kapo glanced around the block without looking directly at any of them. 'Růžičková,' she said.

There was a small snort of derision. A third of the families in the camp used the name Růžička on their papers. It was absurd to call that name and expect a response.

'Anna,' the kapo snapped, 'registered in Bohemia, three children, František, Lidia and Josef.'

Emil, Parni, Bobo. Oh God.

'It is me,' said Anna, staring at the kapo.

The woman at least had the grace to drop her gaze, and Anna remembered that later. She had looked at the floor. 'Your daughter died this morning,' she said. 'Lidia Růžičková. She died. They told me to tell you.'

There was silence in the block. Several of the women had risen to their feet and stood observing Anna, who remained seated, her hands gripping the edge of her bunk, looking down at the floor.

Silence washed around the small group, like clear water. Nobody moved. The kapo turned and left. The block Elder gave a heavy sigh.

Eventually, the stillness was broken by a small, snivelling sound. At the far end of the aisle, Pavlína Franzová was sitting on the central concrete block, her face crumpled and her mouth a downturned semi-circle of grief. Tears were streaming down, rivers in the deep valleys of age on her brown features. She lifted her hands, once, helplessly, then let them drop into her lap.

Anna raised her head, then in one fluid movement rose from her bunk and crossed the block – the women fell back to allow her through. When she reached Pavlína, Anna reached out both her hands to grab fistfuls of the old lady's ragged shawl and lift her bodily from where she was sitting. She pulled Pavlína towards her until their noses were only two or three centimetres apart.

'Old woman . . .' Anna said, her voice calm, loud as a ringing bell. 'Why are you still alive? Why do you, who add nothing to the world, continue to breathe and walk and eat and shit, while my perfect girl is cold and still? Why are you still alive?'

She released Pavliná from her grasp and the old woman dropped on to her seat. Anna turned and strode from the block.

Outside, she fell on to her knees and cried out, repeatedly, 'Aieee . . .'

The others inside the barrack would hear but know better than to venture outside to comfort her. The men at work around the camp would hear, and lift their heads to glance at each other, recognising the sound. Josef was out at the quarries, so he would not hear. He would be told when the party returned to camp.

When Anna had finished, she rose. Her head swam. She leaned dizzily against the wooden wall of the block with the heels of her hands pressed against her temples. Another kapo passed and went into the block without saying anything to her. There were certain kapos who knew when to ignore prisoners.

Anna pushed herself upright, closed her eyes tightly and wrapped her arms around her body. Her need to hold Parni was excruciating, a deep physical craving. She remembered how she had held her once when she had fallen and cut open both knees, at the age of two or three. She had scolded and washed her first, of course, but Parni had been frightened by the sight of her own blood and inconsolable. Anna had knelt before her and taken her in her arms, and remembered how bony and strong that little body had seemed – at once fragile and invulnerable, as hard as a hazelnut and delicate as a baby bird. Children could do that, be both immortal and fleeting. It was a trick.

She had to hold Parni. She ran across the camp to the children's block. At the door, the *Aufseherin* was ladling out bowls of farina. The children were gathered round the pot, wriggling and crying. Bobo would be amongst them. Anna peered down the barrack but she could see no small bodies laid out, no rises beneath a blanket.

She turned, fleeing past the new barracks to the far corner of the camp and the infirmary.

The infirmary area had been fenced off last week, just after two women had been transported to Brno Hospital. No one knew why. The measure had caused alarm. People who went into the infirmary did not seem to be getting out any more. Tekla was still in there.

A guard stood at the gate. Behind the block, Anna could see the side of one of the mortuary wagons. Her daughter would be there, lying naked and alone amongst a heap of frozen corpses.

Anna stopped in front of the guard, exhaling huge gulps of breath that condensed on the freezing air. Her throat hurt. She struggled for words. 'My daughter . . .' she said, lifting an arm and pointing to the wagons. 'My child . . .'

The guard looked at her calmly. 'No one allowed in,' he replied.

'But . . .' Anna lifted a hand to her forehead, where the sweat was rapidly freezing on her skin. She should have brought something to bribe the guard. If it had been a kapo, she would have known what to say, but she had hardly dealt with the guards. She didn't know which ones were pliable. She tried to recall seeing this one before, to work out the measure of him. It was just a matter of saying the right thing, of persuading him. She had spent her whole life wheedling things out of the *gadje*. Her powers would not desert her now.

'My daughter died, suddenly,' she managed to pronounce, taking a deep breath and opening her eyes wide so that she could gaze appealingly into the man's face. He seemed a kindly young man, not much older than Emil. He had green eyes. Her daughter was waiting for her, naked and cold.

The guard looked back, his face relaxed and open. 'Sorry,' he said pleasantly. 'Nobody allowed in or out. New orders.'

She saw that any attempt at persuasion would be futile, and it was then she lost her reason.

The kindly young guard had to punch her twice to knock her down. She bit the back of his hand and drew blood. Even after he had kicked her three times, on the ground, he still had to summon another two guards to help him carry her back to the women's block.

*

When Emil told his father that Parni was dead, that evening in the block, after roll-call, Josef stared at the floor for a long time. A huge beetle was scurrying amongst the dirt, skittering this way and that.

Josef was sitting on the edge of their upper bunk, shoulders bent, his stick-legs swinging idly, the rough wooden clogs half-hanging from his bony feet. He coughed, then said, 'My lungs are worse, and I was sweating today. But I've also been getting these terrible headaches. It's something quite new. And my arms and legs feel puffy. I think I will go to the infirmary tomorrow.'

*

The list for those to be transported was called out at roll-call at the end of the week. It seemed to be the old, rather than the sick. Pavliná Franzová's name was on the list.

Back in the block, as they prepared for night, Anna pushed her way down to Pavliná's bunk. 'So, Pavliná,' she said simply, 'you are getting out of here.'

Pavliná raised her head. Her expression was pleased but sly.

'Yes,' she said simply, and turned back to arranging her blanket.

Anna looked round to the women who were sitting on the bunks either side of Pavliná's. She gave them a hard stare. They glanced back, then jumped down from their bunks and moved away. By the time Pavliná Franzová turned back from her bed, she and Anna were alone.

Anna stepped up to her. The old woman barely reached her chest.

'You will go to the Commandant tomorrow,' Anna said quietly and simply, 'and you will plead with him, as if your life depended on it. You will tell him that Emil must be allowed to accompany you on the transport. You cannot manage without him. He is a good boy. He will help with the other old and sick people and when you get to the sanatorium he will become an orderly. You will refuse to leave the Commandant's presence until this is granted. You will tell him Emil is your only child.'

Pavliná Franzová's eyes widened. 'Anna Růžičková, I cannot say that. They will know I am lying. They have records.' She began to wring her hands. The thought of even speaking to someone as godlike as the Camp Commandant was clearly having a shuddering effect.

'Tell them the records are wrong,' Anna said. 'Tell them when we were picked up we said Emil was a Růžička because you thought he would be safer in a big family. Tell them whatever you can think of to tell them.'

'You don't understand,' Pavliná's voice became a harsh squeak. 'These Czech police, they answer to the *Germans*. They may be running things here but it's the Germans giving the orders. You don't simply, you can't . . .'

'You can. If the Germans come to escort the transport then all the better. You are fluent. You know how to speak to them. It gets things done. I've seen it.'

'No, no, you can't tell a German their records are wrong. They have the identity papers. All they have to do is check. Whatever is written down is written down. I could plead until the moon drops out of the sky . . .'

Anna grabbed Pavliná by the shoulders. If she had to frighten a weak old women to save Emil, she would do it. 'You will go,' she said, each word calm and clear. 'You will go and do this thing. My daughter died alone, locked inside a stinking *gadje* prison hut. She gasped out. No one heard her. She was trapped. My Bobo will be next. Josef is ill already. Tekla. Who knows which of us will live or die? But I can save one, and I *will save him*. Emil will be on that transport with you. If he is not, I tell you, you will suffer the same fate as my daughter. You will die, trapped in a room, suffocating. Your ghost will wander forever amongst the *gadje*. Do you understand me, old woman? You will die *trapped*.'

She let go of Pavliná and pushed her way back to her bunk. Behind her, the other women returned silently to theirs. Pavliná was superstitious and terrified of curses. Anna knew she had frightened the life out of her, and she knew that it had been in vain. Pavliná could no more convince the Commandant to change his mind than she could turn water into wine. Even if she tried, she would fail, and Anna doubted very much whether she would try.

The night before the transport was due to take place, an announcement was made, at roll-call. The following men were to line up at the gates the next morning, by the trucks: six names were called out. Emil was on the list, and Jan Malík, Marie's father.

Anna looked for Emil and Josef as they were dismissed but couldn't find them in the dark. She was forced to trot back to the women's block for lock-up, along with the others. In the crowded barrack, she forced her way to the back but Pavliná's bunk was empty and her blanket gone. The block Elder was pushing around instructing everyone that nobody was to sleep in the vacated bunks. They would be allocated the next day. 'Where are the women for the transport?' Anna asked the Elder.

'They're in the new block for the night,' the woman said shortly, 'being discharged. They have to do the paperwork and check identities and all those *gadje* things that *gadje* do.'

'Why did they call out those men's names at roll-call?'

The woman shrugged. 'How should I know?'

After lights out, in the pitch dark, there was time for a whispered conversation with Marie.

'Marie, why was your father's name called?'

'I don't know.'

'Does he have money, could he have bribed someone?'

'No, he has nothing in here, unless my uncle is trying to get him out.'

'The other men, you know of them?'

'No.'

'I do.' It was Líba, Marie's mother.

'Who?' Anna was surprised to hear the woman speak.

'The other Růžička, not your son. My husband fought him, at the quarry. I'm not sure, but I think the others might have joined in. Two of them are in and out of the punishment block the whole time.'

It didn't make sense. Why would trouble-makers be rewarded with a transport out of here? Afraid to talk further, Anna lay in the dark, listening to the scratching noise to her left. It was Ludmila, who had taken to picking bits of wood from the barrack wall at night, to chew on while she tried to sleep.

*

Dawn was breaking as Emil and the other men crossed the deserted *Appell-platz*. It was so cold that his toes began to freeze as they walked. His eyes watered.

It was the first time Emil had had the opportunity to speak to Marie's father, but the man was taciturn, his face closed. *Hey, brother, I've been talking with your daughter.* On the outside, such presumption would have earned a beating. Perhaps Jan Malík knew already. Emil had had nothing but black looks from him. But everyone got those. That was how Malík got in that fight at the quarry. Emil had missed it. It had been something, they said. Jan Malík and three others.

They lined up as instructed, by the trucks, while the Old Ones shuffled over from the new block, each with a bundle. Pavliná was towards the front of the queue. She did not meet Emil's gaze. Dr Steiner and the Commandant were waiting at the back of the first truck, and as the line approached, each old man or woman came forward to be examined.

One of the men next to Emil said to his companion. 'We're here to take the place of anyone who isn't fit, you'll see.'

Emil turned to speak to him, to ask, 'But why us?' At that moment, he felt a rough hand on his neck and was pulled backwards, out of the line, tumbling to the ground.

'Not you, my boy!' boomed a familiar voice. Emil was on all fours on the frozen mud. The ice burnt the palms of his hands. Čacko placed a boot on his backside and gave a shove that sent him sprawling face down on the freezing ground. 'On your feet!' Čacko laughed. 'You're going nowhere!'

Emil lay sprawled on the ice and closed his eyes, allowing himself a moment of pure, cool despair. He had been first in the line. If just one of the old people turned out to be too sick to travel, then he would have got on the truck. *That man is the Devil, O Beng himself, crouched on my back.*

Čacko lifted him with one hand and set him on his feet, then brushed down the front of his uniform. 'Don't look so despondent, boy. You could've gone, given your behaviour, but

I explained to the Commandant, we need you!' He shoved at Emil's shoulder with his hand. 'Go to the hut and get your drink, then come back and wait for me here.'

When Emil returned from the hut, the process of loading up was almost complete. Two of the old people had been declared unfit and sent to the infirmary: there were only three men left in the line, Jan Malík amongst them.

Emil stood with his shoulders hunched while the last of the Old Ones was helped up over the tailgate. Pavliná Franzová had already been swallowed by the truck. Emil was glad. He could not have watched her climb up without giving her the Evil Eye and his father always said that the Evil Eye came back to the sender, in the end.

The last of the Old Ones, a skinny Ancient with a gummy smile, was given the nod by Dr Steiner and passed to two waiting guards who lifted him up bodily. As the doctor turned from the trucks, he saw Emil waiting and gave him a long, sad look.

The Commandant was holding a ledger, open in his hands. He made a final mark on it, then slammed it shut with a satisfied sigh. The other guards turned away. The trucks' engines ground into life.

Jan Malík and the others were dismissed, but Emil had to stand waiting while Čacko chatted to two other guards, standing in a confidential huddle a few metres away, until they were called to help open the gates.

It was full light now, another white and freezing morning; above, a solid sky. A bitter wind blew the front of Emil's uniform jacket flat against his chest. The cold made his upper jaw ache, above his damaged teeth. He bit at his lip in misery, shoulders still hunched and hands dug deep into his pockets. *I want to die*, he thought, as he watched the trucks trundle and bump from the camp, their huge wheels jumping and settling over the frozen, rutted mud. The trucks tipped down the hill, on to the road towards the village, their rear ends rising as if they were rabbits escaping down their holes.

*

Report on Reception Camp at Hodonín, near Kunštat
in the German Protectorate of Moravia
by
Camp Commandant and Senior Administrative Clerk
(first draft, typed and prepared for signing
15 December 1942)

An examination of all camp inmates has now been completed by Camp Physician MUDr Steiner and the following results recorded. (For simplicity's sake, the main figures are included here. For his comments and addendum, see Appendix I.)

Total number of inmates at present: 1,273. Total sick as follows:

Disease or condition	No. of prisoners (adults)
Trachoma	256
Tuberculosis	21
Syphilis	19

(Eight of the syphilitics are in the advanced stages of the condition)

Disease or condition	No. of prisoners (children)
Measles	272
Whooping cough	8
Chicken pox	16

As the reader will see in Appendix I, 2 female prisoners have recently been sent to Brno County Hospital with suspected typhoid fever. Their removal from the camp was naturally of some urgency, and all infirmary patients will remain in isolation until further notice. Doctor Steiner appears to believe this may be the commencement of an epidemic. His prognosis may be unduly alarmist. He also estimates that by the New Year, only between 5 and 10 per cent of prisoners will be free of some disease or other. He is including pneumonia, scabies, scurvy and diarrhoea in his estimate. These illnesses are not included in the above figures.

The results of the work parties continue to be satisfactory. The quarry manager at Štěpánov n. Svratkou reports that earthworks and overhead works are proceeding with 20 men assigned on 10 hour shifts to the loading of narrow gauge pit cars and a further 20 assigned to the unloading and breaking of the stone on its arrival at the building site. We also have teams of women assigned to adapting subgrades under the banks, sodding the trenches and laying drains, while the girls and youths are clearing snow and assisting with the draining of the trenches.

Other work parties assigned to other tasks are also performing satisfactorily. (See Appendix II.)

The early onset of winter this year did not unduly affect production rates. This is due to the diligent organisational capacities of our Chief Purser. It is hoped that the quarry work will be able to continue until the end of January.

As agreed with the Protectorate Road Haulage Company, prisoners are assigned a wage of 1.77 Czech Crowns per hour, which is paid into camp funds prior to the transfer of payment to Brno County Council on behalf of the Ministry of Internal Affairs for the Protectorate. First such payment was made at the end of November and totalled 415,017.40 Czech Crowns, such payment representing the work period from 2 August to 30 November 1942, a figure which will compare favourably with any other camp in the region, certainly with the Penal Workhouse in Brno, where prisoners are not subjected to such extreme weather conditions. (For a full financial statement see the attached report of the Chief Accountant, Appendix III.)

The health of the prisoners requires close observation in view of the fact that gypsies seem particularly prone to lethargy. The general situation of imprisonment appears to have a particularly negative effect on them and many of them appear to be becoming quite indifferent to their surroundings. With the severest part of winter yet ahead of us, this will have a negative effect both on the rate of disease and upon the productivity of the work parties.

Feeding costs per prisoner have remained steady at 4.20 Czech Crowns per day.

The overcrowding problem mentioned in the previous report has been alleviated somewhat by the transportation of 75 prisoners (45 male and 30 female) to the Main Camp of Auschwitz I. Overcrowding in the sick-bay is likely to increase, however, and the situation generally remains far from ideal. Further admissions must be restricted until more transports can be arranged to Auschwitz-Birkenau or elsewhere within the General Government.

CHAPTER 18

Anna was crossing from her block to the workshop. As she looked down across the *Appell-platz*, she was just in time to see the last of the trucks descending the hill, and her heart twisted. Her son was free of this place; she might never see him again; she hadn't even been able to bid him goodbye, to bless him. She had succeeded. She was heartbroken.

Her gaze fell upon a small, thin figure being berated by Čacko, close to the gate. Her first thought was – *so, that Evil One has already found another victim*. The boy was partially obscured by Čacko's bulk, and it was only as Čacko moved away, shouting and waving his arms, that Anna recognised the pitiable form as Emil. She stopped, then turned quickly, crossing her arms over her chest as she hurried to the workshop. *Dear God*. She was desolate that Emil was not on the transport – yet to see him again, just to glimpse him, when she thought he might be lost to her forever. *Dear God – kill me, or turn my heart to stone.*

I understand now, she thought, how hatred can make you dull rather than keen – how it can weigh you down until it is impossible to feel any other emotion, until there is nothing else to be bothered about. The hatred she felt toward that *gadjo* Čacko, towards all *gadje*, was like a solid lump in her chest, a great weighty rock. She had always wondered why men like Václav Winter were so heavy with their hatred, why their venom towards white people made them so solid and hard. Now, she understood. She hated Čacko so much he had ceased to be a person: she hated all of them. Show her a wooden hut full of pretty little white girls with plump cheeks and senseless smiles and she would pour kerosene over it and set light to them herself. It would do the whites good to watch their children being tortured for a change.

In the workshop, the rest of her group was already seated. Eva and Ludmila were holding their work up close to their faces. Eva's sight was failing but she dared not admit it for fear of being sent to the quarry. They only had two more days on the sewing detail before their group was back to breaking stones for another fortnight. The weather was worsening every day.

'Am I all right?' Anna asked quietly, as she took her place on the bench next to Ludmila, meaning, *Have I been missed?*

Before Ludmila could answer, the woman kapo sitting by the stove said, 'And where have you been?'

Anna disliked this particular kapo, a German Romni who was stupid and lazy. She thought nothing of sitting between them and the stove to keep herself warm, although she could just as easily sit on the other side and allow a little of its poor glow to reach them.

Anna reached for the pile of cloth on the long table in front of them. It was a jumble of nightwear, striped pyjamas and flannelette nighties with ribbons, a great heap of it that stretched along the length of the row of tables filling the large block. Some of it had been expensive, once. Where had they got all this stuff? The women were assigned to groups; some tearing seams open; others stitching the pieces into jackets and trousers for the children.

'My son, he almost got on the transport to the sanatorium,' Anna replied matter-of-factly to the kapo, 'but they pulled him off.'

The woman stared at her. Anna selected a garment, a pair of men's trousers, and began ripping up one leg. She sighed inwardly. Now she would get a reprimand for not speaking German. She was beyond caring. Why didn't they just make up their minds what the rules were?

The kapo did not reprimand her. She shook her head. 'Golden God,' she said quietly in Romani. 'You haven't got a clue, have you?'

Anna glanced at her fiercely. She was about to respond but the woman's expression stopped her.

Eva and Ludmila lifted their heads from their work. The woman kapo was giving them a strange, pitying stare. She was dark-eyed but fair-skinned, her eyes a light brown flecked with gold. Her voice was measured: the way she spoke, she sounded more like a *gadji*. 'You think you're suffering,' she said simply, her eyes glazed. 'You haven't got a clue. You are like children. In Germany . . .'

Anna rolled her eyes. The German Roma all went on and on about how tough things were in the Reich.

The woman saw the action and her expression hardened. 'You'll find out soon enough,' she said dully. She leaned back and folded her arms, giving a light snort through her nostrils. Her eyes had re-acquired their bored expression.

Eva and Ludmila lowered their heads. Ludmila was having

trouble ripping a cuff. Anna took it from her and wound her fingers around it, lifting her elbows and tensing the muscles in her arms to pull. The fine cloth dug into her joints and as she pulled she grimaced, wondering which might break first, her finger tendons or the cloth.

Ludmila leant back on the bench, so as not to get an elbow in the eye as the cuff gave. Anna handed the pieces back to her sister and then returned to her own garment. *We may well be like children*, she thought, *but at least none of us have co-operated with the gadje. These people are scum. They deserve everything they get.*

That night, there was a scramble for the bunks which had been vacated by the transport. A fight broke out. Anna and the others kept out of it, although with Pavlína gone, they could have tried to claim her bunk as one of theirs. Anna had no intention of moving to the far end of the block and Eva and Ludmila would stick with her – they had moved to Tekla's bunk while she was in the infirmary. Líba and Marie stayed in their bunk next to Anna, holding on to each other and watching the fight with wide eyes, until the block Elder strode past them, shouting at the women to break it up.

No one had yet been moved into the larger of the new blocks. It had been standing empty for four weeks now. No one knew why.

It was a few days later. They were at the quarry. The overseer stood at the top of the ditch and shouted at them and called them whores and demanded of the sky how he was supposed to meet his targets when they gave him nothing but women and girls. Women and girls and babies, the whole damn camp was full of them. But soon, thank God, that would change.

They were getting some men from Lety, at last, so they could finish the stonework before the end of the month.

'Did he say Lety?' the woman next to Anna asked. They were on their knees in the frozen mud, trying to work their fingers beneath a huge stone.

'Yes,' Anna replied between her teeth, grunting with effort. Her fingers were bleeding, but they were numb so she felt no pain. That would come later. Lety was in Bohemia, wasn't it?

'My husband is in Lety,' the woman said, her face lighting up. 'Did he say they were sending some Lety men *here*?' She dropped her side of the stone and clapped her hands together, squeezing her eyes tight shut and turning her face to the sky.

'Wooden God,' muttered Anna, sucking the blood from her frozen fingers.

One of the women on their detail had something going with the overseer. Normally, the others refused to talk to her, but when they were allowed to sit on the frozen ground for half an hour at lunchtime, she discovered a new-found popularity. 'Tell us what you know, sister,' said Anna's work partner, 'and we will sit round you and keep you warm.'

They huddled down, their heads bent to the middle of the circle where the woman sat enjoying her new importance. 'The overseers have been complaining for ages,' she began. 'They can't possibly meet the targets by the end of January unless they have more labour. After that, quarry work has to stop until spring. So many of the men are sick, but we have a contract. It's impossible. So last month the Commandant agreed to request a hundred men from Lety. A hundred.'

'Where is Lety?' Anna asked the woman sitting next to her, but the woman shushed her with her hand.

'Only the fittest are coming,' the overseer's woman said, 'he was most specific about that. The best that Lety have got.'

A call from a nearby group announced that the soup had arrived. They scrambled to their feet.

'Where is Lety?' Anna repeated her question as they shuffled into line.

'It's a camp in Bohemia,' the woman in front of her said impatiently. 'It's where they sent all our People who lived in Bohemia. When they rounded everyone up. My son is there. And my uncle.'

Václav and Yakali, and the others . . . Anna thought. If Václav was in the Lety camp, he would surely be amongst the men sent here. Václav was like a bull. She would find out what had happened to Božena and the girls. Yakali's sons, Justin and Miroslav, they were young and fit. Maybe they would be sent too.

The trudge back to the camp was normally undertaken in silence, but now there were whispers all the way. One woman had four sons she thought might be in Lety. Would the men be allowed to bring food parcels, or clothing? Things must be better there, if they were sending men over. Did the men know they were coming yet? When would they arrive? 'It will be almost as good as a harvest!' one woman said out loud. 'At least, there will be *news*.'

As they re-entered the camp, Anna learnt something else. It was 1943.

*

Emil had had no news of his father since he had gone to the infirmary. His mother had managed to get in, once – there was a particular kapo she had been working on, she said. But now the infirmary was quarantined, the bribes were getting bigger.

She came to Emil after roll-call one evening. They only had seconds, in the dark, during the brief, milling confusion that preceded the return to the blocks. The men got their bread ration after roll-call. Emil had just placed his carefully in his jacket pocket. He always ate it as soon as he got back to the block. Some saved theirs for the morning – which was what it was for, officially, to have with your *ersatz* coffee. Some saved theirs for bartering. He regarded either of these options as too risky. Better to have it safe inside your stomach.

His mother did not even greet him. Her hand gripped his forearm, clawlike and demanding. 'Give me your bread,' she said. 'I'm going to try to see your father tomorrow.'

For the briefest flicker of a moment, it occurred to him that he had the power to refuse. Then he handed her the bread. She turned away.

When was the last time he had heard his mother speak his real name? She was the only other person on earth who knew what it was. If she did not speak it to him, who would?

He wrapped his arms around himself and trotted back to the block, nauseous with hunger. The cold bit at him, now his bread was gone. *I thought I knew about hunger, before, on the outside*, he thought. He had gone without often enough. *But now I know I did not know. It was just ordinary hunger, hunger that niggled at you all day long. Now I know hunger that hurts, like a knife in your side, hunger so hard you cannot think about anything else.* Inside the block, before climbing up to his bunk, he removed his shirt and carefully turned the pocket inside out. A row of tiny grey lice nested in the seams. He brought the shirt up close to his face, and pushed the lice aside with one finger, looking for any crumbs that might have dropped from his lost piece of bread.

Don't scratch, Dr Steiner had told him. *You scratch, you break the skin, the lice shit on you and the shit enters your bloodstream. Typhus.* Emil paused with his finger half-raised to his mouth. He closed his eyes, took a deep breath, and forced himself to wipe the finger on his trousers, turning his shirt back the right way, shaking it, and putting it back on.

Settled down in his bunk, he squeezed his eyes tight shut in an effort to forget his pains. He comforted himself with thoughts of Dr Steiner. Last time he had seen him, he had told him a funny story about how his wife had stopped him leaving the house that morning. He had put on an old, un-ironed shirt. You're not leaving the house in that! his wife had told him. What does it matter, woman? he had said, there is a war on! It matters! she had replied. When he tried to put his coat on top, she had come up behind him and grabbed at the shirt, pulling the tails out of his trousers and ripping the shirt right up the back. His daughters had gathered round and joined in, and together the women had shredded the shirt from him, leaving him standing there with tears of laughter running down his face.

Tears of laughter had run down Dr Steiner's face as he told Emil the story, standing in his hut, miming his wife's action – and Emil, in return, told him the story of how Čacko had ripped the shirt from *his* back on the day they had arrived in camp, and they had both laughed and slapped their legs, even though there was nothing to laugh about, and Dr Steiner had given him a small piece of charcoal to chew on, for his diarrhoea, and somehow even that had seemed funny.

Emil lay on his bunk, his teeth chattering with cold and his stomach so hollow and painful it felt as if it was folding itself over and over inside him. He replayed Dr Steiner's jokes in his head, until he had exhausted every detail and the thought of them lost the power to distract him.

The kapo moved down the block, extinguishing the lamps. The men around Emil settled down to sleep. In the extra privacy afforded by the dark, Emil thought of Marie. He had only been able to talk to her twice since they had fed the pigs together – both times facilitated by Čacko, who seemed amused by their friendship.

He pictured her small smile, her assuredness. He imagined meeting her at a harvest gathering. He imagined her secretly to be Kalderash – it was the only quality lacking in her, after all. Once or twice, after lights out, he had reached down to hold himself between the legs. There was never any more than a faint stirring there, but he liked to feel it, to remind himself of what it used to be like once upon a time, when he would touch himself so often at night he worried that he might be doing himself damage. It will be like that again, one day, he thought, when I get out of here. Just watch how strong I'll grow then.

Marie: her neat little mouth, her teeth, her infrequent smiles. He never knew what she was thinking, or what she thought of him, but thinking of her made him forget other thoughts. There were the endless days. And then there was Marie. She and Dr Steiner were the only ones who talked to him of things beyond the camp – they seemed to believe the rest of the world still existed. Not like his own family, who were dying, sick, taking bread from his mouth – who had forgotten his name.

The next day, Emil was at the water pump, with Čacko standing next to him. It was around noon. Two large details of women had just left the workshops behind the pump, when Emil heard a sudden, excited holler. He lifted his head to see that the women had broken ranks and were racing across the *Appell-platz*, their mouths open, shouting, arms waving in abandon. Behind them, two women kapos ran in furious pursuit.

Emil looked round. The gates to the camp stood open and

two trucks were reversing into position beside the staff hut. In a moment, the women were upon the trucks, banging on the sides, calling out.

Two guards raced across the *Appell-platz*, batons in hand. Four more jumped down from the step of the staff hut, one blowing frantically on a whistle. Emil stared as they set about the women, beating them back. Several women were on the ground, crying. Others were openly defiant, waving their arms above their heads and shouting hysterically.

Čacko was watching too. He shook his head. 'There's no point in them getting het-up,' he said chummily to Emil. 'They're going to find out who's arrived soon enough. Let's go and see, shall we?' He clapped his hand down on Emil's shoulder. 'We can pretend we've got to shift that pile of logs round the back. We have, actually. Let's go and see what's going on.'

As they approached, the Commandant was restoring order, shouting and waving his pistol in the air. A row of guards stood with their backs to the trucks and rifles held across their chests, blocking the women's way. The women were clutching at each other, one or two at the back were jumping up repeatedly to catch sight of the Lety men as they descended. The Commandant was shouting at the women to move back.

The driver of the first truck had jumped down from his cabin and was trying to get the Commandant's attention, waving a piece of paper. Eventually, the Commandant turned to him, leaving the guards to keep control of the crowd. The women were talking to each other. The Commandant looked up at the first truck and windmilled his hand. Two guards jumped down from the back of the truck. The tailgate dropped with a resonant, metallic clang that echoed round the camp.

As he and Čacko approached, Emil saw the first Lety prisoner peer out from the truck and gaze around, over the heads of the people below. He saw a grey face, bald head, and bony shoulders from which hung a ragged, filthy shirt. The man's eyes were huge, dark and staring in fear. He lifted a hand and scratched at his head, peering out at the women in alarm. The women fell silent.

Emil and Čacko stood to one side and watched as the men descended; thin, filthy skeletons, each recently shaved, their uniforms even more ill-fitting and threadbare than Emil's. Several were shaking uncontrollably. Two of them fell to the ground as they jumped down from the truck and were unable to get up. The Commandant strode forward and shouted at the other prisoners to help them up but the men just stood staring at him, their mouths agape.

'Sit down, then!' the Commandant barked, and the other prisoners dropped down obediently, on to their haunches.

Some of the women had begun to weep and moan. Čacko leaned forward and whispered to Emil, 'There'll be hell to pay for this, mark my words. They were supposed to send us the *good* ones. Look what we've got.'

The Commandant was pale and quiet. He went over to the drivers of the trucks and ordered them into the staff hut. Then he told the guards to disperse the women.

When the women were told to go back to their work, they stood their ground at first, some still craning their necks to see the men, others weeping or shaking their heads. One was on her knees, arms outstretched, praying loudly: but none of the men was making any gesture of recognition. With a little prodding from the guards, the women turned away. Emil now had a clear view of the group of men sitting on the ground, shoulders hunched. *These men are half-dead already*, he thought. *We have better in our infirmary*. A couple of the men stared back at him

with hollow, incurious gazes. One clawed at the ground with a
rigid, palsied hand, as if there might be treasure beneath the ice.

Beside him, Čacko let out a low whistle. 'Go and help in the
kitchens, we can move the logs later. I'm going to see if I can find
out what's going on.'

Čacko did not come to get him from the kitchen until the end of
the afternoon. He was grinning with glee and keen to impart
what he had learned. He stood over a huge vat of soup, rubbing
his hands together in the steam, face alight with self-
importance. 'Guess what?' he said to no one in particular – there
were three orderlies hammering dough for tomorrow's bread
while Emil was picking bits of stone from a bucket of grey flour.
'Those skeletons they sent from Lety. They *are* the best they had!
The boss is beside himself. He asked for their fittest men but
didn't bother to find out how fit they were! Imagine what the
rest must be like.' One of the orderlies turned and spat into the
corner. 'There was the most almighty row,' Čacko continued.
'The boss has refused to admit them. We've got quite enough
problems as it is, he says. Says they've got to go straight back.
They can't even stay overnight. They've been sitting in the snow
all day and he won't even put them in the new block. It's only a
corporal in charge of the convoy. He doesn't know what to do.
The trucks were supposed to be in Brno by nightfall. The boss is
on the phone now, sorting it out.'

One of the orderlies had stopped kneading dough. 'Well,
they'll just get sent up north, won't they?' he asked rhetorically.

Čacko continued rubbing his hands. 'I suppose so . . .' he
glanced over at Emil, at the orderly, then back at Emil, '. . . to the
sanatorium.'

Another of the orderlies gave a short bark of a laugh, slapping
his dough.

After a while, Čacko tossed his head at Emil and they left the kitchen together. 'Better get those logs shifted before it gets dark,' Čacko said. 'That was my excuse for hanging round.' As they approached the huddled men, Čacko lowered his voice and said, 'I thought they might be gone by now. The boss wants them off the premises before the work parties get back, otherwise there'll be another riot. He's swearing if they don't take them away then he'll make them sit right there all night, the corporal too. There's no way he's admitting them.'

The logs were piled up against the side of the staff hut. Some of them had been chopped already, short fat chunks, and these Emil moved with ease to the tin fuel caddy at the back. The rest of the logs were uncut and far too heavy for him to move alone. He and Čacko stood staring at the pile for a few minutes, then a look of mischief came over Čacko's face. He glanced around. 'Get one of those to help you,' he indicated the men with his head.

Emil looked at him. Had he gone mad? What would the Commandant say?

'Go on,' said Čacko. 'I'll go and speak to the guards. Get the job done.'

Emil turned, shaking his head.

The afternoon was so gloomy, cold and grey, it seemed as though night could fall any minute without warning. As he approached the group, Emil tried to imagine what it must be like for the men to be sitting there, in agony from the cold, waiting to learn whether they would be allowed into a block for the night or have to travel on in the miserable dark. I bet they haven't been given any rations, he thought. There must have been thirty men in the first group, but he could not see a single one who would be any use in lifting logs. They had the beaten look of men who had observed his approach and determined to remain unnoticed. It was cruel to select one.

One of the squatting ones, the nearest, glanced up as Emil approached. He was the only one who looked at him, so Emil said, *'Bruder. Bitte. Hilfe.'* He gestured over to the pile of logs.

The man stared past him, where Čacko was waiting, glanced wearily up at Emil, then stood.

Emil saw at once that his choice had been a huge mistake. The man was enormously tall and skinny as a pine tree. He and Emil were completely mismatched. When they shouldered the logs, Emil would bear the brunt of the weight, unless he persuaded the skinny giant to walk on his knees.

He sighed and turned, flicking his head to indicate that the man should follow him.

As they walked back to the logs, the man said to him in Romani, 'You are thin, *phrála*, but strong-looking. Do they give you extra food for this?'

Emil noted the man's Vlach accent, then glanced around. Čacko had wandered over to the guards. He made sure he was out of earshot before replying, 'No, *phrála*. They make me do everything because that filthy *gadjo* pig hates me. But it makes the time go quicker. I have to follow him around all the time making him feel good about himself. But it's better than being at the quarry for ten hours like the others. He gives me extra rations sometimes. Sometimes it's a beating.'

They reached the pile of logs. The tall skinny man looked down at them, then down at Emil. He gave a mirthless chuckle, then knelt in the snow.

It was easier than Emil had anticipated. He placed the end of the log on his shoulder, and the skinny giant rested it against his chest, supported by his large bony hands. They had to move forward slowly, with Emil at the front, but the skinny man worked steadily without complaining. Only his breathing betrayed his exertion. When they dropped the logs down beside the fuel caddy, he gave an exhalation which sounded from deep inside the cavity of his thin chest.

The last log was the longest. They paused in front of it, as if weighing up the easiest way to lift it, while in fact giving each other a short rest. Emil looked over at Čacko but he was still talking to the guards by the truck.

'In Lety, I moved stones,' the man beside him said. 'I was the strongest man there. The boy next to me, he was beaten to death for not being strong . . .'

Emil looked up at the man. His chin was harsh with grey stubble. He had no teeth. His eyes glistened.

The man saw Emil observing him and repeated, 'I was the strongest man in Lety. Hard for you to believe perhaps, hard for me too, until I look at the others.' He looked down at himself, then gave another mirthless grin, as if noticing for the first time that his prison trousers only reached to just below his knees and that his huge feet were as white as bone, like ancient creatures. Then he sighed, an endless sigh. He shook his head.

'Once upon a time, *phrála*, I owned the finest pair of boots in Europe. They came up to here.' He indicated his legs vaguely with his spidery hands. 'They were of softest pigskin. It took the cobbler in Manchester longer than it took my blacksmith in Madrid to make my horse's harness. He advised against pigskin, told me it would spoil, so I had him make an extra boot for each foot, just in case. The English. They are like slugs, you know.'

Behind them came a shout. Emil glanced over. The other men from Lety were clambering slowly upright. Two guards were trying to lift one of them to his feet but he looked as if he was frozen stiff. The Commandant had emerged from the staff hut and was pulling on a pair of leather gloves. Čacko was still talking to the other guard.

Emil felt sorry for the skinny man with his empty, stubbled face and white bony feet. He said vaguely, 'It looks like you're going, to the sanatorium.'

The man stared at him blankly. 'Sanatorium . . . ?' he said eventually. He exhaled through his nostrils, a gentle, tired sound, then shook his head. 'Keep working, *phrála*, keep being hated. It is keeping you pure.'

He turned towards the truck.

'*Dja le Devlesa*,' Emil called after him. Go with God.

The man stopped, then turned back. He bowed slightly and replied, '*Ač le Devlesa*.' Stay with God. Then he looked at Emil again, his eyes narrowing.

'You are a Vlach Rom,' he said.

Emil nodded.

The man frowned, then said thoughtfully. 'What was your father's name?'

'My father is Josef Maximoff. We are Kalderash. His father was Nikóla Maximoff.'

The man stared at Emil, his eyes dark and shining. Emil could sense thoughts swimming inside the man's large head.

'Jonó Maximoff, my brother . . .' the man said eventually, looking at the ground and slowly shaking his head. 'I heard you had escaped to Slovakia.' He looked up. 'He is here, in this place?'

Emil didn't know who he meant. He glanced past the man anxiously, to where the last of the Lety inmates were being helped up into the truck. If the man didn't go over to the truck straight away, the guards would come and get him, which would mean that Čacko would come and get Emil.

One of the guards shouted at them. The man started, glanced over to the truck, then back at Emil.

'When you see your father,' he said, his voice faltering, 'tell him something. Tell him you met a man who was once Todór Maximoff.'

The skinny man with the grey stubble hurried back to the truck, as if suddenly keen to continue his journey.

CHAPTER 19

It was difficult to sleep now it was so cold. Emil still occupied a bunk near the door. The stove was extinguished at the same time as the kerosene lamps and its meagre warmth vanished instantly. The men around him gave off no body heat at all: they were all bone. The insides of his wrists itched. In the crevices around his eyes and between his toes, the skin was coming away in great white flakes. Sleep came and went, brief moments of cold unconsciousness. For the rest of the night, it was a process of awakening and re-awakening and realising, too quickly, that he was not asleep.

Morning. The door flew back with a crash, the kapo blew his whistle, air like freezing water flooded the block. Emil rolled over, trying to pull his blanket tight around his body, to enjoy a brief second more of nothingness. Instead, he felt a flame of pain along the left-hand side of his back, as if someone had thrown burning oil at him. He gasped, sat up and cracked his head on the roof of the block. His skin was on fire. He craned his head but could not see what was on his back. It was only when he looked back at his bunk that he saw something, a glistening strip. During the night, his uniform jacket had ridden up and his exposed flesh had adhered to the frozen wooden bunk. The sudden movement had ripped the skin from his back.

He clambered down from the bunk, gasping with pain. The kapo ignored him, blowing the whistle repeatedly. His neighbour on the bunk was cursing him for not moving out of the way more quickly. Emil clenched his teeth, wincing and gasping as he tumbled out of the door towards the washroom.

After splashing his face and urinating, he hobbled over to the *Appell-platz* for roll-call, only able to walk if he twisted an arm behind his back to hold his uniform jacket away from his raw skin. The freezing air stung him but numbed the burning. After roll-call, he found Čacko and showed him the raw patch. Čacko dismissed him with a wave of his hand.

A queue had already formed outside the doctor's hut. Emil joined it. He closed his eyes and, experimentally, lowered his shirt. As long as he stood still, the rough cloth would not come into contact with his skin – but it was too cold to stand still. Finally, his turn came. He entered the hut.

Another man was sitting behind Dr Steiner's desk. His jacket, also with a yellow star, hung on the back of the door instead of Dr Steiner's long black coat. Emil was too disappointed to be polite. 'Where is Dr Steiner?' he demanded.

The new doctor stared at him. He was dark-eyed, hollow-cheeked; a bald, elderly man, with the huge gaze of a child. He did not smile. After a pause, he said quietly. 'Dr Steiner and his family have been sent to Terezín. How may I help you?'

Descending from the hut, Emil paused and sat for a moment on the stone step, ignoring the man who was next in the queue and had to push past him muttering.

Dr Steiner was in Terezín. And his family; the wife who had ripped the shirt from his back, the daughters who had helped, the son whose dog had been taken away. He imagined Dr Steiner in Terezín. It was bigger than this camp, apparently. Huge, they said, with a theatre and flower-beds and a proper hospital. But the Jew he had met in the woods didn't look like he had been spending much time at the theatre. He thought of the Jew, the one he had not helped.

He frowned to himself, taking a moment or two to identify the precise nature of what was troubling him. Was he worried about Dr Steiner and his family? Only a bit. Terezín had to be a lot better than here. And anyway, surely nothing bad could happen to a man like that, such a sunny sort of man?

No, it was the thought that the student he had left in the woods back in the summer, the one who had asked him for help, had probably been recaptured and sent back to Terezín, and maybe one day he would meet Dr Steiner and Dr Steiner would tell him how he had been a doctor in one of the *gypsy* camps. Then what would the student say? *Gypsies*! Pah! It's true what we've always thought of them. I could have escaped but this *gypsy* boy lied to me. He never came back. And Dr Steiner would say, but there are some good *gypsies*. I met a nice boy in Hodonín camp. And they would talk, and realise they were talking about the same boy, and Dr Steiner who had liked him would not like him any longer.

Emil buried his head in his hands. Then he gave a deep groan,

an elemental sound that came from the pit of his belly. The
scenario was absurd. He was not worried about it. He was
hoping it might happen. That would mean that the Jew he had
left in the woods had survived, that the boy who was also called
František had not been left to die alone, that Emil's father and
mother and brother and sister and all the rest of his family were
not being punished for what he had done or not done; that Dr
Steiner was alive somewhere, chatting away, cheerfully – that
there was hope. All his thoughts, all his dreams, were so much
mist. He just wanted to believe that what was not true was true.
How else could he continue? *A sanatorium . . . ?*

There were whispers around the camp, whispers about what
was really happening to the Jews. *Whatever they do to the Jews they
will do next to us.* But the things they said – you could not believe
that anyone would really do those things, not even the Germans.

Suddenly, Emil turned and smashed his head against the
side of the hut, his temple making contact with the wooden
planks with such force that he bounced away and staggered.
The man emerging from the doctor's hut at that moment
sprang back, exclaiming in surprise.

Emil's back did not hurt any more. Nothing hurt any more.
There was nothing but a blackness that blotted out all the other
thoughts, all the confusion. He smashed his head again, and
again, until two men in the queue grabbed him and pushed him
to the ground, cursing his stupidity.

Later that night, back in his bunk, the grazes on his forehead
were at least a distraction from the agony of his back. He felt
angry with the men who had stopped him from cracking open
his skull.

*

Anna was at the head of the squad coming back from the
quarry, so she didn't actually see it happen. She paused when

she heard the commotion, and had a moment to appreciate the excuse to pause. The kapo at the head of the squad had run back to see what was happening and a group of women were clustered round by the side of the road. Anna dared not sit, but she rested a hand against the rough trunk of a pine alongside the track and lifted her foot as if she needed to check one of her clogs. She closed her eyes briefly, but that made her lose her balance. I am so tired I want to die, she thought simply, too exhausted to articulate the thought beyond those words.

'Anna, Anna . . .' Ludmila rushed up to her, her eyes glistening. 'A woman just dropped dead. I mean, she just *dropped dead* . . .'

'Not really,' muttered the woman next to them. 'She sat down first. I saw it.'

'She didn't,' said Ludmila. 'She *sank* down, then just keeled over, now she's dead.'

Anna walked back a few paces with the others to see. A huddle was around the woman on the ground by the side of the track and the kapo was shouting at them to lift the corpse. It was a tiny, thin woman who had died, hardly more than a girl, but after a day at the quarry, the three or four women around her were struggling to lift her bony frame. Dear God, thought Anna, a day's work and now we are expected to carry each other to and fro. Were they sure the girl was dead, hadn't just fainted or something?

'Put her down! Are you stupid!' A woman guard was upon them. A guard went out with each work party, the kapos not being trusted as sufficient, but this one had fallen behind on the walk back. Now she was running towards them. The kapo turned to the guard. The guard grabbed one of the women who was attempting to lift the corpse and pulled her away by the arm, hurling her aside with such force that she spun away and landed on all fours on the track. The other women dropped the corpse back on to the frozen mud. The dead girl's head snapped back as she fell, mouth open.

The guard turned upon the kapo, her face a few inches from the other woman's, hissing furiously. 'Are you *stupid*! Don't you listen to anything you are told?'

'All prisoners must be accounted for . . .' the kapo began feebly.

The guard lifted both hands and gave an angry shove at the kapo's chest, using the heels of both hands. 'For God's sake! For God's sake!' she shouted repeatedly, before turning away with an exclamation of despair. She stormed off down the track, ahead of them, abandoning the prisoners she was supposedly escorting back to camp.

'Form up!' the kapo called unconvincingly, her voice shaken.

'Did you see that?' Ludmila asked Anna, 'That guard was in tears.'

The woman next to them gave a sceptical snort. 'She doesn't care about us, not that one!'

'She isn't crying for us,' Anna replied as they began to march in pairs.

'What do you mean?' hissed Ludmila.

Anna shook her head. She did not want to frighten Ludmila.

Her group was the first of the work parties back at the block. It was empty but for two small groups of women at the far end, near the stove, stitching blankets in the poor light.

One of them lifted her head as Anna entered. 'You! Hey!' she called across the barrack.

Anna glanced at her dully as she sank down on to her bunk, too tired to acknowledge the call.

'They say your husband is worse!'

Anna lifted her head.

The woman was a dark-skinned, toothless girl of indeterminate age. Her face was creased and her brow furrowed but her eyes twinkled.

'My husband is sick too. He's at the other end, near the door – they put the worst ones at the far end because of the smell. I was talking to the kapo earlier. Your husband was moved there in the night.' She paused. 'It's not good.'

Anna rose. She brushed down her skirt. There was a dull ache between her shoulder blades. She was hugely thirsty. She only had a short-time before evening roll-call.

As she turned to leave, the woman called. 'You'll have to give that Dumb One your bread ration, sister, but if your husband is dead already then when you come back you can have a bite of mine.'

Outside the barrack door, Anna stopped, drew breath. From where she stood, she could see across the camp, past the children's block to where the infirmary huts and the wagons they were now using for the overflow were packed next to each other, close to the perimeter fence. It was a kapo on duty at the gate sectioning them off, rather than a guard. She could probably get past him. She had no bread left but two weeks ago, when she was on sewing duty, she had managed to unpick a length of gold thread from a nightgown she had been shredding in the workshop. She had rolled the thread into a skein and tied it with a piece of lace.

It was nearly dark. The work parties were arriving back – a group of twenty men were jostling each other slowly into one of the men's barracks and the main gate was opening to admit another detail. Roll-call would be soon, then lock-up. If she went straight to the infirmary she might miss her only chance to visit

Bobo. She hadn't seen him for four days. If she went to see Bobo she would miss Josef.

She had visited Bobo less since Parni's death, and he seemed less and less anxious for her visits. He would look up when she entered the block and stare at her solemnly, as if he wasn't entirely sure who she was. His eyes had been weeping pus for several weeks now – most of the children's were. At first, she had managed to hold him down and squeeze a drop of her breast milk into each eye but her milk had dried up completely because she was so hungry. It wouldn't make any difference anyway. He would be re-infected by the other children soon enough.

He didn't cry when she left him any more, just turned his head away, his gaze indifferent, misty, his suffering beyond her comfort. And her own attitude towards him was changing. Once, he had been her favourite, her perfect plump one, the one she wished would never grow up. Now, when she thought of him, she thought of how quiet and serene Parni had always been, the smoothness of her brown skin and the solemnity in her gaze. *Thank God she is dead*, she thought sometimes. *She did me that favour, put herself beyond all suffering.*

She hesitated, then she strode firmly past the children's block, to the infirmary.

*

Josef Růžička, Jozef Maximoff, *Phrála* Jonó, Branko, Limping Boy, my son, grandson – *Kakó*, the *Rom Baró* . . . Sometimes he rehearsed all the names he had been called, as if in that litany he might find a part of himself that was the essential core, the heart of him, the part lost when he had been admitted to the camp. *Branko*. His real name. He never used it, even to himself. He had never felt the need, until now. How strange a thing to have forgotten oneself, to have become a shell, a husk, to know intently that there was another self somewhere, in a place where he had really existed, lost in the past.

My name is Branko Maximoff, common name of Josef. I am *Rom Baró* of my *kumpánia*. We winter in Moravia, not far from Třebič, but in the summer we move around the Czech lands. Harvest time finds us at the cherry orchards. They are owned by a good man. I forget his name. He keeps a fine table. The Tent-Dwellers antagonise the other Roma but I always make sure to smooth things over. I believe we are all brothers. We once held a *kris* for over three hundred men. I was allowed the honour of speaking first. There was a new law afoot. Grave news . . . the men listened to me. They showed me great respect.

Josef knew why they had moved him to the far end of the hut in the night. One's progression along the bunks was indicative of deterioration. The healthiest prisoners, the ones who could get up to relieve themselves, were placed near the door because that was where the kapo's table was. The kapo had nothing to do all day except keep an eye on everyone and ensure that nobody sprang back to ruddy health and scrambled out of a window and over the perimeter fence. He wasn't even obliged to fetch them water.

It was not logical that the weakest should be furthest from the door, and this lack of logic bothered Josef. If he wished to relieve himself, and he wished it every half hour or so, he had to call out in the hope that a patient further down the block would hear him and pass the call down – via several other patients – so that such information might at last reach the kapo, who then might, if he felt like a little exercise, take his feet from his desk, amble next door to the orderlies' hut and inform them that someone, somewhere, needed to be lifted to the latrines. By which time it was too late.

I wonder what day of the week it is, Josef thought, what month? What year? How strange that I cannot remember the year. I know there is a war on, that much I know.

There was a dull, hot pain in his abdomen. I stink, he thought miserably. Of course I do. I stink. The orderlies will be angry when they eventually come.

His fever had reached a plateau. For days, his temperature had been soaring up and down, bathing him in sweat, then freezing him. Then he had been delirious for a short time, an almost-pleasant, drunken state. Now there was a simple constancy while whatever raged inside his body raged away. It was peaceful.

He lay watching the ceiling, where a long, blurry column of insects was tramping up a diagonal beam, a rope of them, twisting and bulging over the wood. Every now and then, one or two dropped down.

I used to have good eyesight, he thought.

He allowed himself to think of all the things he used to have.

How strange a thing it is, he thought, the way you comfort yourself when it comes to loss. You turn away from it, show it your back, face and embrace what you still have. When we had to sell our gold I thought, ah well, we can always buy more gold, as long as we have the wagon and the horses and can still travel then we will be fine. Then they stopped us travelling and burnt our wagon and I thought, well, we still have one horse and we can build a cart, and we have a roof over our heads. Then we had to flee our roof and I thought, we still have good clothes and boots, so many people don't have boots any more. Then they took the bundles from us as we stood in line on Registration Day and I thought, well, we have the clothes we stand up in. When we got here, they took those. They even took the hair from my head. I thought, at least we are all together in the same camp. So many people have been separated from their families. Now my family are kept from me, even though they are a few metres away and I would give the world for my wife to come and bring me water and my son to sit by my head and talk to me, and the Small Ones to play beside my bed, arguing perhaps, until their mother scolded them.

He frowned to himself at the thought of Parni and Bobo. Thinking of them was painful. Had something bad happened to them? He pushed the thought away.

It is just me, just my body and my soul and that is all I have – skin and bone and this nightshirt they have given me which is owned more by the lice. He tried to turn his head to call out again, but realised he could no longer move.

If I cannot even move my limbs, let alone raise my body to relieve myself with dignity, then I cannot really call my body my own either. All I have left are my thoughts – and breath, each small breath that comes so shallow and strange into my lungs, as if my body hates air and can't wait to expel it. Soon, my thoughts will go.

I am reduced to this. All else is gone.

I am nothing. But the next small. Breath.

It is all

I am.

Perhaps

All

I ever

Was.

*

At the door of the infirmary hut, Anna found her way barred by another kapo, a squat man with red cheeks and a mirthless smile. She had given her gold thread to the one on the gate, so she said, 'My bread tonight. You can follow me after roll-call.' He stared at her for a moment, then stepped aside.

Josef was at the far end of the hut. His deterioration was so severe that for a moment her heart refused to accept that it was him. His face was waxen and his eyes closed, the red rash still livid on his neck. The stubble on his head and cheeks was completely white. She could detect no movement of the chest cavity, no sign that he was breathing. There was a foul smell.

Then, she saw his Adam's apple move in his throat, slowly, effortfully, twice up and down. He opened his eyes.

His gaze did not focus upon her, so she moved closer to him. Last time she had come, the kapo had warned her not to touch him, but she reached out a hand and placed her fingertips lightly on his shoulder, feeling the hard bone through the thin, tattered nightshirt. Slowly, the strain showing on his features, he managed to move his skull so that his face was turned towards her. His eyes were still unfocused but the muscles around his mouth moved.

He whispered something. She bent down until her face was just above his. The words were incomprehensible and the effort of speech emptied his lungs. He gave a huge, heaving breath.

Anna looked down at him, lowering her face so that he would be able to see her. She smiled at him, her face a few centimetres above his, and her smile became broader and broader, just as it had in the warm darkness of the wagon on the summer night he had taken her from her family after all that bargaining between their parents, the matter of the copper pans finally settled.

Josef was looking up at her, and she thought maybe he was glimpsing the smile through his misted vision, seeing it widen and widen as if it could swallow the world.

Anna Maximoff maintained her smile until she was certain
that her husband was dead.

*

Emil learnt from one of the other prisoners that his father had
died. The man didn't know when, or what Josef had died of. He
only knew it was Emil's father because there were no other
Kalderash in their block, and Emil had a certain status now,
because of Čacko. Most people knew who he was.

'Your father's gone,' the man said casually, as they were
standing next to each other, pasting pitch on to the new block,
'Last night.' His tone suggested he was making a passing
observation, about the weather, or the price of hay. The new
block was still uninhabited. Emil bent to dip his brush into the
black, viscous tar. They had built fires to warm the pitch but the
weather was so cold that it became glutinous almost
immediately. At first he thought the man meant, *your father has
escaped*. Gone?

Seeing the questioning look on his face, the man shrugged. 'I
thought you knew. I suppose they've given up telling people.
Too many dying now.'

Emil shoved his brush into a gap between two wooden
planks. It was important to work the pitch deep into the gaps if
the wall was to be sealed properly from the cold. He worked the
large brush up and down in the crack, the rapidly cooling tar
forming tiny brown bubbles on the surface of the wood.

He did not see his mother for some days after that, then was
surprised to find one day, when Čacko sent him to the kitchens
to pick up lunch for the quarry workers, that the prisoner
waiting to accompany him was Anna. A kapo stood next to her,
so he could not ask her how she had managed this. With the
kapo walking close behind them, they left the camp at the main

gate and began to climb the track up the hill towards the quarry. They were each holding a handle of the huge tureen. The handles were made of a thin strip of hard-edged metal which dug into Emil's hand – he tried to walk slowly but Anna set the pace, striding ahead, as if determined to prove that they did not need to take things easy for her.

Behind them, Emil could hear the hard, ragged breathing of the kapo, who had some sort of chest problem, panting away as he followed doggedly close to them. At the top of the rise, they paused and set down the tureen. The kapo did not object, dropping his sack to the ground and resting both hands on his knees.

They stood next to each other in silence, gazing down across the snow-laden fields. This was the best bit of the walk: the worst of the rise behind them, and an uninterrupted view down to the nearer and smaller of the quarry sites. Work had already stopped at Štěpánov, because of the freezing weather. The prisoners called the small quarry site Little Cauldron because it nestled in a hollow at the base of low, long rise. Work would finish here soon as well. To their right, the woods rose darkly but the camp itself was hidden by the trees. A prisoner could stand and gaze at this view and forget that the camp, and the world of the camp, even existed. It was cold, but there was the smallest hint of sun lightening the sky, a freshness in the air. It was almost a beautiful day.

'Come on then,' growled the kapo, heaving the sack of bread on to his back and stepping past them. They bent to pick up the tureen.

As they descended along the path that ran alongside a farmer's fence, the kapo picked up pace and got ahead of them, as if trying to prove he could beat them to it. They both slowed down slightly, until he was far enough ahead to allow them to whisper to each other. It was necessary to walk more slowly now. The ground of the path was deeply rutted, frozen, and covered with a light frosting of snow, making it easy to slip. The soup slapped around inside the tureen. They stumbled on for a moment or two in silence, as if embarrassed by the possibility of speech.

Emil was suddenly full of words, so confused by all he wanted to say that he hissed with undisguised spite, 'You did not think you could find me and tell me my father had died? You thought it would be better to learn it from a stranger?'

Anna did not reply for a few moments. Then she said, very quietly, 'It is difficult.' Her sorrow and exhaustion were so apparent in the words that Emil was overwhelmed with guilt. They walked on some more, and he thought, how long do we have before that kapo turns? A minute? Two, perhaps? How foolish of us to be tongue-tied when time is so short.

'You are well?' he said in a conciliatory tone. Only when the words were spoken did he feel the stupidity of such a question.

'I am not sick yet.' His mother spoke swiftly. 'You?'

'No, not sick . . .' apart from the diarrhoea and the pain in his jaw and the cracked flesh on his feet and hands where the cold seemed to take slices from him. 'No fever, not yet. Many of the men . . .' His voice dwindled. She knew how many were sick.

They were walking steadily. The kapo glanced back once, saw they were still there, then continued down the path.

'There is more pneumonia every day now. The children are nearly all sick, and there is talk of typhus,' Anna said. 'Yenko. You must go.'

Emil glanced over at her but she did not look at him.

'You must leave, escape,' she said, her voice low and firm. 'It is your only hope, and mine. Your father is dead and his ghost condemned to live among the *gadje* forever. Your sister too.

Bobo's eyes are almost closed. He is near blind. You and I are the only ones in our family not yet sick. You must leave while you still can. I know it's difficult to survive in winter but you must do it. You are the man now.'

'If I am the man then I cannot leave you.' He had promised his father. He had sworn by the moon and the stars.

'I command you to go!'

Emil's knees were suddenly weak. He heard himself say, pleadingly, 'Come with me.'

His mother hesitated for a moment, then replied firmly, 'You know I cannot. I cannot leave Bobo, or Ludmila and Eva.'

'Then we'll all go.'

'Ludmila and Eva are too weak. We would have to carry Bobo. That woman who escaped last month with her daughters and grandchildren. They would have starved if they had not been caught. Did you see them when they came back? The children were both dead within a week.'

This was true. Most of the escapees got no further than a few kilometres. Sometimes they gave themselves up rather than starve.

'Kill a *gadjo*.' Anna's voice was sharp.

Emil looked at his mother. She continued staring straight ahead as they walked.

'Pick a poor one,' she said, 'a farm worker or a peasant out in his field. Then you must bury the body so it won't be found. Kill him in the morning and spend all day burying him, then travel at night. If they find the body before you're out of the district, you're as good as dead.'

Emil thought about killing a man.

Anna said, 'That's where the others have gone wrong. They have tried to stay away from people, afraid of being caught. You need to hunt one down. I picked up a piece of metal at the quarry last week. It was sticking out of the ground. It's hidden behind my bunk. It's sharp enough to kill. I've been rubbing it, at night when the others are asleep. Each time I do it, I think about you killing a white person, just one *gadjo* for all the lives they have taken from us; Parni, your father, the hundreds of others in here. When you are killing him, think about your father gasping for breath and his soul trapped forever because I couldn't even open a window to let it out. His ghost will wander forever about this place. He will be in torment always. There was blood at your birth, Yenko, a knife. Maybe that meant something. A sign.'

'I don't know if I have the strength,' Emil replied. He meant the physical strength.

She misunderstood him. 'I know your hesitation. Your father would not have said what I am saying. Even if he had watched us burned alive, he would never have said you should lower yourself to kill in return. He was a good man, your father. But he is *dead*.' She paused. The urgency of her speech was making her breathless. He noticed that one of her upper eyelids was red and badly swollen. Our bodies are rotting, he thought. *I'll rot if I stay here any longer. Soon, I won't have the strength to escape.* 'It is not against the law to kill in self-defence. Even the *gadje* laws say that. You need clothes. That's why the others failed. How could they leave the woods dressed as prisoners? The clothes are more important than food. You can always steal something to eat. But you must look like a *gadjo* if you are to stand any chance. As soon as you are out of here, then grow your hair and rub sand in it to lighten it. Praise to God for giving me one light-skinned child. You'll pass. You speak Czech like a *gadjo* and your German is not bad. You are an educated Rom. Most of our people are stupid. We've always been stupid, I see that now. Stay away from our people. If there are any Roma still free they will be rounding them up soon enough, so stay away, however lonely you get. Live amongst the *gadje*. Become a *gadjo* for the rest of the war. It is no sin when you are doing it to live, to live for all of us.'

They were nearly at the bottom of the rise. The quarry site was visible ahead, the pale heaps of stone and the small black shapes of the prisoners at work. They were near enough to see that two had stood up and spotted their approach. The kapo who was accompanying them glanced over his shoulder.

'I don't know when we will be able to speak.' Anna said. 'So start preparing now. I will try and get this piece of metal to you but if the opportunity comes in the meantime then just go. I've been round the fence. There's a place at the top behind your block where you can burrow underneath. Where can I leave this piece of metal?'

'There is a pile of stones at the side of the doctor's hut. They are blocking a hole where the wood is rotten at the bottom.'

'How will you be able to get it without being seen?'

'I can do it.'

'It might take me a day or two. Don't wait for it if you get the chance.'

'I will come back for you,' said Emil. 'In the summer, when the weather is good and we can survive in the open air with Bobo. The war might have finished by then anyway. Stay in the area so I can find you. I will come back, I swear it on my father's soul. If it isn't all over I'll get work round here so I can come and get you. I'll look different by then. I'll come to the gates like a *gadjo* and just stroll in, as if I was looking for workers just like the quarry owner. Just make sure you stay in the area if you get released. The Russians might be here by then. Who knows?' The words were pouring out of him.

'Yenko . . .' Anna said. She paused, and they lowered the tureen. 'Go with God.'

The kapo had stopped and was waiting for them. Emil said, 'Stay with God.'

They stood for a moment.

The kapo was frowning and beckoning. Behind him, Emil could see a group of prisoners striding up from the quarry to meet them.

CHAPTER 20

He did not see his mother for another week. In the meantime, he collected the piece of metal with its sharpened point and hid it behind his bunk, and as he fell asleep each night he reached out and touched its roughened surface, as if it was a charm. He couldn't imagine killing someone with it. It was more like one of the icons his grandmother used to keep in her wagon, or the little gold cross she wore, hidden amongst the large coins of her necklace.

At first, he did not like to plan his escape because he was frightened of failing – then he realised, he was also afraid of success. He had so resented his family for keeping him in Hodonín – it was always the young men without families who tried to get away. But now his mother had given him permission to go, he realised that he had forgotten life outside the camp. How did they used to get food? His mother was always preparing something. Where did their blankets come from? He had never slept alone, even on summer nights there was his father or some of the other men at arm's length beside him on the grass. It was madness to think of escape in the heart of winter. He would simply freeze to death.

There had been a slight increase in rations, an extra piece of bread with the evening soup. Some said it was because the camp authorities were worried about how many people were falling ill. The man who had the bunk below Emil insisted that it meant the war would be ending soon. 'They are ashamed . . .' he told Emil one evening before lights out, waving his extra piece of bread. 'They are trying to fatten us up. They know we will be released and tell everybody how they have treated us, then the Russians will give them what for. The Russians will say to the Czechs, whose side were you on anyway, ours or the Hitlerites? I tell you, they are going to be in dead trouble for running these camps. Just you wait and see.'

Emil snorted sceptically, wanting to believe the man. 'The Russians won't care . . .' he said.

'Don't you believe it,' the man said, swallowing his dry bread with an upward tilt of nose. 'The Russians are the bravest of all the *gadje*, they'll fight to the last man. And they believe in justice. Comrade Stalin, he's the one for us. Next time you see a German, any of those soldiers who come by or any of the ones who turn up with their notebooks, look at them and say one word to yourself inside, *Stalingrad*.'

'Is that in Russia?'

The man shook his head. 'Brother, this is the problem with our people. We haven't been paying attention to what's going on. *Is Stalingrad in Russia?* Let me tell you about Stalingrad.' A few of the men around them stopped what they were doing to listen. The man noticed and nodded, glancing about, warming to his audience. 'Stalingrad is a huge white city, with enormous buildings, as big as hills, all shiny-white, built in honour of the Big *Gadjo*, Comrade Stalin. It is the cleanest city in the world – well, as clean as a city full of *gadje* can be, that is. It is on the edge of a vast flowing river.'

'Where is this white city? What's he talking about?' said the man next to Emil.

'Russia,' Emil replied.

The man shook his head, 'The Soviet Union, where all men are brothers!'

At this, the men exchanged sceptical looks.

'It's true, I tell you. Even the *gadjos* are brothers. Anyway, I'll tell you about that another day. This story is about how the Germans have just lost the war. Stalingrad is in the east, way beyond where you can imagine, across rivers and mountains and huge plains of grass. The plains of grass stretch as far as you can see, for days and days. The plains are so huge a travelling *kumpánia* would have to navigate by the stars, like sailors on the sea. That's how far east the Germans got. But at Stalingrad, they met their match. The citizens stood their ground and trapped them and forced them into the river. The German army was swallowed whole. None of them are coming back. And the Russians are sweeping west, towards us, even as we speak.'

Some of the men shook their heads or pulled sceptical faces. Others looked impressed. A couple shook their hands at the wrist to show they were washing themselves of this nonsense. Emil believed the man: there was the light of truth in his face, he was sure of it. *It will be finished by the summer*, he thought. This man is right. All we have to do is sit tight until the summer. It would be madness to try and escape now. Isn't the winter nearly through, already? It was always at its worst just before the weather improved.

One day, Emil returned to his bunk mid-afternoon. Čacko was unwell and had dismissed him for the day. The block was empty but the block Elder had left the stove alight, which meant he would be back soon.

Emil checked to see that the piece of metal was still in place behind the loose plank, as he always did. It was still there, but the plank was damp. He investigated further up the wall and found a single thread of water filtering down the wooden crevices. The wood was blackened by the damp and already spongy in places. The expanding ice on the roof must have cracked the tar paper. Now, with the winter sun beginning to shine each day, the ice was melting and water leaking in. A thaw, Emil thought, pressing his fingertips against the pliant wood. It would soon rot. Winter had come early that year – surely Righteous God would now give them an early spring.

It was the next day that he was able to talk to Marie, for the first time in weeks.

Čacko sent them into the small wooded area behind the dog kennels, to dig a hole for one of the dogs who had died, he said. He had sent them off with a cheery, complicit wink at Emil. *Make the most of this opportunity*, the wink seemed to say. *I'm prepared to turn a blind eye*.

As they crossed the camp, shyly silent, Emil wondered whether he should perhaps follow Čacko's suggestion. Should he grab Marie? Force her down? He was fifteen years old and had never had a woman. When else would he get the chance? The normal rules didn't apply here. There was Marie's father to think of, but he had been moved to the new men's block and spent half his time in the punishment shed. Would she complain to him anyway? Marie had told Emil what her father was like back in the settlement. Emil thought he would like the opportunity to fight Jan Malík, to show how a Rom should behave. A man like Malík didn't deserve a daughter like Marie. It would serve him right if Emil took her.

They were out of sight behind the kennels: Čacko's plan, Emil thought, his breath deepening. The dogs could be heard scratching and whimpering. The kennels had been insulated from the cold with piles of brushwood, which made them look like bonfires. How nice it would be to pour kerosene over them and put a match to them, to warm their hands on the flames from a crackling dog.

They had been given a spade each, but Marie made no pretence of attempting to dig. She sat down on a mound of frozen earth and wrapped her skirt tightly round her legs, lowering her head on to her knees and huddling down against the cold. At least they were sheltered from the wind.

Emil lifted his spade and tried to jab it into the frozen earth. Let her speak first, for once. After a few moments, he had made only a small dent. Damn the ground. He was not enjoying looking weak and incapable in front of Marie. Damn her for her silences. It would be nice to shake her, just like Čacko was expecting him to. He stood upright and wiped at his brow with his sleeve. 'This spade is blunt,' he said. 'Let me try that one.'

Without raising herself, she reached forward and lifted her spade, extending her arm towards him.

He stared at her for a moment, tossed his own spade aside and crossed to her in two strides. He placed his hand on the shaft of the spade, but she did not immediately relinquish it. She looked at him. He stared at her without moving, a hard stare that made his intentions clear. She stared back for a moment, acknowledging him, then dropped her gaze.

He took the spade from her and stepped away. 'You know, Marie,' he said, as he raised the spade to strike the earth, 'it does not kill a woman to give a man a word of encouragement.'

She remained silent. He glanced at her, but she was staring at the patch of earth in front of her feet, her expression thoughtful.

'It wasn't your tonsil you swallowed,' muttered Emil. 'It was your tongue.'

'There's nothing wrong with my tongue,' said Marie swiftly, then clamped her mouth tight shut, as if to stop more words escaping.

Emil glanced around. 'Marie, we are out of sight. What are you afraid of? You're not in the settlement now. Your father won't come after you with a stick. He's probably forgotten you exist.'

'The forest has eyes,' Marie said quickly.

Emil dug furiously. 'Don't give me proverbs. No one is looking and no one cares. All anyone in this place cares about is the gnawing in their bellies. Do you think anyone notices us? Don't be so big-headed.'

'My father notices everything.'

Emil made a face. He chewed at his lower lip to prevent himself from saying something rude about Marie's father. However much a person might hate a member of their own family, there was no surer way to make them love them than to agree.

He could not afford to criticise Jan Malík himself but he wanted to prompt Marie into disloyalty against her father, to make her feel the two of them were complicit. She was only using propriety as an excuse. She knew that as much as he did.

'So, what does your father say about us, the Kalderash?' he

asked casually, continuing to dig. Emil knew exactly the sort of the thing a man like Malík would say about the Vlach Roma, but Marie would feel embarrassed if he forced her to say it.

She seemed relieved that Emil had changed the subject. She smiled, then shrugged.

'Go on,' said Emil. 'I won't be offended. I can guess.'

'He doesn't like anyone,' she said, in a casual tone of voice to indicate she did not share her father's prejudices. 'He says the Vlach Rom are backward.'

'Including the Kalderash, eh?'

'He doesn't distinguish, Kalderash, Lowari, Čurara . . .'

Emil threw down his spade. 'He puts us in the same group as the sieve-makers? My grandfather owned twenty horses!'

Marie looked straight at him and said calmly, 'You promised you wouldn't be offended . . .'

Emil picked up his spade again and resumed his digging with vigour. 'Go on then . . .'

'No, I won't. You promised but you were not being truthful with me.'

'No. I want to know.' Suddenly, he did want to know. It was still a game, but not just a game.

'He says some of you marry *gadje* and forget your Romani . . .'

'Some do, not us,' huffed Emil, panting a little due to the ferocity of his digging. He was still making little headway. 'There are a couple of Boyash in our block. Nobody can understand a word they say . . .'

'. . . And that means you are Unclean. We are Roma but you are . . .'

Emil whirled round, hurling the spade from his grasp. It spun in the air and bounced off the pile of brushwood up against the back of one of the kennels. The dogs inside leapt to their feet and began barking furiously and scrabbling against the walls of the kennels.

'How dare he? How dare he!' Emil's hands were fists. He shouted above the clamour of the dogs. 'Unclean? *Us?* The Kalderash are the best Roma in the whole world. Our women are the most beautiful . . . you, you don't even have braids! Our men can craft any metal! Copper, iron, tin . . . You live in a *cottage*, with whitewashed walls and chairs and tables. Tell your father from me, he can come to our block any day and stand in front of me and tell me I'm Unclean. I'll knock him to the ground. My father *died* in this stinking place.'

Marie had jumped to her feet in shock when he had flung the spade. Her eyes were small and dark with fury. 'You lied to me! You said you wouldn't be angry! You lied!'

Emil sank to the ground, kneeling on the hard, frozen earth, unheeding of the damp that soaked rapidly through his thin trousers. He hung his head. '*Taté* . . .' he said. Dad . . . He was overwhelmed with grief, a sudden and tender, yawning and gaping sense of loss. His father; his kind, gentle father, who never hurt a man or woman or child in his life – a wise, soft man who had died slowly because he was so wise and soft, while his son had done nothing but observe. He had never given his father so much as a single turnip peeling. He had thought, there is no point when he is going to die anyway. Now, he was dead. He could see the point, now.

The revelation drained him of all energy. He stayed kneeling, his head hanging, and neither of them spoke for a long time. The dogs fell silent. No one came to investigate. A few sparse flakes of snow began to fall. How pointless it seemed, all the struggling.

'I am sorry for your father's death . . .' Marie said eventually. 'For many reasons . . .'

Emil looked up at her.

Marie shook her head. 'Even if your father was alive, to talk to mine . . .' she said. Then she drew a deep breath. 'My father would never permit me to marry a Vlach Rom.'

Sitting in the mud, mourning his father, Emil felt a strange, drunken rush of happiness; a heady, illogical joy. I am going a little mad, he thought. The air around was light. *Marry.* It was a word full of future, a stupid word, idiotic, a word that had wings. To pronounce it at all was an act of such daring. All at once, Marie seemed heroic. She was right. There was a world beyond. *Marry* . . . He threw back his head and gave a short, hysterical laugh – and Marie, seeing this, smiled and smiled at him, and for a moment they were united in their amusement at their own absurdity. *So this is how it is,* he thought, *between men and women, to be thinking the same thing but in different ways. There was I thinking of pinning her down, and she was thinking of it too in her womanly way, and the gulf between us is so huge and strange at the very time when we are both thinking the same thing.* And he laughed again, feeling the gulf between them, and he loved Marie for laughing too, for believing that she understood.

That night, the inmates stood for a long time at roll-call. A rabbit had gone missing from the hutches at the west side of the camp. Emil stood in line with the other men in a sweat of fear that someone might make a link between his and Marie's sojourn behind the dog kennels and the missing rabbit. Čacko was not on duty and some of the guards had a vengeful streak. Being a favourite had hazards as well as benefits.

They all stood, men and women in separate rows, while the blocks were searched. The Commandant was in a fury, storming up and down and shouting that he was prepared to turn the children out of their block into the freezing night to search if the culprit did not come forward. Some of the women were crying. They had all been told to stand still, to attention, but two women collapsed and were taken to the infirmary. One awoke as she was being pulled along the ground and kicked and screamed as she was dragged away. They were all terrified of the infirmary now.

Emil worked his toes in his footwraps to stave off frostbite and tried to calculate how long they were being made to wait. The night was clear. The stars were out. His breath condensed on the air in white clouds. His toes began to ache with wriggling but if he stopped they went numb. The man next to him was shaking uncontrollably with cold, his head making tiny juddering motions up and down.

Eventually, the guards who had searched the block were all gathered together, shaking their heads. Two were showing the Commandant other items that had been found during the search – in the dark it wasn't possible to see what they were showing him. Emil closed his eyes and said to himself, *O Del, blind the evil gadje and let me keep that piece of metal, and I promise I will hide it in my shirt from now on and use it when I get the chance. Give me the chance.*

The guards had summoned the block Elders and were trying to identify the owners of the bunks where the items had been found. At last, two men were selected from the lines, one at the front, one right behind Emil, and taken away.

Normally, the whole camp observed the beatings; the victims would be bent over logs, stripped, and water poured over their buttocks, but it seemed that tonight even the Commandant had had enough. It was pitch dark. The floodlights above gave each prisoner a huge black shadow. He announced that the search for the rabbit thief would continue tomorrow. The culprit was not to imagine he had escaped detection.

A collective groan of relief ran through the men and women as they were dismissed to their blocks.

Emil was shuffling away in a group of other men when he felt a fierce clutch at his elbow, a pinch. He turned – it was his mother. Her face was contorted. She gave a shriek, 'Aieeee . . .' and collapsed. He bent over her.

'Take me to the infirmary . . .' she hissed, her voice quite normal. 'Tell them . . . alone . . .'

Two other men had bent to help. A kapo was striding toward them. Emil stood and waved them all away. 'It's my mother, she's sick, she has a fever.' The kapo halted his approach.

'I'll take her . . .' Emil added unnecessarily, pulling Anna by one arm and lifting her with his other arm around her waist.

The kapo turned away.

'If I take you to the infirmary, you'll get sick . . .' Emil hissed to his mother as they limped away, her leaning on him, head down.

'Never mind that, I'll talk my way out tomorrow. Just listen. Walk more slowly. Give us time.' Men were streaming past them in the dark, keen to get back to the block.

Emil and Anna limped along together, their breath condensing in the night air and mingling into a single cloud. When she spoke, her voice was low and urgent.

'I was cleaning by the administration block. There was a guard and some girl, a *gadji*, out back, one of the secretaries, his whore. She was crying and he was trying to comfort her. She was making him promise not to tell the other guards.' A kapo walked past and Anna stopped talking until he was out of earshot. 'There's going to be a quarantine. The order has come through but nobody is supposed to know yet. The whole camp is going to be sealed off from the outside world. Everyone. The guards have been expecting it for weeks, that's what this guard kept saying, well we all thought it would happen. She was crying and crying. They are all trapped here now, like us. Leave is cancelled and nobody will be relieved. No one will be allowed in or out. They're making the final preparations. They are going to re-route the road and deliveries will have to be left at least two hundred metres from the main gate. It's typhus. They are sealing us all in, prisoners, guards, everyone, and leaving us to die.' They were almost at the infirmary gate. A guard stood at attention. Beyond him, a tiny electric bulb cast a weak yellow light over the fresh snow which coated the concrete step up to the hut. 'You must *go*,' Anna said. 'Once word gets out about this, no one will get out of here. I don't know how long you've got. A few days, maybe less.'

He wanted to say something but she pushed him away and hurried up to the guard, who looked at her. She spoke to him, clutching her stomach and groaning. He opened the gate for her, closing it after she had passed.

Emil watched as she mounted the step, opened the door without looking back at him, and disappeared inside. The door closed behind her with a bang which shook its weak wooden frame. A thin shower of icicles detached from the lintel and dropped soundlessly on to the snow-covered step. It was the last time he saw his mother.

That night, Emil lay awake in his bunk, shuddering with the cold but hot with excitement. His piece of metal was now tucked into his right footwrap, where it lay flush with the sole of his foot.

There could be no more vacillation. It was die here or die out there, in the open. At least give me the chance to lie down in the snow and die of cold, he thought, at least spare me dogs or bullets. That's all I ask. Dying of cold must be painless, he thought. You would just go numb. The difficult part was trying to stay alive – but if you knew you were going to die anyway . . .

The secret of courage – he had discovered it: to resolve to die. After that, it was simply a matter of preferring one method or another. He preferred to lie down in the snow, go numb, sleep and die rather than stay trapped in the camp and die of typhus. His mother urged it. His father and his sister were dead, his brother beyond help, his mother and his aunts wanted him to do whatever he chose. His conscience was entirely clear.

Marie. He frowned to himself in the dark.

I will take her with me. His thoughts ran with the idea. We could pretend we were married. It's probably easier that way, than a man on his own. Less of a threat. We could pretend she was pregnant. We'd get taken in somewhere.

Then he thought of having to run . . . Marie, her little feet. How would she manage if there were dogs on their heels? She would hold him back. He bit softly at the inside of his mouth. Marie would hold him back, no doubt about that – she would be an asset once they were safely away, but how to get away? How to even get her out of the women's block?

Would she agree to go? There was her mother and father to consider. Could he trust her not to warn them if he told her about the quarantine? He fell asleep deciding he would have to go alone.

He awoke resolved to take her with him. To be alone was terrible. He would need support on the outside, someone to talk to. Then, when spring came, he would come back and rescue his mother and his aunts and Bobo. The quarantine might be lifted by then. He would get Marie's parents out too. Together, they would all form a new *kumpánia*. He would speak to her today. He would find a way.

At morning roll-call, it was announced that all prisoners would be collectively punished for the theft of the rabbit by the cancellation of all food for that day. As they fell out, Emil looked around for Čacko. He had given him the impression that he had had a man's way with Marie, the previous day. He would ask for the opportunity for another go, chummily, man-to-man, then he and Marie could plan their escape. Night would be best, if she could find the courage.

Čacko was nowhere to be seen. He went over to the staff hut. 'Officer Čacko is sick,' one the guards informed him shortly. The next sentence ruined his plan. 'Go and join Work Detail B. They are leaving soon. Go.' It was a disaster. He would be at the quarry until nightfall. There would be no way of speaking to Marie.

'Go,' said the guard, seeing his face. 'Now! Go, go!' He flapped his hands.

Emil ran across to the gate where the detail was waiting, and gave his name to the guard in charge, hoping that there would be too many men, but he was told curtly to join the line. They would leave in ten minutes.

As he fell in, a prisoner looked over his shoulder and said, 'So, Wallach, godfather not on duty today, eh? Doing some work like the rest of us?'

As they marched out of the gate, Emil told himself that at least that night, at roll-call, he would be able to find out whether his mother had talked her way out of the infirmary.

The guard in charge of Work Detail B was a friend of Čacko's and put Emil to work chipping smaller pieces of stone into shale. It meant he could sit down at least, unlike the other men, although he got cold quickly. The stone shattered easily under the small hammer, scattering chalky powder over his coat and trousers. The guard lingered next to him, bored, chatting in Czech. 'They are talking of keeping this site open through the winter now,' he said idly to Emil, as he watched over the other

men, 'just because it's been a bit better the last few days. I don't
think it's a good idea myself, but then I'm not in charge . . .'
While the guard was speaking, he noticed that some of the
powder from the shattered stone had landed on his uniform
trouser leg. He batted at it ineffectually with his hand. 'The
weather's going to be bad for weeks yet.' He reached out and
pulled Emil's woollen hat from his head, then used it to rub the
stone powder from his leg. When he had finished, he tossed the
hat into Emil's lap. 'It's not as if anything is being achieved, apart
from keeping them busy.'

Emil put down the hammer and replaced his hat, then
resumed work. 'And look at them . . .' the guard shook his head.
'Every one of them sick . . .'

'What's wrong with Čacko?' Emil enquired casually.

The guard gave an amused snort. 'Nothing that a short break
from the moonshine wouldn't cure. Have you tasted that stuff?'
He shook his head. 'He's trying to tell them he's got a fever but
they're not stupid. He'll be back on duty tonight, you watch,
clutching at his sore head. I'd steer well clear if I were you.'

Emil sighed. The guard turned his face up to the sky,
squeezing his eyes tight shut and frowning. 'It'll be a long day
for them today.' He meant, with the cancellation of lunch. Emil
hoped that the use of *them* implied that maybe he would be
getting a lunch break after all, perhaps even a bite of the guard's
rations.

At noon, the guard ordered them all to stop, reminded them no
food was coming, then sat next to Emil and opened his pack. The
men huddled down together, a short distance away, several
glaring resentfully at Emil. Emil glared back. He was just as
hungry as they were. A couple of the men had pulled their
spoons from their pockets and were eating snow from the

ground, letting it melt in their mouths before they swallowed, as they had all learnt to do if they wanted to avoid the cramps. Emil wondered if he dared do the same with the guard sitting next to him.

The guard had unwrapped a piece of cloth which held a large chunk of bread and a fat slice of white cheese. He ate for a moment or two, then looked inside his rucksack. He frowned, pushing his hand around the contents. 'I forgot my bottle. *And* no one will come out here with coffee either . . .' he muttered to himself.

He sucked at his teeth, then looked at Emil. 'I tell you what,' he said thoughtfully. 'Go back and get my chicory coffee. Go to the staff hut if there's none at the kitchen and remind them that there's an officer out here too, freezing his bollocks off. If you can make it there and back while it's still warm I'll give you a bite of my bread, maybe even a piece of cheese, eh?'

Emil was on his feet and nodding before the guard had finished his sentence. He avoided the gazes of the other prisoners as he turned and trotted up the path, towards the farmer's fence and the woods.

Later, he tried to remember exactly what had happened when he reached the fence. He tried to imagine himself pausing and looking left and right; right to where the rutted path led up the hill, turning just before the top of the rise that led back to the camp; left to where it ran parallel to the fence and disappeared into the woods. He tried to recall staring into the woods, where a cold mist soaked the trees, making their trunks look soft, almost lilac-coloured, in the poor light. The lower two-thirds of the trees were almost bare, the sparse green pine branches only beginning high up above a man's head. They seemed to aspire to something, those trees.

The snow beneath the trees lay white, untrodden, in patches

here and there. The foliage above was dense enough to provide a canopy in places. A thick brown carpet of dead pine needles lay directly beneath the branches. They gave beneath his feet with an encouraging motion. He jumped from tree to tree, avoiding the patches of snow so as to leave no tracks. He observed how, around the edges, there were puddles of ice where the snow had melted, then re-frozen. Twigs and pine needles were trapped in the ice. He moved swiftly but carefully, wanting to cover ground but also wanting to feel what he was doing, to know it intensely, to enjoy the sharp contrast between the dark brown earth and twigs and the white snow, the delicate crackle of the pliant ice beneath his feet.

There was no pause at the fence. There was no moment in which he made his decision. He had reached the rutted path, and his feet had turned him left without hesitation: and now he was half-running, half-jumping through the forest, away from the camp. Even now, it wasn't too late to turn, to run back and get the guard's coffee, but even as he thought this fleetingly, his feet were moving over the ground and the freezing air was fresh in his lungs and he knew it was already far too late. He had escaped.

PART 6

1943

CHAPTER 21

He walked until the forest ended. He gave no thought to the direction of his walking, or to anything other than the need to place one foot in front of the other. He did not think of anything. He scarcely breathed. He knew that if he stopped to consider the possible consequences of his actions his legs would turn to water and he would collapse. So he concentrated on moving the legs, to and fro, one after the other in that strange scissor motion which he realised he had never before examined. Odd to think that there was still enough muscle somewhere beneath his pallid chicken-skin to move his bones and propel his body forward. He could almost hear the joints of his legs grating together. How long was it since he had walked anywhere of his own volition?

My name is Yenko.

He noticed the ground. The ground proved interesting; thin layers of ice, fresh and crackling, bright as glass; leaves and twigs and pine needles packed together; a sponginess beneath his step. He noticed the sky; a blue which looked as though it wanted to be more blue but was not yet convinced that winter would one day be over. The air was fresh and clear, the branches of the trees so sagging that small breezes sent snow showers floating down.

The edge of the forest came as an unpleasant surprise. The open fields that led away and upwards were fallow, bare. He skirted the forest to the top of the rise and saw with relief that on the other side of the hill there was another wooded area. That would be the place to spend the night. He paused on the edge of the wood, then bent and scooped up a small heap of fresh snow with his fingers, closing his mouth over it and letting it melt before he swallowed. It took a long time to quench a thirst that way. The light was beginning to fade.

A squirrel was scrambling down a nearby tree, making its way towards the ground in spiralling fashion around the trunk. It saw him and froze, legs splayed, tail a furry question mark. They will probably find me and kill me, Yenko thought cheerfully, cocking his head to one side at the squirrel, as if to answer its query. They will come after me with guns and dogs – they are probably behind me in the woods right now, searching. There will be some brief panic and then it will all be over. I will die and I won't have to worry about anything any more. I will die in the open, bravely, screaming my head off. I have chosen to die this way. I am not waiting to rot, not like my father. My mother always told me that my father was a gentle man and made it sound like a good thing. But he rotted. He let them do it to him. I'm making them do it. There's a difference.

He turned, then dropped low to run, crouching fashion, across the open fields. Beyond the shelter of the trees, an icy breeze was blowing. Would he dare to sleep once it got dark? He might never wake up.

The second forest was more sparse. There was no foliage between the trees and nowhere to shelter. He would have to keep walking for as long as he could.

Just before dark, he decided he must rest. He wasted the remainder of the daylight layering branches criss-cross fashion so that he could lie on them to sleep and be raised from the icy earth. He made another layer of branches and twigs to pull on top of him. When he crawled between the layers, the one beneath him collapsed, dropping him on to the spiky, frozen mud. He jumped to his feet and shook himself, laughing out loud at his folly, then looked around, as if there might be witnesses to hear his laugh and think him deranged. All at once, he was overcome by a wave of loneliness. He had never been alone before. He felt a sudden urge to sing, for the sake of hearing a human voice and convincing himself there were still humans in the world. He thought of how his Aunt Tekla had let him try her pipe once, when he was a very small boy, and how he had pretended to like it. They had nodded at each other, smiling and smiling. Then he had vomited in her lap. She had cuffed him, then rose to change her skirts. When she returned, she cradled him and stroked his forehead and sang him a song about a deer.

> The deer ran on and on and on
> The deer-with-an-arrow-through-his-heart.
> The deer ran on and on and on
> Little deer-with-an-arrow-through-his-heart.

If he lay down to sleep, he would die.

He squatted on the ground, his back up against the tree, a few of the branches pulled around him, then closed his eyes and let his head fall to his chest.

He was woken by the sound of something scurrying in the undergrowth nearby and jumped up, heart thumping, convinced that the noise had been the skittering of dogs' feet amongst the branches. It was pitch black. His breathing echoed so loudly in his head that he could hear nothing else. Only when his heart steadied did he realise there were no dogs. Whatever small animal had scurried by was gone. The forest was silent. He thought, if they had dogs on my scent, they would have found me by now. They would have found me before nightfall. Something must have gone wrong for them. They are not going to catch me.

It was too dark to keep walking – he would end up going in circles. He squatted down again and closed his eyes, but the thought of the dogs had rendered sleep impossible. He had stomach pains from eating nothing but snow and his toes were numb. He wrapped his arms around himself and tried to think about counting to one hundred in a mixture of Romani, German and Czech.

Towards dawn, the cloud cover parted to reveal a weak moon. He stood, stiffly, the pain in his frozen joints making him gasp aloud. He began to limp through the forest, his feet crackling with agony. The euphoria of the previous day, the joy of walking, was gone. Each step sent flames shooting up his legs. His rib-cage was enclosed by bands of iron. It won't be so bad once I've got going, he told himself. It won't be so bad, if I can just keep going.

He kept going, pausing only to eat snow, throughout that day. The forest was so vast that he began to wonder if he had lost the ability to navigate and was wandering aimlessly. When he finally reached the edge of the wood, he approached cautiously. Perhaps he would gaze out over the open countryside to see the first wood he had traversed, across the rise, and Čacko and a squad of gendarmes striding out to greet him. But when he reached the edge of the wood, he saw that the landscape was reassuringly different from the one he had left.

It was still light, but soon dusk would come. The frail blue of the sky had bled and faded: it was now a dying, almost-white. The even whiter shadow of the rising moon hung high. A cold wind blew. Before him were more open fields, wide, high flatlands, uninhabited. Farms or villages would be tucked away in the valleys, he reasoned. There couldn't be much up here. He turned to the left and skirted the forest for a few metres, trying to judge the best place to leave cover. The ground descended sharply and he followed it until it dropped away to reveal a tiny, tinkling brook. He sat down and worked his way carefully down a steep incline to the bank. The brook was actually flowing, with icy meltwater. Grey patches of ice still floated on the surface, like frogs' spawn. Icicles hung from the opposite bank, clear as crystal, the single beads of water at their tips shining like stars. He stared at them for a moment.

He knelt and scooped water from the brook to quench his thirst. It tasted even colder than the snow he had been eating. He swallowed carefully and the small gulp shivered painfully down his throat.

As he stood upright, he felt a wash of pain across the sole of his left foot and lifted it to see that his foot-wrap was worn through and the layers next to his skin soaked with icy water. If his foot-wraps were falling apart, they would have to be abandoned, which meant going barefoot. Going barefoot meant frostbite, which meant the end.

It was time to find his *gadjo*.

He tucked the worn ends of the footwrap inside the parts of cloth that were still holding, then clambered alongside the brook until he found a place where he could cross by leaping from one stone to the next. He could not risk getting wet when he might have to spend another night in the open.

Now is the crucial time, he thought, the next few hours are the pivotal period when the small things that will help me live or die will happen. If I am lucky, find food or shelter or someone to help me or to steal from, I will live. If I am unlucky – find no one or nothing, meet a patrol – then I will die. The whole of the rest of my life will be decided in the next two hours.

He thought of the Jew he had left in the woods near Kladno. The hours after he had left him must have been like that for him, if he had waited. He must have thought, if that boy comes back, I have a chance. If he doesn't, I don't. At what point would the *biboldo* have realised he wasn't returning? Perhaps he never admitted it to himself because to admit that would have been to relinquish hope, to imagine the unimaginable – one's own non-existence. That's why people don't run or fight more, Yenko thought. They are paralysed by disbelief.

After leaving the brook, he skulked across the frozen fields, crouching low next to the hedges. The ground was rough and broken and he was bent double, so he made little headway. Every now and then, he risked standing to look across the fields. As he descended into the valley, the fallow land gave way to neater, bordered terrain – there had to be a homestead somewhere near, somewhere in the shadow of these bleak hills. It felt so remote, but the fields were hedged and tended. Once, in the far distance, he thought he glimpsed a horse standing next to a single tree, but the light was fading and when he looked again, the horse had gone. With darkness, the temperature would drop. He was shivering; a deep, shuddering sort of shiver. Time was running out.

It was heavy dusk by the time he saw it; a shack tucked into the corner of a field, no more than a poor hut, with a low fence that bounded it from the surrounding farmland – a smallholding perhaps, or hermit's shack. It was too small to be a family home.

Yenko squatted and observed the shack through a gap in the brown-twig fence. He was close enough to see that there was a pair of boots outside the door.

The door opened and an old man emerged on to the step. He was small and round-shouldered, bare-headed but still wearing his winter coat. He picked the boots up and banged them together, then took them inside, closing the door behind him. A soft yellow glow appeared in the one small window. The old man had lit a paraffin lantern. Then a dark wing flapped behind the square panes. He was hanging a blackout curtain.

Yenko pictured the scene inside the shack. The old man would be lighting a fire, warming some stew perhaps. Yenko felt himself tipping forward slightly as he squatted, as if his body was being pulled involuntarily towards the warmth and sustenance he imagined inside the hut. When had he last eaten? He felt sick and faint at the thought.

He pressed the heels of his hands over his eyes and forced himself to think. If there had been anyone else in the shack then the old man would not be lighting the lantern and hanging the blackout curtain. He must be alone. *He has to be.* Yenko reached down and unwrapped the right-hand foot wrap, prising away the two layers of cardboard which were frozen stiff together, fumbling with his numb fingers for the small, rusted piece of metal that his mother had sharpened so laboriously.

He re-wrapped his foot, stood. It was almost dark. Even if the old man looked out of his window he would not see him. He's an old man, Yenko thought, starting to breathe deeply, letting his shoulders rise and fall to work the stiff muscles. He has lived his full quota of life already. My father never got the chance to do that, nor my sister – nor will I unless I am allowed to rest and feed and disguise myself so that I can travel openly. If he doesn't struggle, I can make it quick.

He began to bend and stretch, trying to work his muscles. He was weak from hunger and lack of sleep but he was young and furious. The old man would be tired at the end of a long day's work, and shocked by Yenko's appearance. He would not have time to gather himself.

He stepped carefully over the picket fence, lifting his legs extravagantly. Walking up a *gadjo*'s path, obsequious smile in place, was a habit familiar from his childhood. The obsequious smile stayed on his face as he neared the door and tightened his grip on the piece of metal, the sharpened tip just protruding from his fist. He knew he should be skirting round the hut first, to make sure there was no escape route out the back, no dog slumbering in a kennel, but he was worked up to do the thing now and could not afford delay. His breathing was already sharp and fast. Sweat had broken out on his brow. He felt overcome with a fierce recklessness.

As he lifted a foot to kick in the door, he thought, what if the old man has already locked up for the night and I can't break in? Then he kicked anyway. The door flew open with startling speed and crashed back against the wall. After the darkness of the fields, the interior of the shack was bright yellow and it took Yenko a second to adjust his gaze.

The old man was sitting at a small square table in the middle of the room. He had removed his winter coat and was wearing a shawl over his jacket and trousers. He had a piece of rough cloth tucked into the shawl and was hunched over a bowl of pale-coloured soup, his spoon clasped awkwardly in a hand which was bent at an odd angle, as if he was a child who had only just learnt to hold a spoon. He raised his face and Yenko saw that soup was dripping from his beard.

They both moved. The old man scrambled clumsily from the chair and turned towards the back of the shack. Yenko was upon him before he had moved a step from the table. They were both calling out, guttural cries that held a twin rage and inarticulacy. Yenko grabbed the old man's shoulder and pushed him to the floor but he resisted. Yenko clambered on to his chest, kneeling on him to pin him down, and pressed the piece of metal to the base of his throat, just above where his collarless shirt protruded from his jacket.

The skin resisted at first. It was tough and speckled, like animal hide, with a few sparse white hairs sprouting up from the chest. The piece of metal pushed deeper and deeper and it seemed the skin would never give – but then it did. The tension against the knife released. Pale flesh fell away on either side and the blood burst forth, pouring over Yenko's hand. The old man gave a bubbling cry. His legs kicked and twitched, flipping over the chair on which he had been seated. Yenko realised he was shouting.

Afterwards, he stood above the old man's corpse, panting. He lifted his bloodied hands and looked at them. The rest of him was shaking from head to foot, but his hands were completely steady. He wiped them on his prison jacket, rubbing them up and down absentmindedly while he glanced around the shack. There was a small stove with a cast iron pan on top; another chair; a chest; bedding in an alcove. He righted the chair that the old man had kicked over and then went to the back corner of the shack, where the old man had tried to run.

There was an alcove which held a long-handled shovel and a broom made of twigs, and another door, this one barred. He opened it and in the light from the doorway saw a small yard with a low coop in which two scrawny chickens stood gazing at him, jerking their heads in alarm.

He returned to the shack and lifted the old man by his shoulders. His head flopped back and blood made an audible splatter on the floor. Yenko averted his gaze, and dragged the body outside, locking the door behind him as he re-entered.

He must clean up, the front door was still ajar – he thought these things as he headed inexorably for the soup, sitting on the chair and grabbing the spoon with one swift movement. As he raised the first mouthful, his hand trembled so much that the soup spilled back down into the bowl. He threw the spoon aside and it clattered against the wall of the shack. He lifted the bowl to his mouth and tipped its contents down almost in one movement. The soup tasted of potato and cabbage, thickened with flour and milk. As he lowered the bowl, he thought he had never tasted anything so wonderful in his life.

Something made him glance up, a sense more than a sound, the sense of a shadow perhaps, and the sense sent messages rushing to his head before his eyes had time to tell him anything.

There is a huge crow standing in the doorway.

He turned.

It wasn't a huge crow. It was a woman, a tiny old woman, wrapped in a long dark shawl that fell almost to the floor, her shoulders hunched, her in-turned feet clad in muddy boots with no laces, her face a mask of bewilderment – as if she was wondering whether she could have wandered into the wrong shack. Her eyes gazed at him, hugely round, with a grey, liquid stare.

Yenko stared back at her. When he saw the grey eyes widen further, he knew she had seen the blood on the floor.

He was out of the chair as she turned back towards the door, her small feet shuffling, a cry of fear and panic trapped somewhere in her throat. His hands found easy purchase in the weave of the shawl. As he flung her round he over-balanced – she was so light he misjudged the movement. He was still full of adrenaline after killing the old man. He and the woman fell together, her face near enough to his for him to feel the warmth of her breath and moistness from her cold little nose. He shoved her away and heard a dull crack as her head snapped back against a leg of the table. He was kicking out at her with his legs, thinking, her skull will be as thin as a blackbird's. She will be easier to kill.

Afterwards, he sat down at the table again, and licked up the last remainder of the soup, his tongue rasping against the rough texture of the bowl. Then he threw the bowl to the ground, where it bounced twice before spinning to a halt on the floor. He gave a great heaving sigh. He was sweating. He rushed to the front door of the shack, wheeled round the corner in the dark, and was violently sick. He wiped his mouth with the back of his hand as he went back inside, shaking his head in dismay. He closed and locked the door behind him, and saw by the soft paraffin light that the old woman's head had bled in a huge puddle beneath the kitchen table. He sat down on the other side of the table. He had two bodies to bury now, and blood everywhere meant that when the neighbours came to investigate there would be no chance they would think the old couple were out somewhere. He would never be able to clear up that much blood. By the time he had dragged her corpse out back to join her husband's, it would be everywhere.

He averted his gaze from the old woman's corpse. He had the whole night to think of that.

He went to the one small window and made sure that the blanket the old man had tacked up was firmly in place. He didn't know how far the shack was from any tracks or roads and he couldn't risk a patrol dropping by. Then he began to search.

There was more soup on the stove. He lifted the lid of the old cast iron saucepan eagerly. Steam rose in a cloud, misting the large wooden crucifix that the old man had carved and nailed above the stove, as if to remind himself of the suffering of his Christ every time he went to sup. Yenko felt suddenly nauseous again. He lowered the lid quickly. He would try to eat in a minute.

The old man had clean clothes hanging on the wall; a white collarless shirt, frayed at the cuffs but stiff and fresh; baggy brown trousers and braces. Yenko left them where they were for the time being. In the wooden chest beneath the window, he found some spare clothes belonging to the old lady and, wrapped carefully in tissue paper, two lace nightdresses the colour of weak tea. Underneath the clothes were some family photographs in silver frames. He turned them over and slid the catches back, letting the glass fall into his hands so that he could remove the photos, which he tossed aside without looking at them.

On a crude wooden shelf next to the stove, there was a pot of flour and half a black loaf, a wicker basket with two wrinkled onions. Yenko looked around but there was nothing else, no cupboards or shelves. He bent over the dirt floor thinking, even this poor pair of *gadje* must have a cellar of some sort, somewhere where they keep things. He could find nothing. Then, as he stood upright – his head momentarily reeling – he glanced upwards and saw there was a square door in the rough-beamed ceiling. Of course.

He looked around for a ladder but found none, so he placed a chair on top of the table, knelt up on it, then punched the trap door back with his fist and pulled himself up. Then he nearly fell out again leaning down for the lantern.

At one end of the attic, a few pine cones were laid out, the last of the old couple's winter fuel, and some wizened apples, which he dropped down on to the table below before realising it was stupid to bruise them. Next to the cones was a wicker basket with two loaves of black bread covered by a cloth and a clay vessel with a wooden lid. He lifted the lid and put a finger into the white, opaque wax inside; goose fat. The vessel was almost full and would be too heavy to drop down. Maybe he should lighten its load a little before he lowered it. He sat with it between his legs and broke a piece of black bread from one of the loaves. Fat, a whole jar of fat . . . The bread half-lowered, he stopped. If his stomach had rejected the soup, then what would it say to goose fat? It took every ounce of his remaining strength for him to dab the bread gently into the jar, allowing himself no more than a smear, before replacing the lid.

At the other end of the attic, he found a wooden box with an iron clasp. In it were the old couple's papers; identity papers with illegible scrawls of black ink on the rough yellow card, ration books, a small leather-bound diary with empty pages and a dried-up bottle of brown ink. At the very bottom of the box was a Bible with gilt lettering, and two prayer books.

A wave of exhaustion flooded over him. He closed his eyes and let his shoulders sag, realising that he was thinking, for the first time since he had turned left into the woods near the quarry, that his escape might possibly be successful.

He wanted to sleep so badly. He wanted nothing more than sleep. But with the thought of success, the fear began. It had not been so bad when he had been resolved to die. There had been nothing to lose. Now that he saw the possibility of survival, he was gripped by anxiety. Re-energised, he put everything he wanted to take at the edge of the hatch, then lowered himself down.

It took him nearly two hours, he estimated. He dragged the old woman out to the back yard by her feet and laid her next to her husband. He searched their clothes. The old man had nothing on him, but the old woman had a leather pouch in her pocket. As he pulled it out, it made a gorgeous clinking sound.

He sat and ate the soup left on the stove, slowly this time, and anchored it with a little black bread. Then he went back outside and wrung the necks of the two pathetic chickens and brought them in. He found a sack for his bounty and divided the things up into two piles; things to be carried in the sack that could be abandoned if he had to run; and valuable things to be hidden inside his coat – the purse and the papers, the silver frames, a portion of the fat wrapped in a few pages torn from the empty diary. When he had scooped the fat out with his fingers, he pushed the fingers into his mouth and fastened his gums over them. His mouth watered deliciously, catching the scent of juices from the long-dead goose. The clay jug would be too heavy to carry. He would have to risk eating some of the fat before he left – and rub some on his feet and hands and lips, to insulate them from the cold.

Eventually, he realised that he had been staring at the clay jug for some minutes without moving, and he knew that if he did not sleep, he would collapse where he was on the floor. He hauled himself up, found a small stack of wood by the front door and shoved it into the stove so it would stay alight while he slept.

The old couple's bed was in an alcove next to the stove, the sort of alcove where most people kept firewood. It was narrow but high, with a paper mattress and a bolster pillow. Just an hour or so, he thought as he climbed up, then I will have time to bury them and leave before dawn.

The old people were too poor to have an eiderdown, but they had several thick blankets and, he discovered, a layer of stiched-together rabbit skins between. To sleep beneath fur . . . he thought, in the fraction of a second before he was swallowed by oblivion.

When he awoke, it was broad daylight. White light streamed through the thin blanket over the window. He was instantly awake, his heart thumping, then throwing himself out of bed, jumping down expecting the height of his upper bunk in his block at the camp and confused when his feet met the floor sooner than expected. He stumbled. His hand touched the floor. He looked around and saw the pool of blood, already black, beneath the kitchen table.

He ripped the blanket from the window. What clearer sign that something was amiss than a blackout curtain still up in broad daylight?

He peered anxiously across the empty fields but there was nothing but the bleak expanse of brown soil and white snow. A few crows wheeled in the sky. He guessed it was midday.

What should he do? He could stay here, clean up properly and wait until nightfall to set out – but what if someone came by?

How wonderful it would be to stay for a few days, to sleep and sleep underneath the rabbit skins, to cook the chickens and eat bread and goose fat.

It was too risky. He had no idea whether the old couple might have visitors or not. He didn't even know which day of the week it was.

Suddenly, the idea came to him. It would save a great deal of time and simplify everything. It would throw everybody off the scent. He wouldn't even need to bury the corpses.

He began to search.

He waited until it was almost dark, by which time he had changed into the old man's clean clothes and shoved the hated prison uniform and foot-wraps into the stove to smoke on the near-dead embers. He had packed the bags, eaten more bread and a little fat, and one of the wizened apples. He had dozed again.

He had ransacked the shack; overturned the table, ripped and flung the blankets, broken apart the chest and smashed the small amount of crockery he found next to the stove. Most importantly, he had taken down the wooden crucifix, and thrown it into the fire, along with the Bible and prayer books from the box upstairs. He watched them burn, thinking, our God needs no books to live in our hearts, foolish *gadje*. We worship him with deeds, not words. We live honest lives and we only kill when we have to – not because we enjoy it, like you.

As dusk was falling, he broke off a chair leg and scorched it in the dying embers of the stove. He had been unable to find any paint or whitewash, so this would have to do.

He opened the door and peered across the fields, then stepped outside the cottage. On the front door he scraped in charcoal a Star of David. How many points did they have? Five? Seven? No, six of course, two triangles. He had to go back into the cottage to burn more of the chair leg, twice. He etched deeply on the door. He wanted to make sure it would not wash off if it rained.

When he had finished, he pushed the chair leg into the stove.

He put on the old man's coat and tied the belt. He lifted the sack. It was heavy. He stroked the rabbit skins regretfully. He had tried to fold them into the sack but they were bulkier than they looked – walking around with a sack that bulged would look suspicious. He folded one of the blankets and tucked it into the belt.

He left the door of the cottage swinging on its hinges.

When the neighbours eventually came, when they saw the Star of David, and found the old couple's bodies unburied out the back, they would not question why they had been stabbed and bludgeoned rather than shot. They would not wonder why the shack had been ransacked and everything stolen or broken. Nor would they run to inform the authorities in shock and panic. They would simply wonder why, in all these years, they had never guessed that the reclusive old couple were Jews.

CHAPTER 22

As he descended into the lowlands, he walked into a heavy mist and once he had been found by it, the mist would not relinquish him. Even when it lifted from the fields, at dawn the following day, it stayed inside his head, took up occupancy there and destroyed the links between things. He saw pictures, as he walked westward, but how he got from picture to picture was mysterious. He covered ground quickly, but each step took an eternity. He could no longer remember when he slept, but never felt fully awake.

He knew he must stay away from the roads, but as he descended into the valley, a road was what he found and it, too, clung to him. He turned back up and climbed a steep meadow, crossed a copse – where the mist was hiding amongst the trees – descended, and found the same road had twisted round the hill to lie in wait for him in the next valley. He found a track that led away from the road, attempting to escape from it like him. When he followed it, it turned itself into a path and petered out amongst open farmland. He was so bewildered by this that he stood like a fool, like a scarecrow, in the middle of an open field, for some minutes, turning and turning beneath the naked sky. Eventually, he gave up, returned to the road, and commenced a steady trudge along it. The pictures continued.

It was mid-morning. The sun was high. He was tramping along the road, chewing at a piece of the black bread, his feet flopping loosely from the ankles. Just as he thought, *if a vehicle approaches, I will hear it in time to leap into a ditch*, the roar of an engine was upon him. A car swept around the corner, blared its horn when the driver saw him, then shot past, the sound of its motor vanishing as swiftly as it had appeared. He stopped for a moment, swaying with surprise, then continued.

Later, he came to a fork in the road. There was no sign to indicate where he might be. He took the smaller, left-hand fork. The road led downwards. At the bottom of the hill, it turned sharply, and as he rounded the bend, he saw that a truck had tried to take the bend at too great a speed and turned on its side in a gully that ran alongside the bottom of the road. Yenko stopped. No one was around: the truck had been abandoned. From where he stood, he could see that the windscreen had shattered but not broken, the cracks in it radiating outwards from the centre, like a spider's web. He scrambled down the edge of the gully and searched the cabin, finding nothing but a few dirty boot prints on the seat.

He clambered over the soil and dead branches to the back of the truck, and saw that its contents had been disgorged across the floor of the gully: wheelchairs, thirty or forty of them. Some were upright, some were on their sides. Some had shiny chrome armrests with cushioned grips covered in deep red leather. Others were older models, with big iron wheels. He stood for a while by the pyramid of chairs, trying to work out how they might be useful to him – could he make a bicycle out of them? He shook his head to rid himself of such an absurd thought. He sat down in one, just for a moment, one of the expensive-looking ones, and imagined the luxury of being pushed everywhere, of never having to get up. Then he thought of having no legs, of his body simply ending, stopping in thin air beneath his waist, and the thought was so terrifying that he leapt up and scrambled back up the side of the gully and strode off down the road without looking back.

That night, he found himself walking along a railway line. Suddenly, the countryside fell back and he was approaching a tiny, rural station with a small goods train parked for the night between two empty concrete platforms. In the starlight, he could just see the small, square shape of a guard's hut. He approached it slowly, then stopped. From inside, there came a single male voice, raised in song. He turned back and skulked along the platform, until he came to a sliding door in the train. It was securely padlocked.

Above him, the stars were fading, one by one. The night was old.

The door of the shed banged open.

He ducked beneath the train. It smelled of oil. Supporting the carriage above him was a pair of diagonal iron girders. He climbed up on them, resting his stomach on the crossing point and, stretching his legs along the rear struts, grasped the forward ones with each outstretched arm. His bundle was strapped to his back, as if he was a beetle. He waited.

The train was hurtling along the track. It was daylight. Dirt and grit flew up from the wheels and stung him in the face. Metal screeched. He kept his eyes tight shut and clutched at the iron girders for his life, his teeth rattling and his whole body shaking so much he thought his bones would fall to pieces. His bundle had slipped sideways and hung from his back, threatening to drag him from the girders.

The train entered a tunnel and the screeching metal noise became deafening. He opened his mouth and let out a scream as long and loud as the tunnel itself. The train shot out into daylight but he continued screaming. The dirt and grit flew into his open mouth and he coughed, choking.

The train was stationary, in open countryside. The only sound was the soft, ghostly chuffing of the engine. His arms and legs were so stiff he thought he might not be able to extricate himself, but by rolling his torso, he managed to tip himself down on to the wooden sleepers between the track and clamber carefully over the rails. Without looking up at the train, he scrambled on all fours to a nearby tree and hid behind it, back against the trunk, the soft bulk of his bundle cushioning him. He stayed there until the train began to creak, to move away from him, first with excruciating slowness, then with sudden noise and speed. When it was gone and the countryside around was silent but for the birds, he rose and tried to walk. As he moved from the support of the tree trunk, his arms and legs shook so much that he fell to the ground on his hands and knees. He remained there for some minutes, shuddering from head to toe. There was still grit inside his mouth. He spat it on to the ground. The tiny grey stones lay in a puddle of spittle, darkening the soil.

He stopped by a stream, and drank from it. His food was gone but for the dead chickens, which he must save for barter. He picked the scabs from the palms of his hands and nibbled at them. He thought of the heavy clay jar of goose fat back at the old couple's cottage, of the stale black bread and wizened apples. He pictured them, then saw a huge black crow looming over them, and jerked awake with a cry. *I have no food*, he groaned to himself, head in his hands. The misery of the fact was harder to bear after having provisions for a while. It overwhelmed the luck of the train and the mellow sky above and not being shot or discovered. *I have no food . . .*

Having no food meant one thing. *Gadje*.

He hid his bundle before he entered the village. He washed his face in a stream, and put on the shirt and trousers he had kept carefully folded away while he travelled. He cleaned the old man's boots with grass and made sure that his cap was pulled down low over his head to hide his stubbly hair. He strutted around the trees for a moment or two, practising insouciance. He sat and counted the old woman's coins. Did he really need to barter the chickens? It was hard to know. But he couldn't light a fire to cook them and he would need as much real money as he could find, later.

As he walked down the lane to the row of houses, the first person he saw was a bread-seller, a tall young woman with a dozen loaves threaded on a piece of string slung across her chest. She was walking towards him. He had the chickens in his hand, clutching their necks, and he raised them to her and gave a cheery smile. She smiled back and lifted her hand. I must be in Bohemia, he thought.

After she had passed, he waited a few moments, then turned and followed her. From behind a low stone wall, he watched as she tapped at a door, and was turned away. She went to the next cottage, and this time was admitted. The door closed behind her. After ten minutes or so, she emerged, waved at the woman who saw her off from the step and continued her journey.

Yenko stayed crouched low behind the wall and counted to a hundred, five times. Then he jumped the wall and walked up to the second cottage, whistling loudly.

He tapped at the door. There was no answer. He tapped again, waited. He took a few steps back down the path, then stepped over an empty flower-bed to peer into a small window. The interior of the cottage was too dark for him to see inside.

The door opened as he was still peering in the window. He jumped back. A heavy-set, dark-skinned woman barked at him, 'Yes?'

Caught off-guard, Yenko stammered, 'Good morning, madam. It's a lovely day, isn't it? Yes?' He held up the chickens, feeling ill-prepared for this, his first encounter. Perhaps the woman would think he was a simpleton. That was a good idea. 'Chicken! Chicken!' he said, grinning, raising them. 'Only two left!' He made a clucking sound.

The woman glared at him. 'How much?' she snapped.

Yenko stood, dumbfounded. How much? He hadn't got a clue. How much was a chicken? He was horrified at his own stupidity. How could he not have thought the encounter through? How much, how much? If he got the price wrong then the woman would be suspicious. He stared at her in panic, breathing heavily.

The woman continued to glare at him. She leaned backwards, opened the door to the house and called inside, 'Bohumil!'

I should run, Yenko thought, but his feet were planted firm and wide on the woman's path and he was turned to stone.

A large, jowly man with a bald head and full moustache came to the door, wiping his hands on a cloth. He was dressed only in a long-sleeved vest and breeches, despite the cold, his braces hanging loose on either side of his legs. He wiped his mouth and stared at Yenko.

The woman indicated him with one hand. 'He's got two chickens but he doesn't know how much he wants for them.'

It was then that Yenko saw the red piping down the seam of the man's trousers – *a uniform. I am done for.*

'Boy,' said the man. Yenko looked up. 'Why are you holding your face?'

Yenko lowered his hand. *I have been holding my face for days,* he thought, surprised by the knowledge. He had become so used to the pain in his jaw that the gesture was automatic.

He stepped forward and opened his mouth. The woman made a noise and turned her head in disgust but the man leaned forward from the step and peered at him. 'Those teeth are grey and the gum is swollen. You are getting an abscess,' he said.

'It wasn't my fault . . .' Yenko faltered.

The man exhaled through his nostrils. 'Give the chickens to my wife and I'll take those teeth out. If someone doesn't, you're going to be in big trouble.'

'One chicken,' said Yenko.

The man snarled, 'Don't haggle with me, boy.'

Yenko stepped forward meekly and handed over the chickens. The man's expression softened. 'Give the boy some bread and dripping, and some salt,' he said to his wife, then, turning to Yenko, 'Wait here.'

The man and woman went inside and closed the door behind them. After a few minutes, the woman returned with a rough-cut slice of bread smeared with dripping and a twist of brown paper. Yenko divided the bread into two, withdrew a handkerchief from his pocket, folded and wrapped one half of the bread and replaced it in the pocket. Then he balanced the remaining piece of bread on his forearm while he unwrapped the twist. Realising he was about to put the salt on his bread, the woman snapped, 'No, no, are you stupid?' She snatched the paper from his fingers and re-twisted it firmly. 'Put it in your pocket.' He obeyed. She watched him while he ate the bread. He forced himself to chew slowly. When he had finished, the woman said, 'My husband is a volunteer in the night-watch.'

'Yes,' said Yenko. They know what I am, he thought miserably, and they have just stolen my chickens. 'I'm only passing through,' he said.

'Good,' she replied.

The man re-emerged and, with a toss of his head, indicated that Yenko should follow him around the back of the cottage.

Behind the cottage was a small yard and a garden with tidy rows of sticks ready to support the vegetable plants when they began to grow. Six snow-white geese wandered gracefully around a wire pen. The man indicated to Yenko that he should sit on a tree stump, then went over to a wooden shed and came back clutching a large pair of pliers.

Yenko closed his eyes and opened his mouth, thinking, *I'm used to pain. It will be all right.* There was a tugging sensation in his jaw, then another, and another. He opened his eyes and saw three teeth lying in the mud at his feet.

'Didn't even hurt, did it?' the man said. 'Thought not. There was no blood in the cavities. Those teeth were stone dead.' He was wiping the pliers on a cloth. 'Open up.' Yenko looked at him. 'I took out the three which were discolouring but you might have some other dead ones in there, I'll give them a tug if you like, we'll soon know.' He held up the pliers.

Yenko shook his head. The man shrugged. 'Please yourself. Rinse with salt water as often as you can. Hot water, if you can get it. So how come you're on the road, boy?'

The question came casually, the sentence hanging off the one that preceded it. The man wasn't even looking at him.

Yenko could think of no reply that wasn't an obvious lie.

The man sighed, glancing up at the sky. 'They took our son away. He's somewhere in Germany. The last postcard we had was from Magdeburg but he said they were about to move him. That was eight months ago. He's making anti-tank shells, I believe. People die in those factories. Lots of accidents. It's dangerous work.'

Yenko sat very still. The man fell silent.

The back door opened and the woman stepped down. She was holding a large earthenware bowl. She did not look their way. She crossed over to the geese and lifted the lid of the wire cage, then began to throw in handfuls of the feed; potato shavings, cabbage stalks and tiny white strips of fat. Her hands were large, red-raw with the cold.

'You'd better get going,' the man said, and turned away.

He found the railway line the next day, on the outskirts of a town. This was no tiny rural outpost, but a wide-gauge double track with goods coaches stacked in a siding – the main route west. Behind the siding was a thorn thicket. He snapped a pair of thin branches from a nearby tree and used them to part the thicket and crawl carefully to the centre of it, where there was just room to unroll his blanket. It felt good, to be surrounded by thorns.

He had to wait two days, timing the patrols of passing soldiers and leaving his hiding place only once, when he managed to steal a loaf of bread and a small pie from a windowsill not far from the station. The pie was filled with almost-liquid fat and grey, gristly meat. As he sat eating it amongst the thorns he thought, I can't wait to tell the others about this pie – after the war, when it is all over, when we are well-fed and safe again and can joke about things and listen to each other's stories. I will tell them how the *gadji* must have shouted at her husband or dog and put the pie on her windowsill, for safety, for me to come along and take it. He paused, looking up. The sky was just visible through the thicket; blue, a good sign. Spring was coming, and he was having luck. *Baxt.* God meant him to succeed. After the war, he thought, we will all have our stories. Everyone will talk about the luck they had. It will seem as if everyone was lucky, as if there was always a loaf of bread on the windowsill or some eggs in a corner of the barn that the farmer's wife had missed. We will seem so lucky that the people who come after us won't believe our tales, but what they will forget is the ones who aren't around to talk, the other ones, the ones who froze to death huddled under bushes or starved crouched over streams or just gave themselves up and were shot. He stopped eating. The sun had gone in. *The trees and bushes will be full of the ghosts of the ones who didn't survive. After the war, people will be afraid to go near trees and bushes, because of the ghosts.*

That afternoon, he was woken by a train thundering into the siding. He crawled forward on his belly, to the edge of the thicket. The train was huge, dark brown, tall-sided, with an uncountable number of carriages stretching either side of where he lay. This had to be the one. He waited until dusk, terrified that the train would move in daylight and he would have missed his chance. *This has to be it*, he thought, *my train*. Darkness was gathering as he ran, crouching, alongside the track, glancing up at each carriage in turn, to find an unpadlocked door.

He had nearly reached the front of the train when he located one. The side of the carriage was so high that he could not reach the handle to check. Instead, he had to prise his fingers between the edges at the bottom of the door and push with all his might, sweat breaking out on his forehead and prickling his back. If anyone saw him doing this, there would be no story. Eventually, one of the doors slid back with a dull, wooden sound, echoing in the dying afternoon. He threw his bundle in, then, without looking round, hauled himself up and slid the door closed behind him.

It was dark inside, and smelled of hay. He felt around behind him until he found a bale, wrapped in some sort of cloth. He sat leaning against it with his legs drawn up, clutching his bundle to his chest and panting after the exertion of opening the door. He closed his eyes and thought of his mother, back in the camp, of the lines on her grey face as she had ordered him to escape. He thought of the barbed wire and the constant fear of being beaten. Then he thought of how glorious it was to be hidden away somewhere dark, to know with absolute certainty that nobody knew where he was, and to feel that he was being born again, as a man of action, a true Rom, with a plan in his head and a future ahead of him. He began to pray.

CHAPTER 23

All through the night he forced himself to stay awake, peering anxiously through the wooden slats of the carriage into the pitch blackness, trying vainly to decipher the train's progress. His efforts to stay awake were so successful that he fell asleep just before dawn, as the dark was melting and the fields forming grey shapes in the gloom.

He awoke with a jolt as the train braked heavily and he was thrown from a hay bale to the floor. He jumped into a crouching position, heart thumping. Shouts were approaching from the outside. The shouts stopped. Booted feet crunched on gravel, passing. After a few moments, he dared to peer out between the slats. All he could see were large, grey-cement buildings, two or three metres away. He stood, shaking his head. The train's lack of motion had a finality about it, he thought. He braced himself and slowly eased back the sliding door.

The train had pulled into some sort of goods depot. Before him was scrubland, dissected by rusting railway tracks, overgrown with grass and weeds. The grey buildings were huge engine sheds, with tiled roofs and vast green doors. He could hear voices on the far side of the train. He jumped down. It was further than it looked and he stumbled as he hit the ground. He glanced swiftly from left to right. Alongside the nearest shed was a row of old oil drums. Bent double and clutching his bag to his chest, he leapt across the rusting railtracks until he reached the drums. He crouched down beside them, catching his breath.

The cement block was disused, the windows boarded, long brown tentacles of weeds clambering up the cracks in the mortar. To his left, a blackened construction of pipes and cables led to an adjacent block. In front of that was a pile of iron chairs and trolleys that had been left in a haphazard, corroding pyramid. Next to it, there was a tall pink chimney. Beyond, he could see row upon row of buildings ascending into the distance and a black dome, the blocks and curves of the city arching around as far as he could see in all directions. He was in the heart of it, this place that he had never even dreamed of. The light was bright white – full dawn but still early. The air was fresh and the birds calling a discordant cacophany. *So*, he thought, *this is Prague*.

When he had caught his breath, he crawled out from behind the drums and along the cement block until he found that this one too had loosely boarded windows. He glanced around; still no one about, but there were distant voices, threatening in their casual rise and fall. Above him was a window with dark wood planks nailed loosely over it. He put his bundle down and reached up, to see if the lower one would come free. He managed to loosen one end and worked it back and forth to free the nail that was holding it on the other side. The protesting creak of wood against metal was excruciatingly loud in the silent dawn. He had almost succeeded when he heard a voice, just the other side of the buildings. There was someone standing by his train. Perhaps they had discovered that the sliding door of his carriage was no longer securely fastened. He heard a shout, and an answering shout, some banging. If the man wandered around this side of the building, then he would be discovered.

He abandoned the plank and crept swiftly around the building to the shorter side, where he found that the huge wooden door was rotted clean through at the bottom. There was no time to be cautious. He pushed his bundle underneath, then got down on his belly and crawled under. After the white light outside, the interior of the block was indecipherably dark. Only as his eyes adjusted did he see that he was in some sort of empty holding shed. It was freezing cold and his breath condensed in ghostly clouds. He sat on the dirt floor with his back against the wall and his bundle clutched to his chest, panting, waiting until it was quiet outside.

After cleaning himself as best he could, he crawled back under the door. He crouched for a moment, checking that there was no one in sight, then stood and strolled openly past the train, picking his feet high over the rusting railway tracks. He reached the tall, open gates that led on to the street before he was seen by anyone, a workman on the far side of the tracks who greeted him with an enquiring shout. Yenko looked over at the man, gave a broad smile and a cheery wave. The workman lifted his hand to his eyes to peer at him. Careful not to quicken his step, Yenko strode through the gates and out on to the pavement. He crossed the empty street with unhurried confidence and took the first turning left, without looking back.

After two more turns, he found himself in a busy street. Men and women were on their way to work, rushing for the early morning shift; heads down, concentration pinching their features. He adopted the same look, the weary hurriedness – he must not hesitate or seem lost. Glancing around as he strode, he saw that tall buildings lined the pavements. They had a dirty, faded grandeur; stone portals with carved scrolls for porches, vast wooden doors with brass handles and the moulded plaster shapes of women draped in layers of cloth. He had never seen such big buildings. They made him feel dizzy.

He kept his head down, only glancing up once in a while. There were no soldiers around and the workers were dressed in their factory clothes, swaddled tightly in scarves and hats. After a few turnings, he was in a commercial district. The surge of workers thinned and fell away. The occasional shop appeared, still closed, amongst the grander buildings. As the streets quietened, his anxiety grew. He turned down a sidestreet, found a low wall, glanced around, then jumped over it.

He was crouched in the backyard of a windowless building. Chipped, apricot-coloured plaster revealed the bare stone, here and there. He thought, when the war is over, I swear I will never crouch again, not if I have to splint my legs to break the habit. He closed his eyes and pressed the heels of his hands against his forehead. *Which way from here, Father? Celetná, the street with the black tower.* He couldn't think. He was hungry. He extracted his small, remaining piece of bread and ate half of it. He closed his eyes for a moment. The effort of climbing back over the wall seemed insurmountable. Eventually, he forced himself to rise.

The further he got from the station, the tidier the streets became, more great buildings in cream and beige and peachy colours, with huge carved doors. The workers had all disappeared and most pedestrians were men in smart suits and overcoats, women with feathered hats – some glanced at him as he passed. This was all wrong, his being in this district. He was becoming more obvious with each step. He began to sweat, despite the chill. Turning a corner, he saw a patrol advancing down the street towards him, a squad of Czech policemen marching with a sergeant at their head. He turned swiftly into the dark entrance of a nearby alley. It smelt of smoke, and piss. Head down, he hurried along it.

As he progressed, the alleyway narrowed. The black stone walls closed in on him. All that was visible at the end was a sliver of white light and some brown cobbles. As he reached the end of the alleyway, he stopped dead.

Before him was a huge square, the opposite side scarcely visible through the throng of people, motor vehicles and trams. Everyone on the pavement seemed to be hurrying, except for the soldiers on street corners. There were German soldiers everywhere, some cruising past on long, low-slung motorbikes, others standing guard. The central part of the square was some sort of tram interchange or terminus. Four trams were drawn up in a row, a fifth clattering to join them. The sky was transected with wires.

As Yenko stood staring, a tram shot past, its red sides flashing an advertisement for toothpaste. The first car was nearly empty, just a few civilians and two soldiers. The second was crammed to overflowing by men and women in grey and brown with blank, unsmiling faces. The door had already opened and the conductor was shouting the name of the stop in German. The tram's brakes were screaming.

He fell back into the alley and turned but at the far end, where it broadened, he could see two German soldiers who had stepped just inside, their backs to him, peering out into the road and glancing from side to side. Satisfied they were unobserved, they leant against the walls of the alley and removed their helmets, chatting to each other. One was smoothing his hair while the other pulled a packet of cigarettes from the top of his boot.

Yenko pulled his cap down on his head and shoved his hands into his pockets, then stepped out on to the pavement. He walked with his shoulders hunched and head down, keeping close to the walls. Suddenly, a black shape rushed upon him and he felt the breath slammed out of him. He staggered backwards, wheeling his arms. 'Look where you're going,' snarled a large man in a woollen coat, before continuing on his way. Yenko turned his back to the square to smooth down his jacket and straighten himself.

Directly in front of him was a small restaurant with a glass conservatory protruding out on to the street. In the corner, a group of SS men and three women were gathered around a heavily laden table. One of the SS men was standing, making a speech. His companions were gazing at him, smiling. It was a celebration of some sort. Paper streamers had been pinned to the dark wooden frame and the SS men were wearing conical hats with streamers cascading from the top. Their caps were clustered on a nearby hat-stand.

A silver coffee pot stood on the table with several smaller silver jugs around it. Each guest had a white china plate before them – the woman nearest to Yenko had not eaten much of her cake, a crumbling confection with a thick wodge of cream at its centre. A discarded silver fork lay resting on the plate.

The noise and clamour of the square behind him had faded into nothing. The people rushing past were phantoms. He could not prevent himself from staring at the cake. Cream, and sugar. He ran his tongue around his mouth, trying to capture some mirage of those tastes in his saliva, possessed by a craving so hollow he felt as though his insides were caving in, as if he would fold down upon himself and collapse like a pair of empty trousers on to the pavement. Involuntarily, he tipped forward on his toes. And that woman could not be *bothered* to finish it.

She was on the periphery of his vision – all he could gaze upon was the cake – but he had a vague impression of her. She was smiling up at the SS man. She was in a silver gown, incongruously glamorous for morning, bare-shouldered. Her upper arms were slender. On the table next to her plate was a purple velvet handbag with a gilt chain strap. Yenko felt himself tipping, tipping. The cake lay scattered on the plate like a derelict building, crumbled walls of stiff sponge crushed and broken. The men and women around the table were laughing at the speech, their faces distorted by the glass. The paper streamers teemed from their hats. One of the white china cups was sitting in its saucer in a puddle of black coffee. The wall behind the group was painted in broad stripes of blue and gold. A waiter was approaching, starched white linen hung over his arm. He bent to remove the cups. The woman threw back her head, displaying a smooth white throat. She placed a hand on the arm of the man sitting next to her. Yenko had a sudden image of his mother placing her hand on his father's arm, restraining him as Yenko was being beaten by Čacko in the admission queue at the camp.

He felt the palms of his hands crash against the glass as he fell forward. His face was pressed up against the window, his vision blurred. The woman's face twisted in alarm. One of the SS men was shouting. Yenko was still staring at the crumbled cake. *It cannot be*, he was thinking, madly. *I cannot be seeing this*. His head was full of pictures of the camp; the wooden boards he had slept on, his father's grey, carved face; the insects scurrying to and fro along the edge of the bunk. *It cannot be*. He could not make his thoughts any more coherent than that one, lunatic assertion. *If I am seeing this, then the camp did not exist. This and the camp cannot both be.*

The waiter had him by the shoulder and was dragging him backwards. Yenko felt a rough, open palm slap him across the face, spinning him away from the restaurant and sprawling him across the pavement. When he was on the ground, the waiter kicked him twice in the stomach, then lifted him up by pulling at one of his arms.

He dragged him bodily back down the street. Yenko felt his trousers being pulled down and had to grab at them with his free hand to prevent himself being stripped, the other hand flailing as he clutched his belongings to his chest. The waiter deposited him in the mouth of the alleyway and, when he tried to rise, slapped him down again. 'You fucking fool!' he hissed viciously, bending to him.

'Don't . . . don't . . .' was all Yenko could say, weakly.

The waiter's voice was hoarse with rage. 'I've saved your life, you fucking, *fucking* idiot. What did . . . ? In the name of God!'

'Please . . .' Yenko gasped, reaching out a hand and grabbing at the waiter's perfectly creased black trouser leg. 'Please, I . . .'

The waiter was trying to shake him off. Yenko managed to gasp out hurriedly. 'Please, which way is Celetná Street, it's by the Old Town Square . . .'

The waiter peered down at him as if he was deranged, his face a furious frown. 'I know that, you fucking little fool!' he hissed ferociously as he shook his leg free.

I *must* find out from him, Yenko thought wildly. I daren't stop anyone else. 'Please . . .' he repeated, almost weeping.

The waiter stood upright and waved his hands, to rid himself of this mad boy. Before he turned, he gave him one last, half-hearted kick in the legs, and waved an arm in a northerly direction, towards other side of the square.

Yenko crawled back into the alleyway, out of sight, huddling down on the ground. He clutched his heaving chest and discovered his belongings were still strapped there. He glanced down the far end, but the soldiers had gone. He leaned his head back against the wall and closed his eyes. His ribs ached and there was a sharp pain in his right hand. He lifted it and looked at it. It had dragged along the pavement and the rough stone had taken the skin from the back of the hand, blood was pricking in the pink flesh. He winced, and closed his eyes again. The pain felt good. It made sense.

He recognised the street called Celetná from Josef's description but walked the length of it twice looking for the right sidestreet to turn off it. It was a busy shopping street, crawling with off-duty soldiers, but by then he was reckless with exhaustion. Some of the shops were closed, while others seemed extravagantly open. He passed one set back in an archway with a trestle table in front of it on which were heaped elegant piles of lace tablecloths; snow white, creamy-white and beige. The greengrocer's next to it had only one small box outside containing two large black mushrooms, crinkled with age. A sign above the mushrooms said, *Edible Goods*.

The street curved gently round. When he reached the black tower at the end, he knew he had gone too far and started to make his way back.

He was less than halfway back when he looked up and saw, ahead, two German soldiers who had stopped to observe his approach. One of the soldiers had his arms folded and his legs planted wide, blocking the pavement. The other had withdrawn a pistol from his holster. The people walking along the pavement ahead of Yenko were parting either side of the soldiers, like a river dissecting itself to avoid a midstream boulder. There was no point in turning or running – he could only walk towards the soldiers, towards the inevitable. *Forgive me for failing you, Father*, he thought.

From the other side of the street, there came a shout. A shopkeeper was standing outside his premises – a glassware shop – and shouting at a woman who was clutching a large blue vase. She was shouting back in German, calling him a dirty crooked Slav. The shopkeeper had his fists clenched and his face was purple with fury.

The two soldiers turned and ran across the street. Yenko passed the empty space on the pavement where they had been standing, his body miraculously sliding through the air where the boulder had been.

He took the next sidestreet, and the one on the left after that, then several other turns, back on himself and around, before he found what he thought must be the right place, a deserted alleyway off one of the sidestreets. Halfway down was a narrow, black stone building squeezed between two bulkier, paler neighbours. The ground-level front of the building was a small shop with a single grimy window. Yenko approached and lifted his hand to shade his eyes and peer inside. The display was no more than a row of wooden shelves, bare but for a row of empty glass bottles, scrubbed clean, their old, tattered labels showing pictures of apricots. Behind the window, the shop was empty and dark. The door to the left had a printed sign nailed to it, the card brown and buckled from weathering. In small letters – first in German, then Czech – it read *Closed for the Victory of the Reich*. On the other side of the shop window was a low passage that led beneath the building, crouching down under a stone archway of black brick.

Yenko stood in front of the building, hands in pockets and shoulders hunched. He had expected something grander. He had expected the shop to be open. He could not stand around in the street like this for long, however quiet it was. How long would his luck last? He glanced up and down the alley. No one was around. He withdrew to a doorway on the other side of the street and sat down on a step. He leant his head against the stone portal: a moment of tiredness, that was all he could permit himself.

He was woken by the scraping sound of shoe upon stone and his heart jumped inside his chest as his eyelids sprang open. How long had he been asleep? A minute? A day? He glanced quickly around and saw that the street was still deserted, the sky bright white.

Then he saw, opposite, a hunched dark figure standing in front of the narrow passage by the shop. The man was wearing a greatcoat that came almost to the ground and leaning with one hand resting on the stone portal, as if weak or exhausted and needing to catch his breath before proceeding down the passage. He was hatless, despite the cold, and a few sparse hairs fluttered lightly in the breeze, clinging half-heartedly to his reddened scalp.

Yenko scrambled to his feet and without waiting to look left or right, crossed the cobbles. He no longer cared that he might have the wrong street or the wrong building. He felt it hardly mattered if the man turned and withdrew a pistol from his greatcoat and put a bullet through his heart. It was finished, his flight. He had arrived – or ended. It hardly mattered which.

'Prosím . . .' he said weakly. Please . . . His voice sounded pathetically thin.

The man turned.

He was fat – no, not fat, flabby. He had been fat once but ill-health or old age had made his flesh sag without reducing its bulk. Heavy bags of skin hung beneath the watery eyes. There was white stubble on his chin. His lips were purple and he stank of alcohol.

'Yes?' he said wearily. He was of indeterminate age. His voice was deep and gravelly. It had a loose sound, like pebbles in dirty water.

Yenko was overwhelmed with disappointment. This could not be the man. The man his father had described was upright, proud, amusing – and hugely rich. He was looking for a tall, friendly *gadjo* with a beaming smile and open arms. This could not be him.

'You live here?' Yenko gestured feebly towards the closed shop. 'You are the owner?'

'So?' muttered the man gloomily, ending his question with a cough which spluttered towards Yenko; the stink of cabbage, half-digested, alcohol.

What was the point of asking further questions? This man would not help him. Yenko hovered, on the point of turning.

'Who are you?' the man demanded suddenly, his voice surprisingly strong, his gaze sharp and suspicious.

'My name is František,' Yenko said. 'František Růžička. My father is Josef Růžička, formerly Maximoff, of the Kalderash.' Yenko blinked. White spots had appeared before his eyes. He struggled to remember what his father had told him, in a different life, a year ago, as they sat up on the front of the cart on a moonless night, passing through the Moravian forest, the only sound the soft clink of the horse's harness. His father had made him learn three things: an address in Prague, the directions to reach it, and a speech. The address he had recalled successfully but the speech was beyond him. He shook his head and took a deep breath, so deep he felt it might be his last. 'My father is Josef Růžička,' he repeated, emphasising it as if the man might disbelieve him. 'He used to work for you. The orchards. He calls himself your friend. He asks you in the name of honour. . . No, no. He sends his greetings to you, hopes you are well, brother, and asks you . . .' The rest of the speech was gone. It had been long, and formal. But all he could think to add was, 'My father is dead.' He hung his head and gave a hollow, breathy sob.

The man was staring at him in disbelief.

Yenko said weakly, 'I am looking for a man called Ctibor Michálek. Landowner, farmer. Perhaps . . .'

The man lurched towards him and grabbed his face between his plump, clammy hands. He drew him in and Yenko fell forward, too weak to resist. The man's watery eyes stared into his face.

'You are Josef's son? Josef's boy . . . ?' He shook Yenko's face a little, as if to make sure he was a real person.

Yenko gave a gasping sound, a sob with depth this time. He felt his knees buckle. 'My father is *dead* . . .' he cried out.

The man released him and turned away quickly, bending double over the gutter. Yenko fell to his knees, dizzy. There were more white spots before his eyes. He blinked hard and they disappeared.

After a moment, the man straightened himself and turned back to Yenko. Yenko scrambled to his feet and rested a hand against the stone portal to support himself.

'I beg your pardon,' the man said in his deep voice. 'You must excuse me. I have consumed a deal of home-made wine this morning on an empty stomach and feared it was about to decide that there were better places to ferment.' He coughed, then brushed down his coat. 'You have not come upon me at my best.' He stopped and stared at him. 'Your father . . .'

'He is dead . . .' Yenko said again. 'They killed him. The rest of my family are in a camp in Moravia. I escaped. I am the only one.'

The man drew himself up to his full height and regarded Yenko. 'You have suffered a great deal.' It was a statement, a simple observation, plain and unpitying.

Yenko looked down at the cobbles.

'Come,' the man said, lifting an arm and gesturing down the passage. 'I am Ctibor Michálek, landowner and farmer no longer – but human being, still, just about. This is my home.'

CHAPTER 24

The old man lived on the top floor of the building above the shop. The entrance was down the alleyway and across a tiny courtyard, through a rough, blackened door. A dark brown staircase led up to a long hallway, the far end lost in gloom.

They stumbled along the hallway, their boots clumping on the wooden floor. Ctibor stopped at the end, leaned against the wall and began a complex procedure of checking each of his many pockets until, with a belch of satisfaction, he located a large, wrought-iron key. As he fumbled it into the lock, a door down the corridor behind them creaked open. Yenko turned. At the far end, by the stairs, there was a single small square window of opaque, etched glass. Just visible in its light was an elderly woman who had come to the door of her room to peer at them. Ctibor lifted his hand without turning. 'How nice to see you, Mrs Talichová,' he said solemnly, 'this is my nephew Jan.'

The woman went back into her flat, slamming the door.

'We will have to come up with a few details for Mr and Mrs T. . . .' mumbled Ctibor as he succeeded in turning the key.

The interior of Ctibor's apartment was only slightly less gloomy than the hallway. He gestured for Yenko to walk in, kicked the door shut behind them, then shuffled over to the single window and opened the wooden shutters. White light flooded in, revealing the dusty interior of the room. 'I call it *my rooms*,' said Ctibor. 'I say to my friends at the Spotted Pig, time to go back to *my rooms*. As you can see, it is but one room. The lavatory is down the hall.'

The room was cold but airless, musty-smelling. The walls seemed to lean inwards. Yenko thought of the number of stairs they had climbed and how long and complicated it would be to get out again. He had never been inside a building where you had to exit through more than a single door. 'Excuse me . . . sir . . .' he asked, hesitating over how to address this *gadjo*, 'may we open the window?'

'It doesn't open,' replied Ctibor, as he shuffled over to the two-ring stove in the corner. 'And you'd better get used to calling me Uncle.' He paused. 'Uncle,' he repeated, cocking his head on one side and smiling. 'I like that.' He opened a cupboard. 'Make yourself at home, Nephew.'

There was a single bed with a brown, stained eiderdown and large square pillow – and a low armchair next to the empty fireplace. The four walls of the room were covered with dusty pink wallpaper. It had a repeated palm-tree pattern, the trees a slightly deeper pink. The floorboards were bare.

Ctibor turned from the cupboard holding a small tin box. 'Sit, sit.' He held it up and rattled it. 'You won't believe what I have here . . .'

Yenko sat in the chair. Ctibor came forward, prising the lid off the tin and holding it out to reveal ten or so wizened coffee beans. 'Don't ask me how I got them,' Ctibor tapped the side of his nose. 'I was saving them until the end of the war, but I think your arrival demands something special. Now . . .' he turned back to the cupboard. 'I know it's here somewhere.' He muttered to himself until he located a small wooden coffee grinder. He unscrewed the lid ceremoniously, dropped the beans in one by one, then stood beaming at Yenko while he wound the handle.

'Thank you,' said Yenko.

After making the coffee, Ctibor reached up to a high cupboard above the sink and brought down a small brown bottle. 'One or two little drops, just to liven it up . . .' he murmured. He brought the cups over, handed one to Yenko and stood next to him, waiting while he lifted it and took a sip. The liquid inside was brown, hot, not unpleasant. Yenko tried to smile.

Ctibor chuckled benignly. 'You think it tastes burnt,' he said humorously. 'That's because it tastes of coffee. That's what coffee tastes like! *Na zdraví!*' He raised his cup, took a sip himself and pulled a face. He perched his bulk on the edge of wooden crate next to the sink, nodding and nursing his cup between his large red hands.

'Who owns this block, the Talichovás?' Yenko asked, lifting his cup to indicate the room. On the wall, there were square, less faded patches of wallpaper, where pictures had once hung. In the corner, the tap dripped into the sink with musical precision.

'No, I do,' said Ctibor.

Yenko looked at him in surprise.

'In practice I do, on paper, I don't,' Ctibor corrected himself. 'The farm was forfeit, courtesy of the Reich Commission for the Strengthening of Germandom, and actually this whole building belonged to my farming business, but they burnt the paperwork along with all my furniture, so they don't seem to have quite

realised it. The tenants on this landing have been here since before
the war, downstairs there are some newcomers. I think you'll be
able to come and go without too many questions being asked.
How long for, I don't know. We'll worry about that when we come
to it. For now, you're my nephew, up from the sticks.'

Yenko looked down into his cup. He remembered his father
telling him that Ctibor had a wife, but sensed it might not be a
good idea to mention her. 'You ground up these coffee beans, for
me . . .' he said, and Ctibor nodded solemnly. There was a long
silence, broken only by the dripping of the tap and Ctibor taking
occasional small but noisy sips from his coffee dregs.

Eventually, Ctibor clapped one hand on his knee and said,
'So, what are your plans while you're in Prague?'

Plans? Yenko shrugged. 'I don't know,' he said. 'I don't know
how long I'm here for. When summer comes, I'll go back to the
camp and get the others out. That's if the war's not over by
then.'

Ctibor frowned. 'You really think you can get them out?'

'I got myself out, didn't I? I got here, to you, with nothing.'

'You must tell me all about it!' said Ctibor.

It wasn't a game, Yenko thought, with a sudden rush of
bitterness. *It wasn't an adventure. Gadje. What do they know of the
war?*

Ctibor must have noticed the dark look on his face. He looked
at the floor. 'I heard the Gypsies were all gone,' he said quietly.
'I have a couple of friends left in Kladno. I heard about the
round-ups. A bad business. And what they did in those
villages . . .' He shook his head slowly, then took a deep breath.
'I decided I was better off away from the countryside, after a
while. It was too painful. In Prague, you hear things, but it's
different somehow, when it's people you don't know. That's why
I like being here. Somehow you feel safer among strangers. It

should be the other way round.' He paused, and shrugged. 'I am sorry, about your father. Very sorry. He was my friend. I had hoped . . .'

'Can I stay, here, with you?' Yenko asked bluntly.

Ctibor lifted his head. His gaze was direct. 'Of course,' he replied.

Yenko unpacked his few possessions – his spare clothes, his tin cup . . . He hesitated as he unwrapped the last small lump of bread, no more than a bite. He ran his tongue over the gap in his gums. The swelling had gone down. He had used up the salt.

'Uncle?' he said tentatively, lifting up the scrap of bread, thinking he would die if he had to share it.

Ctibor was at the sink, rinsing their coffee cups. He turned. 'Oh no, no thank you. I still eat the goulash at the Spotted Pig, though God knows what they use for meat. Sometimes I forget to eat at all. Other things . . . Now you're here I suppose I will have to get in some supplies.'

Yenko ate the bread quickly, before Ctibor changed his mind.

When Ctibor had finished clearing up, he turned. 'We can make up a bed for you out of cushions, over there,' he waved his hand vaguely in the direction of the fireplace. 'Our main problem is your appearance.'

Yenko looked down at himself.

Ctibor was wiping his hands on a dishcloth. 'I normally wash in the sink.' He glanced over and saw the look of disgust on Yenko's face, misinterpreted it. 'You want some privacy, of course. I'll show you where the bathroom is. You'd better do it now. There's no window in there and we can't use the electric light so you'll have to prop the door open with a brick which we keep in there specifically for that purpose. We have an agreement to whistle. There's no soap either, I'm afraid, just caoline, which leaves you dirtier than before, but even so. It's here in this tin. Make sure you bring it back.'

Yenko smiled to himself. This Unclean *gadjo* who stank of alcohol and washed the dirt from his body in the same sink he used for cooking utensils – that he should be worried about *his* hygiene . . . it was almost endearing.

Ctibor saw the amused look and growled at him. 'I know, I know, I'm hardly a swell. We'll have to get you some papers, I suppose. God knows how. I know a man who gets me office supplies on the quiet, confiscated stuff, he'll know someone else who'll know, that's the way it works these days. There's a bit of a problem with payment, though. I don't have much in the way of disposables.'

'I have these . . .' Yenko said, pushing his hand inside his jacket to find the two silver picture frames he had taken from the dead couple in Moravia. He handed them to Ctibor.

'Well, that's a start,' murmured Ctibor, turning them over. 'You wouldn't believe the price of silver these days . . .' He paused, glancing up at Yenko, looking at him afresh. He is going to ask me where I got them, Yenko thought. I will tell him, tell him I stole them.

Ctibor shook his head. 'Life has been very dull . . .' he muttered, inconsequentially. Then winced, as if he had just said something both stupid and true.

When Yenko returned from washing, Ctibor was shrugging on his coat. He explained that he had to go down to the shop, 'Just for a couple of hours. I still call it the shop, even though I only use the office at the back. Then I'll try and get us something to eat. I'm sure you're hungry. Stay away from the window.'

After Ctibor had gone, Yenko lay down on the floor and tried to sleep but he was too nervous. Ctibor could be going straight

to the authorities to report him. Maybe he should just pack up
his things and leave now, while he had the chance. He wished
Ctibor hadn't told him to stay away from the window. It made
the window irresistible. After pacing the room for a while, he
went over to it and pressed himself against the adjacent wall,
then turned his head so that he could peer out without being
seen. Ctibor's room looked out over the back of the block and a
deserted, narrow street. The buildings opposite seemed to lean
towards him – the fluted terracotta tiling almost close enough to
jump to in a single leap. It was as if the buildings were in a
confidential huddle, whispering to one another, gossiping about
his arrival. He shrank back and slid down the wall into a
squatting position, arms wrapped tightly round his knees. He
closed his eyes and waited.

Ctibor returned at the end of the afternoon, triumphantly
clutching a brown paper bag containing some dry, hard biscuits
and a glass jar of milky liquid with white lumps in it. 'Home-
made cheese,' he said. 'At least, that's what they called it.' There
was also a single pickle; a small bent gherkin, which he halved
with scrupulous fairness. After they ate, they sat talking about
the cherry harvests of Yenko's youth, their shared memories,
both avoiding the topic of his current predicament. How good it
feels, Yenko thought, just to spend a little time pretending the
war does not exist. It grew dark outside. Ctibor closed the
shutters. They would go to bed early, he explained as he hung
the blackout curtain. Everybody went to bed early these days –
nothing else to do. His tone was apologetic, as if he thought
Yenko might want to go out on the town. Yenko nodded. Every
bone in his body ached for sleep.

   They made a makeshift bed, a rough arrangement of cushions
of varying depth and consistency. Ctibor tried to persuade him

to use the eiderdown but he insisted he was fine with a blanket –
in which case, Ctibor said, then he must have the pillow. Yenko
took it to please Ctibor, and found as he settled down that it was
a most uncomfortable object, a soft cloud that lifted his head at
an ache-inducing angle. He would push it aside as soon as
Ctibor was asleep.

He closed his eyes. Ctibor was still getting ready for bed. The
last sound Yenko heard before he fell asleep was a bubbling and
swooshing noise as the flabby old man, his saviour, gargled
ostentatiously and spat into the sink.

In the morning, he woke to find Ctibor fully dressed and moving
quietly around the room. He had removed the blackout curtain
and thin pencils of white light shone between the shutters.

Yenko blinked from beneath the blanket, wrapped around his
body like a cocoon. He felt a strange sense of peace, and realised
he was unable to move. He never wanted to move again. Dying
must be like this, he thought calmly.

'I have to go down to the shop,' said Ctibor, buttoning the flies
on his voluminous trousers and lifting his braces over his
shoulders. 'You'd better stay here until we get you some proper
clothes. I have coupons. I never use them. I've got some old stuff
but it would be a little large on you. There's tea in the cupboard
when you're ready, and I saved a bit of bread. It's in the tin with
the blue pictures on it. I'll try and get some more cheese later. And
I can bring back a bottle of beer from the Spotted Pig at lunchtime.
It's quite normal for me to do that, won't raise any eyebrows.'

Yenko did not reply. He was wrapped in a warm blanket.
Later, there would be tea and bread and cheese. He wouldn't
have to do anything. Someone else was going to just bring them
to him, for no reason. I could die right here, he thought, just slip
away right here, and my life would be complete.

After Ctibor had left, he closed his eyes and dozed, making himself wake every few minutes, just to confirm that he was still there in Ctibor's room, lying on cushions and swaddled. Nobody was beating or shouting at him. Nobody was blowing a whistle. Nobody was going to make him run. He thought he had escaped the camp when he left it. But now he realised he had only truly escaped when he arrived here in Prague; wonderful, anonymous Prague.

He dozed and woke for a couple of hours, until his bladder forced him up. He stood for a moment in his crumpled clothes, shivering. There was an old iron hook on the back of the door with a huge knitted robe on it. He pulled it on, on top of his clothes, its hem trailing across the floor behind him. He unslid the bolts at the top and bottom of the door, slowly, and turned the handle.

He was no more than halfway down the corridor when a door opened a fraction and a white-haired, wide-eyed face appeared in the gap. He felt Mrs Talichová's gaze on his back as he shuffled towards the bathroom, clutching the huge robe around his body with his arms. He urinated hurriedly, rinsed his hands in the cold water from the single tap over the cracked sink, then shuffled back along the dim corridor. The door was still open, just a fraction, and the same face was still staring.

He quickened his step, fumbling with the loose handle to Ctibor's room and rattling it in his haste. Inside, he slid back the two bolts and, still in the robe, hurried to his makeshift bed, curling up on the cushions and pulling the blanket over his head, eyes closed, hands over his ears.

He did not leave Ctibor's room for four days. His only forays were the brief shuffles to the bathroom, usually under the watchful eye of Mrs Talichová.

One day, as Ctibor was returning, he heard the murmur of voices on the corridor and pressed his ear against the door to hear Ctibor's low rumble of a voice explaining, 'Yes, poor lad, he's rather ill . . . no, he won't be . . . nothing else . . .' When the voices stopped talking, he skittered back to the armchair and crouched in it, feet tucked up beneath his body.

Ctibor raised the matter after lunch. 'I know you are afraid,' he said. 'It's not surprising. But if you stay in here much longer it will arouse suspicion. Everyone is supposed to be conscripted into the arms factories, men and women, except for the old ones like me. Pregnant women get off so the birth rate is shooting up. I had to tell Mrs Talichová you've been ill, you're recovering, but that will only hold good for so long. You must be seen to be acting as if you are what we say you are, it's dangerous otherwise. Come down to the office with me this afternoon.'

When he saw the look on Yenko's face, he added, 'I promise I won't make you go out into the street. Just the office. I promise.'

Yenko nodded.

The office was a large, wood-panelled room behind the empty shop at the front of the building. As Ctibor showed him round, he became nostalgic about the former glories of his business. 'I used to employ fourteen people here. I had two girls just for the filing . . .'

He showed Yenko the ledgers, where, he said, he kept records of fruit production in Bohemia, sent to him by the local *Landrat* and sometimes the farmers themselves – and the forms he filled in on behalf of the Protectorate authorities. 'I used to be a farmer. When they took my farm away from me they gave me a consolation prize – I'm now a minor civil servant. That is why I have become ugly and fat. Still, it beats doing ten-hour shifts making grenades. This file here,' he thumped down a huge box-file the colour of dried blood. 'This here contains copies of my extensive correspondence with the Bohemian-Moravian Sugar Beet and Sugar Control Board, the most contrary bunch of buggers you'll come across outside the Castle. If anyone walks in through that door – not very likely, so don't panic – you sit at this desk, and you re-arrange these papers. You put them in date order. You file them alphabetically – er, let's say the first letter of the second paragraph. When no one's around you can make paper aeroplanes out of them for all I care, as long as they're smoothed out and back in the file by the time we lock up for lunch. That, my friend František, I mean Jan, is your work. In payment, you'll receive board and lodging. You just have to keep your head down while we try and work out what the hell to do with you.'

'Are you sure no one will come in?' Yenko asked.

'Highly unlikely,' Ctibor replied. 'We had more visitors when I had Antonin, my old manager. We were partners. We used to do a bit of real business when he was around, as opposed to filing. He got put away just before Christmas and it's been downhill ever since. I haven't quite got around to hiring anyone else yet. Trusted him, you see. We had an understanding. Paper aeroplanes.'

'What did he do? I mean, why did they put him away?'

'He was in a bar one day, after work, and was telling the barman about how we'd had a visit from a couple of black hats from the Petschek Palace, asking if we knew you could make bombs out of jam. They wanted copies of all the purchase orders. Antonin told the barman it just went to show how stupid Germans were if they thought you could blow up a railway line with a litre jar of blackcurrant conserve. There was a guy at the end of the bar listening.' Ctibor shook his head. 'Poor old Antonin, a year and a half for *endangering the good name of the*

German people by untrue or grossly misrepresented assertions. Got off lightly in my opinion, silly sod. The barman got four months just for nodding in reply.'

Yenko sat down on a stool. So the Germans were putting Czechs away just for laughing at them. So it isn't just Us, he thought. Mostly Us, maybe, Us and the Jews, but a few of Them as well. Out of respect to Ctibor, he tried not to feel pleased.

Ctibor turned away and started piling ledgers and box-files on to a desk. Yenko shoved his hands deep into his pockets and wandered through the office door into the empty shop. The long wooden counter was covered in a thick layer of grey dust. He ran a finger idly along it, grimacing with distaste. Now he was less afraid he allowed himself the luxury of disappointment. Ctibor would shelter him, for the time being, but how would he lay his hands on the resources to get back to Moravia? He had thought he was coming to Prague to befriend a rich man. He wouldn't have undertaken such a risky journey just for shelter. He had to use this opportunity, somehow – but it was too early to work out how. He sighed. This would have to do, for now. He still felt numb. He needed a rest from being frightened, from having to use his initiative. Once Ctibor had found him some identity papers, then he would have to think of what to do next.

He took a step towards the window with its few sad old bottles, peering through them carefully at the empty cobbled street. The buildings were misted by the layer of grime across the glass. No one was around. Out there, in the open, there were people who just went about their business – walking to work, jumping on a tram and off again. There were people who had supper with their families, and went to concerts in the park at weekends, and raised umbrellas when it rained. There was the whole, huge, turning world. He tried to tell himself that in that world there were also soldiers somewhere, men with dirty faces and guns, hiding in holes. Russians freezing to death. Sailors drowning. It was hard to credit. He felt like the only person on earth who was in danger.

'Funny, you know.' Yenko turned at the sound of Ctibor's voice. He had come to the office door, silently, and was leaning against the frame, watching him. He had a cloth in his hands. He looked down at it as he wiped his fingers. 'I was just trying to clean up a bit in there. It's funny, you know. For years I begged your father to come and work for me. It was a standing joke between us. But I meant it seriously, and he knew I meant it. I had no one else, you see. No sons, no brothers. And you Gypsies, your tribes and your great big families. I always envied you.' He was wiping each finger in turn. 'And now, here you are, after all this time.' He turned back into the office, shaking his head in wonder.

CHAPTER 25

It was April. The air was light but cold. Ctibor told him that down by the river there was a lilac tree in full bloom. Yenko struggled to remember lilac blossom. He still had no identity papers. Lilac blossom, and rivers – these things were abstract as angels.

His world consisted of Ctibor's *rooms*, the stairwell, courtyard and the dark brown wooden office with the dirty window where he spent his days moving bits of paper from one file to the next. When Ctibor went out, he sat with his elbows on the desk and his hands covering his face, sunk in gloom. Ctibor had sold the silver photo frames for him, given him the proceeds and promised that the man who had bought them would come to see him soon, but the days passed without progress. It was difficult, Ctibor said.

To stop himself from going crazy, Yenko read the newspapers and magazines that Ctibor bought, and practised his German. It didn't seem as though it would be over by the summer, after all. What were the Russians playing at? Surely after Stalingrad they should have just stormed westward? Where were they? In March, *Národní Politika* reported vicious Allied attacks on defenceless unarmed civilians in Berlin. Many women and children had been killed, the reports said. One of the targets had been a new maternity hospital in the centre of the city. Ctibor said that meant the British were giving back as good as they were getting, for once. Maybe they would land in France soon. If the Russians were going to be so slow about it, maybe the British or the Americans would get to Prague first.

There was never any mention of the camp Yenko had been in. Sometimes, he wondered if he had really been there at all. He would lift his head from the newspaper and pick things up from Ctibor's desk, like a fountain pen, stroking the smooth, tortoiseshell surface and wondering. *What is happening? Right now, as I sit here holding this pen, looking into the brown swirls of its surface and thinking how well it is crafted, what is happening to them?* He thought of his mother as he had last seen her, climbing the snowy step into the infirmary hut, the door banging shut behind her, the soundless shower of icicles. *Dalé. Stay strong for me. Stay alive.* Then he would put the pen down, closing his mind against the thoughts.

Other stories in the newspapers made him shake his head in disbelief, like the one about a little Indian man who was starving himself in order to hurt the British. Apparently, the British were hated so much in India that people thought it was a good idea *not to eat.*

The news only took up the first one or two pages. The rest was supposed to be more cheering stuff. Yenko was up-to-date on the latest women's fashions, and the ice-hockey results.

When he couldn't be bothered to read, he looked at the pictures; line sketches of ladies in extravagant hats, curved like falling chimneys; photographs of smiling SS men dancing to traditional Moravian folk tunes, of Hitler receiving King Boris of Bulgaria.

The world turned.

One lunchtime, as they were preparing to leave the shop, Ctibor said, 'I need you to stay down here for a bit, while I go out. Maybe you could, I don't know, sweep up or something . . .'

Yenko looked at him. Ctibor raised his bushy eyebrows up and down, twice in quick succession. His eyes were twinkling. 'I have to go to the Spotted Pig. Hopefully, I am meeting a man who may be able to help us. I'm planning on persuading him to come back here to meet you . . .'

At last.

'Why don't I wait upstairs?' asked Yenko.

Ctibor wrinkled his nose. 'My friend, Mr Blažek, has a certain reputation for being, how shall I put it, not entirely above board. I don't think it's a good idea for him to bump into Mrs Talichová. Wait here. I won't be long. I'll lock you in.'

Yenko knew that Ctibor would be long, and he was. He was asleep with his arms resting on the counter-top when he heard the key rattle in the shop's front door. He raised his head sleepily as the two men entered the office and saw they had been drinking. Ctibor's face had the carefully composed look that Yenko had come to recognise over the last few weeks, the look of a man who believes intently in his own sobriety.

Blažek was short and stocky, in his thirties, balding, dressed smartly but without ostentation. He looked like a man with expensive tastes who thought it wise not to advertise them. His brown eyes stared back at Yenko in frank appraisal.

Ctibor raised both arms to display two large brown bottles. 'We haven't forgotten you, Jan!' he declared happily, placing undue emphasis on *Jan*. Of course, he and Yenko had not discussed how much Blažek was to be told.

'My good friend Blažek, this is my nephew Jan. Jan, meet another Jan. Jan Blažek, a businessman of extraordinary capacities! Without him, I would never have any paper to put in my unread files.'

Blažek leaned over the counter to shake Yenko's hand. Ctibor pulled over another two tall stools, then fetched three glasses from a nearby shelf. They were all silent while he poured the beer, then they toasted each other's health.

Yenko took a solitary sip and put the beer down quickly. He saw Blažek observing him.

Ctibor said, 'Well!' with an air of great satisfaction, and wiped his mouth with the back of his hand. 'Jan, I have explained our problem to Mr Blažek here and he seems to think he can help. Jan . . .' he nodded to Blažek.

Blažek drained his glass and allowed Ctibor to refill it before saying quietly, 'I understand you need new identity papers.'

Yenko nodded.

Blažek returned the nod. 'Let me explain a few of the difficulties involved . . .'

Yenko sighed inwardly. This was a bargaining chip as old as the hills. Before offering someone what they wanted, you gave them a great long story about how difficult it was to obtain, to soften them up for the price. *Cut the wind-up*, he wanted to say to Blažek, *and give me a figure. You are dealing with a Rom*.

'Official channels are out of the question,' Blažek began, 'as I'm sure you know. Far too many questions for anyone with something to hide. For instance, you have to give them a family tree going back to your grandparents which proves you're not a

Gypsy or a Jew.' He paused and glanced at both of them before continuing. 'Back in '41 you could have tried the Underground but since Heydrich it's been hopelessly compromised. Half the Communist Resistance are Gestapo double agents. I used to do some of my deals with Resistance people but I wouldn't touch them with a long broom handle now.'

Ctibor belched, then said, 'Oops!' and put his hand over his mouth.

Blažek continued. 'The only realistic method is to get hold of an existing card and adapt it. As you can imagine . . .'

'I have one,' said Yenko bluntly, and was rewarded by the look of surprise on both men's faces.

Blažek recovered quickly. 'Well there are still a lot of hurdles. We need to get a photo of you, that's not difficult, we can do it ourselves, then we need to find a man with a friendly printing press. I know someone. He's good but his price is high.'

'Ah . . .' said Ctibor. 'I think the time has come for me to relieve myself. Getting down to business always makes me nervous.' He clambered down from his stool and went into the small cubicle at the back of the shop. There came the distinct sounds of him unzipping his fly, and the heavy spatter of urine against the porcelain.

'Anything else to drink back there?' Blažek called over the sounds.

There was a pause, then Ctibor shouted back, 'I might have just the thing . . .' A series of ostentatious bangings and clumpings commenced as Ctibor began opening cupboard doors and closing them again.

Yenko became aware that Blažek was staring at him. He glanced at him, then dropped his gaze. Blažek's stare was not friendly.

Blažek leaned over the counter so that his face was close to

Yenko's and he could lower his voice. 'You could at least pretend to drink the beer, son,' he said. 'If you're going to go out in the big wide world you've got to act like the rest of us.'

Yenko lifted his glass, discomforted, and took a sip.

Blažek sat back on his stool, but after a moment leaned forward again. 'Listen. I've nothing against you personally, you know. You've been having a hard time. But I like Ctibor. He's an old fool but he's been good to me. I don't like seeing him taken advantage of.'

Yenko looked at Blažek and said, 'What do you mean?'

'Come on, don't play innocent with me.'

It occurred to Yenko what the problem was. Blažek thought he was Jewish. He wasn't sure whether it would be better or worse if Blažek knew the truth.

'Have a good look at the newspapers some time,' Blažek said, taking a paper packet of cigarettes from his pocket and lighting one, 'the lists of people who get taken out to the stadium and shot? Whole families, eight people with the same name. Mostly, it's for harbouring people like you. I daresay there were plenty of places you could've gone but you went to Ctibor because you knew he didn't have a family. More likely to help you out, wasn't he? But what about everyone else in his block? How long before someone on the floor below decides he can earn a few extra crowns by reporting the new pair of feet upstairs?'

I need this man, Yenko thought. I need him to respect me, if not like me. He's my only chance. 'What do you think I should do?' he said, in a calm, low voice.

'Get on your own feet and sort yourself out with your own place as quickly as possible. Don't help Ctibor commit suicide.'

Yenko steeled himself and lifted his beer, taking a large gulp. It was disgusting. He would never get used to it. 'For that I need help.'

Blažek grimaced. 'I can help. If you are prepared to take risks. I'll be honest with you, I don't like taking risks myself. But someone like you doesn't have much to lose.'

Yenko stayed silent.

'I need a runner,' Blažek continued, 'someone to take stuff from place to place for me. If you are caught you get taken to the Petschek Palace and they pull your fingernails out. But you don't know anything about me so you can't tell them anything, which makes you interesting to me. In return, I sort out your papers.'

'And pay me,' Yenko said, reaching out and helping himself to one of Blažek's cigarettes. He picked up Blažek's lighter from where it sat on the counter top. He had watched other men do this often enough. All it took was confidence.

Blažek watched impassively while Yenko lit the cigarette, inhaled without coughing, and blew the smoke out again as swiftly as dignity would allow. Eventually, he smiled again, and this time the smile contained a little mirth. 'You're a fast learner, boy. That's good.'

'Got you, you beauty!' Ctibor's triumphant shout came from the cubicle. He returned, flourishing another bottle. 'The real stuff this time!'

Blažek smiled and reached for his empty glass. Yenko knew that he would leave soon, now that business was concluded. He would be left to deal with Ctibor.

Blažek departed half an hour later, having drunk one small glass of the colourless engine fuel that Ctibor had poured for them. They had supposedly been making small talk but Blažek had revealed nothing about himself; where he lived, his family, his business. Yenko couldn't talk about himself either, which left only Ctibor, who fortunately seemed happy to talk for all three of them.

After Blažek had gone, Yenko rose hopefully. 'We'd better get back upstairs,' he said. 'It's getting late.' There had been no mention of what they were going to eat that evening.

Ctibor was too drunk to care about food. 'Jan's a good man,' he mumbled, pouring himself another glass and spilling the colourless liquid on the counter top. 'Some don't like his kind but the world wouldn't keep turning without them. We're all doing it, more or less. If a girl wants a pair of stockings she has to get her hands dirty. You can't even get hold of an inner tube for your bicycle these days. People like Blažek, well, they're sticking two fingers up at the Germans in their own way and what if they do make a bit on the side? Good luck to them!'

'Come on, really, we should . . .' said Yenko, taking Ctibor by the elbow and easing him off the tall stool, whereupon the strength of gravity surprised them both and Ctibor plummeted sideways. Yenko grabbed at him and hauled him upright, wrenching his back. He gasped in irritation.

'Oh, for God's sake . . .' said Ctibor, pushing him away and reaching out for the bottle.

Outside the shop, Yenko snapped, 'Give me the keys.' Ctibor fumbled for a while, until Yenko's patience broke and he pushed Ctibor back against the wall and commenced the distasteful business of searching his pockets.

'German bastards . . .' Ctibor was mumbling, eyes half closed. 'A man can't even go to a tavern when he wants. Has to go to bed early like a child. I don't *want* to go home yet. Why can't I walk the streets in my own city?' He levered himself away from the wall and lunged forward. Yenko grabbed him and pushed him back up against the wall. He pinned him there with one hand and found the keys with the other. 'Don't move!' he hissed viciously while he locked the shop.

As they crossed the courtyard, Ctibor began raising his voice.

'They all betrayed us, František.' Yenko unlocked the door and pushed Ctibor in and up the stairs. Ctibor paused after a few steps to bend double and beat at his chest. 'We are the very heart. Us, here, right here, slap bang in the middle. The beating heart! Cut out the heart, and what do you have left? Take a look at Jan Hus, next time you're passing. Big guy, covered in swastikas at the moment. Can't miss him. They abandoned us.' Yenko pushed him up the stairs.

At the top, they both stumbled. Yenko fell to his knees and Ctibor dropped back against the wall. He flung his arms wide. The drink from Ctibor's open bottle showered Yenko's head as he scrambled upright.

'*BASTARDS!*' hollered Ctibor, in a huge, booming voice that echoed down the wooden corridor. This time, more than one door opened.

'Ctibor . . . Uncle . . .' hissed Yenko, trying to pull him away from the wall and propel him down the corridor.

Ctibor pushed him away. 'I am *perfectly* capable of walking, thank you, František,' he said sneeringly, then staggered down the corridor on a diagonal, his shoulder sliding down the wall.

Yenko followed behind, nodding at the half-open doors, his stomach hollow, quite certain that all of the tenants had now heard Ctibor call him František.

Inside the room, Yenko kicked the door shut behind them and turned to help Ctibor, but he had already collapsed on the bed, fully dressed. His mouth was open and his eyes closed. As Yenko stood over him, wondering what to do, he began to snore.

Yenko sat down in the armchair and buried his face in his hands. After a moment or so, he sat up and looked around the room. What a disgusting place to live; safe and dark, horrible and filthy and full of things that he and Ctibor had not told each other about. While Ctibor slept, he would try to tidy up a bit.

Ctibor slept for an hour, motionless as a corpse. Then he jerked awake, sitting up suddenly and shaking his head.

Yenko was trying to wipe down the grooved wooden counter-top alongside the sink. It was covered in a thick layer of grease, sunk into the crevices of the wood. The rough cloth was coming away black, impossible to rinse clean under the tap.

Ctibor sat on the edge of the bed and watched him silently.

When Yenko had finished, he found a large, chipped mug from the shelf above the sink and filled it with water. He took it over to Ctibor. Ctibor took the mug from his hands then rested it between his thighs, gazing into it gloomily, fearfully, as if it might contain secrets. Yenko remained standing in front of him. Ctibor did not lift his gaze. 'What do you think is happening to her?' he asked, still staring into the mug, his voice sober and even. 'I ask myself that every day, even though I know she must be dead by now. Most of them probably are. Except she isn't "them". She's my Sarah. God forgive me . . .' He lifted the mug to his lips and drained it, wiping his hand across the back of his mouth. 'I'm never sure whether it helps or not, you know.' He meant the water.

Yenko took the empty mug from him and returned it to the sink. He came and sat on the arm of the chair, facing Ctibor. 'Did the Germans take her?' In all the weeks he and Ctibor had been living together, the old man had not once referred to his wife, until now.

Ctibor gave him a look of infinite sorrow. His face remained steady but the lines on it seemed etched deeper by his expression. He looked down at the floor. 'No,' he said, then gave a deep sigh. 'Is there any bread? I forgot to eat.'

Yenko went to the kitchen cupboard and found a half-loaf, pulled it into pieces and put it on a tin plate. He took it back to Ctibor, pushing an upturned box with his feet so that it could act as table between them. They both took a piece of bread and Yenko realised he had stupidly divided it into three pieces, not four. As Ctibor leaned forward, he said, 'You know, I have heard of people torn from the arms of their families, everyone screaming in sorrow, but sometimes I envy them.' He chewed the bread with his mouth open. 'You wouldn't think anyone would wish that upon themselves, but I do.'

He swallowed, reached forward and picked up the last piece of bread, raised it to his mouth and paused. 'Two pieces each, right?'

Yenko nodded, chewing the inside of his lip.

Ctibor bit into the bread. Then he stopped and looked down at his hands, suddenly seeming like a very fat and very miserable child. 'Sarah left me of her own accord, back in '39, as soon as the harvest was in. I came home one day from the orchards, and she was gone. I thought at first she had been taken. I ran from room to room, but then I saw she had packed and taken her things, clothes, some sheet music, a few photos of her family – a terrible one of them all together after some holy day, touched up terribly, I mean. The photographer gave them all bright blue eyes.

'I was so distraught I didn't see the note until later that evening, even though it was in the middle of the table. She had gone to find her family, to be with them, she said. She begged my forgiveness. She begged me not to follow her. She couldn't stand it any more. We had been arguing a lot, ever since the spring. Things had got worse and worse between us. She said why had Hácha just let them march right in and I said what chance did we stand when Chamberlain and Daladier and the others had just handed us over and she said us, you mean you, and I said what, suddenly, you're not Czech any more? And she said no, I'm not, I thought I was but I'm not . . . oh, well, I won't bore you with the details . . .'

He swallowed the last mouthful of bread and Yenko gave an involuntary, imitation swallow.

'The thing is, I think she said all that to protect me. I think she ran away because she thought I would be safer without her, that it was better for me not to have a Jewish wife any more. But she knew if she told me that was why she was going then I would come after her, so she put all these other reasons. She made it sound as though she hated all us Gentiles for what the Germans were doing, as if we were all complicit. She knew that the best way to protect me was to pretend she no longer loved me.'

Ctibor shook his head restlessly, his face a mask of doubt. 'At least, I think so, I think that was what it was . . . but I didn't go after her, when there was still a chance I could have found her. I thought maybe she'd come back of her own accord. I didn't . . . and then when the deportations started, I knew it was too late.' He crashed his fists against his forehead. 'Two years. Two years I waited for her to come back, for things to get better, while all the time they were getting worse and worse. Not a word. Then the deportations. I knew it was too late. Now I'll never know. Why did she leave me? Did she really hate me or was she protecting me? I'll never know.'

'Maybe you will be able to ask her one day, maybe her family escaped.'

Ctibor shook his head. 'František, I don't live that way, not like some. Let me tell you something.' He leaned forward and lowered his voice. 'Just in case you think like she did that we've all been sitting by while these things have happened, I'll tell you

408   LOUISE DOUGHTY
a story. The patriots who killed Heydrich . . .' He crossed himself. 'Want to know how the Germans found out where they were hiding? Someone sold the Gestapo the names of the Resistance members who were supplying the patriots with food. The Gestapo paid a visit. It was a couple and their teenage son. The mother heard them coming up the stairs and managed to get a cyanide capsule between her teeth. I don't know what happened to the father. Anyway, they take the boy to Petschek Palace, and they torture him, all day, they don't even give him a chance to confess, they just torture him, beat him, all the usual stuff. Then, when he is half dead, they open his mouth and hold his nose and pour whisky down his throat. They give it a minute or two to take effect, then take him into another room. They have cut off his mother's head. It is floating in a tank of water. They show him the head and ask him where the assassins are hiding. He looks at the head and he says, *the Church of St Cyril and Methodius on Ressel Street.*'

Ctibor gazed at Yenko, his eyes large and watery but without expression. 'We're not supposed to know this story, so how do we know? Someone talked. Someone let someone talk. They were *proud* of it. They wanted us to know. And the students? And the people they take to the stadium? They publish lists, you know, they don't try to hide it. They advertise it in the newspapers. And those are just ordinary people, not even Resistance or Jews. The ones they shoot quickly are the lucky ones.' He shook his head. 'My wife is dead, František. All her family too. It doesn't matter whether she left me to protect me or because she hated me. I'll never know. My wife is dead.'

There was a long silence. They both sat motionless. Eventually, the spell was broken by the slow clip-clopping of horse's hooves on the cobbles of the alley below, a horse-drawn

cart passing beneath the window. Yenko ran his tongue over the
gap in his mouth where his missing teeth had been. It had been
a relief when the man pulled them out; worth losing the chickens
for, in retrospect.

'And your farm . . .' he said, with an effort. 'What happened
to the farm?'

'František, I can't do this . . .' groaned Ctibor.

'What happened to the farm?'

Ctibor sighed. 'When they finally came, it was early in the
morning. I was sitting at my kitchen table, alone, drinking coffee,
thinking about Sarah, and about nothing, the only two things I
have been able to bear to thinking about since this war began.
There were four of them, a councillor from the *Landrat*, I'd met
him before, a policeman, a couple of SS who looked me over then
began wandering through the house. One of them removed his
gloves to pat the stove. I could tell he was thinking, *my wife will
like this stove*.

'I had been expecting it, so in a way it was a relief. I had to sign
all sorts of things and officially they paid me. I didn't care. I even
made them coffee. They were perfectly civil. I had two hours to
pack my things. I was lucky. They'd been clearing out the farms all
over the place and half my neighbours were new Germans, mostly
shipped in from the Balkans. One family had come all the way
from Bessarabia. Most of the previous owners got sent off to the
Reich as slave labour. I was too old and decrepit, I suppose. My
friend from the *Landrat* knew I had a place in Prague, so he
persuaded the SS to let me move up here and take an
administrative job overseeing jam production for the good of the
Protectorate.'

Ctibor rose, got down carefully on his knees and pushed a
hand underneath his bed. He grimaced for a moment or two,
then withdrew a thick, brown glass bottle with a home-made

cork. He pulled out the cork with his teeth and offered the bottle to Yenko.

Yenko shook his head. Ctibor shrugged, then took a deep draught.

'As I was loading my bags into their car – the councillor was dropping me off at Kladno station – truckloads of soldiers arrived, scores of them. Why so many? I turned to the councillor and said. Is it going to be a billet? I had assumed they were giving my house to one of those high-ranking SS men. I had heard one of them talking about whether or not a grand piano would fit in the corner of the drawing room. The councillor said, they are here to cut down the trees.'

Yenko looked up. 'The whole orchard?' he asked.

Ctibor lifted his hands. 'I know. It must have taken them days. Your father and I walked through those trees each time you all came, talking things over. As the harvest began each year, the old women would spend the first morning going round to pick the first cherries and hand them out to children of other tribes. Do you remember that? They always gave the first cherries of the new harvest to unknown children . . .'

'To feed the Ancestors . . .'

'To feed the Ancestors . . . It took me twenty-six years to build up that orchard. Black beetles and white mould had failed to destroy it. It had survived the winter of '29 and the Depression and the floods.' He took another swig from the bottle. 'The German army cut it down in less than a week.'

Yenko did not reply. He was thinking of his father, and his father's father, and grandfather and great-grandfather and all the Maximoffs back through the centuries. For all he knew, he was the last one.

Ctibor looked at him and took a long swig from the beer bottle. He licked the foam from his lips. 'I know what you are thinking, Father Confessor. What are a few trees? I know. I've thought it too. A week after I came to Prague, there was a shooting in the street, not far from here. It was a girl, about twenty years old. I heard the shot and there she was on the pavement, right in front of the Powder Tower. Two soldiers were standing over her. I couldn't help looking as I passed. She was very tidy, hair still in plaits like a teenager, shoes scrubbed clean, her arms flung and a neat hole in her forehead. The blood was running into the gutter. I thought of her mother. Raising a child – well, I've never done it myself but I've seen it. Meals to be cooked, lessons to be taught. All that effort wasted because in a moment some soldier twitches his finger and BANG!'

Ctibor stood suddenly and shouted, clapping his hands together and slopping liquid from the neck of the bottle. Yenko jumped. 'It's all gone! In a moment! Just like that . . .' Ctibor slumped back in his chair. 'It's so easy . . . so easy . . .'

Suddenly, Yenko felt desperate to get away from Ctibor's misery, the mirror being held up to his own. I want to run across a field, he thought wildly. I want to feel my feet striking the earth and a breeze on my face. He looked around the room, as if a door might open in the wall and reveal a meadow.

Ctibor had emptied the bottle and was holding it against his cheek. 'You and me,' he mumbled. 'You and me, and the girl's mother and the hundreds they killed to get the farms and the thousands they arrested after Heydrich, and the Jews . . . and, hey, František, we're just the civilians. We haven't even *started* on the soldiers yet. Each one of them has a story, each one of them took twenty years to grow. Sometimes I forget there are soldiers in this war. Sometimes I forget there is a front line at all. It feels as though the war is happening right here, in Prague, here . . .' he lifted a finger and placed it on his temple. 'Here inside my head.

Is it really a World War? That's what they tell me. I don't believe them. They've invaded *me*, that's what they've done, and the League of Nations didn't give a damn, they just handed me over. I'm dispensable, you see. They thought, let's hand over old Ctibor Michálek and maybe Hitler will stop there . . .' He was drunk again.

Unable to bear any more, Yenko rose and strode to the window. The afternoon was grey. Darkness would come soon, curfew, another evening trapped in the room with Ctibor. The old man was right. Take each of their stories and multiply it by millions, how could you imagine that much human suffering? Best not to think of it, otherwise you would go mad, or take to drink like him with his veined nose, mumbling about his wife and his cherry trees.

On the windowsill, in the gloom, a sparrow was hopping expectantly, pecking at the stonework now and then, then turning his head sharply from one side to the other, confused there were no crumbs.

Yenko had no idea how long he had been asleep when he was awoken. The room was in darkness and hot. He had rolled off the cushions and was lying on the bare boards of the floor with the blanket wrapped tightly around him. His head was resting on the floor, and as he lifted it, he felt the vibrations that had awoken him.

He sat up, breathing hard. There was a low rumble. Above it, he heard Ctibor stirring too.

All at once, he was violently awake, heart thumping.

Ctibor was out of bed, sensing his alarm, saying, 'Hush, hush, I think . . .'

They stood close to each other, listening.

It became apparent that vehicles were approaching, very

slowly. Yenko stepped over the cushions and shuffled towards the window, slowly, hands outstretched so as not to bump into anything in the dark.

'It's not safe!' Ctibor hissed.

Yenko crouched beneath the sill, lifted the edge of the blackout curtain, then the hook which fastened the shutters together. Ctibor hissed, 'František!' but then came and crouched next to him. Together, they slowly creaked the shutters ajar, just enough to allow them to peer over the sill.

The vehicles, lorries and jeeps, had almost passed beneath the window, bumping in single file along the cobbled street, its walls so narrow they could only just squeeze down it. The convoy was lit by the white headlamps of motorcycles, driving in two rows. As Yenko peered to decipher the inky black night, he saw that behind the motorcycles was a long, thin column of people, civilians: men, women and children, loaded down with goods, bundles, suitcases. There was a man in a smart coat and Homburg hat, with a huge roll of blankets tied up with string on his back and a saucepan in each hand. An elderly man clutched a suitcase to his chest and worked his jaw soundlessly as he walked. Two women in headscarves went by, heads bent, arm in arm. A man in a flat cap and galoshes carried a boy on his shoulders.

'Where are they going? At this hour?' he whispered to Ctibor.

There was a pause. 'They are Jews.' After another pause, he said, 'More Jews. In the name of the Holy Father, more Jews. I did not think there were any left. I thought they were all gone by now. I did not think there were as many Jews in the world as I have seen pass by this window at night.'

Yenko watched them. A young girl went by, staggering beneath the weight of a child not much smaller than herself.

'Why do they move them at night?'

'So that the rest of us won't see, so that we won't realise how many are being deported. For the first few months, I used to watch all the time. I used to think I might see her.'

'Are the stories really true, do you think, about what they are doing to them?' *Whatever happens to the Jews will happen next to us.*

'No one ever comes back,' Ctibor said slowly. 'I have realised that now. For a while, I hoped. But I am not a fool. They set dogs on them at the railway stations. They shoot them if they don't climb up quick enough. The stories . . .' His voice dwindled.

Yenko thought of a saying the *gadje* had in the East. *My house is outside the village. I don't know anything.*

There was a small commotion beneath the window. One of the motorcycles had sputtered to a halt and its headlamp had gone out. Some of the deportees also halted, confused. Soldiers began shouting.

Afraid that in the confusion someone might look up, Yenko withdrew, sitting down with his back against the wall.

He looked over at Ctibor, expecting him to do the same, but Ctibor seemed to have lost all fear and remained where he was, peering below. Yenko wondered how many times Ctibor had done this.

'Do you know what the worst of it is?' Ctibor said, without turning his head. 'The worst of it is the ones who look hopeful, determined. I see it in the mothers, clutching their children to their chests. They are trying so hard to fool themselves. As long as I can hold on to this child, then somehow I will be able to protect it. They make themselves believe that. I think they believe it right up to the edge of the abyss.'

Ctibor's face was no more than a dark-grey shadow in the tiny light that came up from the street. Yenko heard the throaty growl of the motorcycle engine coming back to life, more shouts, the footfalls continuing. He closed his eyes. *Dalé*, he thought. *Mum. Don't die. Don't die before I come back for you. I'm coming. I'm sorry it's taking so long but I have to save myself before I can save you. And I'm being so slow because I'm frightened and don't know what to do. I'm trying not to think of you. I have to try all the time. If I think of you I will go mad.* What would be happening back at the camp? It seemed so far away. Would the quarantine be lifted yet, or would they all still be locked in to die? They must have done something about the typhus. They wouldn't have abandoned the staff, at least. Maybe they would. Maybe they were all falling sick, one by one, as he hid safely in a Prague backstreet, doing nothing. *Don't die, Dalé. Please don't die.*

It seemed to last forever, the low murmur of the engines, the rumble of the feet against the cobbles. What did you put on your feet when you had been warned that you would be deported? Your best shoes, the most valuable? Or did you wear the sturdiest? Did you stop and think that the choice was pointless? Or, as Ctibor had said, did you continue to delude yourself until you stood at the edge of the abyss, until delusion was no longer possible? The *Biboldes* have it worse than us, he thought. We have never expected anything but death from the *gadje*. The Jews have lived with the Gentiles all these centuries, in this city, making things for them, doing business with them, marrying them, and where has it got them? A night stroll through the stony streets of Prague, a choice about which pair of shoes is better for the walk into oblivion.

He closed his eyes and put his hands over his ears. Would it never cease? The engines, the feet, a river of murmurs, ceaseless, already-ghosts – and he and Ctibor lost in their own misery; Ctibor's wife, his family.

Yenko squeezed his eyes tight, pressed his hands against the side of his head, and wished profoundly that he was back in the camp with his people, whatever was happening there. Anything was preferable to this, this knowledge. He hated himself.

There was a shuffling in the dark. Ctibor had crawled beneath the window to where he was sitting. Yenko felt a rough, plump hand fumble for his arm and squeeze it. 'Thank you,' Ctibor whispered hoarsely. 'Thank you for coming to me.'

*

Blažek visited two weeks later with a present for Yenko: a suit, brown pinstripe with wide lapels and turn-ups on the trouser legs. The identity card would take a little longer, he said, but the suit meant he could at least walk down the street without looking as though he had a sign hung round his neck saying *illegal*.

They were all in the back room of the office. Ctibor sent Yenko into the toilet to change into the suit. When he emerged, Blažek and Ctibor both stared at him. Yenko looked down at himself. The suit was too large around the waist and the legs of the trousers were far too long.

'Those will need taking up,' said Blažek, pointing with his cigarette.

'I've got a needle upstairs, I can do it,' said Ctibor.

'I'll do it,' said Yenko.

The jacket was roomy round the shoulders but the arms were just right.

'Brown,' said Blažek, thoughtfully. 'It suits you.' For some reason, all three of them laughed.

'Socks. Shirt. Braces. I can manage those with my clothing coupons,' said Ctibor.

'I'll pay you back,' Yenko said.

Ctibor flapped both hands, 'Ach! What do I need with clothes?'

'Shoes are difficult,' said Blažek. 'Shoes are important. Shoes are what gives a man away.'

'Can you sort it out?'

'Of course,' Blažek said with a smile. 'But you will pay me. The suit is a gift. But you pay me for the shoes. I'll put it on your tab, underneath the identity card but above the spectacles, hair ointment and cigarettes. Your own father won't know you by the time we've finished with you.'

Yenko said. 'I'd better get this off,' and turned away.

When he emerged, Blažek said, 'There's something else.' He picked his cigarettes up from the counter-top and tossed them across the room to Yenko, who caught them neatly, withdrew one and tossed them back. 'We need to cripple you.'

When Yenko had lit the cigarette, he inhaled deeply and said, looking at his fingers, 'How, exactly?'

Blažek shrugged. 'Take your pick. We can get a crippling disease put on your identity card, tuberculosis maybe. We'd need a doctor's letter as back-up. Trouble is, you will still get stopped and your story checked out. It's better if it's something visible. You could strap up one arm and keep it inside your suit, or limp.'

'You just don't see any young men on the streets these days,' said Ctibor apologetically.

'A limp,' said Yenko.

'Good choice,' said Blažek. 'I'll find some sort of brace and surgical sock so you can strap up each morning when you get out of bed. You have to do it every single moment. Don't even go to pee or answer the door without it.'

'I know how to limp,' said Yenko shortly, frowning at his cigarette. He brushed a few flakes of ash from the sleeve of his shirt. Already, it seemed old and worn, unsuitable. He missed the suit. He wanted everything else as soon as possible. At last;

to look like the people around him, to be able to walk down the street . . . 'Get me a stick. With a silver top.'

Blažek gave an ironic bow. 'Whatever you say.' The two older men chuckled indulgently at Yenko's newly acquired air of authority.

Yenko tipped his head back and blew a long stream of smoke towards the ceiling.

CHAPTER 26

Yenko was standing outside the main railway station. He had removed the shoe on his 'bad' foot and was tapping it against a nearby tree and frowning into it. Passers-by ignored him.

There was no stone in his shoe, or any other object, but he needed a moment or two to collect himself. It was one thing to limp into bars behind Blažek, smoothing back his oiled hair and lighting a cigarette while Blažek did the talking. He had even got used to walking past German soldiers. It was another matter to go up to a ticket counter and say, 'Single to Brno,' as if he bought railway tickets all the time. The last time he had travelled on a train, he had been an escapee in a goods car. Now, only a few months later, he was going to hobble past the soldiers on guard, make his way slowly to the counter, purchase his ticket (you didn't even have to show your identity card) and board the train. *You are a cripple, but a confident cripple*, Blažek had told him.

Practise your look. Damaged but suave – the girls will love it. Injured men make them feel patriotic. Play your cards right and I'll introduce you to some girls. It was complicated, being a *gadjo*.

He tipped his head to the sky, closing his eyes against the sun. It had risen fast that morning, hard and bright in a blanket of blue. No blue was as positive as the blue of early summer, as if God had something to prove.

The heat on his face returned a memory to him: the evenings when he would lean against his mother as they squatted next to the fire, listening to her and the other women singing softly. He could remember lifting a hand to stroke her cheek, amazed at the texture of her dark brown skin, so much darker than his, bathing in her indulgent smile. Their wordless unity – that was what he remembered. His mother was a tall, smooth-skinned woman, with gold coins in her braids, not the grey-faced skeleton he had last seen in the camp. It was that other mother, that early one, he was going to find. *The mother you remember no longer exists.* He squashed the thought.

He pictured himself on the train. He would sit on a seat, his bad foot resting upon the other knee and his stick across his lap, playing with an unlit cigarette and staring out of the window at the countryside flashing in the sunlight. The train was going to carry him back through time as well as distance, the harsh spin of its iron wheels rolling back the years to the life he had had as a child before the war, before all the white people had gone mad. If he thought beyond that, he would lose his courage and go and hide beneath Ctibor's eiderdown. *My father died. He did nothing. He just curled up and died.* He opened his eyes and bent to pick up his small case.

He spent the night in Brno; and the following morning at the tiny district railway station trying to get a train to Nĕdvedice. At first he was told there were no passenger trains stopping at all that day, but a few crowns to the stationmaster soon elicited a different story. There were passenger trains going up that way but because of travel restrictions in the area no one was allowed to get on them. Once they had begun to talk, the stationmaster was curious as to his business up there. Yenko fobbed him off with a story about visiting relatives. Why was it a restricted area? he asked the stationmaster, pretending he had not been up there since the Occupation. The stationmaster changed the subject to warn him about how long the train would take. He could probably walk there quicker. It would be nearly evening by the time he arrived.

I can spend the night in the woods, thought Yenko. No more fat bouncy pillows for me. They can keep their beds. Soon, I will become a Rom again.

He walked from Nědvedice, taking the track that led up to the camp, following it until he judged the time was right to turn into the woods and climb upwards so that he was above and behind the camp. The light was beginning to fail when he found a suitable clearing with a springy cluster of new-growth ferns and bracken beneath a tree. He opened his case and extracted the thin sheet he had brought with him from Prague. It was a concession to the *gadje* world, laying a sheet down before he slept on the forest floor – but he only had one change of clothes. He removed his jacket and hung it on a nearby twig, then sat down and smoked a cigarette, feeling profoundly comfortable. It was a mild night.

When his cigarette was finished, he sat for a long time with the stub between his fingers, listening to the tiny cracklings of the forest, like noises from a dream. The dusk began to gather. *The forest has eyes.* He rose, took his water bottle from his case and tucked it under his arm. He walked a few metres, to piss against a tree, then poured a little water over his hands and rubbed them together, apologising to the Ancestors for his many recent breaches of the laws of decent behaviour. He would be seeing his mother soon. She would want to know he had done his best to keep himself Clean.

He replaced his water bottle and closed his case, then lay down with his arms bent sharply at the elbow and tucked under his head, as he used to when he was a boy. He was tired. He thought he would fall asleep quite quickly.

After a minute or so, he sat up and brushed a few stray pine needles from his sleeves. What was wrong with him? Had a few months of *gadje* beds made him soft? Here he was, back where he belonged, in the open air. Perhaps he needed just one more cigarette.

As he smoked, he pulled small strands of tobacco from between his teeth and tucked them into the top pocket of his shirt. His father had never wasted a single strand of tobacco. He closed his eyes, blew smoke into the air, and thought about Josef. *Oh Dad*, he thought, a well of soft sorrow opening in his chest. *I am not letting you down. I found the gadjo Michálek, and I survived – and everything you said about Prague is true, by the way. It is a den of snakes. But there are other things I didn't expect. I didn't expect to like seeing big buildings, after a while, and sitting in a bar in a suit, and having gadji women glance at me with glances that seem to mean something. The gadjo Blažek says I look much older than I am. It's the missing teeth and weather-beaten skin, he says. I know differently. I know it is the things I have seen. I could have stayed in Prague. I could have turned into a swindling gadjo like Blažek but I didn't, although it was getting easier and easier with each passing week. I stopped starting to become whatever I was becoming. I even have a limp now. Isn't that enough for you?*

He gave a sudden shudder. Was he cold? He looked around

at the darkening forest. His father had died locked in a hut full of sick and dying souls. His ghost would have been unable to escape. Would it have returned to his body and been buried with him, in the pit above the camp? Perhaps it would have slipped out of the winding sheet and even now be wandering around the camp's perimeter, in Hell, unable to leave, moaning for his surviving family and bewailing their inability to set each other free.

Yenko's breath began to deepen at the thought. He wished he could ask his Aunt Tekla. She would know what had happened to his father's soul.

The air between the trees was grey. Patches of mosquitoes were just visible in the gloaming, floating like blouses drying in the wind. Distantly, a fox barked, was silent, and barked again. His father's soul might be nearby. It might stumble upon him in the night, its eyes dark and disbelieving, its mouth an open hollow. *My son, why did you allow me to be trapped, rotting, for all time?*

Aunt Tekla. Yenko jumped to his feet. His need of her was overwhelming. She was already sick by the time he ran away from the camp. What were the chances she had survived? Perhaps these woods held her spirit too, joined with that of his father, aimlessly united in their misery: and Parni, small Parni, transformed into a malicious sprite. Her tiny fingers would pluck at his eyes. Who else? Bobo: a small, plump demon? His Aunts Ludmila and Eva: their slim, wavering figures would be like flames in the dark. *The forest has eyes.*

Dei. Mother. She would still be alive, no matter how sick the rest of the camp had got. She would not have let him down by dying.

He snatched his jacket from the twig where he had hung it and shrugged it on. He picked up his case and shook it free of forest debris. He could not wait a moment longer. The camp was just over the rise. He had to go and look at it, just look. He could not spend the night sitting and waiting and staring into the dark.

He left the sheet where it was and hurried through the trees, up the rise, then turned to skirt the fence with the old quarry lost in gloom to his right. He tried to console himself by thinking of the look on his mother's face when she saw him, when she realised he had come back. How many other sons could have achieved what he had? The perilous journey, the transformation, the return . . . Even she would find it hard to hide her amazement.

After skirting the low fence that bordered the farmland, he headed back up into the forest, so that he could approach the camp from behind. He would go to the edge, where he could look down on the perimeter fence and find a safe place in the trees. Then he would sit up all night, awake, watching the camp, so close to his family that they would probably hear him if he stood up and shouted. The next morning, he would walk down to the road that led past the camp. If the quarantine was still in force, there would be signs on the main gate, which would be visible from the road. If anyone challenged him, he had a story ready: he was a businessman, Jan Michálek, interested in the possibility of cheap labour. ('Here is my identification. Would you care for a cigarette?') But he wouldn't get challenged unless he got too close. When he had taken a good look at the camp, he would return to the woods and plan how to get his family out; a ruse, bribery – perhaps it would be simplest to dig beneath the perimeter fence one night and force the lock on the women's block. *Dei*. Marie? He could hardly remember what the girl looked like – when he thought of her he had only an impression of smallness and self-possession. *Dei*, she was the important one. He would save her, and then she would be able to save him and together they would save the others. He must find a way of talking to her, at least. But until he knew whether or not the quarantine was still in force, it was pointless to plan.

He thought of walking past the camp in daylight, just strolling down the road. He was confident the guards would not recognise him. They knew him only as a shaven-headed *gypsy*, bony and weak, in prison uniform. Now, he had hair and creases in his trousers and collar studs. Even so . . . Perhaps he should take a closer look at the back of the camp now. It was almost dark.

He could soon make out the perimeter fence from his vantage point on the edge of the forest. It had changed, he thought. It was not quite where he remembered it – it was nearer the trees, and not as tall. It had been untended in his absence, the barbed wire hanging loose in places. The sentry towers were unoccupied. They must be changing shift.

The absence of sentries gave him the courage to skirt closer – the patch of scrubby ground between the fence and the trees was no more than ten metres wide. What a poor state of repair the fence was in, the wooden planks broken and skewed. I could scramble under that in an instant, he thought scornfully. Could he really be at the same place? That fence looked so short. Emboldened, he glanced left and right, then stumbled in the growing darkness over the rubble-strewn ground to crouch by the fence and peer through a gap in the rotting wood, into the camp itself.

It was difficult to make things out in the gloom. A thin line of smoke was coming from the cook's hut on the far side of the camp but he could see no one from the narrow angle afforded

him by the gap in the fence. Everybody would be in their bunks
by now, the lamps extinguished. Nearest to him was the men's
barracks. He had the sudden, mad idea of creeping in there and
starting an uprising, a mass breakout. That would give them
something to think about. If only there were six of me, he
thought. Six men could do it. If he had a pistol he would do it
on his own. It would be so fine to stroll in there now, to greet
that Jan Malík with a casual grin. He wouldn't recognise him at
first. When he did, his eyes would pop out of his head. He'd
soon change his mind about whether Yenko was Rom enough
for his daughter. Yenko felt his breath quicken. It was so
tempting.

Odd there were no patrols. He remembered the night-sentries
wandering the camp continuously, skirting the inside of the
fence and weaving between the barracks, on the constant
lookout, especially in the summer. There were always more
escape attempts in summer. He could see no one, in fact.

Fear began to creep over him, a dread as cold and heavy as
any he had felt alone in the woods, surrounded by ghosts. Could
it be so quiet because *everyone* was sick now? Were they all lying
in their barracks, their faces black, dying, even the guards?
Would the authorities really have let the sickness get that bad,
just shut them all up in there to die? There was a gap somewhere
in his comprehension, an inability, a yawning. A hole was
opening up – a chasm – but he couldn't work out how or where
or why. He crossed himself.

He remained crouched for one brief breathless moment, then
he got down on his belly, pushed his case through the gap and
began to work his way under the fence. On the other side he
stood upright, panting. The strange dread that gripped him had
dissolved any last scrap of caution. There was still no one in
sight. He strode to the nearest block, the one he had spent so

many nights locked into desperately trying to sleep, the one he remembered packed with coughing, starving, dying men, crawling with lice, the air alive with misery. He strode to the door, grasped the handle and turned.

It was unlocked. He gave a light push. It swung slowly, with an infinite creaking sound, like the groan of the dead. He remembered a dream he used to have in Prague; a body wrapped in cloth, inhaling and sucking its own shroud into the open hollow of his mouth. He remembered his father lifting his shirt one day, when he was still well, and saying, 'Emil, my back is itching. Can you see anything?' *The lice feed on you*. Dr Steiner's face had been fierce. *They feed on you and they shit. You breathe in the shit*. Yenko blinked. Ctibor Michálek had looked at him strangely and sadly when he had said, 'I'm going out. I'm going to take my case. I'm not sure when I'll be back.'

The block was empty. The wooden bunks were square shadows in the gloom, scrubbed clean. There was a chemical smell. He could see right through to the far end of the block where a small square window formed another lighter shadow. There was nothing, not even a hastily abandoned blanket.

He turned and ran down to the next barrack, the children's block. He slammed back the door – nothing. For a moment, he thought he saw a movement in the shadows and his heart leapt, but it was an empty, unlit paraffin lamp hanging from the ceiling, swinging minutely in the breeze he had created by throwing back the door.

He wheeled away, one hand clutching at the corner of the block for balance. The camp was deserted. They had all gone, left him. He had come all this way, risked his life, for nothing. They were gone. It was only then that he looked down the camp, across the *Appell-platz*, and saw that the main gate stood wide open. *The cooking hut* – there had been a little smoke drifting up.

Somebody had been left behind to keep an eye on things. He would force them to their knees and press his thumbs against their throat until they told him where they had sent his mother and his little brother.

He turned swiftly around the corner of the block, and came face to face with Čacko.

The two men froze, no more than a metre between them. Čacko was holding a paraffin lantern which had almost run down. His expression was one of surprise, bemusement. He frowned, then swayed lightly. Then frowned again.

'You're early,' he growled, wiping the back of his mouth with his hand. Then he coughed, and the stench of alcohol was so overwhelming that Yenko wanted to reel backwards. He steeled himself not to move. He became aware that he was clenching and unclenching his fist.

'We were expecting you tomorrow,' Čacko continued. 'I don't know what you're doing. You can't price it up in the dark. They should have sent you back to town. Who was on the gate?' The words *who* and *was* were stretched and slurred into one. He was drunk.

Yenko's voice sounded strange and light in his ears. 'Just thought I'd . . . look around.'

'Well, *I'm* the only one on duty tonight and *I'm* not helping you.' Čacko's tone was petulant. He swayed again.

He's more than drunk, Yenko thought. He is comatose on his feet. He pushed his hand into his trouser pocket and withdrew his cigarettes. He offered the packet, trying to steady his breathing. The wild thumping of his heart was subsiding.

'Oh for God's sake, come and have a drink in the hut then,' grumbled Čacko. 'I assume you're staying at the staff quarters? You're not planning on walking all the way back to the village tonight?'

'No,' said Yenko.

'I'll tell you what I know,' Čacko said, as he leaned forward for Yenko to light his cigarette. 'Unofficially, of course . . .' he chuckled, then waggled a finger in front of Yenko's face. 'Don't go getting me into trouble, now. I'm planning on being out of this godforsaken hole by the end of next week. God help your men, that's all I can say.' He tipped his head back to exhale, then looked at the cigarette. 'Where did you get these?'

Čacko's face was still close to Yenko's. The orange glow from the paraffin lantern ballooned his features. It was really Čacko, so civil, confidential. No, it was more like the opposite of Čacko, his genial inverse. He was regarding Yenko with a slight air of puzzlement, as if the sight of this smart young man was making his brain itch. Yenko lit his own cigarette. When I have found out what has happened to my family, he thought steadily, I am going to kill you. God was on his side, for once. He had served up Čacko on a plate.

Čacko turned and they crossed the camp to the small hut down by the main gate. As they passed the other buildings, Yenko saw that they were all empty; the women's block, the staff hut – the infirmary across the *Appell-platz*. The small white wisp of smoke from the cook's hut had been extinguished but there was a thin line of glowing orange on one side of the blackout curtain.

Yenko remembered that his stick was tucked beneath his arm. He swung it into his hand so he could lean on it while he walked. 'You still have a few gendarmes here then?' Yenko asked, indicating the cook's hut.

Čacko shook his head. 'Just my relief, and they're at the staff quarters,' he waved a hand loosely, 'that low building there, beyond the gate. There's a cleaning detail in that hut. We kept some of the *gypos* behind to help us fumigate but they followed the others in trucks last week as soon as the DDT boys had finished. You wouldn't *believe* what this place was like . . .'

Last week. There were Roma here as recently as last week. They had reached the steps of the hut. 'Where have they been sent?' Yenko asked casually as they mounted the steps.

'Oh, you know,' Čacko replied. 'Up north, like the others.' Inside the hut, he reached up and hung the dying paraffin lantern on a hook in the centre of the low ceiling. The shack remained in semi-dark. 'Used to be a boot store, but I've made it *quite* my own little cabin. Sorry if I didn't seem too friendly. S'been a long shift. Nice to have a bit of company. Makes the time pass.'

In the corner of the hut there was a small desk with a collection of tin plates and mugs. 'I thought I had a little glass, with gold lettering on the side, a tiny little one. S'nice. I think I've . . .'

'Whereabouts, up north?'

'Aha!' said Čacko, locating the glass. 'Here you are, little one, just *waiting* for a visitor.' He reached up for a bottle made of thick brown glass which sat on a high shelf above the desk. 'Not bad this stuff.' He handed the glass to Yenko, then turned and poured himself a large dose into a tin mug. '*Na zdraví*!' The two men looked at each other over their drinking vessels as they sipped.

The liquid in the glass tasted of nothing but heat. Dear God, thought Yenko, *Wooden God*, am I to spend the war indulging drunks?

'So,' Čacko said, sitting on the edge of the desk and gesturing Yenko towards a low stool. 'Now you've taken a look, what d'you reckon?'

Yenko pulled a non-committal face as he sat.

'Between you and me,' Čacko continued, taking another swig from his mug. 'I would let the Werhmacht have it. If you try and put workers in here, how long are you going to have to keep them here? Then you've got to transport them each day, and the cooking facilities are *completely* inadequate, I can tell you. Let the Germans do what they like.'

'How was the cooking managed before?' Yenko asked. He had only taken two sips of his drink and already it was giving him a headache.

'Oh well, we didn't have to do much for the *gypsy* vermin, they were used to it. Most of them were in a pretty bad state when they arrived, that's why they kept dying. During the quarantine we lost a load. Tell you something funny, though. When the Kripo' arrived they said they weren't taking them in that state and we had to give them two extra slices of bread a day to make them look better.'

'So where have they all gone?' Yenko put his glass down on the floor beside him, staring at Čacko.

Čacko lowered his mug. 'You are . . . interested . . .' he said slowly, with a slight frown. Yenko felt for his case with his foot. It was right beside the stool. The door to the hut opened inwards. The main gate was close but running that way would mean running towards the staff quarters just outside the camp, past the relief guards. It would be better to head back up through the camp and under the perimeter fence.

Yenko stood and hitched up his trousers. 'Well, thanks for the drink,' he said. 'I suppose I'd better get myself settled for the night.' Čacko did not move. He was watching him. Yenko bent and picked up his case. 'Nice to have met you,' he said, as he swung the small but heavy case in a wide arc that made contact with Čacko's face in the region of his left cheekbone.

Čacko sprawled backwards, arms flung wide. The mug flew from his grasp and hit the wall. Yenko dropped the case and threw himself forward, trying to grab the man's throat. Čacko recovered his balance quickly and shoved back. As Yenko fell back, one of his hands knocked against the low-slung lantern and its arc of dim light began to swing loopily from side to side, as if they were on a boat tossed by a river.

They crashed to the floor together but Čacko's head smacked against the stool as they fell so Yenko had the advantage. He rolled on top of him and pinned his elbow across his throat. Before I kill him, he thought clearly, he must know who I am.

He pushed his face close to Čacko's, which was bright red, deepening to purple as he gasped for breath. '*Where are they*?' Yenko hissed viciously. 'Tell me where they have been sent. *Where are they*?'

Čacko coughed desperately. Yenko loosened his grip slightly to allow him to speak. Čacko took advantage to inhale deeply, then used all his strength to shove Yenko off and fling himself upwards, his hands reaching for the small desk. Yenko grabbed the back of his uniform and shoved him to the ground. He scrambled over Čacko, stamping on his face with one foot as he pulled open the little drawer in the front of the desk. There was a small pistol inside, still in its holster. Čacko was so lazy he didn't even bother to put it on when he went patrolling the empty camp. Yenko snatched the gun from the holster, turned and pointed it down at Čacko's head.

Čacko was collapsed on the floor again, face down, realising he had lost. A small amount of blood was leaking from his face, over the dusty planks. 'You've broken my nose, you fucking lunatic,' he muttered. 'Who are you?'

Was there a safety catch on the pistol? Yenko didn't have a clue and didn't dare take his eyes from Čacko to look. He had never held a gun before. He kept his arm steady. 'Keep your face down. Now tell me, where have the prisoners been sent?'

'Same place they all get sent. Same place they send the *yids*.

Poland. *The General Government*. That's where they all end up.
You can't make a silk purse out of sow's ear. Anyone could have
told them that.'

'Where in Poland?'

'I don't know. The Germans take over the trains at Ostrava.
What difference does it make? The same thing's going to happen
either way. Two slices of bread a day, for God's sake.'

'What? What's going to happen?'

Čacko paused, as if he was finally realising the importance of
his answers. 'Well, you know. You know what people are saying.
The camps they have there. They are as big as cities . . .'

'Tell me . . .'

Čacko's gasping breath had finally subsided. His voice was
suddenly dull and hopeless. He lifted his face. A little blood ran
from his nose. 'You know, surely. You work for the Labour
Department, don't you? You must have seen the paperwork.
Return undesired. Isn't that what the lists say at the bottom? I
suppose they kill the weak ones straight away but I think they
hang on to some of them to work them. Shouldn't think they
kept any of ours. Ours were all weak ones by the time they left.
They gas them. That's what the Croats said. I'd heard they shot
them and burnt them but they said, no, it's gas.'

He sat up gradually, wincing with pain, glancing up at Yenko.
He brushed down his hands, then stopped in the middle of the
action. He looked up, staring at Yenko full in the face. 'You don't
work for the Brno Labour Department do you?' he said slowly.

'No,' Yenko said. What would happen if he pulled the trigger?
If the safety catch was off, then he could blow Čacko's face all
over the hut and be out of the door and across the camp before
the relief guards came to investigate. If the catch was still on,
Čacko would be upon him.

Čacko was not looking at the pistol. He was looking at Yenko.

Then he said, very softly, 'František. It is you, isn't it?' He shook his head, still gazing at him. His expression became soft, pleading. He spread his hands. 'František. Put the gun down. This isn't necessary. Not for me.' He looked at the floor, where blood was dripping from his nose. He shook his head slightly and gave a small exhalation, as if amused, then looked up at him again. 'After all, I saved your life, you know.'

'*What*?' Was the safety catch on or off?

'I saved your life. More than once, actually.' Čacko wiped his nose with the back of his hand, then looked at the smear of blood on it. His voice was still quiet, philosophical. 'The first time was when they were going to send you on that transport, back in December. Your name was on the list because you were down as a troublemaker. I came and pulled you off the truck, remember? I told the Commander you were useful. Otherwise you'd be cinders by now, like the rest of them.'

Yenko blinked hard. It was taking all his effort to keep his arm steady.

'When you escaped, I was disappointed you'd run out on me but I said, ah well, it's in the boy's nature. You can't blame him. Poor old Lojza caught it, I can tell you. He said he thought someone had kept you back in the camp and that's why you didn't come back. That's why you weren't missed until the evening. They wanted to send the dogs out but I told them it wasn't worth it. You had too much of a head start. They would've, you know, if it wasn't for me . . .' He looked up at him, and Yenko saw there were tears standing in his eyes. 'I always looked after you, didn't I? You were like a son to me. Well, I lost my temper now and then but every man does that once in a while. But I protected you. Always. I could have chosen any of them but I chose you.' He lowered his head again. 'I hate the fucking Germans. We all do.'

Yenko said, evenly, raising the pistol slightly, 'What has happened to my family?'

Čacko lifted his head again. 'They're dead, František. Of course they are.' Yenko stared at him, the bulbous features, the fat neck, the red rise of his cheek where he had been struck . . . 'We had some Croatian guards sent down as soon as the typhus was under control. They came straight from their tour of duty in Poland. So many of ours had fallen sick and Brno Police was refusing to send any more. These Croats, they'd been working in one of the big camps. They are like factories, they said, factories for killing people who aren't needed any more. They gas them. It's quite quick, they said. In they go, and out they come. They burn the bodies.' He stopped. He looked up at Yenko and gave a little, helpless grimace. His voice began to whine, piteously. 'František. I'm not saying I approve of it. It's not us, you know. The Germans . . .'

Yenko's arm began to shake with the effort of keeping the pistol steady. Čacko lifted his hands, pleadingly. 'Come on. You've always got your old friend Čacko, you know. I know it's hard, but you've always got me.'

Yenko squeezed the trigger. Nothing happened.

Čacko threw himself at Yenko's legs. Yenko tried to sidestep him. As Čacko's fat arms encircled him, he brought the pistol down on his head, twice. Čacko loosed his grasp enough for Yenko to kick him aside and reach for his case. As he stepped away, Čacko managed to grab one trouser leg. 'I won't tell,' he gasped, desperately. 'I promise I won't tell a soul. You could be safe with me. You could come with me, when they transfer me next week. I'm going back to Brno. Nice little cushy number they've promised me after a whole year here.' Yenko cried out with disgust, flailing out with the pistol. 'I saved you!' Čacko shouted. 'I saved your life!' Yenko stamped on Čacko's arm. 'František!' Čacko sobbed.

Yenko finally freed his leg and reached out for the door. The
pistol fell from his grasp but he didn't stop to pick it up. The night
outside had never seemed so sweet. He tumbled from the hut
with his case and walking stick clutched to his chest. As he
jumped down from the step he heard Čacko behind him shouting.
'František! Come back! We're friends, aren't we? We've always
been friends!' As he ran up the slope to the perimeter fence, he
heard the voice still hollering across the darkness, 'Fran-ti-šek!'

He found the broken planks and scrambled underneath. He
flung himself across the scrubby patch of earth and dived into
the safety of the trees. His feet slipped on some loose stones and
his stick fell from his grasp. He snatched it up and pounded on,
one arm raised to protect his face from branches as he crashed
through.

Finally, when he reached the heart of the wood, where the
ground rose, he fell down on to the slope between the trees,
down upon the soft, dead pine needles and unrelenting earth.

He lay for a moment, gasping with the effort of running
uphill. Then he rose, upright on his knees, threw back his head,
exposed his face to the unresponsive sky – the calm moon – and
let out a long, undying howl.

It seemed to last for minutes in his head, flying up through
the trees and racing over the surrounding countryside. At some
stage he must have drawn breath and howled again but
somehow the tail of each howl was welded seamlessly to the
mouth of the next. It echoed so loudly he imagined Čacko, alone
in the camp below, would turn his head in fear. In Brno they
would hear the howl, in Prague – even in Poland, hated Poland,
where his family had been taken to be ripped out of the world
and turned to ashes.

He howled until there was no longer within him the capacity
for sound.

When he had finished howling, he rose unsteadily to his feet. He could have fallen down again, wept – but instead, he stood.

He was empty now.

He gazed upwards at the still-calm moon, a new moon, a broken promise.

They were all gone. His father gone, gasping his last on a pallet bed. His mother, beloved *Dei* gone. Parni gone, eyes blank with bewilderment. Aunt Tekla was gone. Bobo gone; Aunt Eva and Aunt Ludmila; and the others captured in Bohemia, Václav and Božena Winter and all their daughters; Yakali Zelinka and his wife whose name he couldn't think of and Justin and Miroslav and their wives and children and old Pavliná who would have known before any of them; and all the other Kalderash in all the other camps and the Lowari and the Polska Roma and the Sinti and Boyash and Marie, tiny beautiful Marie, and her silent mother and her brutal father and *Dei* ... his beloved *Dei*, his mother, the strongest woman in the whole world. Dead, all dead. Pushed into the trucks, climbing up willingly perhaps, believing that nothing could be worse than the camp, not knowing that the worst still lay ahead.

He gazed upwards, dizzy with grief, his face an upturned, broken wheel, turning beneath the night sky. After the howl, there was silence; not even a breeze; moon but no stars; and the blackness of night everywhere. He was the only Rom left in the world.

PART 7

1945

CHAPTER 27

Yenko was in his hotel room in Beroun when the phone rang. He was standing in front of the full-length mirror on the door of the wardrobe, buttoning his flies and baring his teeth at his reflection. His shirt needed pressing and he had lost one of his cufflinks. Maybe it was on the floor somewhere. The woman had pushed him back on to the bed before he had had time to undress. Stupid *gadji* whore. She hadn't even re-applied her lipstick afterwards, a true sign of contempt and carelessness. Neither of them had said goodbye.

Yenko turned and sat down on the bed, knees wide to avoid creasing his trousers. He picked up the phone and stuck it in the crook of his shoulder, muttering, 'Yes?' while reaching forward for the pack of cigarettes on the bedside table. As he upended the packet on to the bed, he grimaced. There had been eight in the packet, now there were only five. The whore must have lifted three while she was at work. He revised his opinion of her. She was a clever *gadji* whore. A stupid one would have tried to take the packet.

'A call from Prague, Mr Michálek,' The receptionist's voice was distant and bubbly.

'Put him through.'

While he lit the cigarette, there was a series of clicks, then Blažek's gravelly tones. 'Jan. How's it going?'

'Not bad. Not that good but not bad.' Yenko had two paper packets of wizened sausages in his suitcase and four eggs wrapped in handkerchiefs nestling in his hat. Judging by how light the eggs were, they were rotten. There were also three watches in the false bottoms of his brogues, straps removed, and two signet rings sewn into the folds of his long-johns, around the crotch. It wasn't what you'd call a big haul, hardly worth the risk of the journey, which took so damn long these days, but just enough to make it worthwhile. The eggs and sausages would be sold when he got to Prague, or used for bribes, and the watches and rings would go to what Blažek called *our retirement fund*. Valuables had become more and more easy to acquire as the food shortages had worsened. The retirement fund was bulging.

'Been busy here,' Blažek replied. That meant prices were up again. Coffee had been eighteen hundred crowns per kilo when Yenko had left Prague, a couple of days ago. He wondered if it had gone over two thousand yet. The cigarette ration was down from thirty-five to twenty-five a week and you could get twenty crowns for one smoke. To say nothing of the booze. On Monday, he'd sold a bottle of brandy to a restaurant on Strosmayer Square for eight hundred and fifty – well, some of the liquid in the bottle was brandy. The owner wouldn't complain. He'd spent the last two years cleaning out snail shells after each serving of *escargot* and refilling them with chopped dog.

Yenko drew on his cigarette, pursing his lips to exhale in a fine, speedy stream.

'Has your cousin collected his wages yet?' he asked. They had an informant inside the police who let them know which of the black-market boys had been pulled off the streets recently. If it was anyone they had done business with, they off-loaded their stock and went quiet for a while.

'Yes. He's grateful to us. Things are very slow for him.'

'Good. I'll drop by when I'm back then.'

'Safe journey.'

The journey was never safe. Trains were cancelled all the time because of the coal shortages, and those that ran were dangerously over-loaded. The Allies had started to bomb the railway lines, now they were within range; the civilian trains as well as the troop carriers. (The Americans had dropped one on a tram on Schwerinstrasse last month.) No, the journey was never safe, but as Blažek said, 'Jan, it beats doing twelve-hour shifts in a tank factory.' Blažek was happy to sit in Prague doing the deals while Yenko performed the more dangerous task of travelling out to the country. Yenko didn't mind. He liked to be on the move.

Sometimes, on nights when he couldn't sleep, he would lie in his dark hotel room, the rough blankets up to his chest, smoking and exhaling upwards, thinking that maybe he would just walk into the woods one day, somewhere, in the middle of nowhere, and strip off his smart suit and shiny shoes and ruffle his pomaded hair – start growing a beard, perhaps. He could do it, any time. That was why he didn't worry like Blažek.

He never did walk into the woods. He always went back to Prague. In Prague, there was no time to think.

The war would be over soon. The Russians were already in

Brno and the rest of Moravia would be theirs within weeks. It
was just a question of who would get to Prague first, them or the
Yanks. In the meantime, everyone was keeping their heads
down. He and Blažek had the field to themselves.

Blažek treated Yenko like an equal partner now. He never
went short of cigarettes. In return, Yenko happily handed over
his weekly ration of a quarter of a kilo of meat, especially once
Blažek had told him it was horsemeat. Blažek had a lot of mouths
to feed; a wife and four children in Krč and a mistress in the
Little Quarter. The mistress came from a German family who
had their bags all packed, ready for the dash to the American
lines once the Russians got too close.

Yenko stubbed out his cigarette in the tin ashtray and lifted
the phone. The receptionist answered politely, 'Yes, Mr
Michálek.'

'I'm leaving in a few minutes. Would you prepare my bill
please?'

'Yes, Mr Michálek.'

He liked this receptionist. She didn't look askance at him, the
way some did, and she gave him the only hotel room in the
whole district that had its own phone. The only people using
hotels these days were businessmen like him, and Germans.
Blažek barricaded the door at night when he stayed in a hotel.

Yenko rose and took his jacket from the wooden hanger on
the back of the door. He didn't like the brown pinstripe any
more. He had a smart grey suit now but he never wore it for
travelling. He hoped there would be a train that day. If there was
a troop carrier passing through, he would bribe the guard to let
him ride up front.

He was back in Prague by late afternoon. He had left his bicycle
in the safekeeping of the stationmaster at Smíchov and rewarded

him with an egg. Bicycles were valuable these days. There was
no fuel for cars and the trams kept breaking down and crashing
because there were no spare parts.

He strapped his case and his stick to the back of the bike with
the long strand of string that he kept in his pocket. With the hat
containing the three remaining eggs balanced carefully on the
handlebars, he cycled slowly north, parallel with the river. He
would cross over into the New Town so he could cycle past
Charles Square. It had been dug up last year for the planting of
vegetables, and one of the workers there was a friend who
occasionally passed on a little something.

The day had turned out sunny. As he crossed the bridge, he
glanced north along the river, squinting in the bright light. There
seemed to be more soldier activity than usual at the foot of the
bridges. He hoped they were not going to close them – they did
that more and more frequently these days. He wouldn't be able to
get over to the Little Quarter later.

As he passed along Ressel Street, he saw more soldiers
grouped on the corner. Something was up. He slowed down.
Four women were standing by the Church of St Cyril and
Methodius, clutching bunches of flowers, dandelions and spring
daisies. The swastikas which were usually draped over the
entrance to the crypt were lying crumpled on the pavement. The
Germans were gathered around the women but the atmosphere
was quite calm. They seemed involved in some sort of
negotiation.

Yenko sighed to himself at the women's folly. It was far too
early for that kind of gesture. They would be all right dealing
with ordinary soldiers but just wait until the Ordnungspolizei
turned up. They would catch it then. Didn't people realise that
now was the most dangerous time? They would get dragged off
to the basement of the Petschek Palace, all for a few dandelions.

Why couldn't people just sit tight and wait for the Americans to come?

There was no sign of their friend amongst the diggers at the Charles Square vegetable patch, so he continued cycling past. As he crossed Wenceslas Square, he saw that some of the shopkeepers had taken down the German versions of their signs. He shook his head.

He was renting a small apartment in the Old Town, not far from Ctibor's place. He didn't see much of Ctibor these days. He told himself it was safer for Ctibor that way but in truth the old man embarrassed him. He was still drinking, still becoming maudlin. He never seemed to eat anything but never got less flabby. When Yenko went to visit, he would open a bottle of some disgusting rubbish and drink himself unconscious while Yenko sat in the armchair, smoking and nodding. Yenko would let himself out later, after he had emptied a few beans of coffee from a small brown envelope into Ctibor's tin. He wondered if the old man ever guessed that it was Yenko who gave him the coffee, or whether he awoke from his stupors and thought it miraculous that there always seemed to be just enough coffee for one cup, to sober up.

When Yenko reached his lodgings, he cycled up to the door and dismounted carefully. He unstrapped his suitcase and stick from the back, put them under one arm and the hat with eggs between his teeth, then hefted the bicycle up on one shoulder. He unlocked the door with his free hand and used his foot to push the door open.

As he manoeuvred inside, his landlady emerged from her ground-floor apartment. 'Mr Michálek, Mr Blažek came by just an hour ago to see if you were back yet. He seemed a little agitated.'

Yenko attempted a grin with the hat still clenched between his teeth. He put the bicycle down, propping it against the wall, and removed the hat. 'Mr Blažek is always agitated,' he replied nonchalantly. The last thing he wanted was to get stuck in conversation with Mrs Stropová. She always wanted a chat when he returned from one of his trips. Leaving the bike, he carried the hat and suitcase up the stone staircase. 'But thank you anyway . . .' he called over his shoulder.

'Do come down for some tea if you're thirsty,' she called up after him. 'I bought my new ration today . . .'

'I have to go out straight away, Mrs Stropová, but thank you anyway . . .' he was nearly at the top of the stairs.

'Well, later perhaps . . .' her voice echoed up the gloomy stone stairwell.

Yenko muttered to himself as he let himself into his room. Maybe he would drop in for tea on the way back from seeing Blažek. It was always a good idea to keep your landlady happy.

As he put the hat and suitcase down on his small iron bed, he wondered what Blažek was agitated about. Probably just woman trouble – his perpetual problem – but it might be something more serious. He checked his watch. If he went over to the Little Quarter straight away, then he would be in time to catch Blažek following his afternoon exertions with Heda.

Blažek and Heda had a love-nest, dangerously close to her family home – a room above a bar, with oak shutters and a wrought-iron balcony. The patron underneath also let Yenko and Blažek use his cellar to store the retirement fund. He was well paid, although they had been careful not to let him know the real value of what he was hiding for them. They pretended it was bolts of cloth and cutlery. Blažek's affair with Heda was a good cover for their other activities. All the gossip about Blažek was about his *Fräulein*.

Yenko left his bicycle at his landlady's, cutting on foot behind the Old Town Square through the deserted Jewish Quarter. As he limped past the Pinkas Synagogue, the crows nesting in the trees above the walled cemetery were cawing wildly to one another. The late-afternoon light was golden but it had turned unexpectedly cold. He shivered.

The bridges were still open. He crossed at Mánesův, keeping pace with a crawling, clanging tram, and headed down Letenská. When he had started walking around Prague he had tried to avoid streets like Letenská, with high walls either side, affording no escape. He didn't bother now. Two soldiers patrolled past but they ignored him. Past the square where the trams stopped, he took a couple of left turns into a deserted courtyard – it could hardly be called a square, with a black stone statue of a weeping angel and a single bar tucked into the corner.

The bar was deserted, not even Old Stano was around, so Yenko went to the bottom of the tiny wooden staircase and shouted up. 'Blažek! Blažek, are you there? It's Jan!' Then he returned to the bar and sat at one of the empty tables by the open door, where he could see out into the courtyard. The weeping angel cast a heavy shadow.

He withdrew a cigarette and tapped it on the table. After a few minutes, he heard a light step on the stair and turned to see Heda descend, barefoot, in a thin dressing-gown, her hair in disarray. Her expression was sleepy and annoyed. Her grey eyes gazed at him. He returned her gaze.

'He'll be down in a minute,' she said eventually, then slunk over to the bar where she helped herself to a beer. She turned back to the stairs.

'What's up?' asked Yenko, as she trailed past him.

Heda made a small huffing sound. 'He'll tell you.'

Yenko returned to watching the square.

After a while, Blažek descended, fully dressed but for his jacket, smoothing his few strands of thinning hair back over his head and frowning heavily. 'You've been back to your place then?' he asked rhetorically, as he pulled them two small beers. As he sat down at the table, Yenko lit the cigarette, then exhaled, waiting for Blažek to explain.

Blažek stared at him for a moment or two, then exclaimed, 'Ah, Jan! Are you made of stone? Have you never been in love? I know you're only young but even so! The whores tell me you are like a machine. I don't understand you.'

Yenko gave him a level gaze.

Blažek drained half his beer and wiped his mouth with the back of his hand. 'I wish I was like you. That girl is driving me crazy. I'm beside myself. I don't know what to do.'

Yenko sighed. Had Blažek really dragged him all the way over here just to discuss his tart?

Blažek observed his impatience. 'No, hear me out. Listen. Since you've been away, things are moving. There are all sorts of rumours. Toussaint has put the army on a state of alert. The whole city is chewing its fingernails. The Resistance won't wait for the Russians.'

'So?' said Yenko, swapping his full beer glass for Blažek's empty one. He still hated the beer.

'What am I going to do about *her*?'

As he spoke, Heda descended the stairs. She had dressed in a pale blue dress, cut just above the knee, with a row of lace daisies about the cuffs and collar. Her hair was drawn back with a white ribbon. She took her beer glass over to the sink behind the bar and rinsed it.

Blažek lowered his voice.

'Just look at her, Jan. She's eighteen. Have you ever seen anything so perfect? Imagine what's going to happen to her and girls like her if the Russians get here first?'

'I thought she was getting out.'

'The father wants to. The mother refuses to go. *My family's lived in this city for three centuries.* You know the kind of thing. You know what those old German families are like.'

Yenko didn't know and didn't care. He shrugged. Heda was still at the sink, scratching lipstick off the glass with a fingernail.

'I think I can persuade them,' Blažek said.

Yenko raised his eyebrows.

'They know all about me and Heda. I've been helping them out, since things got bad. I think I can persuade them to clear out but I have to promise them I'm going to look after their things until they've worked out whether it's safe to send for them.'

Yenko was beginning to see where he might come into all this. 'So . . .' he said slowly.

'I need the basement. You wouldn't believe the junk they've got. But the mother's hysterical. She refuses to try and take the heirlooms out on a cart. I said wrap them in cloth and pretend they're sacks of bedding but she said no. And she's probably right. They'd get lynched if they got caught with it. Stano says it's all right to move our stuff up to his attic but he won't let me do it unless he gets your permission as well.'

'When do you want to do it?' Yenko asked wearily. Blažek hadn't even asked to see what he got in Beroun.

'Right now. Stano has gone to Helichová for pickles. He'll be back any minute. If he unlocks for us straight away, there'll be plenty of time to empty the basement and let you get back over the river. I can get someone else to help me move Heda's stuff tomorrow.'

Yenko shrugged again.

'There's one other thing . . .'

Yenko looked at Blažek.

'We'll have to pay him a bit extra.'

Yenko leaned back in his chair, exhaled, then said with gentle, mock-amused emphasis, '*We?*'

'Well, I can hardly tell him the stuff belongs to Heda's family. He hates her. He'd be down in that basement before they'd left the city limits.'

It was dangerously late by the time Yenko left the inn. Curfew would start soon. He took a short-cut down the set of steep stone steps that led out of the far corner of the courtyard and down to Lázeňská. The quickest way back was across Charles Bridge, which he didn't like using in the evenings. It was always crawling with SS. He cursed Blažek for holding him up. Moving the stuff had taken longer than they had expected and he had had to leave Blažek to secure the attic and escort Heda back to her family. The man had gone quite mad. To risk everything for a *gadji* whore, and a German one at that.

The sun had gone in. The evening would be dull and chilly. He noticed as he hopped down the steps that the silver head on his walking stick – his *rovli* – was wearing smooth.

*

What a man in his haste could not be expected to notice were the rows of basement windows which accompanied each stone step, at foot level, narrow glass rectangles covered with sets of iron grilles.

Peering out of one of the windows, at his hasty, stick-aided descent, was the small face of a young woman, a girl. The girl knew she was not supposed to peer out of the window, but she had been inside all day, as she was most days. Now the streets were quiet, she could not resist the temptation to look out, just

for a moment. She saw the smart-looking young man as he came
hobbling down the steps: or rather, saw his legs and his stick and
his shoes. She noticed that although the brown brogues were
polished to a deep shine, one lace was black and the other
brown. Even smart young men were having difficulty getting
hold of matching shoelaces. She found the thought reassuring. In
her predicament, it was hard not to believe that every single
person in Prague was better off than herself. The girl
considered herself to be the most unfortunate person in the
world, although the thought filled her with guilt, as she also
knew she was lucky to be alive.

Yenko had already passed when she glanced up at the rest of
him, so she only saw a back view; the brown jacket and the
leather gloves clasped in one hand; the trilby tipped back on his
head. But even if she had been able to see his face from her
subservient angle, it was unlikely she would have recognised
him. He was just a smart young man with a limp, in a hurry to
get home before curfew.

She turned away from the barred window with a deep,
sorrowful sigh.

CHAPTER 28

Yenko rose early, that day. He wanted to track down Blažek –
he hadn't seen him since their drink at Old Stano's place, a week
ago, and they had things to discuss. In the last few days, business
had become impossible. Everyone was terrified. The SS had
taken a new batch of hostages over the weekend. One of them
was the manager of the restaurant on Strosmeyer Square where
they did regular business. Who knew what a man might say to
get himself out of trouble?

He stood before his closet, in his vest, wondering which
trousers to wear. If he couldn't find Blažek in the Little Quarter
he would have to come back for the bicycle and cycle all the way
out to Krč.

In the last few days, the tension in the city had become a
physical thing, in the air, like a smell. Everyone hurried,
everywhere. Children were being kept off the streets altogether.

The German soldiers were as unpredictable as dogs – and German civilians were fleeing in droves, making their escape while their soldiers were still there to protect them. Every day, another group of families could be seen heading out of the city with wagons or handcarts. Anything that still had wheels was piled high with belongings. They wouldn't have to go far to reach the American lines. Some said Patton had occupied most of the Sudetenland, others that he was poised to take Pilszen any day.

The rest of the city waited – but some were already taking matters into their own hands. Yesterday, Yenko had seen a group of men and women surround an SS jeep in Bethlehem Square, jeering openly. The driver of the jeep had had to reverse quickly to get away. Afterwards, Yenko had stopped to talk to an old man in the crowd. He said the Germans would never leave without setting fire to the city. All the bridges had been prepared for demolition. 'They will tear down the buildings and kill us all before they go, mark my words,' the old man said.

Even the weather was erratic, alternately hot and cold, the light so bright in the mornings it seemed unnatural to sleep.

He made himself coffee, standing over the stove and watching the black liquid bubble in the green enamel pan, warming his hands and letting his fingers bathe in the steam. He remained standing while he drank, as was his habit, sipping noisily, the coffee just off the boil. It scalded his tongue.

He picked up his *rovli*, locked the door of his apartment behind him and slipped downstairs. He let himself out of the building, closing the door quietly, so as not to disturb his landlady, standing on the step for a moment to inhale the cold air and enjoy the emptiness of the sky.

At the corner of Masná Street, two SS Ordnungspolizei were standing talking to each other. No one else was about. Yenko stopped, tucked his stick under his arm and reached into his jacket pocket for his identity card. The Ordnungspolizei had gone wild recently, pulling people off the streets and breaking down doors in the hunt for Resistance workers. The Russians were dropping parachutists into the Protectorate, they said – so were the British, apparently. The wireless was broadcasting constant warnings: spies were everywhere. The Germans were crazy with paranoia. Quite apart from the hostages, they were picking people up, almost anyone, and forcing them to dig anti-tank ditches on the outskirts of the city. Yenko wasn't sure a pronounced limp was much protection under the current circumstances.

As he hobbled towards the two men, the identity card clasped securely and visibly in his palm, he felt a thrill of fear. If this pair had a quota of arrests to make before they came off their shift, then he could be in trouble. As he passed them, he turned to give them an open smile. There was no point in scurrying past trying to look insignificant. You might as well paint a target on the back of your jacket.

The Germans ignored him. They were talking to each other quietly, shaking their heads.

As he turned the corner, he stopped by the newspaper stand. The seller had just arrived and was bending down outside his closed kiosk, cutting the string from his piles of papers. Yenko stuck his hand in his trouser pocket and pulled out a handful of change, picking through it for seventy hallers. As he passed Yenko the paper, the newspaper seller nodded once and said quietly, 'There's a couple of SS behind you on that corner, so don't react.'

Yenko turned from the stand, flapping open the paper. The front page was dominated by a large photograph of Hitler. It was a studio portrait, head and shoulders, in profile. His military cap was pulled low over his forehead, his nose a sharp angle. The photograph, and accompanying story, were surrounded by a thick black border.

Yenko stood for a moment, staring at the paper, his gaze running over the newsprint in an effort to gather in information as quickly as possible. The Führer had died, the article said, fighting to his last breath against the evil of Bolshevism.

Yenko turned in the street, and turned again. The SS men were gone. The newspaper seller had disappeared inside the kiosk. He bit at his lip, overwhelmed by the urge to run through the silent streets waving the paper and shouting up at the windows. *Hitler is dead! Wake up, everyone! Hitler is dead!* No, no, that wasn't what he wanted to shout. He wanted to shout, *Hitler is dead but I AM STILL ALIVE. That man, that evil colossus – the gadjo to end all gadjos who spread poison over the earth, he is dead and I, whom he thought to squash like an insect, I AM STILL ALIVE.*

He thought these things standing perfectly still, glancing nonchalantly around as if someone had just told him that rain was expected later that day. He tucked the paper under his arm, and turned back towards Masná Street. The one person he could disturb was Ctibor.

Ctibor's shop and apartment building were still firmly locked and no amount of banging raised the inhabitants. Yenko paused in the courtyard, looking up at the firmly shuttered windows. He could go round to the other side of the building, the one that looked out over the street, and shout up, but that would attract the attention of any patrolling SS. It would be absurd to get himself shot now, on this day of all days. Come to think of it, that was probably why nobody was answering. They were probably wide awake but cowering under the bedclothes. He laughed at his stupidity. You didn't go banging on people's doors just after dawn, not unless you wanted to give them a heart attack.

He turned out of the courtyard, towards home, abandoning his plan to go over the river. He would go and make himself some more coffee, and then take his landlady a small present from the cache he kept at his apartment, a couple of sausages, perhaps. He could read the paper to her while she fixed him some breakfast. He could always go over to the Little Quarter later.

It was only when he was back in his apartment, the newspaper spread across the wooden counter-top while the coffee bubbled, that he calmed down enough to wonder whether, actually, most people would stay at home today. *Who knows what is going to happen out there, with the SS in this mood?*

His landlady answered the door in her dressing-gown, frowning. When she saw him, she smoothed the dressing-gown down and tightened the sash. Yenko said nothing, merely raised the front page of the paper to her.

She broke into a smile, 'I came up last night but your light was off!' she declared, opening the door for him. 'I couldn't sleep until the small hours. You didn't hear the broadcast?'

Yenko shook his head as he entered her tiny parlour and offered the two sausages in their paper packet. 'Breakfast, Mrs Stropová, to celebrate.'

'Wonderful!' she said, turning to her stove. 'I can't believe you didn't hear it.'

'I've given up listening to the wireless,' he said cheerfully, seating himself at her little square table.

'You'd better start again,' she said. 'Things are going to move pretty quickly now.' She bent to lift her frying pan from the cupboard beneath the stove. Then she stopped, the cast-iron pan loose and heavy in her hand. Her frown returned.

She straightened and stared at him. He stared back. 'My dear Mr Michálek,' she said sombrely. 'Do you really think it's true, this time? I haven't been outside or spoken to anyone last night and all night I lay awake thinking maybe I would go mad with wondering if it was really true.' Mrs Stropová's husband had been in the Czech army. He had escaped just after the Occupation began. She had had word later that he had been killed in France. She always wore her sorrow lightly in front of Yenko, but he sensed she was about to let go of something, to put down a burden she had been carrying for over five years. She was a plain, decent woman, who had never asked him anything about himself. He had been grateful for her discretion. Tears stood in her eyes as she asked him, 'Will it really all be over soon?'

Embarrassed by her candour, he looked down at the newspaper on the table and coughed. 'I suppose everyone will go a little mad now,' he muttered.

Rebuffed, she placed the heavy pan on the front ring of the stove and unwrapped the sausages from their greasy paper packet. 'How kind of you . . .' she murmured. 'Sausages, to celebrate. The whole city will be celebrating today.'

It is a little early for that, Yenko thought.

Later, she asked him to escort her to her brother's shop off Wenceslas Square. She was afraid to go out on the streets on her own. Yenko agreed. It would be good to take a look around, see what was happening, and he could go on to the Little Quarter later.

He went upstairs while she got dressed. He wondered whether he should have suggested going out later in the day, to give him time to drop in on Ctibor – but if Ctibor had heard the broadcast last night then he would sleeping it off right now. It would make more sense to call in on the way back.

They skirted the Old Town Square. The clusters of loudspeakers on the corner of each building were blasting out sombre music. As they left the square, they passed an elderly man and two German soldiers involved in a confrontation. From the corner of his vision, Yenko saw one of the soldiers reach out and snatch the hat off the old man's head, throwing it to the ground. The old man was expostulating. As Yenko and his landlady hurried away, they heard a single shot.

Mrs Stropová gasped. Yenko grabbed her elbow and hastened their step. 'That poor man,' she whispered, 'just when it's nearly over.'

Železna Street was crowded. Everyone was heading towards Wenceslas Square. Yenko looked around for more soldiers but the Germans seemed to have withdrawn. From a second-floor window above their heads, he saw a man hanging out the tricolour flag. A group beneath the window stood looking up and cheering. At the window next door, another man was tossing out handfuls of paper, official documents of some sort, which flapped and flew above the heads of the passers-by.

The mood was infectious. By the time they reached the Square, they were both smiling. His landlady detached herself from his arm and said, 'I'll be fine from here, thank you, Mr Michálek,' and disappeared into a cheering, jumping crowd. On a stone bench nearby, a white-haired man stood tapping one foot and playing the accordion, his head thrown back and eyes closed. A group in front of the bench had formed a circle and in the middle of it a couple was dancing, arms interlocked at the elbow, whirling round. The woman's hair and skirt flew in the wind. The man's mouth was open in a shout of glee. The bystanders clapped in time.

He wandered down the square. Everywhere the shopkeepers were dismantling their German shop signs, or standing on ladders and painting over them with white paint. *It can't be this easy*, Yenko thought, shaking his head. *The Germans will never let them get away with this*. All the same he unbuttoned his jacket and the top buttons of his shirt as he strode, swinging his stick and smiling back at the glad, grinning *gadje* around him. So white people did know how to celebrate, after all.

At the top of the square, he looked up at a tall block that loomed over the Bat'a shoe shop. The upper floors were offices with wide windows that curved the corner of the building. Leaning out of one of them was a man in dark clothing, watching the crowd with binoculars.

After an hour of wandering around the square, he set off up National Avenue, to see if it was possible to get over the river and into the Little Quarter. All along the boulevard, he passed smiling Czechs walking past him to join the crowds in the square: the end of the Avenue marked the end of the celebratory atmosphere. As he approached, he saw a barricade made of sandbags with a narrow opening in the middle guarded by German soldiers.

There was a small queue of people at the opening, waiting to be searched and have their papers checked before being allowed through. A few others were hanging around, debating whether or not it was worth joining the queue. A woman was walking just ahead of Yenko, pushing a baby in a pram. She came to an abrupt halt when the barricade came in sight, turned the pram sharply and started striding back the other way. Her about-turn was too hasty: two soldiers on guard in front of the barricade spotted her, withdrew their pistols from their holsters and ran after her.

The milling crowd parted to allow the woman to flee. She glanced once behind her, then stopped and snatched up the baby, abandoning the pram to run down a side street. The crowd closed up. The German soldiers began shouting and pushing people aside. Then one of them pointed his pistol at the sky and fired. Everyone dropped to the pavement. Yenko crouched down against a nearby lamp-post.

While the two soldiers pursued the woman, another two ran forward to the abandoned pram, now standing alone in the middle of the boulevard, surrounded by crouched passers-by. One of them lifted his foot and kicked the pram over. It crashed to the pavement and Yenko stared as a pink knitted blanket tumbled out, followed by half a dozen pistols, two larger weapons and two square metal objects. Radio transmitters, maybe? he thought.

The crowd was rising cautiously. The German officer was shouting at them to line up. Yenko stood and, with one or two others, began strolling casually back down the Avenue.

Ctibor was not at home. Mrs Talichová told Yenko she had heard him go out half an hour ago. Who knew when he would be back? She lifted her hands resignedly. Yenko walked back to his own lodgings, feeling deflated. Today was the one day he might have been prepared to open a bottle with the old man.

The loudspeakers were still going in the Old Town Square. The music had stopped and they were broadcasting threats in alternate German and Czech. *Public order must be maintained . . . Anyone caught sheltering traitors would suffer the severest penalties . . . The German army would never surrender to the terror of Bolshevism . . . The sanctity of German civilians must be respected . . . Reprisals would be severe . . .*

Back in his apartment, he lay on his bed with the window open, listening to the loudspeakers' indistinct malevolence. He blew smoke rings in the air and thought about turning on the wireless. The next few days will be like this, he thought idly, one arm bent behind his head, a brass ashtray resting on his stomach; a little risk, and hours of boredom. Some people will stay on the streets. Most won't. All over the city, there are people waiting, just like me. The key thing – the most important thing – is not to get involved.

The next day he tried to cross the river, again in search of Blažek, and again failed. This time it was not the German army who stopped him but a group of three men who came running towards him as he cut down a small street called Anenská. One grabbed him by the shoulder of his jacket and hustled him down two steps into a low stone doorway. While he pinned Yenko against a recessed wooden door, another stood next to them clutching a short iron bar and the third kept a look-out back down the alley.

'Which way have you come?' the man holding him hissed.

'Řetězová,' Yenko responded.

The man' s grasp on him was urgent. He was panting for breath. Yenko smelt fear.

'Any activity?' said the second man.

Yenko shook his head.

'Come, come!' the second man snapped at the one keeping a lookout, grabbing at the back of his jacket. The first man released him. 'Stay away from the river,' he said to Yenko. 'They are lining hostages up across the bridges.'

The three men turned and ran down Anenská, back the way Yenko had come. Yenko waited in the doorway and a few minutes later, a patrol of Germans came pounding down the street. Just after they had passed, there was a burst of automatic gunfire which echoed and spun in the confined space of the alley, the cracks and whizzing and *phutting* noises of the bullets sounding as if they came from in front, behind, above and below. Yenko put his hands over his ears. He stayed in the doorway until it had fallen quiet, then strode swiftly back down the alley, turning right to avoid Řetězová and cut across Bethlehem Square. As he rounded the corner, he nearly ran into two Germans standing over the body of the man who had grabbed him. He was face down on the cobblestones, the top portion of his head blown away, and blood pouring in a dark river down to the gutter. The other men were nowhere to be seen. One of the soldiers glanced at Yenko as he passed but he raised both hands and backed swiftly away. They let him go.

Beyond Bethlehem Square, in the sidestreets north of Wenceslas, it was business as usual. One or two of the shops had opened and women were queuing for their rations. At a tram stop, he saw two Czech policemen chatting with a couple of German soldiers, laughing. Beyond the stop, a man in a smart overcoat had openly set up a large suitcase on a bench and was calling out that he had bars of real shaving foam. Yenko's professional pride made him hesitate and wonder if he should ask the man's price. Then he thought better of it.

He made himself tea when he got home, hoping the routine of the task would get the picture out of his head – the top half of the young man's head, blown away into the gutter; the blood, a little grey matter. *The crow in the doorway. The old man's cry.* He shook his head. *Don't think about it. Don't go out. Stay at home, working out how much those gold watches in Stano's cellar might be worth when it's all over.* The Germans would either respond to the disturbances or pull out. He would stay at home from now on.

Blažek could look after himself, so could Ctibor. What was he to any of them? *Don't think about it*.

His resolution lasted until the following day. He was listening to the wireless and heard Prague Radio announce that henceforth it would broadcast only in Czech. He sat down on the edge of his bed, pursing his lips. This was it. This was different from hanging a tricolour out of a window. It was different from the tram conductors refusing to announce the stops in German and the shopkeepers rejecting Reichsmarks. This was someone, somewhere, declaring the independence of the city. It was war.

He felt an odd mixture of confusion and relief. It would all be over soon. The Germans could not possibly tolerate this – already the radio station was requesting all citizens to come its defence. Today would be the day. Today was *truly* the day to stay at home, preferably in a basement with a flask of tea, a loaf of bread and several packets of cigarettes. No one in their right mind would go out on the streets today.

He wondered if he should go down to the neighbourhood shelter, but the thought of being shut in a cellar was more than he could contemplate. He decided to inspect his wardrobe. Now he had smart clothes, he had become quite fastidious.

He took the jacket of his best grey suit from its hanger and turned it inside out. The silk lining was worn through, where the left arm was stitched to the armhole. It was beginning to fray. If he didn't stitch a new seam, he would have a hole soon. As he examined it, the Prague Radio announcer said, *Citizens of Prague! Citizens! The attack has begun. Come and defend the voice of freedom from the forces of evil. Now is the time to avenge yourselves against the German murderers. Think of our innocent dead.*

He was threading the needle – holding it up to the light – when he heard the sounds of gunfire, some way distant, then a low booming noise. *It has begun. The crow. Dei. Don't think about it.* The stitching took him over an hour. At first, he continued listening to Prague Radio's increasingly frantic requests for help. Then he turned the wireless off. He replaced his one precious sewing needle, carefully, in the little leather needle holder, and put the holder back in the box with his two reels of thread – one brown, one black. He turned the jacket the right way round, replaced it on its hanger and brushed it down. There was a burst of machine-gun fire in a neighbouring street; loud, staccato and brief. *It has begun, round here now, too. Don't think about it.*

He rose and went over to the cupboard underneath his sink. In another small wooden box, he kept a tin with his last scrap of dried-out shoe polish. He returned to the bed wearing his right shoe on his right hand and clutching the polish and a rag in the other. He flipped the lid off the polish, one-handedly, and placed the tin on the bed beside him, then dabbed the polish with the rag. He lifted the rag in one hand, and the shoe on the other.

He sat looking at the two items he was holding. They seemed disinclined to meet. He glanced from rag to shoe, and back again. When Blažek had first found him some shoes to go with the brown suit, two years ago, Ctibor had got down on his hands and knees, a fat old man on his knees. He didn't have any polish, so he had cleaned them with spit and a shirt he said he didn't need any more.

Damn the old man. He's only going to go out and get himself in trouble. Yenko dropped the rag on the bed and the shoe on the floor. He pushed his right foot inside it, and bent to lace it up. On the way out, he picked up his walking stick.

The street was deserted. He stood for a moment, on the doorstep, listening to the unnatural quiet. Then he heard, in the distance, the low rumble of thunder. There was bright sunshine. The thunder died, then came again. He walked to the corner of his street and looked down the neighbouring one, in the direction of Celetná. It, too, was deserted, except for some activity at the end, the dark shapes of men in jackets, jumping and leaping. He began to trot towards them. As he neared, he saw that they were in the final stages of constructing a barricade. Already, it was shoulder high, mostly stones and doors, with a few sandbags on top. A heap of furniture lay piled against the stone wall of a nearby shop, and several of the men were throwing chairs and chests and planks of wood on top of the barricade. Two other men were using bars to lever up cobblestones from the street. As Yenko approached, there was the sound of automatic gunfire from the other side of the barricade. Two of the men piling furniture stopped and withdrew pistols, scrambling up the barricade to return fire. The men levering the cobblestones raised their heads. One of them saw Yenko and began frantically wheeling his hand.

Yenko looked back down the street. As he turned his head, a bullet whistled past his ear. He crouched down and ran forward, to shelter behind the barricade. One of the men standing on the furniture above him fell back soundlessly, arms flung wide. His pistol dropped to the ground. One of the other men picked it up and tossed it to Yenko. Yenko caught it clumsily. It slipped through his fingers and made a metallic clatter as it fell. He picked it up. Not knowing what to do with it, he put it in his pocket. The other man on top of the barricade was shouting down at them, 'Go back, go back! Pull back!'

The man next to Yenko grabbed the shoulder of his jacket and hauled him to his feet, and together they ran back down the street. Then something strange began to happen. As he ran, Yenko felt the ground beneath him become fluid, and disappear. The air in front of him shuddered. He heard a roaring noise but his ears seemed to be having trouble transmitting the noise to his brain. He felt, rather than heard the rumble, like a hundred trains rushing past him at once. He fell to his knees, hands over his ears. The buildings around seemed indistinct. He blinked madly, trying to make them come back.

The man running next to him stopped and turned round. He grabbed both of Yenko's hands and pulled them away from his ears. He was shouting into Yenko's face, but Yenko couldn't hear anything – then noise rushed into his head, as if a pair of sluice-gates had opened. 'You're okay!' the fighter shouted. 'You're just stunned! Come on!'

'What was that?' Yenko gasped.

'They are shelling from over the river. It landed close. Come.' He pulled Yenko to his feet and together they ran down to the corner of Celetná. The other men had disappeared.

'Stay back,' the fighter hissed, as he peered round the corner. When he turned back, he said to Yenko. 'They still have most of the street. We need to get a unit behind them. Go back to Masná and tell White Dog to bring some men up Rybná. If it's blocked, we'll have to circle back the other way. I'll stay here.' Yenko stared at him. The fighter stared back. 'Go!' he said. 'Now!'

Yenko turned and ran back down the narrow road. At the crossroads he paused. Maybe he should try and creep behind the Týn Church and get to Ctibor's place. It wouldn't be safe to go back the way he had come.

He turned left, and saw that the narrow road ahead of him was strewn with rubble. A building at the end had taken a direct hit. Half the roof was gone and wooden beams were exposed. Something else seemed to have exploded up from the middle of the street. There was a shallow crater surrounded by huge stones covered with a scattering of earth.

Then he saw, next to the crater, a German soldier, lying on the ground. He was on his stomach, in the shelter of a wall, peering down the street, away from Yenko, down the sights of a machine-gun propped up on a stand. The soldier's helmet and back were also covered with loose soil. He was lying beneath a shop window, an optician's, with rows of spectacles in tiers staring down at him. Suddenly, the glass in the window shattered and the spectacles jumped off their stands. The soldier cried out and began firing the machine-gun, shouting all the time with his mouth open and his face distorted, his words inaudible above the clatter of the gunfire. Tiny explosions detonated in the wall above him, showering him with dust. A ricochet sang past Yenko's ear.

Yenko withdrew the pistol, checked that the safety catch was off, and took a step out into the street. He pointed the pistol at the German soldier, aimed at the side of his body, and fired.

There was a noise inside his head. The German soldier flipped over on to his back and lay still. Almost immediately, two fighters ran down the road, leaping the broken masonry. One seized up the machine-gun and the other turned to Yenko. 'Well done, Comrade!' he shouted joyously.

Yenko felt a wild flush of happiness and self-importance. He was a partisan fighter, a hero. 'I have to get back to the barricade on Masná,' he replied. 'I have a message for White Dog.'

The fighter grabbed him by the shoulder and turned him. 'This way!'

This is how it happens, Yenko thought, his feelings oddly detached as he followed the two fighters leaping from corner to corner. This is how you fight a war, and die in it. It is happening to me.

White Dog was a woman. She was wearing a tin helmet and a bulky brown coat tied with string around the waist. She listened to his message, then turned away to consult a group of men and women seated around a wooden table just behind the barricade. The men who had run with Yenko disappeared into the crowd. He looked around, wanting more congratulations, but everyone was busy. No one seemed to notice him.

There was a lull in the fighting round here – there was no firing from the other side of the barricade. He turned back down the street, and began to walk towards a crowd of about twenty people, halfway down, where it widened out. They seemed engaged in some business of their own. As he neared the group, he saw that they were standing around a German officer, a tall man, who had one hand raised, whether in supplication or remonstration, it was hard to tell. The men and women were around him in a circle, talking to each other. One of the women shouted across the group. 'They've shot the hostages on Mendel Bridge! They've killed them all!'

Someone else called out. 'Vlasov's lot have gone!'

The German officer took a step forward. The crowd closed in. He stepped back. He looked from one face to another, as if trying to work out which of the faces to negotiate with. His stance was imposing, calm and uncowed. Yenko said to the man next to him, 'I've just come from the fighting on Celetná. I had an important message for White Dog.' In the distance, from the direction of the river, there was a series of explosions. Several of the people looked around in alarm, then turned their attention back to the German.

'Has anyone disarmed this bastard?' the first woman called out.

A small, smart man wearing little round glasses stepped forward from the group. He was holding a brick. He approached the officer from behind and, reaching up, brought the brick crashing down on the back of the officer's head. The officer dropped to all fours, and the crowd closed in on him.

Yenko lost sight of him. He stood on the edge of the crowd,
listening to the grunts of effort as they kicked and beat him.

After a few minutes, there was firing from the end of the
street, and everyone looked around in alarm. When it became
apparent there was no immediate danger, they turned back. The
German officer was still alive, up on his elbows and trying to
crawl. Yenko was struck by the slowness of his movements.
Blood was running down his face in thin streams. His
expression seemed resigned, or stunned, it was impossible to
tell which.

Three men on the edge of the crowd moved in. Two of them
grabbed one of the officer's legs each, and they dragged him
backwards towards the edge of the road. As they pulled him,
his chin thumped on the rough ground. One of his high boots
came off in one of the men's hands and the crowd laughed. The
man tossed it into the air. Someone produced a rope. They tied
the rope around the bootless leg and threw it up over the arm
of a nearby lamp-post. It took one, two, three attempts, before
it caught. Then the men sent a boy shimmying up the lamp-
post, to pull down the loose end. Meanwhile, the German lay
face down on the pavement, breathing heavily. The crowd
around had fallen silent, apart from the occasional, lacklustre
cheer.

As they hoisted the officer up, his long coat fell down and
ballooned around him. His hands hung limply, as though he
had given up all struggle. From the edge of crowd, another boy
approached with a jerry can of kerosene. He poured it over the
German's upper body. Yenko turned away. As he took a
turning that would lead him back home, he heard a high,
agonised cry. He glanced back, but the crowd had closed in
and all he could see was a little black smoke rising above their
heads.

He had lost interest in being a partisan fighter. He picked his way across the rubble in the sidestreet that led back to his lodgings, looking down at his jacket and seeing that it was spattered with blood. He tried to recall where it had come from.

His road was quiet, although sporadic bursts of machine-gun fire were still coming from the Old Town Square. He mounted the stairs slowly and let himself in, pulling off his jacket immediately, with a shudder. He was hanging it up, automatically adjusting the shoulders on the hanger, when he heard feet pounding up the wooden stairs to his room followed immediately by rapid banging on the door. A voice he didn't recognise, a woman's voice, was calling, 'Michálek! Michálek!'

He stood very still.

'Michálek! Jan . . . Jan, *please* . . .' the voice sounded breathy, desperate.

'Hold on!' he called. When he opened the door, he saw that it was Blažek's wife. He struggled to remember her name. They had only met three times in the two years he had been working with Blažek. She lived in the suburbs.

She was sweating profusely. Strands of her dry brown hair had come loose from her chignon and hung about her face. She was wearing a flowered day-dress and brown lace-up shoes with no stockings. Heda got the stockings.

He stood back to allow her in, and saw that she scanned the room.

'He isn't here,' Yenko said. 'I don't know where he is. He isn't with you?'

She was panting from her dash up the stairs. He closed the door behind her and gestured at his armchair.

'When did you last see him?' she asked, as she sank into it.

'Not for over a week.'

'What did he say?'

'I'm sorry?'

'Last time you saw him. What did he say?'

Yenko pulled a face. 'Well, he was concerned, of course. But he was relieved you and the children were safely out of the centre of town. He will be most worried to learn that you have come all the way up here. It's not safe.'

She turned to him with a look of plain hatred. 'Don't tell me it's not safe. They've gone crazy in Krč. Those little SS boys are taking their revenge while they've got the chance. They're pulling people out of their houses and killing them in the streets. My neighbour Milada was six months pregnant. They dragged her out by her hair and cut her open in front of my eyes. Her children were watching from the window. Don't talk to me about how safe it is. My children are with my mother, thank God. I've risked my life to come up here and find my worthless *shit* of a husband.'

Yenko was speechless in the face of her venom.

She was sitting bolt upright in the chair, her face shiny with sweat, her eyes glistening. Then the light in her face went out and she dropped her shoulders. She said, miserably, 'It's too late, isn't it?'

Was the woman deranged?

She raised her head again. 'He's gone, hasn't he? He's gone with his little German whore.'

Yenko stared at her, his surprise quite genuine, while knowing immediately that she was absolutely right. As he drew breath, slowly, he knew something else. He knew that when the streets were safe again, when he went to Old Stano's bar, up to the attic, he would find that the money and valuables he and Blažek had been hoarding for two years would be gone, and that the German family's furniture in the basement – if it existed at all – would be entirely worthless.

As Blažek's wife rose wearily to leave, he sank down on the edge of his bed. He lifted his empty hands, to look at them. Somewhere amidst the rubble of the Old Town, he had lost his *rovli*, his walking stick with the worn silver head.

CHAPTER 29

During the night, the gunfire and shelling continued. Yenko lay on his bed, fully clothed. He had closed the shutters in case the window shattered but left the blackout curtain on the floor. At one point, he heard planes flying low over the city, and more bombardment. Then in the eerie silence that followed there was the sound of a woman wailing and screaming, a mad, disordered sound, then silence again. Later, there were more guns. Towards dawn, it fell quiet.

When it was light, he opened his shutter and his window. He went back to bed and dozed for a while in the strange stillness. Later, he rose, turned on the wireless and filled a bowl of water to wash and shave. He was patting his face dry when the announcer broadcast the news of the ceasefire. All hostilities were to stop immediately. The German forces would lay down their arms. In return, they were to be allowed to withdraw unmolested. All citizens were to remain vigilant, however, as pockets of SS were expected to continue fighting. Volunteers were still needed . . . While he listened, he stood by the window, looking at the sky and smoking one of his remaining cigarettes. When it was finished, he stubbed it out against the stone windowsill, closed the window and shutter, and left.

The street outside bore no signs of the previous day's fighting. It was only when he turned the corner that he saw the extent of the devastation.

The building opposite the end of his road had taken a direct hit from a mortar. The roof was a crumpled mass of blackened beams, charred and broken tiling. Every window along the street had been blown out. Three of the shops had been ransacked and furniture, boxes and papers were strewn across the road. There were two pools of blood on the cobbles, one leaking down into the gutter, where it petered out in a rivulet of dirt. One of the shops had a swastika hastily daubed in white paint on the broken doorway. At the end of the street, towards the Old Town Square, black smoke drifted skywards.

A woman was picking her way towards him, over the rubble. She ignored him, looking down at the items scattered across the street. She was wearing three fine woollen coats, one on top of the other, and clutching four hats in one arm. A fox fur was draped over one shoulder. She did not lift her gaze from the street as he passed.

He turned on to the main street that led towards Ctibor's apartment building, and came to the remains of a barricade. A wardrobe had slithered from the top and lay at a diagonal. Its door hung loose. As he passed, he could see that there was a heap of books inside, pages flapping loose. Beyond the barricade, most of the old cobblestones had been prised up from the street to reveal the sandy earth beneath. Two men were sitting on a pile of cobbles, leaning back against the wall, arms folded, drinking tea from tin cups. Four other men were standing nearby, two either side of the low entrance to a cellar. They had rifles slung over their shoulders.

One of the men drinking tea raised his cup to Yenko in greeting, 'Good morning, Comrade.'

Yenko lifted his hand in reply, about to pass, when he saw that the man was one of the partisan fighters who had led him to Masná after he had shot the German.

The man rose and grasped his hand. 'We did well, eh? Those of us who fought. It's not finished yet, but we did well, eh?'

The second man nodded and said. 'The Rat tells me you are a good shot!'

The first man laughed. 'He flipped him like a pancake! Have you been assigned for today?' he asked Yenko.

Yenko shook his head.

The Rat tossed his head in the direction of the cellar entrance. 'Ask if you can come over the river with us. There's still fighting in the Little Quarter. Some of those bastards don't believe it's over.'

Yenko saw his chance to go and look at Stano's place. 'When are you going?'

'In about an hour. We're just waiting for ammunition. It's on its way.'

'All right. But there's something I have to do first.'

He clasped hands with the Rat, and moved on.

Mrs Talichová stood at the top of the stairs, wringing her hands. 'There were three of them,' she said, as he climbed up the stone steps, towards her. 'They pushed him down the stairs. He fell. I begged them not to. They didn't listen. He's old, I said.'

Yenko stopped halfway up, staring up at her.

'I saw you coming across the courtyard,' she explained. 'I said to my husband, it's his nephew, he'll sort it out.'

In the two years since Yenko had first taken refuge with Ctibor, Mrs Talichová's opinion of him had altered sharply: he was now a respected businessman, an upstanding Czech.

'What happened?' he asked sharply.

'They came this morning,' she said. 'I heard them coming up the stairs, and went out on to the landing. They said it was one of the most important tasks of the new order, to root out collaborators. They said some of the Nazis have sworn that Prague will be German forever. They'll hide in cellars and shoot us in the backs.'

'What has this got to do with Ctibor!' demanded Yenko. He ran up the last few stairs and pushed past her. She followed him down the corridor to Ctibor's room. The door was hanging open.

'They kicked it in!' she declared thrillingly, as she followed him.

Vile woman, Yenko thought. *I bet you couldn't wait to tell me. When you saw me crossing the courtyard just now, I bet you couldn't believe your luck.* The room had not been ransacked, as far as he could tell, but the way Ctibor lived it would not have been apparent if it had.

'Where have they taken him?'

She lifted her hands. 'They said he worked for *Them*. They said his office processed their files and he kept important information and reported back to them. Could it be true?'

'Mrs Talichová!' Yenko exploded. 'I've worked in that office too. There is nothing in Ctibor's files but tedious letters about jam production. They burnt his orchards, for God's sake, the SS threw him out of his home and murdered his wife!'

Mrs Talichová gave a melodramatic gasp. *Wooden God*, thought Yenko, *another piece of news for her to pass on. She'll be telling her husband before I've reached the bottom of the stairs.*

'Who took him?' he asked.

Her gaze shifted around the room. She was glancing at the walls.

'Who took him, Mrs Talichová?'

'One of them was from downstairs. One of the new lodgers. I don't know his name. He and Mr Michálek had an argument about the rent. I don't think he'd been paying since the start of the year. He said all collaborators are going to be imprisoned until the Russians get here. The Russians will question them.'

Yenko pushed past her and ran back down the stairs.

The Rat and his comrade were still where he had left them, still drinking from the same mugs of tea. He strode up to them. 'Is White Dog in there?' he pointed at the low basement entrance. The Rat nodded. As Yenko turned, the Rat said, 'The ammunition has arrived. Don't be long, or you'll get left behind.'

The men guarding the basement stepped back for him. The thick wooden door stood open.

Inside, it was gloomy. Two kerosene lanterns had been lit and hung in arches at the far end of the room. Piles of boxes lined the walls. There was a large table around which half a dozen men were seated and a stove with a huge kettle where a woman stood brewing tea. Beyond the large table was a smaller one. The woman they called White Dog was seated at it, next to a man. She had her head in her hands.

As Yenko approached, she looked up. In the gloom, her face looked lined, exhausted. She was still wearing the bulky brown coat tied with string. She did not recognise him.

He stood before the table, and said, 'White Dog. I am one of your fighters. I came through the battle yesterday to bring you the message about bringing men up Rybná.'

She sighed and said wearily. 'I'm sorry. Václav is dead. He was a good man. He fought very hard yesterday.' She looked at him. 'Václav Pernicky. You are the brother?'

Yenko shook his head.

'I was told his brother was looking for him,' she said. Then added sadly, 'Everyone is looking for someone today.'

'Are our men taking people from their homes, people who have been accused of collaboration?'

The woman's expression changed. The man sitting next to her said sharply. 'That is classified information.'

'A man was taken from the top floor of an apartment building in the alleyway behind Jakubská, early this morning,' Yenko said. 'He owned the shop that used to sell fruit and preserves. He didn't do anything. He's a harmless old man. The accusation is malicious. One of his tenants doesn't want to pay the rent he owes.'

The man and the woman glanced at each other.

'His name is Ctibor Michálek. There's been a mistake. He's harmless.'

'Any errors will be corrected when our Russian comrades arrive,' said the man.

Yenko had his feet planted firmly apart. He met each of their gazes in turn. 'This one will be corrected now.'

He saw the man look behind him at the group of men seated at the large table. He had only seconds before he was thrown out. 'I beg your pardon,' he said quickly. 'This is not why I came to you, Comrades. I came to request permission to join the party going over the river. I wish to join with my fellow citizens in killing any SS we can find.'

'What is this old man to you?' the woman asked.

Behind him, Yenko heard some of the men at the large table rising to their feet. 'He is my father.'

The woman glanced in the direction of the men behind him. She picked up a stub of pencil from the wooden table and drew a piece of paper towards her. 'Tell me his name again. I'm not promising anything . . .'

Yenko thought of Ctibor being held in a cellar somewhere, being beaten and questioned by furious partisans. He thought of the old man's innocent bewilderment and of the stupid things he would say. *Well, yes, of course the Gestapo came and asked me about our purchase orders sometimes. Yes, I told them how much sugar each factory foreman ordered.* Ctibor wouldn't last a week. 'Where has he been taken?'

'That is classified information. I cannot possibly tell you that.' The woman was firm. Yenko saw there was nothing he could do. He repeated Ctibor's name, then added, 'Thank you, Comrade.' He looked at the man sitting next to the woman and repeated, 'Thank you, Comrade,' to him.

As he turned to leave the cellar, one of the men who was standing around the large table stepped up to him, confronting him, chest to chest. 'It's not a good idea to come in here throwing your weight around.'

Yenko waited for a moment, without speaking. The man did not move. Yenko stepped past him, out into the light.

As he emerged from the basement, the Rat tossed a rifle at him. He caught it clumsily. About twenty men were gathered in the street, some lacing their boots, others shoving pistols into holsters or buttoning their coats. The Rat was jamming a black leather cap on his head. He nodded at the rifle. 'It's Polish. Know how to use it?'

Yenko shook his head.

The Rat clapped him on the shoulder. 'Neither did the Polish army!'

Two of the men laughed. Another, buttoning his braces, said, 'You're enjoying this, you bloody idiot!'

'Let's go!' shouted the Rat.

They ran down to the Old Town Square, where the buildings were still smouldering. In the corner, at the top of Charles Street, a dead horse lay on the ground, on its side. Behind the horse, a bonfire was burning; a heap of German propaganda booklets and papers, a banner with a Nazi eagle stitched in gold, a tumble of SS caps. Flames flickered about the general smoulder and smoke drifted across the street. Yenko coughed as they ran through it.

They stopped at another cellar, on Liliová. The Rat and two others went in to consult with the unit leaders there. They were inside a long time. Yenko and the others were left waiting, tapping their toes. The sun had come out. Yenko squinted at the bright sky above. Eventually, the Rat and the others emerged, lifting their hands, saying no one could go over to the Little Quarter until an advance unit had checked that Charles Bridge was secure. Yenko squatted down on the cobbles, leaning against the wall, until he noticed that no one else had sat down. He rose. The Rat came over and offered to show him how to use the rifle.

They were still waiting in the street, when the man standing next to Yenko tapped his arm with the back of his hand. Yenko and the Rat lifted their heads from the rifle and looked where the man was gesturing, towards the Old Town.

A column of German soldiers was approaching, all on foot, their heads bowed.

The Rat gestured for his men to stand back against the walls. Then they stood and watched as the German soldiers passed.

Yenko estimated there were over two hundred in the group, all dressed in their greatcoats, despite the heat, and wearing woollen hats instead of helmets. Most of them wore large knapsacks on their backs, with round water canteens bouncing against the sides. None of them lifted their heads or spoke as they passed.

Yenko looked at the partisans either side of him, and the ones standing against the opposite wall, their faces tense. The Rat called across the street in a light, sing-song voice, 'Not a word, Comrades . . .' The man next to Yenko leant forwards and whispered. *'Run like little fieldmice, my fine foolish friends. Our Russian Comrades are coming soon, to catch you by the tails.'*

Yenko stared into the face of each German who passed on his side of the street. He saw a young one, clean-shaven, with very blue eyes. There was another, older, stubbled, with a pronounced facial tic. Another had bright orange hair and pale skin so translucent it was bluish. *What are they thinking?* Yenko wondered to himself. *What runs through their heads as they trudge along? Anger? Humiliation? Relief?* The faces seemed impassive to him, blank. He couldn't imagine them having any thoughts at all. *I hope the Russians won't get you,* he thought. *I hope you get home safely, and find the stinking bodies of your wives and children buried beneath the rubble of your homes.*

When the Germans had passed, an air of gloom descended upon the men. Several of them sank down to squat against the walls, removing their caps and sighing. One or two lit cigarettes. The Rat said, dully, 'We'll be going over to the Little Quarter soon.'

They could not get over the river until afternoon. Even then, they were told to report to the barricade at the bottom of the bridge and wait for orders. After watching the German soldiers retreat unmolested, everybody's spirits were low. Even the Rat seemed to have lost his enthusiasm.

They crossed the bridge at walking pace. Looking down the river, Yenko was surprised to see how undamaged the city seemed to be. The fighting had been in the Old Town and by the radio station, one of the men told him. If he kept his gaze in the distance, Yenko thought, he could imagine that it might be any spring day; warm sun, a light haze over the sky.

They greeted the men at the barricades at the foot of the bridge and the Rat took Yenko with him to consult with the unit leader, a bespectacled man called Koblic. They sat around an upturned chest of drawers while Koblic drew a diagram of the surrounding streets on a crumpled piece of paper.

'There's a unit of SS in this building here.' He scrawled a circle on the map. 'You'll see when you get there, there's a load of dead Germans piled in the square. The SS fired on their own troops. They killed a whole load of them.'

'Why?' Yenko asked.

The two men looked at him scornfully.

'It was probably the column that passed us on Liliová,' said the Rat.

Koblic said, 'The SS would think nothing of killing their own soldiers, for retreating.'

Yenko thought of the clean-shaven young man, and the man with ginger hair.

Koblic sighed. 'It's turning into chaos. It was supposed to be an orderly withdrawal, but we can't control what the SS do, or our own men. There are groups out rounding up Germans who've got separated from their units, killing them. I can't ask them to stop. I had a Russian parachutist killed this morning, my best man. He was stopped walking over here from the New Town. One of my other men shot him. He said he looked like a collaborator.'

There came the sound of artillery fire, along the river from the south; a low booming, dull but resonant.

Koblic and the Rat rose to their feet and pulled their rifles on to their shoulders.

'You'd better wait here until more men come, I suppose,' said Koblic.

'To hell with that!' the Rat responded sharply.

Koblic gave him a tired look, then nodded.

When they neared the square, they split up into single file and approached the corner of it by running down the street, doorway to doorway. Looking ahead, Yenko could see the bodies of the German soldiers. They had fallen one on top of another, mown down while they were marching. There was another scattering of bodies on the far side of the square, where individual soldiers had broken ranks and tried to flee down the alleyways.

To the left was a series of low archways piled high with sandbags, where a small unit of Koblic's men was holding down the SS in the corner building. When his men had been established behind the sandbags, the Rat consulted with the leader of the unit. The SS were stationed at windows on the first and second floors of the building. There was no way to approach it other than across the square. They had sent for a heavy gun. The situation was complicated by the retreating German troops, some of whom had decided to turn and return fire. They were in position behind a barricade at the top of the square. When there was a lull in the firing, civilians who were trapped in the buildings around the square would emerge. The firing would begin, and not knowing which of the three groups of men were shooting at them, the civilians would sometimes run straight towards the SS. The man pointed out a row of civilian bodies just beyond those of the German soldiers. There was stirring from the row, an uplifted arm, but nobody could reach the injured man or woman lying there.

'We can't do anything until the artillery arrives,' said the Rat. 'All we can do is make sure they don't go anywhere while they make sure that no one else goes anywhere either.'

When the heavy gun arrived, dragged by a crew of six, it took another hour to manoeuvre it into place behind the sandbags in a position where it would not kill any of their own people if it recoiled or backfired. Then it had to be loaded with shells, and the few remaining shells placed in an orderly pyramid ready for re-loading.

'Once the first shell hits, they will concentrate all their fire here,' the chief gunner told the Rat. 'Move your men up.'

'Thank you, Comrade,' the Rat said sarcastically, adjusting his leather cap to scratch his forehead. Turning to Yenko he added, 'Does the man think I'm a fool?' He squeezed Yenko's shoulder and said, 'I know. I hate these boring bits too. I wish we could just go in there. The waiting, it's worse than anything.'

The Rat formed them into five squads; two to hold the arches and provide firing cover while the others stormed the building once the artillery had done its job. Yenko was pleased that he was staying in the arches. This was different from the adrenaline of the previous day. There was time to plan and anticipate; time to become afraid. As soon as it is safe to cross the square, he thought, I will slip away. Enough heroism.

The gun crew was preparing to fire the first shell, when one of them turned to where Yenko and the Rat were waiting in the next archway and said, 'Look.'

On the opposite side of the square, a group of women had emerged from a building and were standing up against the wall, peering across the square. There were about ten of them, a mix of young and old, clutching at each other and looking this way

and that, preparing to make a dash for it. Two of them were
waving white handkerchiefs.

'In God's name . . .' muttered the Rat. 'They are crazy, why
don't they just stay put?'

'Can we signal to them?' asked Yenko.

Before the Rat could reply, the women decided to make a
dash for it. They broke away from the wall and ran alongside the
far edge of the square. Immediately, the SS troops in the corner
building began to fire. The line of running women collapsed like
dolls. Coats and arms flapped in the air as they fell.

There was a scramble in the next arch, a lurching pause, then
a huge booming sensation that seemed to fill the low overhang
and blow Yenko sideways. Blasts of gunfire opened up in
response. He saw the Rat shouting again but could not hear him
above the noise; the machine-guns from the SS, rifle shots from
the German soldiers on the other side of the square and the guns
of their own men. To his right, he saw men leaping over the
sandbags and running across the square.

He flung himself back down on to a sandbag, pulling his
Polish rifle from his shoulder. He laid it flat and peered down the
sight. He tried to remember what the Rat had told him to do.
*Squeeze gently like you would with any rifle but when you feel
resistance release and squeeze a second time, otherwise the trigger locks.*
Across the square, four of the women had risen and were
running back to the building. One of them had become separated
from the others. He turned the rifle and aimed in the direction of
the German soldiers behind the barricade. He remembered to
pull the butt of the rifle hard against his shoulder, and squeezed
the trigger. The rifle thumped back in the hollow between his
shoulder and his collarbone. He pulled the trigger again, then
thought, *maybe the Germans behind the barricade aren't shooting at
us, maybe they are shooting at the SS*. He turned so he could take

aim at the corner building but two more artillery shells fired in quick succession. The noise deafened him. He closed his eyes and instinctively flung an arm over his head to protect it. When he lifted his head and opened his eyes again, the square was full of smoke. There was an acrid smell, a burning sensation in his nostrils and an intense humming inside his head.

Bastards, he found himself thinking wildly, about no one in particular. Then the Rat was pulling him by the shoulder, over the pile of sandbags. As he scrambled up, his rifle slipped from his grasp and he tripped over it, tumbling down on to the pavement beneath the barricade, landing heavily on one wrist and crying out. Bullets tore into the sandbag above him, the brown cloth shredding and dirt pouring out. He rolled over. The Rat was lying on the ground, face up, one arm across his chest. He's dead, Yenko thought. *Nearly got me killed too, the reckless bastard*. He waited until there was a pause in the firing, then scrambled back over the sandbag.

The rest of the men were still crouched down in the cover of the arches. The man nearest to him looked up at him, as if expecting orders. Yenko turned and looked across the square. The other units had reached the corner building. Two men were kicking at the door, while two others were standing a few feet out in the square, fully exposed, firing up at the windows. One of them fell.

'Tell them to hold the artillery, for fuck's sake,' the man next to him said. Yenko ran along to the heavy gun arch.

'Hold it!' he shouted.

One of the gun-operators turned with a furious face. 'Of course!' he hollered, waving him away. Yenko ran back.

The first man looked up at him and said, 'What now?'

Yenko looked out across the square. The Germans behind the barricade had stopped firing. Perhaps they were using the confusion to retreat. There was still machine-gun fire coming from the corner building. Through the smoke, he could see that the woman who had become separated from the others was trapped against the wall of a building. She was a tiny old woman. She had her hands splayed back against the wall and her mouth open in a huge scream, inaudible above the firing.

Then the machine-gun firing stopped. Yenko saw that the advance units had broken through the door and were entering the corner building. As he watched, an SS rifleman crouched in a top-floor balcony turned, flipped backwards over the stone ledge and plummeted to the square below. *They've done it*, Yenko thought.

He turned to the other men and waved a hand, shouting, 'Let's go!' I sound like the Rat, he thought. He clambered up the sandbags, jumped over the Rat's body and began to run across the square.

There were three isolated shots as they ran, he couldn't tell where they were coming from. As their resonance died, he could hear that the tiny old woman pinned against the wall was still screaming, crazed with fear and panic. He turned and saw through the drifting smoke that she was running towards them. She was not old but young, and had her hands outstretched, her eyes huge in a pinched, dark face. She was staring at him.

'Emil!' she was screaming wildly, as she ran towards him, *'Emil!'* He stared back at her, uncomprehending. It was only when she had flung herself upon him, crying and grasping his upper arms, that he realised she was shouting out his name.

CHAPTER 30

Marie Malíková had become trapped because of her own stupidity – and been rescued by the bravery of someone else, a woman who didn't even know her. All her life, she was to remember this. For the last three days, she and her parents had not left the basement near the river. They had huddled down with their backs against the damp wall, listening to the bombardment. She had thought, *I am going to die buried in this hole. At least in the camp we were above ground.* Finally, she had pushed herself out of her mother's terrified clutches, and dashed out of the door.

In the open air at last, she ran without reason, feeling nothing but the reckless joy of movement. Her pace only slowed as she reached the square, which seemed quiet. She glanced behind her as she crossed it, and it was then she saw the column of German soldiers. When the shots started she dropped down behind a stone bench with her hands over her ears. Three soldiers ran past her, almost reaching the far corner of the square before the firing opened up again and they fell. One began to thrash on the ground, screaming in agony. She raised her head and looked around, to see who was killing the Germans. The gunfire echoed.

It was then that she saw the young woman in the doorway, wearing a spotted blouse. She was waving frantically, beckoning her.

Marie was incapable of rising. She stretched out her hand to the woman, fingers splayed. The woman continued to wave. There was another burst of gunfire and terror gave Marie the energy to push with her legs and fling herself towards the building. As she reached the woman, she clutched at her. The woman grabbed one shoulder, and her hair, and fell backwards. Marie tumbled on top of her, into the dark. There were other women, shouting. Someone pulled at her leg. The door behind her slammed shut and the light from the square disappeared. Marie tried to rise. She was kneeling on someone's stomach. They cried out. Other hands dragged her up and someone tugged at her arm. She was pushed through another doorway.

She was in some kind of office or ante-room. The windows were shuttered but stripes of white light illuminated the faces of the women around her. She burst out, 'Can't we get out the back?'

The woman in the spotted blouse put an arm around her shoulders and said, 'It's all right, you're safe now.' She pulled her towards a wooden table in the centre of the room and seated her on a bench.

Another woman, an older one, said, 'There's only one back door and it leads on to a street which is overlooked by the other side.'

'The other side of what?' Marie asked. The spotted-blouse woman shushed her.

'The building the SS are firing from,' the older one said.

'They aren't firing out of the back, not now . . .' said a third woman, crossly. 'We should have gone out that way as soon as they started shooting the soldiers. It's only twenty metres to the corner.' Marie looked at her. She was also young. Her hair was curled in careful brown waves.

'You want to try it, go ahead,' the older woman said.

The spotted-blouse one released Marie. 'I think it's best we stay here, until someone comes to flush out those men. There's no point in getting killed.'

'What if they shell?'

'Isn't there a basement?' said Marie. All at once, basements seemed more attractive.

The women shook their heads.

Later, when the fighting was over, Marie thought of those women. She tried to picture them; the spotted-blouse one who had saved her life by pulling her into the building; the older one; the one who was young and cross and wanted to make a run for it; and the others who came in later, from upstairs; the one who stared at her rudely; the one weeping uncontrollably in fear; the thin, brown-haired one who cried to her, 'What is your mother thinking of, little girl?'

It upset her, later, when she found herself getting them confused. (Was the one who cried out the thin one, or the one in black? Was the one who lit a cigarette also the one who said, 'I'm freezing. Why is this building so cold?' And who was it said, 'I can't stay here any longer, I just can't. My husband will be frantic. He will come looking for me, then what will happen?') It bothered her that she never asked the women why they were there. Did they all work in the building? Had they taken shelter there when

the firing started? Which was the one who shrugged and said,
'Helene, why don't we sing that song about the woman and the
man who's gone off on the horse, you know the one?'

Whose idea had it been to leave the building? 'There hasn't
been any firing for ages, for God's sake let's just go.' Which one
of them had said that, and why had they listened?

Most of the women were killed instantly when the machine-
guns started firing. Three, she thought, might have made it back
into the building. (Which three?) The others were shot down
around her, their small group exploding apart in the same
instant as the noise was upon them. As she scrambled back to the
relative safety of the wall, she trod on the arm of the woman
wearing the spotted blouse.

Trapped against the wall, pinned down in the open for the
second time that day, she lost herself in fear and found that
inside the fear, there was release. She screamed and screamed,
unable to hear the sound of her own voice except as a pain inside
her head. She thought in pictures: her mother being beaten to the
ground in their cottage in Romanov; the German soldiers who
had pushed them out of the truck when they got to Brno; the
block Elder in the camp saying, listlessly, 'You might as well
know. Tomorrow at roll-call, they're announcing a quarantine.'
All those times when she had felt afraid, all rolled into one and
turning over each other, as if all those experiences were spinning
her against the wall like one of those mad fireworks she had seen
once at an Easter Day parade. She screamed until screaming was
effortless.

And then she was running. She was running towards
someone, and she could not remember which had come first, the
running or the recognition . . .

When she fell upon Emil, she could say no more than his
name. When he pulled her away from the square, when they ran

together, she thought she had escaped the guns only to die on her feet because her lungs would burst. She made him slow down, once they were away from the square, but continued to cling to his arm as they walked and her breathing returned to normal, as if he might slip away when she let go.

They sat down by the river. For some time, they did not speak. Marie did not feel capable of speech, only of staring. She could not stop herself. *Emil*, she kept saying in her head, over and over again. *It is Emil* . . . He sat with his knees raised, looking out over the water, allowing her to gaze upon him without embarrassment. She wanted to finger the rough cotton of his shirt, to grab at his light brown hair – his hair had been so short in the camp – to punch him in his hard, narrow chest and kick his legs. *It is Emil.*

Eventually, she said, 'Emil,' then paused to savour the word. 'Emil, you look like a proper *gadjo* now.'

His mouth twitched a half-smile, but he did not respond. Instead, he looked down and patted his trouser pockets.

'Have you lost something?' she asked.

'Cigarettes,' he said. Unable to locate them, he reached out a hand and snapped off a long stem of grass, then sat chewing the end.

She looked out over the river. Something dark was floating in the water, a few metres out; a bloated jacket, and just visible behind it, the jutting heel of a shoe. She looked back at Emil, then said, her voice suddenly loud and high, 'Lift your hair up, back off your forehead.'

He glanced at her.

'Please,' she said.

He pushed his fringe back from his face, and she saw what she wanted to see, the small red scar, close to the hairline.

'How are you?' she said, but before the sentence was out he interrupted her.

'I can't talk like that. I can't do that, not until you tell me what happened after I escaped,' he said. 'Tell me everything.'

They were sitting in a secluded clearing close to the water's edge, in the middle of a small patch of earth, surrounded by grasses and a few tall weeds. Behind them, in the Little Quarter, there was still the occasional burst of gunfire. She glanced back at the buildings, then up at the blue sky above. When she looked back at the river she saw that the body in the water had not moved.

'We are safe here,' he said. 'Tell me.'

'I was screaming, back then,' she said, 'when there was all that shooting. It felt good. I thought I would just scream and scream until I died.' She wriggled her bottom on the ground – she was sitting on some gravel. She fanned her skirt out and leaned back on her hands. She closed her eyes and lifted her face to the sky, then began. 'After you escaped . . .' she stopped. What should she tell him? That they stood on the *Appell-platz* for half the night, and that two women collapsed while they were standing? That the Commandant strode among them shouting and three men from the work detail who had been at the quarry were taken to the punishment block and beaten? He has gone, she had thought, *without me*. Of course.

'It gave us hope,' she said, 'the whole camp. And then when they didn't bring you back, we all knew that someone had really got away.' She heard the unnatural timbre of her voice, the strain and brightness, but he did not challenge her.

'When did you escape?' he asked.

'We didn't,' she replied. 'We were released. Me, and my mother and father.'

He turned to her, looked her full in the face for the first time.

'They closed the camp,' she said. 'They transported everyone.' Her voice faltered. He would ask about his family, now.

He turned his head away. He knows and doesn't want to know, she thought. He knows and wants a moment or two of delay before he has it confirmed, just a brief space in which a small amount of self-delusion is still possible.

'When we were first arrested, they held us in Brno prison because of an appeal from our village, a local officer my uncle was friendly with. When we were sent to the camp, we just assumed it hadn't worked. It was only when it came to the transport that we were told there was a list. A few people had reasons for getting out. Contacts outside, appeals against their status.'

'What was yours?' Emil asked.

Marie felt her face twist with the irony of it. She gave a small, almost-laugh. 'It was on our papers, we were down as, well, not really *gypsies* . . .'

'Didn't they look at your *faces*?' Emil said, turning to her again, his expression wide-eyed with disbelief.

'We didn't believe it ourselves,' she said quickly. 'We were all waiting in line. We didn't find out until the day they took everyone. We were standing in the line like everybody else. They had allowed the families to stand together so that they would be in the same truck. Next to us were the Lomeks. The trucks had been waiting forever. The transport police were having some sort of argument with the Commandant. The police were saying that they were only going to take us all as far as Nědvedice and the Commandant was saying the trucks were to go to Brno and pick up the train there. The Germans would take over at the border. As soon as I heard that I began to shake. I didn't know whether we should tell the other families or not. My father told me to stay close to them and keep quiet. We waited.'

'Where were they?' He asked the question quite suddenly.

She did not need to ask who he meant. 'I couldn't see them anywhere, at first. I tried. There was a huge crowd by then. The families were trying to stay together and the children were crying. There were a lot of children who didn't have anyone by then. It was hot. I saw your mother just before she was pushed into the truck.' She halted, thinking, I shouldn't have said *pushed*.

'Marie,' Emil said, without turning his head. His voice was very gentle. 'Tell me.'

'I didn't see them until the end. They were in a group waiting for a truck that wouldn't start. Most of the trucks had gone. The guards were still angry. By then, we had been told we were not going, we still didn't know why. We thought it was because the trucks were full. Maybe we would just have to wait there in the heat until another truck came. I wanted to go and not to go. I wanted to get away from there more than anything. But when they had mentioned Germans, I knew. The people who had been sent on the trucks in December . . .'

'I know,' he said. 'I know where the transports were going.'

'I saw them,' she continued, wanting this part to be over. 'Your mother was there. Your little brother was in her arms. He had been very ill, after you left. Your mother didn't think he would live during the quarantine. He was still very weak.' She would not tell him that by then Bobo was blind. 'Your mother was standing holding him. Your aunts Ludmila and Eva were clinging on to her arms. They were crying but she wasn't.'

'Tekla?'

'She died during the quarantine. Lots of people died. Some of the guards too.'

Emil let out a deep sigh. Marie wondered if he had imagined any of this. She wondered how his vision of what had happened to them all tallied with what she was telling him.

'Eva and Ludmila were holding your mother's arms. She was looking around. She saw me . . .' Perhaps she should make something up, some last words that his mother could have said to her. *If you ever meet my son Emil . . .*

Emil was watching her face. She looked at the ground, the earth in front of her, peppered with gravel. She shook her head.

'She couldn't come over to us. They were in the last group, surrounded. There were German soldiers as well, come to make sure everything went smoothly. I think they thought there would be trouble. They didn't trust the Czechs. Your mother just stared at me, for a moment. I think she knew. I don't know.'

Emil had turned his face and shoulders away from her. She heard his breathing deepen. She lifted a hand, then let it drop, afraid to comfort him. She heard him gasping for self-control.

He began to sob, making a frightening, animal sound, a monotonous *hur-hur*. The great gasps of it shook his frame. 'Emil,' she whispered. He shook his head, refusing her. *I haven't told you any of it*, she thought despairingly. How could she begin to tell him what the camp had been like, under quarantine, how even a simple conversation had become impossible – how they had all become no more than suffering ghosts? He rose suddenly and walked a few paces away, standing with his back to her, his shoulders shuddering. I should not have told him anything, she thought. I should have just told him about our release and said I had no idea what had happened to the others.

He returned to her and sat down again, still turned from her. 'Go on,' he said.

She brushed at her skirt. 'The trucks had already gone when one of the guards came over and told us to go back to the barracks. The place seemed so empty. He didn't say which block, so we all went and sat in the women's block. It was only that night that they came and told us we were going to be released.'

Emil still had his back to her but he had stopped shaking. He sat down again, reached for another blade of long grass.

'Eventually, it was one of the clerks who came. I don't know his name. He was the accountant, I think, the one who did the sums and the paperwork. He stood in the doorway of the women's block. It was us and the Lomeks and four men we didn't know. We were hungry. We just sat staring at the empty stove. My mother and father looked at each other. They had hardly spoken to each other for a year. Eventually, this man came and stood in the door. He had a bundle in his arms. He tossed it over. It was the warm clothing they took from us when we arrived, the things we had wanted so much in the winter. All the time we had been so cold, the bundle had just been sitting somewhere, in a shed. He said, tomorrow you can go, you can go now if you like but it'll be dark in an hour. He gave my father an envelope with official papers inside. We waited for a while after the guard had gone, then my father went over to the men's barracks to see if there was anyone there. Nobody. The four men that we didn't know stood up and said they weren't going to hang around and give them time to change their minds. Mr Lomek was all for setting off straight away as well but two of his children were still quite small and his wife was sick. My father persuaded him to stay. We all slept together that night, in the women's block, with the door open. Mr Lomek and my father propped it open with a pile of stones that would fall and make a noise if anyone tried to close it. We knew we were free to walk around but we stayed inside in case somebody saw us. Through the evening we heard them packing up. At one point I went to the window and watched. It was dusk by then. They had a jeep. They were taking things out of the office, boxes of papers. I saw one of the women come out with armfuls of winter boots. She dropped them into the back of the jeep, then she brushed the dirt off her shirt. My mother told me to come away from the window. I don't think any of us slept that night.'

Emil turned slightly. She could see his face in profile. He was shaking his head. 'You mean after all that time, a whole year, they just told you it was a mistake?'

'It was as we were leaving the next day, a guard told us. We wouldn't have asked but Mr Lomek went up to him and said, where have they sent the others? The guard said, to Poland. They've all gone now, the *gypsies*. Mr Lomek said, the *gypsies* have gone? The guard was one of the older ones, quite friendly. He said, yes, all of them. You don't really count. You were a big farmer before, weren't you, Lomek? It's all on your papers. Some of them were all for sending you with the others, but it's got to be legal. We've got procedures. Get home as fast as you can and see if your homes are still secure. Your gardens will be dug up, you know. You've forgotten what it's like on the outside. There won't be so much as a cabbage. Or something like that. I can't remember. I couldn't believe the way he was talking, all friendly, as if he was concerned how we would manage.' She sighed. 'I don't think my father really worked out what the guard meant until we were walking down the road, towards the village. He turned to Mr Lomek and said, what did he mean, we don't really count? That's when Mr Lomek explained. We had been released because we weren't considered *gypsies*, because someone in Brno who had never even met us had looked at the paperwork and decided we didn't count. Being not-*gypsies* in their eyes had saved us. My father stopped, right there, in the middle of the road. He was shaking his head. We all stopped. My mother was speaking to him, but he turned and started striding back up the road. Mr Lomek realised what he was doing and ran after him. He grabbed his arm and my father turned and hit him. We couldn't believe our eyes. It took Lomek and both his big sons to pin him to the road. My mother was screaming and crying. He had gone mad. He was going to walk all the way back up the hill, into the camp and demand to be put on a train to Poland . . .'

She stopped speaking, suddenly exhausted by her story. In the two years that had passed she had hardly thought of how they had left the camp; the journey back to Orlavá, her father vowing all the way that he was going to knife his brother for having betrayed them and her mother and herself too frightened to remind him that it was probably Uncle Karel's appeal against their arrest that had resulted in their eventual release.

And then, when they reached Romanov; the burnt-out cottages, the little yards full of smashed furniture and the desecrated vegetable patches, the stray cat sitting on the rubble and staring at them with narrowed eyes, hostile to their trespass . . .

They had hidden in the woods for two weeks. Her father went out at night to steal food. One evening, he came back and said he had managed to find Uncle Karel's old friend, Officer Holt, and given him the fright of his life. Holt said the others were all gone. They had been taken two months ago, straight up to Poland. None of them would come back.

Holt was desperate to get rid of them. He had given them the address of a cousin who owned a factory on the outskirts of Prague. He would give them work, he said. It would only take a phone call. It wasn't safe for them to stay in South Moravia. But they could travel quite openly – their papers were legal. He would even give them some money for the fare.

It was on the journey to Prague that her father broke. It had happened quite gradually, as he was staring out of the train window. She had watched it happen. She had looked at him and thought, *all his life he has had the confidence of being utterly right. Now he doesn't know what to think. The brother he was going to kill has disappeared and because we were betrayed by him, we have been saved. My father doesn't understand. He wants to kill someone for saving us. He wants to live, and die. He is ashamed.*

She could not find the words to explain this to Emil. She said simply, 'We got to Prague. It wasn't too bad when we first got here. We stayed in a back room in a factory, out of sight, even though we were legal. The three of us worked like slaves in return for the back room and a little food. We managed there for a whole year. But then it got worse and worse, more arrests, the rations went down, everyone got more frightened. The factory manager said he didn't care if our papers were legal or not, we had to go. He had five children. He couldn't risk their lives. I had to do all the talking. I told him that making us leave was the same as murdering us. I threatened to go to the police and turn us all in and say he had been listening to illegal radio broadcasts. He didn't believe I'd do it until I pointed at him and cursed in Romani. He found us a shed in an allotment but we only stayed there for a few weeks. Too many people came and went.'

Her voice became low and bitter. 'I've had to look after them, to do everything. Move us from place to place. And each time it's got worse. We're in a cellar. It is horrible. We've been stealing dog-food from the German family upstairs. They give their dog the rotting scraps and my father made friends with him so he never barks at us. He would if he knew it was us taking the slimy cabbage and green bread they put out for him. My mother managed some work as a cleaner, for a bit, but we got frightened they would round her up. We buy flour on the black market once a week but we can only make a paste. We can't cook. I do most of the going out but I keep my head covered. My mother rubs flour over my face before she lets me out. My father . . .' As she had been talking, her speech had become faster, like a train gathering speed. Emil took one of her hands between his.

'I'm sorry,' she blurted, her voice cracked and desperate. 'I haven't talked properly for two years. My parents, they don't talk any more. It is like living with ghosts. I've been so desperate. Sometimes I thought I would just abandon them, just crawl out of the basement and leave them to it.'

Emil stood up and held out a hand to raise her. 'Enough for now,' he said. 'It is enough.'

He pulled her to her feet.

'I ought to go back,' she said. 'They will think I am dead.'

She closed her eyes and swayed, remembering the pure moment, as she had run in panic across the square, through the smoke, looking at a man, and seeing how that man's face, without changing, had resolved itself into something she recognised . . . It was like flying.

'They are nearby?' Emil asked.

'Not far from the square.'

'We will go and see them,' he said. 'But there is something I have to do, a place I have to look at. It's just round the corner.'

She nodded. *Anything*, she thought, *anything so long as you do not leave me*.

From the bridge, there came a long, continuous burst of machine-gun fire. It stopped, then started again, and was joined by the sound of other guns, firing repeatedly.

She looked at him.

He said, 'That isn't fighting, it's celebrating. Someone has seen tanks in the northern suburbs, they're saying.' He ran his hands through his hair. 'Let's go and see your parents. Then let's go to Wenceslas Square.'

'You don't have to fight any more?'

He shook his head. 'No.' He turned to mount the bank and stride back up to the street. She hesitated, not wanting to leave the riverside, where it had been just the two of them and she had talked and talked, and been listened to.

He turned back to her, reaching out his hand to pull her up the bank. 'Come. It's all right.' His hand enclosed hers. As he pulled her up the bank, she felt a brief dizziness. It often happened when she stood. She ate so little these days. She wondered where he lived now, if he had food somewhere. His clothes were dirty and torn from the fighting but his shoes were good shoes. My *gadjo*, she thought.

As they climbed the bank, the gunfire on the bridge burst out afresh, and floating towards them, down-river on the breeze, came the sounds of shouting, of song.

CHAPTER 31

At the top of the rise, Yenko told Marie to wait while he walked to the end of the street and checked that it was safe to cross the road. From the corner, he could look up towards the square and see that the smoke had cleared. Four partisans were standing in a group adjacent to the arches.

As he trotted back, he saw that Marie was stock-still where he had left her, staring after him, her eyes as round as the ebony buttons on the long waistcoats his father used to wear. It was how he imagined a child might stare at a ghost. He tried to smile at her, but all he could do was return her stare. He tried to feel emotion but after talking about his family, all he could feel was a rawness inside, a deadness. When he reached her, he touched her lightly on the arm, to turn her, and said, 'This way. Come.'

–

The little square with the statue of the weeping angel was deserted. Old Stano's bar was locked. While Marie waited, he returned to the street and found a short, thick piece of metal. He glanced up at the shuttered windows that overlooked the square, then pushed the piece of metal into the link chain that held the padlock on the door, forcing it open. The chain snapped with a ping that echoed around the tiny courtyard. He turned and beckoned Marie forward. They slipped into the bar.

Inside, the stools were upturned on the wooden tables and a sheet draped over the bar. The empty money-box was lying flat-open next to the bottle rack, to tell thieves there was nothing of value on the premises. Yenko took a stool from a table, turned it upright and told Marie to sit. Then he went up the small wooden staircase, to the attic.

When he returned, Marie was still standing in the middle of the room, looking around. 'Do you work here?' she asked, as he clumped down the staircase.

'No,' he replied. 'I thought I might have left something here, but I hadn't. There's nothing.' He turned to go but she did not move. She was looking at him. He shook his head. 'I have lived like a *gadjo* for two years,' he said, as he ushered her out, 'And I have learnt that they are every bit as treacherous as we were always taught. They would betray each other for a glass of beer.'

The basement where Marie and her parents had been hiding was two minutes from Old Stano's place. They went around the front of the building to enter. As they approached, Marie said, 'My father. He is not as he was. Neither of them are, but my father especially.'

She opened the large wooden door, slowly, and they entered a darkened hallway. They turned right and went down a short flight of stone steps, at the bottom of which was another door. She signalled with her hand that he should be quick.

'If it was a German family upstairs they'll be gone by now,' Yenko hissed.

She waved at him to be silent as she tapped lightly, three times, on the cellar door.

The door opened immediately. The interior was dark but for a little grey light from the barred window on the opposite side of the room. A very old man stood in the doorway, his face lined, his shoulders stooped, his hair a shock of white.

Yenko had been planning to greet Marie's father in formal Romani but was so surprised at the sight of him, that all he could manage was a nod.

Jan Malík looked from his daughter, to the strange young *gadjo*, and back again.

'It's all right, Father,' Marie said kindly, reaching out a hand and placing it on his sleeve. He stepped back to allow them in.

As they stepped forward into the gloom, there was movement from the far side of the basement. Marie's mother came forward. Her hair was streaked with grey. Grey shadows swooped down from the corners of her eyes, either side of her nose. Even her lips looked grey. *They cannot stay down here*, Yenko thought. *They will die*.

As his eyes adjusted to the gloom, he saw that they had made a few small attempts to render the basement habitable. A tin bucket stood in one corner. On the opposite side of the room, a torn blanket had been nailed above an arch. There was a dank smell, a smell of old people, and piss. The wall beneath the window was streaked with greenish-purple, a shininess – a thin slime of damp reflecting the sliver of light above.

In two years, Yenko thought, *I have forgotten what it is like to live like this, to be grateful for this.* (His polished shoes, his black-market coffee – what would happen now his savings had been stolen by Blažek and his livelihood gone?)

Marie's mother was staring at him fearfully, looking from him to her daughter, waiting for clues.

Marie said gently, 'This is Emil Růžička. You remember him, from the camp? Anna Růžičková's son.'

The woman's expression did not change. Jan Malík's face had no expression at all.

Yenko turned to Marie. 'They can't stay here. I'm going to look at the flat upstairs. Are you sure the people who lived there were Germans?'

Líba Malíková answered him by spitting on the floor.

'I'll be back in a few minutes.'

'I'll come with you,' said Marie. As they left the basement she turned back to her parents and said, 'You don't need to lock the door behind us.'

From the hallway, a grand stone staircase swept upwards, keeping pace with the elegant line of a brass handrail, up to a heavy, oak door.

The door had a brass knocker in the shape of a lion's head. Yenko knocked it, hard, and they waited a moment or two. He stepped back from the door. 'It's heavy,' he said. 'I will need your father to help me, if he can.'

'I know where there might be a key,' Marie said. 'I watched the woman go out one day.' She led him down the wide, shallow steps, back to the hallway, where three terracotta vases stood in their own little alcoves, arranged diagonally in the wall next to the front door.

'The top one, not underneath, to the side of the alcove somewhere. I couldn't really see what she was doing.'

Yenko felt around the cold stone until he found a small ledge with a tiny iron hook. On it, was a large, old-fashioned key.

'Let's take your parents with us,' he said triumphantly, holding the key up. 'Come on, even if we have to carry them up the stairs.'

As he opened the heavy oak door, the landing where they stood was flooded with light. Marie's mother gasped. They stepped forward, into the light.

They were in a huge drawing room. Immediately opposite them were three vast windows draped with heavy brocade curtains tied back with plaited golden ropes. In the centre of the room was a round table with an immaculate, shiny surface. A huge vase stood in the middle, with a raised relief pattern in turquoise-blue and red; Chinese dogs, begging.

Marie's father showed no reaction, but her mother stepped forward to look at the vase. She turned back to them, her face full of life. 'This was above us, the whole time?' she said, incredulous. 'They lived like this?'

They have always lived like this, Yenko thought, but he did not want to embarrass the woman.

He opened his arms. 'You are going to live like this, Mrs Malíková, for the time being.'

She shook her head, but he said, 'Get your things from the basement. No one will come. If they do, tell them this. Say, my son is the leader of a partisan unit and you must come back when he is here. Say that and look them right in the eye. Don't smile.'

As he said, *don't smile*, Líba Malíková broke into a huge, gap-toothed grin, turning to her husband, who still stood expressionless, and then her daughter, who nodded and held out her hand.

'Let's find the bedroom, so you can see where you will sleep tonight.'

Líba shrank back, shaking her head. 'We will sleep here on the floor, near the door.'

'No, you won't,' said Marie, taking her by the hand and pulling her towards the double doors on the left. Líba looked back at Yenko as her daughter pulled her out of the room.

They left Marie's parents in the grand apartment; her mother going from room to room, opening cupboards, her father sitting stock still in a leather chair.

The streets leading to the bridge were crowded. Yenko took Marie's arm. 'Look,' he said. 'Everyone is coming out of their houses. The whole city will be heading for Wenceslas Square, you'll see.'

Ahead of them was a group of young women who had put on traditional Moravian costume, red-tiered skirts and puffed-sleeved lace blouses. They were dancing along, arm in arm. Two young men joined them, waving bottles.

At the far side of the bridge, there was a group of ten or twelve militia-men surrounding a handful of German civilians who were trying to cross the bridge in the other direction, to leave the city. A middle-aged man was at the front, clutching a leather bag to his chest. The Moravian girls and the young men stopped to watch and Yenko and Marie joined them. A small crowd surrounded the militia-men who were surrounding the Germans.

The man clutching the leather bag was pleading with the militia, 'Please, my wife and children have already crossed the bridge. If I don't keep up I'll lose them. Please.' One of the young men standing next to Yenko stepped forward towards a large bundle which sat on the ground, next to the group. He drew back his foot, and gave the bundle a hard kick. It rolled away. One of the German women cried out as the man proceeded to kick the bundle to the side of the bridge. Ignoring the shouts of the militia, she ran to it.

A militia-man strode after her. He grabbed her by the shoulder and pulled her roughly backwards, pushing her back to join the group. Then he picked up the bundle and tossed it over the stone balustrade into the river below. 'Line up!' he bellowed to the group, as he returned, waving his rifle in the air for emphasis.

'Are they going to shoot them?' Marie whispered curiously to Yenko. He shrugged. The Moravian girls were clapping.

The man in charge of the militia pushed the eight or so German civilians around so that they were lined up on the bridge, facing the river. Then another man came forward with a tin of white paint. On the back of each one, man or woman, he painted a rough swastika with the paint.

'Time to help clear up the mess!' shouted the leader. 'Follow me!'

Yenko heard the man next to him say, 'They are getting them to help dismantle the barricades, put the stones back where they belong. Let's see how *they* enjoy a little hard labour.'

'Come,' Yenko said, 'Let's look down the river, the view from here is good.'

They saw the group of Germans half an hour later, as they strode down Charles Street. They were lifting huge square cobbles from a pile by the side of the road and carrying them to a rough patch of destroyed ground. They had been joined by two young women who had had their heads shaved and their faces smeared with tar. The one nearest to them looked at them as they passed. She was wearing a long tweed coat. Her fingernails were bleeding. She was weeping.

It was strange to be back at the door to his apartment, unlocking and opening it on to the neat, square room; the single bed, the little enamel pan rinsed and up-ended on the wooden drainer. He seated Marie at the wooden table and made her coffee. When he put the small yellow cup in front of her, she stared down into it. *Of course,* he thought. *She is hungry.* He was hungry too, but in an ordinary way. He knew his hunger could not compare to hers.

He took some stale bread, and the last two sausages, which he had saved from the packet he had taken down to Mrs Stropová – how long ago? It seemed like another age. Marie watched him intently as he unwrapped the sausages. He lit a flame under a pan to cook them, then served them to her half-raw, because he could not bear the intensity of her gaze while they were frying.

He was still wearing his dirty clothes, so he excused himself and took a clean shirt and his spare, old trousers from the wardrobe, then went down the corridor to the bathroom, to wash himself and change. When he came back into the room, Marie's plate was empty and she was staring down into her lap.

'We have not dared to use our clothing coupons,' she said, in a very small voice.

'We will get you some, from somewhere,' he said, reassuringly, wondering, *what will happen now? How will all that work?*

They were descending the stairs, when the door at the bottom opened, and Mrs Stropová emerged. She looked up at Yenko, and he nodded a greeting, about to speak, when he saw her expression change. She had seen Marie, behind him on the stairs.

She looked at him, then at Marie, then turned and went back into her room, slamming the door behind her.

They stopped on the stairs. Marie was looking at her feet. 'That woman . . .' she said quietly, 'she thought I was . . .' She pushed past him, and ran out into the street.

He followed her. She was half-running, half-walking down the road. When he caught up with her, she turned on him. 'You have a life!' she snapped, her voice low and furious. 'You haven't been just staying alive, like us! You have a home. You have a *life*!' Her tone was accusatory. 'Why didn't you tell me?'

He grabbed her arm. 'I haven't,' he said, 'No, I haven't. It's just a room, that's all. It doesn't mean anything.'

She was looking down again. She was so much shorter than him that he had to dip his head to try and see her face.

'Nobody has meant anything to me, these last two years,' he said, holding her upper arms. 'Do you understand me?'

'I should go back to my parents,' Marie said miserably. 'We have to decide what to do, where to go. My mother hates Prague. My father doesn't say anything so God in heaven knows what he wants.' She looked upwards, despairingly, as if importuning the sky.

'Marie, it's still ending. It's too early for decisions. Please, come with me to Wenceslas Square. We have earned some time when we don't have to think about anything, please. If you don't come with me, I will have no one to celebrate with. The man I fought next to today, he was shot dead, before he had time to dance in the square, or drink. They were brave some of these people, really brave. That woman, she's been kind to me. They haven't all been bad. I'll take you back home afterwards, I promise. Just come with me now.'

She nodded.

They crossed Celetná. The sun had come out. Gangs of men were still clearing the rubble. Amidst the chaos, the glass-seller had set up his wares, outside his shop. He had built two towers of rubble, then used planks covered by a cloth to make a table. Over the planks he had lain rows of lace place-mats, overlapping. His exquisite blue vases were set up on the place-mats, and he was seated on a chair by the display, smiling beatifically.

CHAPTER 32

The war was over. Yenko was staying with Marie and her parents in the grand apartment abandoned by the German family. One day, two women visited and showed them identity cards. They were from the Resettlement Ministry. Their job was to take an inventory of empty properties in the Little Quarter. They would be re-assigned to their rightful owners, if the rightful owners could be found. Some would be requisitioned. The women were not unkind. It would take weeks, they said, months perhaps, for everything to be sorted out. In the meantime, they should make sure that their names were down on the waiting list at the Housing Department, so they would have somewhere to go.

After the women had left, Marie said, 'Do you think we should have told them we have been in a camp? I heard a woman yesterday saying that people coming back from the camps will get everything. Any Germans left are going to have to give them their shoes and live off the same rations that the Jews lived off.'

Yenko shook his head. 'What about when they ask which camp, and why? They will write it down. They will write down that we are "gypsies". Since when has that been a good idea?'

Marie and her parents were sleeping in the grand bedroom at the back of the apartment – her parents on the huge, tall bed, Marie on a chaise longue with a pattern of gold chevrons. Yenko was sleeping in what had been a boy's bedroom, a small square room still full of wooden toys, with an annexe for a nanny.

One day, when Marie and her mother had gone out to queue for the new food tickets – the system that was replacing the ration cards – Yenko and Jan Malík were left alone, sitting at the huge circular table in the drawing room. They were sipping weak tea – the women had made it for them before they left. Yenko missed his black-market coffee.

He looked across at Jan Malík. Malík's snow-white hair was fluffy, thin – it stood upright on his head as if he had just received an electric shock. There were deep hollows in the dark skin either side of his collar-bones. His gaze was indirect. Even when he looked straight at you, his eyes never met yours.

I suppose I had better make the situation clear to him, Yenko thought. It must be obvious, but who knows how much he is capable of grasping? He allowed himself a moment of small amusement at the thought of how timid Jan Malík would have made him feel, before.

'Mr Malík,' Yenko said.

Marie's father lowered his cup and looked at Yenko – that same, strange, indirect look.

'I am going to marry Marie,' Yenko said. There was no hint of interrogation in his words. He was not asking for permission.

Malik's wandering expression did not change. He lifted his teacup, paused when it was halfway to his mouth and said quietly, 'Of course.' He sipped his tea.

Marie and her mother were not back until the middle of the afternoon. They were smiling, each clutching two large bags made of brown hessian, one under each arm.

'Liberated sugar,' said Marie, with a flourish, dumping her two bags down on the shiny table, 'liberated flour, and liberated bread. The biscuits are ex-army rations but they didn't say which army.'

'We were lucky,' said Líba. 'We were at the head of the queue. They came straight for us.'

'They had seen our faces,' said Marie, untying her headscarf.

'My black skin. I thought . . .' Líba raised her hands and let them fall on to her skirt, contorting her features.

Marie turned to her mother, mimicking. 'But they said, in front of everyone, *Citizens! You are the thinnest people in the queue! You must have these!*'

Yenko shook his head.

Líba took her bags into the kitchen and returned. When she saw that Marie had put hers down on the shiny table, she rushed forward. 'Daughter, daughter, what are you doing? What will Mr Růžička think about the way you were brought up? Do you want me to die of shame?' She snatched the bags from the table and then flicked its surface with the side of her hand. She gave Marie a despairing look, then disappeared back into the kitchen. For a woman who had spent two years in constant fear of capture, Líba had acquired the habits of the house-proud with impressive rapidity.

Marie turned to Yenko and pursed her lips comically. Yenko smiled back.

'Where is my father?' Marie asked.

'Lying down,' said Yenko, taking his jacket from the chair by the door.

'You are going out?'

He sighed. 'I'd better go to the Housing Department. We can't leave it any longer.'

Marie ran her fingertips over the shiny table. 'My poor mother.'

'We'll find something.'

Marie looked up sharply, when he said *we*. 'I'll come with you,' she said.

'You've only just got back. Aren't you tired?'

She shook her head, stubbornly.

The Housing Department had become one of the most crowded places in a crowded city. As they turned the corner, they saw the queue stretching down the wide street; a thick, fat queue that filled the pavement and spilled on to the road. As they walked to the front, to see what was happening, a group of four men jeered at them without enthusiasm. Two women turned and remonstrated with them. The first group waiting at the open door was a large, emaciated family, the mother comforting the children, the father holding a baby and staring fixedly at the desk just inside the door, waiting for his turn. Glancing at the man's thin, set face, Yenko thought, *he looks like a man who is rehearsing his name, who is afraid that, when his time comes, he won't be able to recall it.*

As they passed the head of the queue, an official emerged from the door and began handing out leaflets. 'It's too hot for this!' he said to a man nearby.

Yenko recognised the voice. It was Josef Kuklak, the head waiter at the Lagoon on Strosmeyer Square.

Yenko said to Marie, 'Go and wait at the back of the queue. I'll join you in a minute.' He waited until Kuklak had turned, then went up and took his elbow, saying softly in his ear. 'Hey, Kuklak, so you've turned civil servant on us. I was hoping to do a little business . . .'

Kuklak turned. His immediate expression was one of dismay but he disguised it quickly beneath a broad smile. 'Jan, Jan Michálek, how's it going?' They shook hands.

Yenko shrugged. 'Very nicely, under the circumstances,' he said with an air of modesty. 'Got myself a nice place in the Little Quarter. How about you?'

'I heard you'd left the Old Town. Hauer at the restaurant thought you'd left Prague altogether. We heard Blažek ran out on you.'

Yenko shrugged again, as if the matter was of no concern. He pulled out a packet of cigarettes and held it out. He was restricted to rations like everybody else now but it wouldn't do to let Kuklak see that. 'So what's going on here then?' he asked, as he leaned forward to light Kuklak's cigarette.

Kuklak gave a tight grin. 'Why, putting yourself on the list?'

Yenko shook his head. 'Looking for something for a friend of mine.'

Kuklak shook his head. 'Can't help you, friend. It's chaos in there. You wouldn't believe it. Suddenly everyone claims to have owned a palace before the war. Nobody has any documents. We get women who turn up with three children and lie down on the floor refusing to go until they're given somewhere to live. Yesterday, one of them *died* in there, just rolled off her chair. She'd been queuing for days, her friend said. They'd walked all the way from Poland after they got out of the camp, and then she dies just as they get to the head of the housing queue.'

Yenko looked back along the queue, the assorted clothing of the people waiting, their blank, resigned faces. 'Are they mostly from the camps?' he asked.

'Some of them,' said Kuklak. 'Some of them have been in hiding, they say, others in prison, others left Prague for their own safety at the beginning of the war to sit it out in some nice little *chata*, and now they think they can waltz back in here and get their old places back.' He leaned forward and lowered his voice. 'They're mostly Jews, of course, even the ones who don't want to admit it. I know the Germans did some really bad things to the Jews but I don't believe all these stories about gas-houses and ovens. Just look, take a look,' he gestured with the hand that was holding the cigarette. 'There must be at least three hundred people here. If they were killing them all, then how come so many of them have come back?'

Marie was waiting at the back of the queue. She looked uneasy as Yenko approached. He shook his head. She left the queue to approach him and took his arm, steering him away. 'I just heard those women talking,' she said. 'I spoke to them.' She hesitated. 'She said there's a wall, just round the corner from here. People are pinning up notices, survivors from the camps, like the messages from the radio. She said she found her cousin. She was sure he was dead.'

Yenko felt a lump of misery well up inside him. He had promised himself he would not let himself be put through this.

Marie stared at him. 'You can read the messages at least. Let's just go and look.'

All he could see, at first, as they turned the corner, was the crowd of people, two or three deep. Towards the far end of the street it thinned out and he saw the messages pinned on the fence. They began at head-height and went down as low as his knees. Some were large, some small – some had no more than a name and address, others had long, complicated messages. The bits of paper were bright white, creamy-white, brown as skin or pale blue. Some were stuck with a single pin, others with neat rows of nails. A few had become detached and fluttered to the floor where they lay at people's feet. An old woman stood next to him. She was bending, very slowly, to pick up one of the fallen bits of paper. Her hand shook with effort, the gnarled fingers trembling. Just as she lowered herself sufficiently, a low breeze from a man rushing past whisked the paper away from her outstretched hand.

Yenko shook his head. The fence stretched the length of the street. It would take days to read them all.

'Go on,' Marie said. 'Even if we don't see a name we know, we might find some other Roma, someone who's been in Poland.'

'You're forgetting something,' Yenko said. 'Hardly any of our people can read or write.'

'You can . . .' she said, but her insistence was fading.

He turned, brusquely.

He strode quickly through the New Town, his hands deep in his pockets, Marie at his side, trotting to keep up. He only slowed down as they approached Charles Square. At the bottom of the square, looking up, he could see more hordes of people, gathered in groups in the shade of the trees. A makeshift encampment had sprung up where the vegetable patches had been. One of the Red Cross groups had set up a tent. As they approached the square, Yenko could see yet another queue, waiting to register at a table. Behind the table was a young woman about the same age as Marie, scribbling frantically as each person gave their name.

More writing down, Yenko thought bitterly, *more questions, more records being kept, more notes on who everyone is and where they come from.*

Marie was standing next to him, facing away. He turned and saw what she could see; the rise of the square, the vast huddle of people covering almost every patch of available earth – some seated on boxes or blankets, others squatting on the dry ground, sleeping children, women talking, men arguing or silent.

'Emil,' Marie whispered from the side of her mouth, 'is the whole world here in Prague?'

Yenko did not reply. He was gazing at the people. Eventually he said, 'None of them are Roma. Not one. There's nobody but us, Marie, there's no point in fooling ourselves.'

'Talk to some of the Jews,' Marie urged. 'Most of them got sent to Poland. Someone will know something.'

Nearby, there was a group of four men, all late middle-aged or elderly, sitting in a small huddle on one of the few remaining patches of grass. They were talking intently. Two of them were wearing striped prison trousers. All four had short, downy hair; the tell-tale recent re-growth. They looked like they hadn't yet taken advantage of the food tents.

Yenko approached and stood over the men, Marie following in his wake. They continued to talk softly amongst themselves. He waited until one of them lifted his head; an old man with a quantity of grey stubble and large sunken eyes, the lids loose flaps of skin. *That camp look*, Yenko thought bleakly. I would recognise it anywhere.

'Excuse me . . .' He didn't even know what nationality they were. 'I'm sorry to trouble you. Are you from Prague?'

'We are Poles,' said another of the men, his Czech heavily accented. 'What is it? What do you want?'

'You have come from the camps,' said Yenko. 'I was in a camp in Moravia for six months. My father died there.' He was anxious to establish his credentials.

The Pole gave a bitter laugh. 'Six months. This man here,' he indicated one of the others, 'was arrested in 1940. Six months is zero.' He gave a grin that revealed him to be toothless. 'How old are you? I'm twenty.'

'Please, where were you, which camp?'

The man shook his head. 'Not in Poland. We were in Buchenwald. We're on our way *back* to Poland. God knows why. Here, the women give us apples and milk.'

'My family was sent to Poland,' Yenko said. 'In 1943. My mother, my two aunts and little brother. I'm trying to find out if they could have survived.'

The men had fallen silent. They glanced at each other. Finally, the second one spoke. His Czech was fluent. 'My name is Roman Blynsky,' he said. His voice was deep, his age impossible to fathom. 'Before the war I was a Professor of Linguistics in Warsaw. When the Germans invaded I was picked up in the first wave. They sent me to Buchenwald, to act as a translator for the Commandant's office there. The rest of my family were in the ghetto, then the camps. My cousin arrived in Buchenwald in '44. He had been in four camps, including Auschwitz, back and forth. He told me many things, things he had seen with his own eyes. Whenever I meet anyone who has been where my wife and children might have been I question them. It's always the same answer.' He looked down and grabbed a handful of grass, tugging at it, struggling to pull it up from the possessive earth. When he had succeeded, he threw it back down. 'Everyone is dead. One or two of the men survived, somehow, like us. The women and children? No. I'm sorry but you must say Kaddish for your family. They burned everybody, the women and children first.'

'I am not a Jew, I am a Rom,' Yenko said desperately. 'I know they killed the Jews but what about *us*, the Gypsies . . . ?'

The Professor stared at Yenko. His expression softened slightly and a little curiosity came into his features. 'What is your name?' he asked.

'František Růžička,' Yenko said.

'František . . .' the man said, and gestured to the grass beside him. Yenko knelt on the grass. Behind him, Marie remained standing. 'František,' the man repeated. 'I thought before the war that I knew all the words a man could know. I spoke six languages fluently and could get by in another four. I could tell you the difference between a transitive and intransitive verb in French. I could write poetry in Finnish, even Estonian. Do you want to hear a new phrase I learned on our long walk from Buchenwald?' Yenko stared at him. The man continued. 'Us camp survivors talk, wherever we meet, exchanging news and names, everyone is desperate to hear their own surname from another's mouth. I have seen a man turn around and head back the way he came after walking three hundred kilometres, all because somebody described a girl who sounded like his daughter. As we came through Leipzig I was talking to a man of words like myself, a magazine editor before the war, a Jew like me. He had been imprisoned in Germany with some people like you, and he said to me, "Know what the Gypsies call us now?"'

The Professor stopped and stared at Yenko, as if he really thought that he might know. Yenko shrugged.

'Smoke Brothers,' said the Professor. 'That's what you Gypsies call us Jews now.' Seeing Yenko's incomprehension, he turned to the others and sighed, rolling his eyes as he might once have done in response to a particularly slow student.

'Smoke Brothers,' he repeated, and he lifted his hands,

spreading his fingers to form a wide cup and then made a *whooshing* motion upwards. One of the men cackled with laughter. 'We went up the chimneys together.'

As Yenko strode down towards the river, Marie followed close behind but made no attempt to draw level or take his arm. Eventually, he turned and sat on a stone bench looking out over the water. Marie sat next to him, at a slight distance. A few metres to the right, a work detail of Germans was dismantling a low, concrete machine-gun bunker. He stared at them. There were six men, in jackets, with swastikas painted on their backs in white paint. They were all wielding pickaxes, bringing them down time and time again with weary imprecision. He was near enough to see that their faces were shiny with sweat, their chests rising and falling with their laboured breathing. Their expressions were set, despairing at the uselessness of their small tools against the huge concrete slabs.

Marie was silent for a while, then she said, 'When we were first released, I was just so numb and grateful I couldn't think about the camp. Then, when I had got warm again, and had a little food, I wanted to tell everyone. It was unbearable. I wanted to grab strangers in the street, the ordinary people we passed on the streets of the city. I wanted to shake them from their dreaming and say, *this happened to me, and this*. It hurt so much inside. I couldn't say it. I had to just keep my head down because we had to stay unnoticed.'

'I nearly smashed a window,' Yenko said. 'In a restaurant full of SS officers, and women. I saw them all eating and laughing. Fat white women like cows. And I nearly smashed the window with my fists. I wish I had, even though they would have killed me. It would have been worth it, to see the shock and fear on their faces, just for a second.'

'But it changes . . .' Marie said. She sighed, then leaned down and picked up a handful of small pebbles from the ground and began tossing them one by one back on to the ground. 'You think when you first get out, you can't wait to tell everyone, they will be so shocked and horrified. And then you realise there is no one to tell. So you stay quiet and then you start to hear everyone else's stories. After a while you realise, there *were* places even worse than our camp, places with ovens, places where they . . .' The pebbles were finished. She was staring ahead.

Yenko felt as though his head would burst if he had to think about it any more. He put his hands over his ears, but Marie wasn't looking at him and continued talking. 'Do you want to know the worst story I've heard? About a man who tried to escape from a camp in Poland, one of the worst ones. I heard this in one of the bread queues. A boy was saying, a man in his camp had tried to escape. He was a big strong man. They put him in a wooden box, so small he was crouched right down, and nailed down the lid, then they drove nails through the box, into his flesh, then left him to die. It took days. He went mad. His screams kept the whole camp awake, night after . . .'

Suddenly, Yenko wheeled away from her, crouching down beside the bench. He began to roll on the ground, as if he were being attacked by a swarm of bees. He thrashed from side to side, making guttural sounds at the base of his throat.

Marie threw herself on top of him with a cry, trying to wrestle his hands away from his face, calling out in despair, 'I'm sorry . . . I'm sorry . . . I'm sorry . . .'

Eventually, he quietened. She sat back up on the bench and brushed at her skirt.

The Germans on the work detail and their Czech guards had stopped to stare at them. Marie jumped to her feet, rounded on them and cursed them in Romani. They went back to their tasks.

She turned back to Yenko and spat on the ground. '*Gadje* . . .' she muttered bitterly, 'Filthy, evil *gadje* . . .'

Yenko stood, brushed himself down and sat back on the bench. Marie joined him, sitting closer this time. He turned to her and tried to smile. She smiled back, and for a second or two he was able to hold the moment. Then the effort of smiling made something inside him collapse and crumble. He rose and turned away from her, walking over to the wall behind them, pockmarked by bullet-holes. He placed both hands flat on the rough stone, leaned forward and let his head hang down. The blood surged, pulsing, in his ears.

Marie came and stood behind him. 'Emil . . .' she said softly.

Yenko shook his head.

He had a vision. He saw how their union would have been in the countryside, in the summer, in another time. His father would have had his mother sew a new waistcoat. The women would have oiled their hair. Members of their *vitsa* would have come from all over the Czech lands, the Carpathians, Hungary, Slovakia – family members they had never even met before. The feasting and dancing, hours of it – the light of the fires in the dark, a whole forest of people to celebrate the wedding of Josef Maximoff's eldest son.

He would never have met Marie had it not been for the devouring of all those people. Could he forgive her that?

He closed his eyes and for one sweet moment wove himself a fantasy; he and his *kumpánia* somehow managing to pass through South Moravia and stopping for water; Marie standing shyly by the pump; him helping her, then running to his father to beg that he find the parents of the quiet girl and bargain for her; his father refusing angrily at first because she wasn't Kalderash, then relenting; Jan Malík transformed into a kind and loving father who would raise his hands and say, 'Well, I had thought to place my daughter elsewhere, but if the two young people really love each other, who am I to stand in the way?' The two fathers would seal the pact by drinking together all evening, ending with their arms around each other's shoulders, singing songs . . .

They are dead. They are all dead, but I'll never know for certain, so they will carry on living just enough for me to be reminded, every day, that they are dead. Every time I have hope, for a minute, they will have to die again.

How will we ever recover? Yenko thought as he leaned against the stone wall with his eyes closed, listening to the fall of the picks from the work detail, an arhythmic chipping and clicking. Whatever happiness comes to us in the future, how will we recover from all we have lost? How will the world live now, with splinters in its heart?

Marie was standing close behind him. She placed a hand gently on his shoulder and said, 'Come. It is enough.'

He turned to her and allowed her to take his hand and lead him away from the bench and the Germans at work chipping stone, as if he were a blind man, unable to find his way.

CHAPTER 33

Summer in Prague, early summer; the air wavers, the sky above the city is an unblemished blue. It is the kind of summer when all the ills of the world seem transmutable, when a person might believe that there is meaning and purpose and that everything can be made whole again, with enough will. It is 1945.

Marie Malíková's heart is breaking.

As they walked along the road above the river, away from the work detail, she thought to herself, *when we were in the camp, we told each other stories about cherry blossom and schnitzels. Now we are free, we tell each other stories about death.*

They walked in silence towards Charles Bridge; the bridge, in all its dark, strange beauty, hung, misted, in the haze of heat. From this distance, the stone statues strung along its balustrade were like black angels, wings raised in benediction above the liberated city. There was no damage to the streets here. The grand buildings set back from the street had large windows overlooking the water. In one, opened wide, a lilac-coloured chiffon curtain flapped.

As they neared the bridge, Marie felt the distance between herself and Emil. *I should not have made him look at the notes on the fence or speak to those prisoners*, she thought. *I have ruined everything.* His silence was beyond ordinary quietness. He was far away from her. His was the silence of a man who has finally realised and accepted something, and is about to say goodbye.

At the corner of Anenská Street he stopped and said, 'Will you be all right from here? I'm going to go this way.'

She felt as if she was dropping from a great height. She was right. He was saying goodbye. He knew all he needed to know now: his family was not coming back. He had decided to cut himself away from all the suffering he had been tethered to – she was his last link with it, after all. He had had enough of living with her and her parents in the grand apartment that would be taken away from them. (What would happen then? Another basement?) He was going back to the life he had had before they had met as the smoke cleared from the Uprising. He was going to go back to being a *gadjo*.

He was looking at her. He said, a little brusquely, 'It's easy from here. You just go over the bridge and you're in the Little Quarter.'

'I know that by now,' she snapped. 'I'll be fine.' She turned swiftly. She did not want kind words of farewell from him, not when he didn't even realise what he was leaving her to; her parents, a future as bleak as a fallow field in February.

She strode no more than a few paces before she regretted her haste. She turned, but he had already walked off down Anenská. She caught a glimpse of his departing back, then he was gone.

She closed her eyes briefly. She should not have been so hasty. Pride had made her turn on her heel, to show him she would be fine with or without him. If she had not been so foolish, perhaps she could have persuaded him to stay, to love her. I love him, she thought, in the same way that a baby blackbird loves a parent bird as it sits in the nest with its tiny beak agape, begging to be fed. I should let him go. He's better off without me, without us. He can do whatever he wants without us holding him back. If he stays with us, he will always be a *gypsy*.

Full of self-loathing and misery, she turned towards the bridge.

*

Yenko strode down Anenská and was soon at the Old Town Square, where one of the cafés was displaying a sign saying, *Get Your Cup of Liberation Coffee Here – One Cup Per Customer While It Lasts (the coffee, that is!)*. He stopped and pointed at the sign, saying to a boy clearing a nearby table, 'Real coffee, eh, *šav*?' The boy frowned at him and Yenko corrected himself. 'I'm sorry, young man – is it real coffee?'

'Of course, sir,' said the boy, gesturing towards a seat.

Yenko sat and lit his last cigarette. After two puffs, he stubbed it out gently by wheeling the lighted end against the edge of the marble ashtray. He would save the rest until his coffee arrived. As it came, he was standing, readjusting his trousers. His good pair had been ruined in the fighting and he was back to the old brown pinstripe which were ill-fitting and, in this heat, uncomfortable. He thanked the boy and sat down, feeling an ache of nostalgia for the war days, when he had been a businessman. Had it really been so bad, the fear of being caught? I am forgetting already, he thought. But that was the thing about such extremity. It wasn't possible to recall an emotion such as fear or pain, not accurately. They could only be felt in the real, the here and now. Once they were past, you could never recapture their precise flavour, thank God, otherwise you would go mad. Time to stop feeling guilty, he thought, as he sipped the coffee. I did what I could. Let's leave guilt to those who have good reason to feel it. God knows, there are enough of those. He re-lit his cigarette. An image came into his head, unbidden; *the crow in the doorway.* He closed his eyes. *Leave me be!* He finished his coffee hastily and stood, looking down at the table, wondering whether or not he had paid. It came to him that he hadn't.

As he left the café, a young man in a leather jacket and cap stopped him and handed him a leaflet, saying as he took it, 'Long live Comrade Stalin!'

There were gangs of men at work in Celetná. Most of the rubble had been cleared from the street, now passable with care, but several damaged buildings were still surrounded by rope cordons. Here at least, there was no pretending that there hadn't been a war.

The easiest place to walk was in the middle of the road. On the pavements there were still piles of rubble and cobbles stacked against the walls, waiting to be replaced in their proper order. The war was the cement that held people together, Yenko thought, as he picked his way carefully. Now we are all loose stones. We must each find our place.

As he turned the corner into Ctibor's alley, he saw that two men were standing in front of the old shop. The door stood open, and they were nodding to each other. He glanced at the men as he passed beneath the low stone archway and through the courtyard. They ignored him. As he mounted the staircase of Ctibor's block, he saw, at the top, two wooden crates and a small suitcase. He walked along the corridor to Ctibor's room.

Mrs Talichová had propped open the door to her apartment and the corridor was full of light. She was brushing the floor with a broom. Her husband was also inside, seated at a table near the window, dressed in a string vest, holding up a small mirror with one hand and shaving with the other. He was humming to himself. A boy that Yenko hadn't seen before sat on the opposite side of the table, head in hands, reading a newspaper.

Mrs Talichová looked up at Yenko as he stopped in her doorway, then resumed her brushing. As he turned away, she said, 'He's been back for over a week, you know. He's been asking after you.'

The door to Ctibor's room was also propped open. Inside, the shutters had been hooked back and the windows flung open. The room was full of light. Ctibor's tins and mugs were gone from the shelf above the sink. The bed had been stripped and the eiderdown and blankets folded and tied with string. Ctibor himself was standing over a large suitcase that was resting on the bare mattress. A pile of clothing lay next to it.

He turned as Yenko entered. 'I finally managed to open that damn window,' he said, 'with Mr T's help. I told them they can have this room when I'm gone.' He lowered his voice. 'Believe it or not, it's bigger than theirs.'

Ctibor had a large, yellowing bruise on his forehead. He seemed a little less bulky. Otherwise, he looked unharmed by his experience at the hands of the partisans. Yenko sat down in the armchair, as he used to do in the war days. Automatically, he patted his pockets, remembering he had just smoked his last cigarette. He leaned back in the chair and then leaned forward again. 'You're leaving,' he said, redundantly.

Ctibor continued packing. 'I hear you're a war hero these days.'

Yenko gave a short exhalation of surprise. 'Who told you that?'

'Mrs Talichová, of course. You should go to the Town Hall and get accreditation. They're giving out certificates to partisans and Resistance workers. You never know when it might come in handy.'

'Ctibor, Uncle . . .'

'Of course, who knows how much those bits of paper are going to be worth? They're probably selling them on the black market already. You might be fixed up with one, I suppose. Sorry. That was a cheap remark. Beneath me.'

'Ctibor . . .'

'But then your line of work is going to keep going for quite a while, I'd say. I heard about Jan Blažek, by the way. I can hardly believe it. You don't know who to trust these days.'

Yenko sighed, resting his elbows on his knees and letting his head hang.

Ctibor still had his back to him but he paused in the act of folding his voluminous dressing-gown and said, without turning, 'I suppose there is nothing I can say to persuade you to come with me?'

Yenko shook his head and said, 'No.'

Ctibor was standing very still.

'I'm sorry,' Yenko added, then asked, 'What will you do?'

'I'm going back to Kladno,' Ctibor said over his shoulder. 'I still have one or two friends there. The German families are all leaving and I should be there to claim the farm. I don't want it, actually, but I'd like to be in the area, just in case there's any news about Sarah.' He sighed. 'If I can sell it, then I'll buy myself a little cottage somewhere nearby. Who knows? Maybe I'll even plant a couple of trees.'

For a long time, there was silence between them. Then Yenko said, 'This room looks different with the window open. It's hot outside. The evenings are long. It's clear now but I think it's going to cloud over. It will rain before nightfall.'

'I haven't been out today. '

'They are still piling up the cobbles. There is scaffolding over the Astronomical Clock.'

'That's been there for a while,' Ctibor said, as he resumed folding his clothes.

Yenko watched him finish his packing in silence.

'For a man who prided himself on having few possessions I seem to have an awful lot to cram into this suitcase . . .' Ctibor said. He threw down the lid and tried in vain to fasten the catch. Yenko rose to help but Ctibor waved him back to his seat. He turned and plumped himself down on the brimming case, bouncing gently. The bed springs creaked in protest.

'The war is over,' he said contemplatively, bouncing lightly. 'And now that the fighting has stopped, us victors can start a little competition. It's a competition called, Who Has Suffered Most? Shall I tell you the rules?'

Yenko smiled grimly and said, 'I think I can guess.'

'The rules are, anyone who talks about their suffering wins. The ones who talk about it loudest and longest will not, of course, be the ones who have suffered most. Those ghosts coming back, you know the ones I mean, the camp people and the soldiers with legs and arms missing and craziness in their eyes. Do you think there is even the language for what has happened to them? But Mrs Hubičková downstairs? You can't get past her door without her coming out of the apartment and telling you how she risked her life to warn the Jewish family across the road and how for the whole of the war she was convinced the Gestapo would knock on her door at any minute. Know what she did? She heard the father had been arrested: he worked with her husband at the paper mill. So she went over the road and told the mother and three children to pack their things and scram before they brought trouble down on the whole street. She was frightened about her own skin and the china dog collection she keeps on the windowsill but . . .' Ctibor threw his hands in the air, 'that woman will be convinced for the rest of her life that during the war she saved a family of Jews.'

You saved me, Yenko thought, *and for the rest of your life, you will be convinced you didn't do enough.*

Ctibor sat glumly for a few moments, although the sides of the suitcase beneath him were showing clear signs of strain. 'I'm not immune, you know,' he said after a while. 'When Mrs Talichová's boy came back – he was one of those ones got taken to the Reich. Well, their boy came back just yesterday, a strapping lad, and I passed him on the stairs and I thought, what do you know? You were safe in Germany working away at your factory, making the guns they used to shoot us, the steel to make them strong. What can those boys know of what it was like for us under occupation here, always waiting for the knock on the door? Know what?' Ctibor lowered his voice again. 'I heard them having a row last night, the three of them, the very first night the boy is home. Doors banging, the father shouting. And the boy comes out and storms off down the corridor. At the top of the stairs he shouts back, loud enough for the whole building to hear, *You've no idea! Nothing has happened in Prague! You've hardly had a single bomb! You should have heard it over our heads! You should have seen the things I've seen!'*

Ctibor paused, then lumbered down from his unfortunate suitcase. 'Who Has Suffered Most?'

As he lifted the suitcase to the floor he said sorrowfully. 'If only you would come with me, František.' He shook his head. 'I don't understand . . .'

Yenko was silent. What could he say? Ctibor had saved his life, but he had been a boy then and now he was a man, with a man's responsibilities. No man could call himself a Rom without a family and people to care for. *I am my father's son, after all,* he thought, and felt a sudden warmth spreading through his veins.

'Ah well,' Ctibor said resignedly. He picked up his case and half-carried, half-dragged it towards the door. When Yenko rose to help him, he waved him away again. 'In the name of Our Lord Jesus Christ and the Blessed Holy Virgin . . .' he muttered between his teeth. 'It is good to be leaving Prague.' Yenko stood and watched the old man as he struggled stubbornly down the corridor, bumping his large suitcase against the doorposts and cursing as he went.

Yenko strode back to the Little Quarter over Charles Bridge, pausing to look down the river in the early evening light. He still felt the new feeling, strange and peaceful. It seemed odd that the city was no different from how it had been an hour ago. The river was flowing as it always did. He realised that he had come to love the river.

As he approached the grand apartment building, he saw Marie sitting on the step of the building opposite. She was leaning against a stone portal with her head hanging slightly and her eyes closed. Her hands were crossed in her lap, resting in the folds of her long grey skirt. Her blouse hung loose on her shoulders. She needs to put on weight, he thought. I must talk to her about it.

He stopped in front of her and she raised her head. She stared at him, her black eyes wide in her clear, small face. She scrambled awkwardly to her feet and he held out a hand to help her up. As they walked up the street away from the building, she said, 'We should go in. They'll be wondering where we are.'

Yenko tucked her arm beneath his. 'Your father knows I will look after you.' They began to walk up the hill, crossing the

square and turning left. 'Can you manage a climb, do you think?'
he asked.

She looked up at him and nodded.

After a while, they reached the huge, grassy slopes of the
Petřín Hill, rising steeply above the city in an optimistic, upward
flush of green. The lower slopes had been dug up to grow
vegetables and there were dismantled German artillery
positions dotted around, guarded by Czech soldiers with open
shirts. As they climbed higher, they saw that amongst the trees
were little encampments of refugees, makeshift tents made of
ropes and blankets and groups of women gathered around small
bonfires. If we get thrown out of the apartment while the
weather is still good we could come here, Yenko thought. This
would suit us just fine.

They climbed higher and higher in silence, Marie panting
gently. Yenko slowed his pace. He had been eating properly for
two years – she had not – but she was determined, and when he
asked her if she needed to stop and sit down, she shook her head
and said, 'Let's go as high as we can. It's good to be away from
people.'

They were still some distance from the top of the hill when
she stopped and heaved a breath. 'All right, my friend. You have
won.'

He took her hand and led her into the trees, along the hill,
until he found a spot where they were enclosed around but still
had a view looking down over the city. They sat and leant either
side of a tree, recovering. He handed her his handkerchief to
wipe her face and neck. The trunks of the trees surrounding
them were green with moss. Dappled light filtered through,
greenish too.

When he had caught his breath, he said, 'I must pray, first.'

She looked at him, then nodded.

He rose, walked a few paces away, then knelt down on one knee and clasped his hands, copying the stance he had observed in his father. He pursed his lips, trying to remember the old words. *Sun and moon bear witness* . . . He closed his eyes. 'Te šai vrakeren mange o Kham thai o Chon . . .' he began. 'Sun and moon, bear witness. Witness this union, and tell God. Tell him I knelt to Cleanse myself and offered him this vow. Dear God, I hereby renounce my *gadjo* ways. If you give me Marie, and she is virgin, I will live from now as a true Rom. She is not tutored in the true Roma ways but I will teach her as much as I can.' He paused to clench his hands together more firmly. 'Dear God, I hereby renounce my *gadjo* ways. I will eat with my fingers so I do not contaminate myself with their implements. I will not eat their foul meat, nor drink their alcohol without offering the Ancestors a libation. I am sorry for the things I did when I was a *gadjo*. I am sorry I cheated and lied when I worked with the black-marketeer Blažek. I am sorry I told that woman in Beroun that her father's watch was worthless, because she looked so upset and wouldn't sell it to me anyway. I am sorry . . .' He clenched his eyes tight shut against the sun. 'I am sorry I killed the old couple in the shack.' He paused and opened his eyes. White light. No, it wasn't true. He wasn't sorry. If he hadn't killed them, he wouldn't be alive now. He glanced back at Marie. She sat waiting, not looking at him. 'Dear God, this is all I can say sorry for. I am sorry that I did not admit to myself, before now: I did it to live, but it was vengeance too. There is hatred in me. I think I will always carry it around with me. I cannot put it down.' Was it enough, to acknowledge something, even if you weren't truly sorry for it? He groaned aloud. He could feel in his bones; it wasn't enough. He looked up at the sky. The summer sun beat down, relentlessly. Where was God? Where was he when they were all dying in the camps? *'Te šai vrakeren mange o Kham thai o*

Chon . . . Sun and moon bear witness . . .' He dug his fingernails into his clenched hands. 'I am not repentant, but I know what I did. I know what it means. I am a man. I will, I will . . .' He heaved a sigh. 'I will take care of Marie, and her parents, even though as a Romni she should care for my parents. Mine are dead. I will take on my shoulders Marie and her mother who is like a little, old child, and her father, who I despise. I will protect these two old people that I do not care for, for Marie's sake, and because I killed the old couple. When we are thrown out of the apartment I will build us a shelter on this hill. I will work in some *gadjo's* factory if I have to . . .' He paused again. 'Don't ask more of me, O Del. You took my family and all my people away from me. How can you ask . . . ?' It was enough. He was empty of words. He looked up at the sky, despairing. There is nothing there, he thought.

He returned to Marie, wearily. She looked up at him from where he sat. He removed his jacket, and laid it on the patch of bare earth immediately in front of them. He gestured with the flat of his hand, an expansive gesture, that she should lie down.

She looked at him calmly, then obeyed.

As he parted her legs and knelt awkwardly between them, pushing up her skirt, he smiled down at her, to reassure her. Her expression was small, scared and resolute. He paused, a slight question in his look, and she gave an almost imperceptible nod. Then she lifted her hips from the ground so that he could push her skirt up further. He half-lay down, supporting himself with one hand flat on the soil while he unbuttoned his flies.

He wondered briefly whether he should kiss her mouth, the way a whore in the New Town had once taught him. It felt like the right thing to do, but he didn't want to risk offending her. He didn't know how to behave with a good Roma girl – he had only ever slept with *gadji* whores. Marie was lying perfectly still with her eyes closed. He closed his own and thought of a small, black-haired woman he had picked up on New Year's Eve. She had worn a peach-coloured silk camisole and matching French knickers, the feel of them as smooth as water.

As he pushed into Marie, she cried out and he clapped his hand over her mouth. He finished quickly, then knelt up, pulling her skirt back down for her and buttoning his flies. She lay quite still. As he resumed his sitting position, leaning back against the tree, she sat up and he saw she was still grasping his handkerchief. She turned away from him, and tucked it under her skirt. Then she shuffled backwards so that she could lean against the tree, next to him.

He dared not look at her. He sat with his knees raised, looking out over the city. The river was a bright ribbon of winding blue, the buildings white and terracotta shapes. People were tiny.

The ground sloped sharply down, away from them, covered with clusters of spiky yellow flowers. He wished that one of them was within reach, so that he could pluck it for Marie without rising. He did not want to move until she spoke.

She was silent for a long time and he thought, I have misjudged it. I thought she wanted me, but I have insulted her.

Then she said, 'I will learn.'

He picked up her hand from where it rested on the soil between them and said, 'Don't be afraid of anything. That is my first order to you as your husband.' He had been sincere, but at the word *husband*, they both burst into snorts of childish laughter.

When they had stopped laughing, she said, 'And I will teach our children to respect their father at all times.'

He touched her arm. 'I will teach them never to let anyone write down anything about them, and to remember that the *gadje* hate us.' We will call our first daughter Marienka, he thought, after Marie. Our second daughter must be Anna, in memory of my mother. And the third, Tekla. He wanted sons as well, of course, but he liked the idea of a few daughters first. He saw himself in old age, bewhiskered and white-haired, sitting beside a fire while his girls argued about which of them should have the honour of bringing him his lime-blossom tea.

'You must not frighten them until they are older,' Marie said, her voice lightly scolding. 'When they are little, we must just hold them and hold them and feed them so much they get as fat as puppies.'

'Marie,' he said, thoughtfully, taking her hand and rubbing one of her fingers between his forefinger and thumb, 'what is your real name?'

She looked at him, querying, then shrugged. Yenko frowned. 'But didn't your mother whisper your real name into your ear when you were born, didn't she put out bread for the Three Spirits on the third night?'

Marie smiled and shook her head. 'We lived in a cottage like everybody else. Nobody keeps up those old customs any more.'

Yenko was silent.

She dipped her head and moved closer, tipping her face so that she could put it close to his. 'You can teach me if you like . . .'

He shrugged. 'I don't know, do I? I'm a man. I don't know the women's secrets.' There was a pause. 'Anyway,' Yenko said, picking up a stone from the grass and tossing it on to the path in front of them. 'They were only superstitions . . .'

'Have you got a real name?' Marie demanded, suddenly interested.

He thought for a moment, then said, 'Yes.'

She waited, but he shook his head.

Marie stood up carefully, wincing a little. 'Turn your back,' she said. He looked at her, then turned. After a moment, she said, 'All right.'

He looked at her. She was standing straight in front of him, hands on her hips and an expression of pride on her face. He saw, on the bush next to her, his handkerchief, blood-stained and draped over a twig. He nodded solemnly, knowing this was her gift to him, the only one that she could give, and hoping his face did not betray his distaste. He looked up at the empty sky. *Is this your sign, O Del? It isn't enough.*

Marie had turned from him, to look out over the city. 'It's still warm,' she said. 'It's going to be a lovely evening.' She stretched her arms out wide. 'Oh, Emil,' she said. 'This air, being able to breathe, up on a hill.' She tipped her face upwards. 'I could grab the sky!' Her hands clenched and unclenched in the air.

Yenko gazed at her expression, her small face with the light upon it. He looked upwards, struggling for the strength to believe her optimism. The sky was still an honest blue, still empty. A few low clouds were drifting in from the east.

POSTSCRIPT

Estimates of the number of Roma and Sinti people killed by the Nazis have varied from 250,000 to 500,000, although some historians regard these numbers as massive under-estimates. In the Czech lands of Bohemia and Moravia, there were 6,500 Roma at the start of the war. Fewer than 500 survived.

The internment camp at Hodonín near Kunštát was opened in 1942 and closed in 1943 following a typhus epidemic. The majority of its occupants, all Roma, were transported to Auschwitz where they perished. The names and characters of the prisoners and staff that appear in this novel are all fictional, but the events that take place are based on historical fact.

The camp at Hodonín was re-opened later in the war as a billet for soldiers of the Wehrmacht. After the cessation of hostilities in 1945, it was used as a holding camp for German civilians who were being forcibly repatriated to Germany. Later, it was used as a prison camp for dissidents of the communist regime. The site still exists and, following extensive refurbishment, is now used as a holiday camp. A swimming pool has been built. Only one of the original concentration-camp barracks remains. It houses a table-tennis table.